To Shata

I hope you will enjoy this beautiful story of an injured dancer (as Stephanie was) and a football player.

Love,

Denise Bell

Second Wind

STEPHANIE RENÉE BELL

"You have turned my mourning into dancing"
Psalm 30:11(NKJV)

~

Teach me the second wind, teach me to live again
Teach me to understand, teach me to be a man
Teach me to never fear, promise me that You'll be here
Teach me to stand up strong, show me where I belong

Second Wind

Stephanie Renée Bell

Back cover painting: Elizabeth Abram ©2012. Used with written permission.
Cover design: Brandon Bell and Denise Bell, M.D.

Back cover photograph: unknown

Scripture quotations are the New International Version 1984 of the Holy Scriptures. Zondervan and The Holy Bible, New King James Version Copyright ©1982 by Thomas Nelson, Inc.
Grand Rapids, Michigan 49530, U.S.A.

Notice of rights

Trademarks

In this book trademarked names are used. Rather than put a trademark symbol in every occurrence of a trademarked name, we state that we are using the names only in an editorial fashion and to the benefit of the trademark owner, with no intention of infringement of the trademark

ISBN -13: 978-1470103781
ISBN -10: 1470103788

Foreword

"I consider that our present sufferings are not worth comparing with the glory that will be revealed in us."

Romans 8:18(NIV)

My youngest child, my daughter Stephanie Renée Bell, was on the earth for approximately 654,969,000 seconds, i.e. 20 years, 280 days and 16 hours. At the age of 10 years, she prayed a prayer to accept Jesus Christ into her heart as her Lord and Savior. Total immersion baptism during her teens was her public profession of faith. As a Christian, I *know* that she went to heaven on March 25, 2010.

"Jesus said to her: I am the resurrection and the life. He who believes in me will live, even though he dies; and whoever lives and believes in me will never die."

John 11:25-26(NIV)

"It's all about Jesus." In November of 2009, during one of many hospitalizations, Stephanie was urgently writing on her blanket with her right index finger. When we gave her a pen and paper to decipher what she was writing, she repeatedly scrawled that sentence, superimposing it on one spot on the paper. That was one of the final sentences of her prolific writing career . . .

In April of 2008, I was reduced for several weeks to sitting in a chair, leaning back; the only position that afforded me relief from continuous, excruciating abdominal pain. This was due to a large liver cyst pressing on my stomach. My appointment with a surgeon specializing in liver disease was weeks away. Surgery was finally scheduled for May of 2008. Stephanie spent the night in a chair in my hospital room the night after my surgery. As time went by I was recovering and requiring less narcotic painkillers. Stephanie had just completed her 1st year at a local community college where she had an "A" average, earning induction into Phi Theta Kappa International Honor Society of the Two-Year College.

On June 1, 2008 Stephanie told me that since her May 17, 2008 birthday she had experienced severe headaches. I took her to the local hospital Emergency Room where an MRI revealed a brain mass. She was transferred to Vanderbilt Medical Center in Nashville, Tennessee, where most of the mass was removed and discovered to be a malignant brain tumor, glioblastoma multiforme. Stephanie told us that the night before surgery angels came to her in a dream, telling her to do what they said and be very still and they would protect her, not allowing her to awaken during surgery; this had been her fear. The procedure was done June 2, 2008, 1 year to the day after she gave her Middle Tennessee Home Education Association High School Graduation speech.

In July of 2008 my husband William, myself, Stephanie and our 2 sons Sean and Brandon embarked upon the first of numerous over 1100 mile round way road trips Duke University Medical Center in North Carolina where Stephanie enrolled in a clinical trial that was to be administered by them in conjunction with the local medical center, where all of the radiation treatment and most of the intravenous chemotherapy would be given. She also took oral chemotherapy at home. Before heading for home after the first trip to Duke, we went to the coast since Stephanie had never before seen the ocean. We ended up on Carolina Beach on the 4th of July. During a later trip we were sideswiped on Interstate 40 in Knoxville, on the way to an appointment; the window next to my seat shattered; my shoulder was injured; no one else was injured and there was body damage to our vehicle; we continued on to Duke.

Stephanie was unable to attend school during the Fall, 2008 and Winter, 2009 semesters. However, as MRIs and PET scan began to show no evidence of tumor, Stephanie enrolled for the Fall, 2009 semester at the only local university where Speech Language Pathology (her chosen major) classes were offered at the undergraduate level. She joined the National Student Speech Language and Hearing Association and maintained an "A" average in her coursework and attended classes even when MRIs started to show recurrent tumor and her left arm began to just hang at her side and flail around. She continued to attend until she began to literally stumble and fall.

During that November, 2009 hospitalization she became bedridden. She was discharged to home where we cared for her between ambulance rides, ER visits, further admissions at 3 different hospitals. William and I spent every day and night in her hospital rooms, including the critical care units; Brandon spent most days and nights there. Low blood counts, platelet counts and aggressive tumor growth caused doctors to stop further chemotherapy. Among her requests, I read to her the book of Luke and other Scriptures; her brother Brandon read to her from the book of Ezekiel and other scriptures. Her brother Sean and many others also read the Bible to her. Our family, church pastors and members as well as other friends held prayer vigils and worship sessions at home and at the various hospitals. The Lord held us up during those times as He does now. Our Strong Tower Bible Church family provided a tremendous level of support. We played nearly continuous music in her hospital rooms. As far as we could tell, God in His infinite mercy spared her from agonizing pain throughout, because after she recovered from the surgery she denied any pain whenever we or her doctors would ask.

On a breakthrough, wonderful day, at Vanderbilt, Stephanie was alert, talking and able to swallow. She began to ask for all kinds of foods. I fed her for hours on end while she ate ravenously. The next day I fed her breakfast but by lunchtime she was unable to swallow or talk. In the final throes of the disease, her brother Sean asked her how she was doing. She replied, "Good." She was semi-comatose and during her final admission at the local hospital she lapsed into a coma, eventually going to Heaven on March 25, 2010. Her faith never wavered.

Stephanie attended a private school until the middle of 1st grade; I homeschooled her through high school, except for 2nd grade, during which she attended another private school. She earned many badges as a Girl Scout and was in the National American Miss Pageant. For many years she was a camper and eventual counselor at a Christian camp promoting unity of all people through Christ.

God supplied Stephanie with multiple gifts. An accomplished classically-trained pianist, she also was a guitarist, music composer (copyrighted instrumentals and lyrics, including Christian rap deliberately written in the vernacular of youth, particularly urban youth, for whom she felt a particular burden), artist and dancer. Some of her music included her pseudonyms "NiteLyte" and "AjiaJade." A petite basketball player with great skills, she played for over 10 seasons in a local community league. She took ballet classes at age 5, stopping because she said it made her neck hurt. When she was older, she attended a church Vacation Bible School and was practicing for a group dance that was to be done during the final day, portraying dancers around the throne of Jesus, but injured her ankle and was unable to be in the final group dance. When we told the nurse at the walk-in clinic the circumstances of the injury, she gave us a card bearing the name of a Christian dance studio. Stephanie subsequently took Christian hip-hop dance classes at that studio, which was owned by that nurse and, along with her brother Brandon, she ministered through dance at local churches, parks, a shopping mall and at the Rescue Mission. Although another injury, a tear of the left knee medial patellar retinaculum in August, 2006 (while doing an exercise routine at home) culminated in open knee surgery and ended her dancing here on earth, she continued to serve as a member and long-time President of the 212 Dance Team of our church where she attended since 1999, becoming a member in 2007. She also served on the church Student Youth Council.

It is, of course, her gift of writing that brings me to this foreword. I have spent much time just trying to find all of her writings and probably still have not found them all. Some were handwritten, others in her computers. Looking back through her home school notebooks I found poetry in spiral notebooks on bound sheets interspersed with bound Chemistry, Biology and Math homework and tests that I had graded. I don't recall seeing this poetry as I was grading the work. She completed 3 novels and started many others.

I was aware of the 3 completed novels but only found the poetry and lyrics to her more than 40 songs after she went to Heaven. She also wrote several installments of "fan fiction" as well as many unfinished stories. In her blogs she speaks of her "secret life" of writing.

The fact that many of her *handwritten* works included the date and time of day (of course, the computer writings automatically do) caused me to arrange them chronologically. For those whose date could not be ascertained, I inserted them where the subject seemed to fit with the writings around it. The dates as well as time of day, in my estimation, lend to the poignancy and urgency of her writings, in light of the length of her life on earth. Apparently, oftentimes, she wrote well into the night. As I found more of them, I realized that this compilation was actually autobiographical as well. Her works reflect the degree to which she felt ostracized, especially as a result of the way people, adults and students alike, reacted to her as a home schooled student. As many of the writings were heartbreakingly difficult to read, I procrastinated in collecting them and typing the handwritten ones; not to mention my cataloguing the recordings of her keyboard renditions of her instrumental music compositions and my typing of handwritten song lyrics. Reading her works, however, also provided me with inspiration and comfort, due to the Gospel that she proclaimed. For me, this has been a humbling, incredible journey.

Stephanie touched the lives of many people, including her family, through her ministry of dance, as a camper and camp counselor, and in many other ways. I accepted Jesus Christ as my Lord and Savior after seeing my children on fire for Christ. Stephanie's faith sustained her, supplying strength and courage through a ravaging illness. She walked well in her purpose, which was to glorify God, always acknowledging that her gifts came from Him. She is now perpetually worshipping the Lord, dancing at the foot of the throne of Jesus without limitations. Like the numerous unfinished stories that she wrote, the story of her eternal life will never end.

Stephanie was a gift to us and I thank God for the honor and privilege of being her mother. I'm sure that I did not convey this to her as I should have. These pages are, by far, the most difficult yet joyous that I have ever had to write, their completion facilitated by the guidance of the Holy Spirit. This introduction does not encompass everything that I could say about her. Since her transition to Heaven, the Lord has been holding me up more than I could ever imagine; I am much better than I thought I would be. We more than miss her but we grieve with hope, knowing that we will see her again when we, too, get to Heaven.

In her autobiography containing the poem "Abandoned" she writes: "Why am I writing poems that no ear will ever hear?" I could not let that happen.

To God be the Glory,

Denise Bell, M.D.

Second Wind

STEPHANIE RENÉE BELL

"*My life is filled with stories, some good, but more are bad, though I won't share them all here. True, they shaped me in one way or another, but I have only one particular story to tell, as it's the one that led me to something new, something different and, as I can now admit, something* **beautiful.**" *– Jet*

"You have turned for me my mourning into dancing; You have put off my sackcloth and clothed me with gladness…"
Psalm 30:11(NKJV)

One
Josiah Seth Carmichael

She was always the expressive one, the girl who starred in just about every drama production imaginable. We didn't go to the same high school; she wouldn't recognize me. But I *remembered* her. It was during one of my adventures to snag a girl that I found myself sitting in the school auditorium, watching a production of *West Side Story*. I saw it once with my brother Jonathan when we were kids, and I knew from the start that I liked it. Minus the dancing, singing, and love story, there was action, tough guys who fought for their turf. That's all I needed. If it was any other play than *West Side Story*, I probably wouldn't have even thought about attending—cute girl or not.

So I was sitting next to Julia, my date for the night. We were hidden away in the vacant back row, and I was making sure my arm was around her shoulders at all times. I didn't pay a whole lot of attention to the play, but instead constructed a plan to get alone with her afterwards. Maybe I was too old for *West Side Story*, or maybe I was afraid to be interested in anything involving guys doing ballet. I zoned out for the first scenes of the play. But that quickly changed when Miranda Phillips came onto the stage. I watched her dance and sing, following her every move (although I tried not to get *too* caught up). She was still one of those "off-limits" girls, you know, the type that are morally grounded and serious about their future.

Miranda had always been like a chameleon, transforming into every role given her. Though I had only seen her in two shows, I knew this off the bat. I remember taking my grandmother to see Miranda in *The Nutcracker Suite*. When I walked with Nana Jo out of the community theater that night, all she could talk about was the "beautiful dancer" who stole the show as the Sugarplum Fairy. She wouldn't stop asking me if she went to my school.

Perhaps it was the fact that Miranda and I once met years ago that caused me to take such notice of her. Nana Jo was always telling me the story of how, when I was a toddler, and while visiting her in North Philly, she would take my mother and me to the park. Somehow, more than twice, she would pass the same lady and child on one of the paths; the little girl, of course, being Miranda. Chuckling, Nana Jo patted my hand and turned to my mother, saying, "I wouldn't be a bit surprised if those two crossed paths someday." My mom shook her head with a sigh, replying, "Momma Jo, what did Clay and I tell you 'bout bein' superstitious?" Raising her eyebrows and hands, Nana Jo said, "Who said anything about superstition, Evelyn? I'm talkin' 'bout the Lord's providence!"

Over a decade later, I'm certain Miranda wouldn't have recognized me for all of the dance competition trophies in the world. She had much more important things on her mind.

Popular as she was on the side of the North Philly neighborhood I lived in with Nana Jo, there was much to be found out about

Miranda—at least by me. All my friends and I knew was that she attended Marshall High, danced and acted, and lived a few blocks down from me in the West Oak Lane neighborhood with her parents—emphasis on parents. Miranda was fortunate to have both her mother and her father at home, and she was envied by many, including myself.

As for me, I was raised in an "okay" neighborhood in the South. While it wasn't the best, it wasn't the worst, either. Everyone held a special sense of community. Homemade ice cream on a neighbor's front porch, bike riding up to the market for some Kool-Aid, and watching the older boys fix up their cars was everyday life for me in Memphis, Tennessee. I felt like my life was normal—I wasn't ever held up on the way to school (unless you count the elementary bullies). I never had an older brother in jail, and I made decent grades. But I didn't come close to learning about the life waiting for me outside of Memphis until the Sunday night my parents had the argument.

Mom and Dad almost never fought, but I guess that changed when the money got low. My father was an elder at our church and a physical therapist. He worked hard to help people who had strokes or injuries to be their best, giving them the confidence to live life. I remember watching him at work one day after school— the way he talked and laughed with the patients as though everything was normal for them. It made me feel proud to know that he was so appreciated. If only those days could have lasted . . .

I was ten years old when my father lost his job. My first real taste of the violence of the streets finally visited my doorstep. My dad was shot in a random drive-by shooting. Now he needed the very help he used to give on the job. He got very sick from complications due to surgery and couldn't work anymore. My older brother and I were heartbroken to see our dad, our hero, so dependent and weak. The doctor bills piled higher and higher, and

16

my young mother, having to take on two jobs in order to support us, soon grew weary. She was quietly carrying the burden of providing for our family by herself, and I suppose she must have eventually had enough, because she was gone the morning after a bitter argument with my dad.

My brother and I later moved in with Nana Jo (Dad's mom) in Philadelphia, and that's when the change in me began. Almost as though it had been waiting to surface, I saw and felt things in me that I never knew were there before. I started to not care about my future and depended only on the present. I wanted to be liked by my new "friends" in Philly, so I did everything they dared me to, tackling every risk without a second thought. I was the "country boy," the kid from the South who would never be anything but soft. I proved them wrong every chance I got. I had to fit in; it was all I felt I had left for me.

At sixteen I was finally "the man" at my high school, just as I planned from the start. Anyone who wasn't my friend feared me, and it felt good to know that I was important in some way. My brother, Jonathan, being four years older than me, was in college, giving me the room I wanted to express myself without the intimidation of his shadow above me. And I ran with it, forsaking my studies and responsibilities more than ever in order to gain respect and "star status." I shoplifted a little here and there, boasted of being a bit of a "class clown," and lied about dating tons of girls (when in reality I couldn't have been shier around them). I tried alcohol in front of my boys once—just in case they thought I was still "soft." Popular as I was with the guys, girls usually steered clear of me (the more academically-focused ones, at least) but I didn't mind. If they wanted to pretend that they were too good for me, well, I didn't care. Who needed a smart girl with morals? Not only was that lacking in "fun," but it didn't earn me any points with the boys.

My life is filled with stories, some good, but more are bad, though I won't share them all here. True, they shaped me in one way or another, but I have only one particular story to tell, as it's the one that led me to something new, something different and, as I can now admit, something beautiful.

Two
Jet

There's one day that's been branded into my mind, burning and searing through my thoughts when I fail to find sleep at night.

Graduation day couldn't have gone any better in the beginning, especially with Nana Jo and Jonathan there to watch me get my hard-earned diploma (my dad, hospitalized in Memphis, was only able to send his love and congratulations). Though there wasn't much for me to be proud of regarding my studies, I had done well enough in football to receive a full scholarship to La Salle University in Philadelphia to play for the Explorers. With a growing ego, having earned the nickname of "Jet" on the field, my goal, as you might have already guessed, was to go to college, meet girls, mess around and make some big money in the NFL someday. That was all I could make of my so-called "dream," until I stumbled onto a path that changed everything.

Jeremy had been my closest friend since day one in Philly. He had challenged me to leave my old country ways and join his crew. He took me under his wing, and taught me all he knew about "hustling." Little did I know what my knowledge could do when allowed to get out of hand.

After a graduation celebration dinner with Nana Jo and other family and friends, Jeremy dropped by, inviting me out with him and some other boys—older guys whom I knew to be important in the hood. Leaving the dinner, I went out with them, our destination unknown but purpose clear. We would find some girls and head to the club, said Nikko, the leader of the pack. I was game for some fun and excited on a night meant for celebrating the end of high school.

We pulled our cars in front of Katalist, the hottest club in the area, and piled out. Jeremy joked about agreeing to be the "designated driver" (which, for us, only meant that he would *try* to drink less than everyone else). He and I rode over in my Mustang, and I remember handing Jeremy the keys. After only a few minutes of being inside the club, while I was flirting with a girl near the bar, Nikko grabbed my shoulder suddenly, enraged and already drunk. Apparently, the girl was reserved by Nikko, and before I knew it, he threw a punch. We went tumbling over the bar, fighting and yelling, until one of Nikko's boys came forward with a gun.

The whole club was sent into a riot of beer bottles, switchblades and fists, and I was barely able to escape to the front of the building with just a few bruises. I felt a hand on my shoulder, and turned to see Jeremy, out of breath and holding my car keys. "Get outta' here!" he yelled over the commotion.

Seconds after speeding off, I heard sirens in the distance, and soon they were hot on my trail. I swerved and avoided them, block after block, not knowing where I was going but understanding full-well what an arrest would mean for my future. Shooting through an alley, I found myself in a secluded parking lot and pressed harder on the gas. I glanced back over my shoulder several times to search for the police cars. But after returning my focus to the road again, I suddenly noticed a figure walking toward their parked car. It was the only car in the lot. Clenching the steering wheel with all of my strength, I slammed on the brakes and jerked the wheel, trying to avoid hitting the person. Still, over the wail of my tires, I heard the crash of metal against flesh and bones—a painful scream. I kept driving, dazed and shocked by what I had just done.

Everything else went by in a flash, but the next morning, alive and a free man in my own bed, I knew that I had been the cause of a hit and run.

Three
Miranda Anastasia Phillips

My life needed direction. It had always been that way for me. Any time I felt that something was out of my hands, it scared me—and I wasn't easily frightened. Okay, maybe I was, but I certainly wouldn't have admitted it at first. Not for anything.

You see, fear of failure was my biggest enemy. I was always afraid of missing the mark. If I set a goal for myself, the only option was to reach it. The goal had to have great meaning, as well. I guess you could say I was terrified of being purposeless.

I wear my formerly-dark, wavy hair in copper braids. I have my father's clay-brown skin and my grandmother's hazel eyes (I can't tell you how many times I've defended the fact that they're *not*, indeed, contacts). My father jokes that everything else is strictly from Momma—my personality, mouth, nose, and especially my love for expression.

Momma was a drama coach for a local theater, until I was five or so, when she decided to go back to school. In my mom's womb, I must have heard her singing, and that's when they say I inherited my passion. In my daddy's arms as a little girl, he and I danced the waltz or ballet before I went to bed. Expression was all around me, itching for me to grow up and fill the large footsteps awaiting my debut. It was perfect, and, most importantly for me, overflowing with direction *and* purpose. All of that changed, though, after the accident.

When I was twelve, I broke my arm in a ballet class, fourteen when I sprained my ankle. Injuries were merely "the pulp in a dancer's orange juice," as my mother had so often said during many a physical therapy session. My volleyball and basketball girlfriends understood my pain, but I knew that they really couldn't fathom how dance could possibly be so dangerous. Each time I got hurt, I decided that I would overcome with flying colors, no matter what it took. I remember telling my mother once on the way to the doctor with a badly-broken toe, that, whatever he recommended about my future, I wouldn't stop dancing. Smiling, she merely nodded quietly, her thoughts probably soaring off to her own days of determination.

Evangeline Phillips was a dancer, singer, actress and teacher. My mother could have been world famous, as my father always said, but instead of money and fame, she chose my dad, sister and me. She told me that she had sat on her bed in her room, holding the telephone in one hand, ready to return a top Hollywood agent's call, and the Bible in the other. She said, "The Book fell open to Proverbs 16:9 (NIV)—*'In his heart a man plans his course, but the Lord determines his steps,'* and I put the phone down." The story sounded heartwarming and predictable—like something you'd see in a movie. But my younger self couldn't find the adventure in her decision, as much as I loved and respected her. After marrying my dad, Momma continued through college, learning more about her passion for drama as she developed a love for teaching the art to others. A few years later, she had my sister, Nina, and then me.

I grew up in West Oak Lane, North Philly, where my parents made a decent living for us through their drama studio and agency. Being the daughter of a businessman, I learned to accept life as a rollercoaster. Sometimes we glided along smoothly, other times we struggled to make ends meet.

I can recall a time when I took my first ballet classes at a prestigious academy downtown. After a while, I had to miss a few of the classes because of the high tuition. When I came back, a few of the girls laughed at me and asked me where I had been. I lied that I was sick, not wanting to admit to them that my parents actually couldn't afford to send me to the pricey school. It somehow made me feel like less of a dancer, but also made me work harder.

I appreciate my dad for how hard he worked to keep me dancing, and I know that if it weren't for his own sacrifices I wouldn't love dancing as much as I do. Wiping the tears from my face after the embarrassing, painful departure from my ballet academy, my daddy told me how things would get better for me. He made sure a long time ago that I would live a successful, joyful life.

Four
Miranda

I didn't know how little I knew about pain until I found myself on a hospital bed, staring up at a tear-blurred emergency room ceiling, wanting for the first and only time in my life to die. It was the most terrifying moment I've ever been in, next to the accident itself. Talking about it has never been easy for me. When I became aware of my mother at the bedside, holding my quaking hand, I saw the tears in her eyes, and that's when I knew it was serious—whatever had happened to me. I couldn't remember anything about the accident, but I was later told all that had happened: my legs were shattered and I might never walk again. When they told me this, all I heard was, "you'll never *dance* again."

This time, my once-determined, headstrong self believed it . . . and accepted it.

It took a whole two years for me to recover, and, yes, I was able to walk again—though not like I used to. I limped, mostly, due to what the doctors diagnosed as secondary osteoarthritis in my knees, which is a form of arthritis that comes as a result of injury. On good days I used a cane, bad ones I stayed at home in bed, battling the pain I would struggle with for years. You may wonder how I was able to walk again after being told it was hopeless, but I decided early on that I was at least going to have that much out of life. The pain of not being able to dance any more cut deeper than anything I had ever felt, but I had to at least walk again.

Pushing myself to the limit, I strengthened my legs through countless hours of physical therapy, and after many prayers of healing from my church, family and friends, the doctors were astounded with the progress I made. Though dancing wasn't a possibility, walking was, and that was enough for those who loved me. I just wish I could say that it was enough for me.

At nineteen, the age that I was once planning on being enrolled in Juilliard or training with the Alvin Ailey dancers, I was working at a local Philly studio, teaching ballet and jazz. All I had to do was call out the move the dancers were to execute (since ballet is made up of terminology) or have one of the students demonstrate it for me. My church supported the studio, my parents' agency as well, thus everyone was like family. But it wasn't always easy. Many times I don't understand why I took the job. Surprisingly, I received lots of offers from studios and schools to teach after news of my injury got out, and painful as it was, I accepted one. Being around dance while unable to actually do it was as painful as being on that hospital bed. However, being away from the art would have hurt me even more. I guess you could say it was my bittersweet escape.

Teaching grew on me over time, and I found a sort of peace in watching the growth and joy in my students. It helped me to show others how to dance. Maybe that's why I loved teaching so much. It gave me a voice where I thought I was mute, and reminded me that

I wasn't the only dancer in the world. It took the focus off of my problem.

Every now and then, a student would arrive, coming from a broken home or as a sort of intervention, usually on a scholarship. The new students almost never struggled with fitting in. The diversity of rich and poor, black and white, professional and beginner, always delighted me, and watching others excel gave me a thrill that helped to distract my mind from my disability.

One night, while finishing up with a class, my co-worker and close friend, Cat, walked into my classroom. I was lifting one of the portable ballet bars and moving it to a wall.

"Miranda, now what're you doing that for?"

I glanced over my shoulder, puffing as I held the bar with one hand and my cane in the other.

"Just cleanin' up," I grunted.

Cat jogged over.

"Here—why didn't your kids do it?" she asked, removing the bar and carrying it herself.

Wistfully, I watched her from the middle of the floor.

"We got out late," I explained shortly, feeling a mixture of sadness and weariness—as I usually did after my night classes.

Cat turned, pulling her fingers through her shoulder-length, reddish-blond hair with a sigh.

"And?" she asked.

I shrugged. "They had to go home—it's a school night. I told them I'd do it."

Cat shook her head, casting me her usual disapproving look. She had never liked me working too hard, and was the person I trusted the most at the studio (even though she could lean on the overprotective side every now and then).

Our friendship dated back to high school, where we used to hold healthy competition for roles and solos in the dance and drama world. As much as I loved her and was happy about her accomplishments, it was sometimes hard for me not to be envious of the life she had . . . the life I almost had.

Cat was your classic "eat, drink and sleep" dance fanatic. Often I joked that she was worse than me. With long, graceful limbs and a lean frame—the "ideal" dancer's body—Cat also had the skills and personality to match it. She was, however, still waiting on her big break, teaching at the studio in the meantime.

"C'mon, Cat, I promise I'm okay," I reassured her as I walked over to a compact refrigerator in the corner. "You forget I'm in shape."

"But that doesn't mean you need to wear yourself out," Cat countered, slinging her sports bag over her shoulder as she checked her watch. "Ten already!" she sighed. "Believe it or not, I didn't come to scold you—"

"Believe it or not," I repeated sarcastically.

We both laughed.

"So what'd you come for?" I questioned, opening a bottle of water as I gathered my things.

"News—remember the guy who won that big game for La Salle Friday?"

I shook my head.

Cat sighed, known for being frustrated when her joy at a news flash wasn't shared.

"*You know*, Mira—that guy, Joe . . . uh, er . . . wait, Gene . . . no—Jordan?"

I laughed, sweeping a stray braid out of my face.

"Cat, you don't even know his name and you get on *me* about not knowing who he is?"

"I just forgot, okay? Anyway, he's number sixty-seven or somethin,' and he won the game for La Salle—"

"You already said that. What's the big deal?" I asked as we locked

28

up, leaving the building and crossing the city street to our cars.

"The *big deal*," Cat began, trying to sound important against my disregard, "is that he's coming here."

"Where?"

"The studio, of course!"

"What? Why?"

Cat leaned against the side of my Pontiac Firebird as I loaded the trunk, sighing heavily at my ignorance on the subject.

"Miranda, where *have* you been, girl? He's gonna take lessons here—somethin' about how he snuck out one night and got in some trouble. So the coach announced this morning to the press that the guy's gotta have some kind of discipline thing to do."

I listened skeptically.

"So the coach told the whole city in his press conference that dance is *punishment* . . ." I laughed wryly. "Um . . . *why* do I not like football again?"

Cat laughed at my attitude.

"No, Mira. You know what he meant." She shook her head. "You are *such* a cynic sometimes . . ."

I shrugged, knowing she was right.

"So now we're gonna have a big-headed, immature, irresponsible football player to worry about," I reported dully. "That's the news flash?"

Cat nodded. "In a nutshell."

I sighed as I lowered the trunk door to a close.

"Well, I'll tell you what, I'm definitely *not* gonna be the one to teach him."

Five
Jet

It all started when I walked through the door. The press, the cameras, the *humiliation*. After managing to escape the mob of media personnel outside of the studio, I walked in, greeted by a host of faces. A short man in his late forties, with dusty-gray hair and tired eyes, stepped forward, extending his hand.

"Welcome, Mr. Carmichael. I'm David Nelson—I'm free to answer any questions you might have. We hope you'll like it here."

I nodded as I shook his hand, noting just how forced his smile might have been. Squinting from a flash from my right, I noticed a camera man from one of the big newspapers. I felt like a publicity stunt. *"Like it* here?" I wondered. I knew I would hate it.

"Do, uh . . . do you have a bathroom I could use?" I asked before I could be led off to the scheduled tour of the building, wanting to be alone to gather myself first.

Mr. Nelson glanced at the other teachers and staff watching me in the lobby.

"Yes—yes, of course. Carl, show Mr. Carmichael to the restroom, please."

A younger teacher led me off down a hallway, and after nodding my thanks, I went inside of the bathroom.

Wiping my face with a wet paper towel, I looked in the mirror, noting how tired I was.

I never thought I was bad looking, but that I was actually quite handsome. My skin was medium brown and my eyes were dark, slanted a little like my mother's. I wore my dark brown hair cut short, having recently shifted from corn rows. Because I played running back, I had to be agile and strong, and I still remember how hard it was for me to build the muscle I had in college.

Twenty-one years old and on my way to the NFL, I couldn't have asked for more in my life, but if it weren't for the football victories under my belt, I don't know if I would have still been popular on campus. I had a few friends with whom I hung out, as well as girls whom I flirted with and dated regularly. But somehow, I still got the feeling that they only wanted to share in my popularity by being my "friend." I couldn't really talk to anyone at school, nor on the team—not even the coach. I ignored the reality of my seclusion, focusing instead on the guarantee of the NFL. What else was there to do?

Finally leaving the bathroom, I walked back down the hallways to the lobby and people awaiting me, my mind drifting to just what had brought me here in the first place.

It was the night of the homecoming game, and we had just won against LSU—thanks mostly, to me. A few of the other guys were going out to celebrate, and asked me to come along. We headed to a few clubs, staying out way past curfew, and soon enough we were caught. The other two guys got off a lot easier than I did, since it was their first slip-up. But me, being the rebellious, free spirit that I was—I had snuck out many a night, breaking lots of other campus rules as well. My name had graced the newspapers more times in a bad way than in the light of a victory for the team. Everyone knew me as the "kid with potential who just needed a swift kick in the"— you-know-what. I guess that's why Coach decided to arrange for me to take dance classes.

Humiliating as it was, I was willing to do almost anything to keep my scholarship. I could only hope that I would be taking hip-hop or breakdance lessons—anything but— no, the thought was too ugly. They wouldn't . . . would they?

"Here are a few of our lesson rooms—we recently remodeled, adding more ballet bars and mirrors."

I cringed as Mr. Nelson spoke. Did he just say "ballet?" What could I care about it? Why wasn't he showing me the hip-hop classrooms?

"And here's the room your class will be held in."

I followed Mr. Nelson into the wood-floored dance classroom, noting the mirrored walls and large, wall-to-wall window overlooking the city streets below. I sighed inwardly. Obviously, I would have to see about getting some curtains put up for privacy. . .

"Your teacher should be here somewhere," Mr. Nelson voiced with a nervous laugh, his eyes darting about the empty room.

As if on cue, though, a door suddenly swung open on the right, apparently leading to a supply room or closet.

I looked over and saw a sight. Standing in the doorway was Miranda Phillips, three years older than I had last seen her at the production of *West Side Story*, and just as pretty as I remembered her. But much to my surprise, she walked with a limp and a cane.

"Ah, there you are." Mr. Nelson smiled. "Mr. Carmichael, this is Ms. Miranda Phillips—she'll be your teacher. Miranda, this is Jet

Carmichael."

Miranda seemed to study me for a moment before holding out her hand.

Clearing my throat, I adjusted the tie of the suit that my coach advised I wear, and then shook her hand.

"Nice to meet you," I said as politely as I could, realizing how odd it felt to officially meet her.

Miranda smiled rather shortly. "Likewise."

Mr. Nelson cleared his throat, feeling awkward at Miranda's lack of enthusiasm.

"Well, now that you two have met and you've seen the studio, Mr. Carmichael, would you like to join my wife and I for lunch?" Mr. Nelson turned to Miranda, who was standing slightly aloof, loosening her braids from their ponytail. I recalled that she used to wear her hair dark and wavy. "You're free to come as well, Miranda."

Miranda shook her head, smiling lightly.

"Um, no thank you, Mr. Nelson. I have a class to prepare for. If you'll excuse me," she paused, turning to me with what I was certain to be a smirk, "Mr. Carmichael."

Nodding, I watched as she left, trying to figure out what two months of classes with *her* was going to be like.

Six
Miranda

"Walking better today, Miranda."

I smiled at my doctor's amiable compliment, limping only slightly at her request to pace the floor.

"Too bad it never feels like it." I sighed, effortlessly pulling myself back up onto the examination table. Dr. Abdul looked on with an impressed nod, her long, brown curls bouncing. She had been my doctor since before my accident, and knew me well—recalling each of my injuries. Dr. Nancy Abdul was first a friend of my mom's, before she became our orthopedist.

"But you can't say your upper-body strength isn't good." Dr. Abdul chuckled, briefly wiggling a pen in my direction with a smile. "That's what crutches will do for you."

I gave a light laugh, rubbing one arm and noting the additional muscle detail. It certainly wasn't there before the accident.

"I guess so," I murmured, distantly watching Dr. Abdul's tiny hand hastily jotting on a form.

"So . . ." she began conversationally, her eyes on the paper, "I hear Mayo's been in contact with you—New York and Chicago too..."

I distantly pulled at one of my braids and finally shrugged, staring at the purple-and-orange-tiled floor.

Dr. Abdul must have noted my silence, and looked up. "Have you talked to your family about it yet?"

When I shook my head, she nodded slowly, setting her pen down and removing her small, metal-framed glasses.

"Well, just be careful about those offers," she admonished, choosing her words carefully. "These kinds of situations have to be handled delicately, and even though they may be onto something with this talk of surgery, you've got to make sure it's the right thing to do."

The day I found out that I would be teaching Jet, I knew that something was going to change for me. Be it good or bad—I didn't know—but I guessed that it would be the latter.

I ambled into my classroom with a headache, nowhere near feeling ready to teach jazz and ballet basics to an obnoxious football player (especially with my prior doctor's appointment on my mind). As I was straightening the room and preparing for class, I paused, staring at the mirror. Usually, I tried to avoid my reflection as much as possible. I guess I never got over seeing myself with a cane in one hand.

That particular day I wore gray, extra-baggy workout pants and my favorite green sneakers, as well as a black tank. My braids were in a ponytail, adorned with a green headband. I also wore my favorite silver hoop earrings. (Just because I couldn't dance any more didn't mean that I stopped believing in looking halfway decent for my classes.)

Massaging my neck, preparing to ignore my headache, I noticed the door opening in the mirror and watched as Bri walked in. A well-trained student at the studio, she was Jet's soon-to-be partner.

"Hey Miranda," she greeted me cheerily, her almond-shaped, Filipina eyes scrunching up.

Eighteen and fresh out of high school, Bri knew exactly what she wanted to do: open and teach at her own ballet studio. Many a night she had brainstormed with me after class, and she was my favorite student. Everything was fresh for Bri—life, and her future. Though we were only three years apart in age, I often felt like it was years ago that I once planned my life as fearlessly as she did. I was Bri's teacher, and yet I still believe I learned more from her than she did from me.

"Feelin' okay?"

I held up my hand before answering Bri's question and finally let out a sneeze. Rubbing my eyes, I nodded.

"Just a crazy allergic reaction."

Bri winced as she sat against the mirror, pulling on her jazz shoes and tying her long, dark hair into a low ponytail.

"I hate those. Maybe it's from lack of sleep. You know, the immune system can go crazy without rest."

I smiled. Bri's father was a doctor, and she never hesitated to remind students or staff to take care of themselves.

" 'Rest' might as well be a forgotten concept for me."

Barely had the words left my mouth before the door opened once more, this time revealing Jet. He was dressed in a wife beater, baggy jeans and sneakers—stylish in general, facetious for a jazz class.

Shaking my head with a sigh, I turned and walked to the tape deck.

A silence lingered as I sifted through a stack of CDs, wondering just how productive the class could possibly be.

Bri spoke up, "Looks like we're partners. I'm Bri."

I sensed Jet's stare, then glanced in the mirror to see him scratch the back of his neck and shake Bri's extended hand.

"Jet . . ." he said slowly, obviously a bit confused. "So . . . we're *partners?*"

Bri nodded. "Well, yeah."

Jet glanced around. "What kind of dancing are we gonna do?"

Bri chuckled, standing up from her seat by the mirror. "Jazz, of course. Didn't you know?"

Smirking as I found a CD, I popped it into the player.

"Jazz . . ." Jet repeated, standing in the middle of the floor with a look of confusion, disbelief and fear. "Not ballet, then?"

I turned, taking hold of my cane as I walked over.

"Not ballet," I confirmed.

Jet relaxed, breathing a heavy sigh of relief.

"Good." He grinned at Bri. "You don't know how worried you had me for a second there—"

"Closely related to it, though," I finished with a saccharine smile.

Jet's lopsided grin quickly faded and he glanced back at the door.

"Listen, I, uh . . . I really can't do anything close to ballet—let alone ballet itself. So maybe I'll just check out the hip-hop class—"

"Mr. Carmichael—"

"*Jet,*" he interrupted, eyeing me evenly. "Jet is fine."

I smiled sarcastically. The idea of changing one's name to a nickname gained from football seemed ridiculous to me.

"Josiah."

Jet cringed. I proceeded.

"I know this is all new to you, but there's a common rule we follow in the dance world—the football world as well, I'm sure: you've gotta give some to get some." I paused with a shrug. "Consider this 'giving some' to get back to your football glory."

A five-second-long staring (or I should say *glaring*) match followed my remark, until Bri, whom both of us had forgotten, cleared her throat.

"We'll start from the top," I said casually, then glanced at Jet's shoes. "And you'll quickly find out it's pretty hard to do jazz in sneaks."

"Well, what else am I supposed to wear—slippers?" Jet complained.

I smiled mischievously.

"If that's what you want—"

"No! I mean . . ." Jet sighed. "Let's just . . . start from the top. I'll get some new shoes later."

Bri and I shared a glance, secretly amused at his paranoia.

"The dance you'll learn," I began, pacing slightly between the two of them and the mirror, "is a story of endurance and strength... "

"Sounds good to me," Jet whispered to Bri with a smile, and she chuckled.

Pausing, having heard his remark, I smiled to myself before continuing.

"But also love. Bri, your role is to be elusive, yet . . . curious." I stopped in front of Jet. "And Jet, your job is to resist and pursue."

"So we have the same role, basically." Jet shrugged.

"No, because you're the one who takes the lead."

Seven
Jet

To be honest with you, Miranda's teaching tactics weren't that different from Coach's on the practice field. If our footwork was off, he'd correct it; our form, our technique, our devotion—all of it was to be carefully refined. Coach never missed a beat, neither did Miranda. Under her watchful eye, I was unable to get away with even the slightest mistake.

"I promise she's not gonna bite, Jet—put your arm around her waist."

Resisting the urge to show my disdain, I did as I was told, taking hold of my oh-so-patient partner Bri's waist before doing my version of a jazz walk across the floor. Miranda's scrutinizing eyes followed my every move from her station in front of the mirror.

"Point your toes!" she called over the cheesy classical music.

"I *am*," I muttered.

"Don't be scared," Bri whispered, displaying her tendency to have my back. It helped having a partner who knew Miranda like a book. That way, I could be told where all the potholes were in the road—which buttons to avoid when it came to Miranda's short temper.

"I'm not," I replied as we walked in the other direction.

Miranda, what with her meticulous nature, had taken no time in getting the basics of jazz dance out of the way. Today we were working on jazz walks, which were far from my style.

"All guys who do this point their toes," Bri assured me.

I smirked as we paused and prepared to walk the other way again. "All guys who do this are—"

"Um, excuse me?" Miranda interrupted my negative remark, shutting off the music with a remote. "When did I say we were talking and not jazz walking?"

I felt embarrassed, as if I was being scolded by my coach for a fumble or misstep. Somehow, however, this was almost worse.

"Don't worry, I promise it gets easier."

I smirked at Bri's faithful optimism.

"Easy for you to say—you've been doin' this for years."

Two hours later, with my third dance class behind me, I was barely able to walk to my car, catching up with Bri as I did so. Believe it or not, my legs, arms and stomach were aching almost as much as they did in football training. Three days of *demi pliés* and *tendus* were enough to make my muscles want to quit—muscles that I didn't even use in football nor did I know existed. Miranda sure didn't take conditioning lightly.

Bri shrugged blithely, running her fingers through her loosened hair. Dressed in casual clothes—jeans and a hoodie—I knew that Bri didn't seem as intimidating as she did in the classroom (at least at first) with her strictly-bound hair, leotard or tank, and toes skillfully pointed. Ballet and jazz were completely new worlds to me, and being around two people who knew it so well often succeeded in dragging my confidence in the dirt. But there was a camaraderie between us that I honestly didn't know in college or on the team, and I hoped we could become friends.

"You've got a natural way with it, Jet. Stop worrying."

I laughed in disbelief as we crossed the busy street to the adjacent parking lot, straightening my leather jacket on my shoulders.

"Miranda sure doesn't seem to think so." I puffed a little as we reached Bri's car—two spaces away from mine. "Here, lemme help." Stepping in, I lifted a boom box from the trunk to make room for her bag.

"Thanks." Bri smiled gratefully as she placed the bag inside. "You can just put that in the back seat."

Opening the door of the car, I set the boom box on the floor. "Miranda can be . . . vague, but that doesn't always mean she's not pleased." Bri spoke slowly, thoughtfully, as she closed the trunk. "Trust me, I had to learn that one day, too—we all did."

I sighed, leaning against the car.

"Well, it sure ain't easy to learn." Exasperated, as cars shuttled by and the busy sounds of the city filled the air, I continued, "So has she always been like that?"

Bri's shoulders lifted in a shrug. "She's just demanding."

I shook my head.

"I mean, did she change after she got hurt?" I responded carefully.

"Oh." She tucked a strand of hair behind her ear, looking out to the studio across the street. "I was fifteen when it happened. I didn't really know her yet—we went to the same school, though." She paused. "Miranda was a really good dancer, to me, the best. It sounds like I'm just saying that, but it's true. You could ask anyone who's seen her dance, and they'd tell you the same. She could have been really successful and even famous."

I was silent as Bri paused, and the memory of Miranda dancing

41

on the stage in high school darted through my thoughts, her very presence lighting up the theater and captivating its audience. I wanted to ask exactly what had happened to Miranda that kept her from dancing, but figured I could always ask Bri another time. No one had brought it up in the short time I had been at the studio, and it seemed to be taboo.

Finally, Bri shrugged, turning to me with a light smile. "I guess she's just a perfectionist, in her own way."

After saying goodbye, I walked to my own car as Bri drove off, silently wondering if the glowing Miranda I recalled had truly shrunken into the past.

Eight
Miranda

A symphony of strings, harps and a piano echoed dramatically through my mind, and almost as though having a life of their own, images of dancers twirled through my dream. My mind was their stage, my thoughts their music.

"Mira!"

Scrunching my nose, I turned onto my stomach, hearing a thud below me.

"Mira, you there, girl?"

Slowly, I opened my eyes and looked around to see my bedside table, the clock which read 6:40 P.M., and near darkness in the rest of the room. My soft-pink night light glowed from my right.

"Miranda—oh . . . oops."

"Nina," I mumbled, pulling the blaring headphones off with a frown. "What do you want?"

Nina sighed as she leaned in the doorway of my room, crossing her arms over her chest. She looked a lot like Momma right then, with her eyebrow raised innately and head wagging disapprovingly from left to right. Nina was older than me by three years, yet was much more of a risk taker. As much as she loved dance, her true passion was modeling. Anything from TV commercials, perfume ads, and even a TV show once, Nina loved to be on display. With her winning smile, medium-brown, crystal-clear complexion and thin frame, her career certainly couldn't have been more fitting.

"Choreographing in our sleep again, Mira?"

I sat up, bleary-eyed, and shut the power off on my iPod, wishing suddenly that Nina hadn't decided to come back home to Philly between jobs.

"Just preparing for tonight's class," I replied after yawning, frowning down to see my history textbook on the floor. I had been trying to study for a test I had the next morning, as well as choreographing a piece in my mind. But I had fallen asleep . . . as usual.

"Tonight's *class*!?" Nina gasped, placing her hands on her hips. "I thought you just got back from the studio an hour ago!"

Panicked, I got out of bed, flicking on a lamp before limping over to my bureau. Glancing at my reflection in the mirror, I shook my head. My braids were sticking out randomly and my eyes were red and weary.

"They sure are askin' a lot of you over there, Mira."

I sighed at her musing, pausing in my rummaging for an outfit to wear to my second trip to the studio.

"No more than your people ask of you," I returned somewhat defensively, beginning to wonder if Mom had sent her up to scold me.

"Well, yeah, but that's diff—"

I looked at her indignantly as Nina caught herself.

"That's what?" I quizzed as I turned around. "Different?"

Nina sighed, twirling a strand of her dark hair in her fingers. "*No...*"

"But that's what you were *gonna* say, Nina."

"Mira, c'mon." Nina ambled over to the bed and collapsed.

As I silently gathered my clothes together and we put the near-argument behind us, Nina distantly played with the ballerina charm bracelet on my bedside table.

"Mayo Clinic . . ." she mumbled, then sat up suddenly, excited as her eyes fell on a stack of mail on the table. "Hey!"

"What?" I grumbled vaguely as I scribbled some notes onto my busy calendar.

"You got the letter?"

I sighed, running my fingers through my hair.

"Yeah, I got the letter."

"Did you tell Mom and Dad?"

"No, Nina, I didn't tell them."

"Well, why not?"

My cell vibrated on the bed, and I quickly checked it to read a text from Cat, asking where I was. Startled, I recalled the staff meeting at 6:30—the one which had started a good fifteen minutes ago.

"Oh no," I muttered, then quickly tossed the phone into my purse and tied my hair into a ponytail.

"What is it?" asked Nina, noting my haste.

"I'm runnin' late."

"Well, what about the letter?" Nina prodded. "You've gotta tell Mom and Dad, it's what you've been waiting for—"

"Nina, I've gotta think that through and everything . . ." I shook my head and grabbed my keys. "Look, I don't have time to talk about this right now. I've gotta go."

After parking my car, I crossed the semi-crowded street to the studio. I moved as quickly as I could, ignoring the persistent aching in my right knee (it never liked to be rushed). Pausing briefly in front of a mirror in the lobby, I pulled a braid out of the ponytail, allowing it to dangle near my face. Satisfied, I continued to the board room, where the meeting was probably just about over.

" . . . So with that said, we'll now adjourn—I believe Ms. Nichols brought some homemade cookies in the lobby as well," Mr. Nelson was saying as I stepped quietly into the board room, and Cat caught my eye with a wave.

Moving through the now standing individuals to where I lingered by the door, Cat touched my arm when she arrived.

"Mira, where've you been? I was starting to worry—you didn't answer your phone," she whispered as Mr. Nelson concluded over the light murmuring of the mingling staff members.

Smoothing my dark-brown, pinstripe jacket, I shrugged.

"I forgot to take it off vibrate—I was asleep. So what'd I miss?"

Cat leaned against the wall, her turquoise eyes moving about the room.

"Just the usual boring stuff. Work conduct, studio schedule, *et cetera, et cetera.*"

I nodded, and Mr. Nelson, who had begun to move away from the wireless microphone at the head of the long, mahogany table, suddenly whirled around.

"I'm sorry," he began in his slightly squeaky voice, catching the attention of the staff, "we'd also like to welcome Mr. Carmichael, our guest at tonight's meeting. As we all know, he's coming along nicely with his classes. Mr. Carmichael?"

Frowning, I quickly scanned the room and finally noted Jet, who was standing in a corner in a tan suit, waving shortly with a winning

46

smile at the applause.

"How is it so far?" Mr. Nelson shot the predictable question, and Jet glided to the microphone.

"It's great," came his short but satisfactory response.

Mr. Nelson smiled, and the whole room seemed to glow with pride.

"I thought this was a *staff* meeting," I murmured over to Cat, watching as Jet received a pat on the back from the vice-president as well as a handshake from his wife.

"I guess I forgot about that part of the meeting," Cat answered slowly, keeping her voice down.

I blinked.

"You mean there was *more* of this nonsense?"

Before Cat could reply, Mr. Nelson gave another question.

"Good to hear. So is dancing easier than football, or . . . ?"

Jet seized the microphone and smiled; though, personally, I would have called it a smirk.

"Definitely easier," he assured with a grin, his tone almost condescending. "In the sense of not having someone tackling you all the time," was his skillful addition, and the room immediately filled with laughter.

Crossing my arms over my chest, I shook my head.

"That's gotta be the best recovery of having your foot in your mouth I've ever heard."

Cat sighed at my cynicism. "Mira."

"And, of course, you have your teacher to thank for that," Mr. Nelson quipped matter-of-factly.

"Oh, right. Of course," Jet quickly stated accordingly with a nod, speaking as though he was being interviewed by an ESPN reporter during a post-game recap.

"Is she here yet?" Mr. Nelson asked someone on his right, and was directed to look at the door. "There she is. Miranda, anything you'd like to add?"

Jet seemed to pause in his sycophancy, his grin slowly fading as his gaze rested on me.

I forced a smile, briefly holding up a hand to gesture my decline.

As the staff members moved for refreshments in the lobby, I slipped away into my classroom, not noticing the pair of eyes following me.

Nine
Jet

After exiting the stuffy board room, I noticed Miranda walking down a hallway and turning into her classroom. I spoke with a few teachers for a couple of minutes, then excused myself to follow Miranda.

Standing in the doorway, I watched as she limped to the portable bars on the wall and picked one up. I shook my head and walked in to give her a hand.

As I took the bar from her and placed it in the middle of the floor, Miranda stood watching me, an expression on her face which I couldn't read.

"The other way."

I turned around after setting the bar down.

"It's supposed to go the other way," Miranda explained in a neutral tone, "perpendicular to the mirror."

I adjusted the bar, then laughed shortly.

"My bad," I apologized, secretly wanting a "thank you" of some sort. But not Miranda. She only cast me her signature half-smirking, half-amused smile before turning and walking to her tape deck.

"So I guess we'll be seeing a lot of each other in the *staff* meetings," Miranda said a little too conversationally as she flipped through her CD book.

I shrugged as I slid my hands into my pockets.

"If they invite me," I replied slowly, reading the sarcasm in her tone. Deciding to shift conversation in another direction, I spoke up, "Teaching again?"

"My night jazz class," Miranda responded shortly, distantly twirling her cane in one hand, a movement that I had come to see as an interesting habit of hers.

I nodded, beginning to feel stupid for entering the classroom only to make a one-sided attempt at small talk. Racking my brain, I searched for another casual question, in the event that Miranda should suddenly open up.

"So . . ." I began, taking a deep breath, "do you teach hip-hop too?"

Miranda paused for a full five seconds, then tossed her booklet before limping past me to the door, leaving the room altogether.

The question was completely ridiculous, the kind of thing you want to smack yourself for . . . yet I realized this much too late.

Of course *she doesn't teach hip-hop, Jet!*

Mortified, I sighed heavily, trying to figure out how I could have messed up so badly.

I woke up while trying to sleep that night, and stared up at the ceiling of my apartment for a while, my fingers laced behind my head.

I thought about the night before, the meeting and the "talk" with Miranda, the way she left me standing like an idiot in the empty classroom. Was she deeply hurt? Did she . . . cry—is that why she left?

I had allowed the questions to tumble through my mind for a half-hour or so, and finally came to the conclusion that Miranda simply wasn't the type to cry in front of people—maybe only those whom she really knew well, but especially not someone she didn't like.

Looking back on my remorse now, I can almost laugh. Sadly, there was a day when making girls cry was something to brag about. As cold as I was, it still didn't feel good knowing that I was hurting people, yet I simply leaned on the fact that I would gain something as a result—respect from my boys. That always helped . . . for a little while.

But Miranda, was she that different? Why was I finding myself dwelling on the words I said, echoing through my mind and inciting my guilt? Why did it actually . . . hurt me this time to know that I had hurt someone else?

Until daybreak, when the pitch black outside of my window transformed into a hazy lavender, I tried my hardest to convince myself that Miranda was no different from any other girl to me. But it didn't work.

Dance class was long and draining the next day. I arrived late due to staying on the phone a little too long with a girl from my past, and Miranda certainly wasn't pleased. We still had to actually *learn* the dance, and it didn't help that it took me five whole days to merely get a half-decent jazz walk down.

Half an hour into the class, after finishing Miranda's grueling workout, I embarked upon the journey to mastering a lift.

"Now, with your palms touching, you'll lift her and turn twice."

The first attempt at the lift was an unsuccessful one, and I was pretty disappointed in myself, because of the strength training I had taken. Bri was a good sport about it, though, allowing me to help her up with a chuckle.

Miranda laughed as well, as she rarely did so—usually only whenever I messed up a classic move to a high enough degree.

"See, it takes not just strength, but technique and timing, Josiah," she explained, calling me "Josiah" as she usually did (she refused to call me "Jet"). "Try it aga—"

"Miranda," a voice called from the doorway, and Cicely, the secretary stood in the doorway, obviously nervous.

"Make sure he doesn't kill you, okay?" Miranda joked to Bri before leaving.

Smiling, Bri positioned herself so that we could give the lift another try.

"Wait for me to lift off," she suggested.

Surprised, I asked, "You mean you play a part, too?"

Bri laughed.

"Well yeah, it's not *all* about you, Jet," she jested.

After trying the move again with a little more success, I paused, glancing at the door, where Miranda was talking to Cicely. They were trying to keep their voices low, but I was still able to pick up their conversation.

" . . . Where's he from?" Miranda was asking, puzzled.

"New York—it sounds pretty big. He talked about a cover shoot and everything."

Miranda sighed heavily.

"Who leaked this? I just got the letter a couple of days ago . . ."

Cicely shrugged.

"Everyone's got their eye on you, Miranda—"

"I know, I know," Miranda said. "I just . . . I don't want this public at all. Could you ask him to leave or something?"

Cicely hesitated.

"He's been waiting for two hours—thought your first class was at

52

three."

"Really?" Miranda shook her head, running her fingers along the handle of her cane, lowering her voice when she spoke again. I had to read her lips to understand her. "I bet this whole Josiah thing doesn't help, either."

Cicely smiled sympathetically. "Want me to tell him to go, then?"

Miranda paused in contemplation, then finally shook her head. "No, just tell him to leave his card," she smirked. "Maybe I'll be feeling a little more daring once I get through this class—we're working on *lifts* today."

Cicely patted Miranda's shoulder before walking off.

"So what was that all about today?"

Bri looked over at me, slightly surprised with my question. She looked down with a sigh as we left for the parking lot.

"Um . . . I'm not supposed to say."

I frowned. "C'mon Bri, we're cool, ain't we?"

Bri laughed as we paused to cross the street.

"You're too much, Jet," she sighed. "I really can't say. I mean, it's like mad taboo around here."

I shrugged. "So bend the rules a little."

Bri retorted, "You sure like to make everything easy."

I chuckled as we hurried across the street, our breath turning into foggy mist in the icy air.

"I have to. It makes life a lot—"

"Easier." Bri finished for me.

I gave a smile.

"Exactly. Now tell me, what's this with Miranda and New York— some movie deal or somethin'?"

Bri sighed again as we approached our cars, holding her black, puffy coat closer around her.

"You promise not to tell?"

"Tell who?" I laughed. "You make it sound like someone's not supposed to know about this."

"Well, it's just touchy." Bri took a deep breath. "Okay, okay. Miranda's situation has caught the attention of some major doctors and hospitals."

I nodded.

"And she's been getting letters from them—requests to do some research on her case. So now the Mayo Clinic—that mega-hospital in Minnesota—is trying to tell her that they've come up with a way to help."

I wondered about this as we arrived at Bri's car.

"What is it?"

"Surgery."

"Wow." I shifted my jaw in thought for a moment. "What are the chances?"

Bri shrugged, popping a stick of gum into her mouth.

"That's what we *don't* know yet."

"She *might* dance again, though?"

Bri smiled lightly.

"That's a pretty big 'might'—Mira's pretty hesitant about stuff these days . . ."

"Stuff involving her condition," I added quietly, sliding my hands into my coat pockets. "So what's New York got to do with this?"

"That's where it gets ugly," Bri replied dryly. "See, Miranda doesn't want any of this going public, but now the media's heard about her offers from Mayo. They've been tracking her story locally for a while now, but I guess she's getting a little upset with New York finding out about it."

"She's got some mad ties, I guess."

Bri shrugged.

"Her sister's Nina Phillips."

"Nina Phillips," I murmured, then nodded. "Oh, the girl from those perfume ads!"

An amused smile slowly inched onto Bri's face.

Noting her obvious confusion, I quickly corrected myself.

"Hey, my grandma works in the perfume department, okay?"

We both laughed, but soon became serious again.

"Well, I've gotta go. Thanks for walking me to my car again."

I shrugged with a small smile.

"Don't worry about it—hey, is, uh, is Miranda teaching another class tonight?"

Bri thought about it, then nodded.

"Yeah, I'm pretty sure she is. It's the advanced ballet class."

"In other words, 'Jet's worst nightmare if he took it'?"

Bri chuckled.

"You could say that."

"Not for you, though. I guess you've graduated."

Bri smirked.

"Not exactly. I don't take the Thursday class—I've gotta pick up my little brothers from the daycare tonight."

"Gotcha.'" I nodded. "I think I'll go check out the class, maybe see what Miranda's like when I'm not in the room," I joked.

Bri laughed, and I walked back across the parking lot as she drove off.

The dimly-lit, coffee-house-style lobby was empty when I entered the studio, with the exception of Cicely, who stood behind the front desk with a smile upon seeing me. Slowly, I strolled down the hall to Miranda's classroom, pausing in the open doorway.

Inside, a group of ten or fifteen dancers, all in their late teens to early twenties, were dancing to a slow yet energetic song—their movements modern and dramatic. I soon spotted Miranda, moving along the edges of the room, her eyes shifting from dancer to dancer, but finally locking onto one in particular.

"Sylvia," she spoke, walking over to the girl—obviously one of the younger dancers. "Lift your elbow more," Miranda instructed as she guided Sylvia's extended arm into a graceful pose, the other dancers continuing with the routine.

Downcast, Sylvia sighed at her reflection in the mirror.

"I can't do it—"

"You what?" Miranda inquired expectantly, at lightning speed.

Sylvia looked down shyly.

"I-I mean, I'll work on it."

"Exactly," Miranda nodded. "Just think of your elbow as hanging weightlessly, and your fingers will follow."

Smiling just a little, I watched as Sylvia grew frustrated once more, claiming that she "never could get the graceful-fingers thing down." Sighing, Miranda finally poised the girl's arm into the position once again, then demonstrated it herself, focusing on their reflections in the mirror.

Tilting my head to the side slightly, leaning in the doorway, I realized how intentional—*beautiful*—Miranda made the simple ballet pose when she held it. For the first time since I arrived at the studio, I caught a glimpse of the Miranda from *West Side Story* in high school, the Miranda who seemed born to dance. But maybe it was just the contrast between her and Sylvia . . .

"You'll get it," Miranda assured the diffident Sylvia with a smile, then limped to the front of the class, leaning against the mirror as she continued to watch the dance.

Watching Miranda, I noticed something in her eyes, her face, that I soon realized to be familiar—since she possessed it many a class with Bri and I. Was it sadness? Maybe disappointment—I wasn't completely sure. Recalling it now, there almost seemed to be a yearning or longing in Miranda's eyes as she watched the dancers, perhaps from being unable to dance herself, but also a longing for something else. I would find out what that something was shortly, after Miranda headed for the tape deck and shut the music off.

"Sit down," she said, and the dancers, looking a bit confused (and slightly anxious) did as they were told, most likely grateful for a break anyway.

Miranda didn't speak again for a full minute, and the room remained silent as she stood at her usual spot in front of the mirror, holding her cane below her chin as she routinely did when deep in thought.

"Someone tell me what sells an idea."

A hand was in the air only a second later. Miranda nodded.

"Chris."

Chris, a thin guy with dark hair, gray eyes and a black bandana around his forehead, shrugged as he leaned back on his palms.

"Confidence."

"Why?"

Chris glanced at a few others with a chuckle, then replied,

"Well, without confidence there's no conviction, and dance is all about conviction," he stated matter-of-factly, proud of his answer.

"True," Miranda noted slowly, thoughtfully, as she moved amongst the dancers. "Anyone else?"

Another hand rose, though not as quickly as Chris.'

"Feeling," a girl, with blond hair and lively brown eyes, spoke up. "Nothing is artistic without feeling—dance *or* an idea."

Again, Miranda nodded. "This dance is supposed to be about direction, about showing how you can't hide behind the emptiness in the world. It's about finding who you are as God made you to be," she paused, "but how will the audience know that if they can't see it in you?" Miranda sighed. "Guys, you know how many times I've told you that dance *can't* be something you just do for nothing.

"Everything in dance has to have *purpose*—especially for you, because of *Who* you're dancing for. So if this dance is about finding who you really are, where you really belong, then I've gotta be able to see that in your face—in your eyes." Miranda rubbed her forehead with her fingertips, listening to her voiced feelings echoing throughout the silent room. As some eyes followed her and others examined the floor, she smoothed her hand over her braids, returning to the tape deck.

"Take it from the top," she voiced softly, almost wearily. "Make it *real* this time."

Slowly, the dancers rose to their feet, each taking their starting positions in silence as Miranda stood by the tape deck.

Minutes passed, two or three, maybe, during which the room remained completely quiet and still.

The song started.

I watched the soloist begin her routine as I had seen when I entered, but this time her face was vivid with emotion. Then came the rest of the dancers, moving with a freedom and level of heart that I didn't see before—even the timid Sylvia.

Somewhere near the bridge of the song, I was surprised to feel my own feelings begin to conform to those of the dancers, almost matching the words of the song.

By the final chorus, I realized that I was watching true expression in in motion, filled with purpose, beauty, and conviction. Just as Miranda said would happen if the moves were given the life only real dancing could grant them, I was taken on a journey, eased into a place where I felt the message of the dance. I believed every move.

As stirred as I was by the dancers, though, I didn't truly feel the song as much as when I finally looked at Miranda, who now stood against the back wall, her eyes closed and a single tear escaping down her cheek.

Ten

Miranda

I walked up my front steps slowly that evening, a little more weary than I originally thought I was. Class couldn't have gone better, and I was very proud of my students, yet an ache persisted in my heart that I couldn't ignore.

Placing my key into the lock on the front door, I quickly dabbed at my eyes, removing the remaining traces of the few tears I had cried on the drive home. Since the accident, I never liked for my family to see me crying.

Opening the door, I was met with the warm, inviting smell of home—the gentle blend of sugar and apple, the essence of familiarity that held no true scent, but to which my nose had grown accustomed since childhood.

My house was small compared to homes in the countryside suburbs, but large for an urban residence. Two stories with an attic that I once used for dance practice, it was an old building, constructed in the early twentieth century or so. I've always loved the dark, hardwood floors and heavy oak doors; the way the creaking steps used to scare Nina and me when we were little girls. Given my mom's unique flare of traditional mixed with modern design, the house was very much my favorite place to be—next to a dance room.

Closing the front door behind me with a sigh, my ears picked up music playing in the den, and I walked down the hallway to see what was up. Off the hall and to my right was the den, where my parents were laughing and slow dancing together. Smiling, I prepared to quietly leave for my room.

"Miranda, there you are."

I turned, moving back to the doorway at Mom's call.

"Well hello, stranger," Dad added with a smile. "We haven't seen you for two whole days."

My parents were like the couple from high school who were meant for each other and always seen together—simply fast-forward a few decades. Momma was a thin woman, with a smooth, copper-brown complexion and dark, laughing eyes. Daddy was tall and husky, with a wide grin and deep brown skin.

As Dad wrapped me in a hug, Mom shut off the turntable, taking care not to step on any of the many records scattering the floor.

"I know, work is crazy these days," I said with a light smile.

"Wait." Dad frowned, placing his finger under my chin. "'Vangeline, are these *circles* I see under your daughter's eyes?"

I cringed.

"*Daddy.*"

Dad chuckled.

"Just playin,' Tutu," he assured as I walked over to Momma,

calling me by the nickname he had given me when I was little.

"Let me look at you," Mom said with a sigh, taking my face in her hands. "Still intact?"

"Yes, Mom," I sighed as well.

"Did you eat somethin' yet or are you fasting again?"

I chuckled at her joke.

"I grabbed an—"

"PowerBar from the machine," she finished for me, shaking her head in disapproval. (As you can see, she's definitely one of those "forever-overprotective" parents.) "Nina made some spaghetti about an hour ago. It just needs to be heated up," Mom suggested with a quick kiss on my cheek before returning to the records on the floor.

"Nina made dinner *again*?" I questioned disdainfully, knowing my sister always put way too much salt in her food.

"Yeah," Dad replied, taking a seat on the floor to help Momma. "But we made sure she didn't try to kill us this time," he added with a wink.

I shrugged, jingling my keys before tossing them into my purse.

"Oh, well. So what're you doing—organizing the geezer records for the millionth time this year?"

"Miranda," Mom began after sharing a glance with Dad, "if you're just gonna stand there and make fun of us, then—"

"Okay, okay." I held up my hand with a laugh. "I'm leavin.'"

"Save some midnight snacks for me!" Dad called after me as I headed to the kitchen.

I shook my head with a smile.

"And we need to talk about that letter, too!" Mom added.

I paused in my steps.

Nina must have told them. Oh well.

About an hour later, I was lying across my bed while trying to

61

finish up some studying. When the doorbell rang, I frowned, wondering who it could be.

Through my open doorway, I could hear my mother's quick footsteps and the front door opening, followed by her sing-song voice when she said,

"Kevin, how nice to see you—c'mon in. It's been so long."

"Thanks Mrs. P. Is Miranda here or still at the studio?"

Mom chuckled.

"No, no. She's upstairs—just a moment. How was your trip?"

"Pretty good."

Setting my pencil down, I rubbed my eyes as Mom came up the steps.

"Miranda, guess who's here."

I didn't look up as she stood expectantly in the doorway.

"Who?"

Mom breathed a laugh.

"You could hear us from up here." She shook her head as she moved off. "Don't leave him waiting too long, now."

"Sure, Mom," I mumbled, running my hands over my forehead and up through my braids.

You know that guy from your childhood, the one who sticks with you and your family for years, with the question of a serious relationship hovering over your heads, until you reach a certain age where everything just becomes awkward? Well, I had one of those. Kevin Cannon was his name, and our families had known each other since before either of us were born. Kevin's mother and mine were roommates in college, and are still best friends to this day. Kevin was born first, a year older than me, and I still suspect that Mrs. Cannon and Momma must have stayed up many a night chattering about how their kids would someday marry, making them *official* sisters.

If any direction was lost in my carefully planned life after my injury, Kevin made up for it, as that much of my life was still subtly "planned."

Rolling off my bed, I limped to the mirror without my cane, and loosened my hair from its ponytail, smoothing my black, three-quarter-length-sleeve blouse as well. While starting to leave, I paused, and quickly opened my jewelry box to remove the silver charm necklace Kevin had given me for my eighteenth birthday. Placing it around my neck, I touched the charm as memories surfaced in my mind. With one final glance and a sigh of satisfaction, I left the mirror and descended the steps.

"I'm surprised you're here," Kevin said as he looked up from where he stood by the front door.

"Where else did you think I'd be?" I asked as I arrived at the foot of the steps, grabbing my coat from a hook near the door.

Kevin shrugged as he helped me put it on.

"Where else are you usually?" he returned with a light smile, then hugged me with a quick kiss on my cheek.

As Kevin and I walked out the door into the chilly, early October night air, his hand gently guiding me on my back, I was reminded of the days when we used to dance together—as official partners. Yes, from junior high all the way up to my accident, we were partners in ballet, jazz and hip-hop.

Kevin was an excellent dancer, having been trained since he was able to walk, as was I. And what my parents loved most about him were his good manners, loyalty, and perhaps most importantly, his confidence. Kevin, unlike other guys who danced, was completely unashamed of his talent, and due to his respect for himself, he almost never received any trouble from anyone. A "strong and sturdy" young man, as my father often called him, Kevin was, well, perfect for me, and had stuck with me even after the accident—when our primary excuse to be together was destroyed.

Though he was, in many ways, like a brother to me (having

grown up with him) I still found Kevin attractive, with his dark-brown complexion, broad grin and three-inch-long, tightly-twisted hair.

"So tell me about the studio and everything—what's all this business about Jet Carmichael taking classes?" Kevin interrogated coolly as we walked along the mostly-empty sidewalk, passing the neighbors' houses with an occasional "Hey, Miranda" or "What's happenin,' Kevin?" from a porch or driveway.

Looking down at the ground, the orange and yellow leaves of autumn which crumpled under our feet, I smiled lightly.

"Just a random surprise from La Salle," I replied casually with a wave of my hand.

Kevin looked over at me suspiciously.

" 'A random surprise' in the form of a dangerous, wannabe bad, good-lookin' football cat who I can only *hope* isn't hittin' on you."

I sighed. If there weren't my parents and Nina to worry about getting worked up over my private life, there was Kevin.

"Kevin, c'mon."

"Hey, Miranda, I'm serious. Jet Carmichael's bad news. Everyone knows it, too. You just be careful, okay?" He paused, then sighed, seeming as though he was about to say more but decided against it.

We continued on in silence when I didn't reply, and I looked up at the hazy, late-evening sky.

"So how was ATL, anyway?" I casually asked, brushing a stray braid out of my eyes.

Kevin immediately grinned at mention of Atlanta, sliding one hand into his suede jacket pocket and the other around my shoulders. "Everything I thought it would be. Rayce was feelin' the choreography, as well as the idea."

I nodded, twirling my cane a little as we paused at the outskirts of the neighborhood park.

"So you think it'll work?"

Kevin sighed as we faced each other, looking intently at me.

"I hope so," he replied quietly, then looked down. "Either way," he took my hand, "I'm hopin' you'll be right there beside me."

I looked away.

Kevin's life-long dream was to start a dance company in Atlanta, featuring every style, but specializing in getting urban, teenage males into dancing. He had set out on his first trip to Atlanta recently, receiving an offer to discuss his idea with Rayce Reed, one of the city's top choreographers. Adding to this, Kevin had been asked to showcase some of his choreography for a Christian hip-hop video being shot for an upcoming group. My father, with his entertainment company, had helped Kevin over the years to get his dream to come to fruition.

"I, uh . . . the studio—" I grasped for an excuse.

"Miranda," Kevin interrupted. "I'd wait for you for a thousand years if I had to." He touched my face. "But I want what's best for you, and sometimes I wonder if all of this teaching and being up and about is good for you, especially when in addition to college—"

"Kevin," I cut in, "you think it's hurting me to . . . *have a life?* The doctors never said I couldn't be normal."

Kevin sighed.

"That's not what I meant, Miranda." He ran his fingers through his hair. "I just . . . it's draining you, I can see it. It's in your eyes, Miranda . . . your smile . . ." He paused as I avoided his eyes. "I don't want this life to hurt you . . . and now with newspapers hounding you over this Mayo stuff—what else can you expect me to say?"

I didn't reply for a moment, and looked out into the park at the playgrounds.

"Some people," I began slowly, "told me I wasn't the same Miranda after it happened. Others . . ." I swallowed, then smirked, "they told me I was only worth who I was as a dancer, and, without it . . . well, I was a nobody." I struggled slightly to keep my voice steady. "And then, some people, still, said to run away from dance—to forget it . . . because it would . . . hurt me too much to even think about it anymore, let alone teach it."

Kevin was thoughtfully quiet for a few seconds.

"I hope you don't think that's me, Miranda."

I sighed, turning to look at him with a small shrug.

"But that's how I feel, Kevin." I gathered a long, deep breath. "I've got so much pressure on me from so many directions . . . I just . . . I-I don't want you to be . . ."

"One of them," Kevin finished for me, nodding slowly as his eyes met the ground.

Neither of us said another word during the rest of the walk, and after turning around and heading back home, Kevin dropped me off at my door.

Eleven

Jet

"Nana Jo, I'm back!"

I puffed a little as I stepped through the back door of my grandmother's urban home, carrying a paper bag filled with groceries for that night's dinner.

Placing the bag on the kitchen table, I reached over to switch on the overhead light. While beginning to unpack the groceries, footsteps sounded in the hallway.

"Took you long enough, boy," Nana Jo sighed, and I lifted my hands in defense.

"Traffic—what can I say?"

After a second, both of us smiled and she kissed my cheek before helping put the items away.

"How was it today?" asked Nana Jo. "Learn anything new, any

leaps or *sashés*—whatever they call all of that ballet mumbo-jumbo?"

I smiled wryly.

"Oh, I learned somethin' new alright," I began as I opened the 'fridge, bending over to place a milk carton inside, "that I couldn't dance if I wanted to."

Nana Jo laughed as she stored a few canned items in the pantry. "Well, do you?"

"What?"

"Want to, child."

"Oh . . . I dunno."'

Nana Jo sighed, wagging her head.

My grandmother was your typical sweet, fun-loving grandma. With sixty-five years behind her, she was still beautiful, with crisp white hair, sharp brown eyes, and a smile and laugh that I couldn't find in anyone else. My grandpa, Nana Jo's deceased husband, used to pick me up, slide me onto his lap, and point at Nana Jo and say, "Jet, that right there is God's handiwork at its finest. You find a woman like that when you're older."

I remembered Pap's words as I watched Nana Jo reading the label on the back of a can.

"Honestly, you'd think all they do these days is try to make old women like me big and fat." She sighed. "Look at the calories in this, Jet."

I glanced briefly at the can, then smiled up at her.

"You don't have anything to worry about, and you know it," I replied, but Nana Jo shook her head. "I hear Mr. Harrison's been askin' about you at the meat market again."

Nana Jo cast me a warning glance before turning to put the can away, but I was certain I caught a blush and smile right before she did so.

"Tell me about your lessons. I only see you twice a week now."

I shrugged, leaning against the side of the 'fridge.

"What do you wanna know?"

"Well, what kind of dance you're learnin,' your teacher . . ." She paused, snapping her fingers suddenly. "That's right, I read about it in the paper yesterday—you've got Miranda Phillips, don't you?"

I nodded, fumbling with one of the magnets on the 'fridge, one which supported a picture of Jonathan and I when we were little.

Nana Jo grinned from ear to ear, setting a pot of water on the stove.

"Uh-huh, what have I said for the past seventeen years?"

"Nana, c'mon—"

"I said, 'if those two ain't gonna cross paths in one way or another, then I'll be doggoned.' " She paused, looking up from the stove with a bit of an enigmatic smile on her face. "How old is she now?"

I shrugged, deciding to help out by chopping an onion.

"My age, I guess."

"Yeah, that should be about right." Nana Jo began slicing a carrot. "You know, I see her mother, Evangeline, pretty often at Bible study." She grinned. "Yes, Reverend Carter always has somethin' nice to say about the Phillips family." Nana Jo looked up again, a thought clearly entering her mind. "You know what? You ought to invite her to dinner."

I blinked as she moved to the stove.

"Oh no, c'mon, Nana Jo—"

"Yep, that's exactly what you should do." She nodded before stirring some salt into the pot, waving a spoon in my direction. "You know it would do you some good to have a friend over—"

"But she's not my friend, Nana," I sighed, struggling with the last of the onion, trying not to cut my fingers as the vegetable grew smaller. "She's just a teacher I've gotta deal with until my coach thinks I'm through." I shrugged, trying to convince myself with my own words. "I mean, after this nonsense, it'll all be over," I chuckled. "I've probably only got a few more classes left anyway 'till I'm free."

Nana Jo knowingly glanced back at me with one of her mysterious smiles.

"You never know, Jet. The Lord works in mysterious ways."

"Only a couple of weeks before the recital."

I nearly fell as I attempted a leap, then looked up sharply at Miranda.

"What? What recital?"

Miranda laughed unbelievingly, lowering herself to sit with her back against the mirror.

"The recital you'll be in."

"Doing this dance?" I questioned, my heart seeming to cease beating.

"Well, what else would you do? Kick field goals?" Miranda laughed again, shaking her head in disbelief as she withdrew her cell phone and assessed her schedule.

Bri, who sat stretching to my right, patted my shoulder.

"Don't worry, Jet. You've got this dance down."

But I wasn't supposed to do it in public!

Miranda's words hit like a blow from a 290 lbs. defensive back. She had to have been joking, right? She couldn't possibly put me, the bad boy football player, into a . . . *jazz* recital . . . could she?

She sure did.

I lied to countless newspapers and reporters that I was looking forward to the recital, and that I was confident that I would do well. Why? Well, one thing I never liked to do was be honest about the way I felt about certain things in public—putting up with coach's discipline, for example. Not only would complaining about it look bad to the kids rocking my jersey on the street corners, but Nana Jo and coach wouldn't exactly be pleased either. (And it's not like I wanted Miranda, of all people, to see me sweat.)

So I stuffed my fear of the inevitable recital, and put all my energy into brushing up my skills and practicing overtime—even in my apartment when my roommate wasn't home. Miranda was, believe it or not, impressed, though she didn't really say it.

Walking out of a challenging class with my head held high and a slight swagger in my step, I had to admit that I almost felt better about myself, simply because Miranda had (finally) applauded the final run through of the dance, even going so far as to call it "impressive."

Tossing my keys upon reaching my car, adding a little Michael Jackson spin (when I was sure no one was looking) I opened the door and slid inside while humming a tune, not realizing at the moment just how much Miranda's view of me was beginning to actually *matter* to me.

Twelve

Miranda

Surprisingly, it was on days when my limp wasn't as strong that I felt worse. The doctors said it was psychological, since when I was walking almost normally, I would think of how within reach dancing seemed to be. In reality, however, dancing still wasn't a possibility due to the severity of my arthritis. It was on days when I didn't need my cane that I would watch my dancers move about with absolute freedom, and feel the most heart-wrenching desire to join them. My obstacle, of course, was that I couldn't.

One of these days came only a week before the recital, and I had honestly considered staying home, and would have, had it not been for the students I had to teach and the football player I had to prepare.

"You sure you're alright?"

Looking at Kevin's hand over mine, I slowly nodded.

"Yeah," I lied, ready to open the passenger door of his red sedan. I regretted allowing him to drive me to class that day (he said he wanted to).

Kevin, obviously, wasn't convinced, and sighed.

"Listen, Miranda, you can say no to all of this just like that. We can go to ATL, run the studio and you'll do administration—safe behind a desk..."

"Kevin," I protested, holding up my hand, "I don't feel like talking about this right now, okay? I'm alright."

Kevin studied me for a moment, obviously unwilling to drop the matter so soon.

"Miranda, when *are* we gonna talk about it, then? You've been putting this off for weeks. Now, I know you're busy with classes and your new friend—"

"What new friend?" I returned defensively, moving my hand out from under his.

Kevin shrugged this time as he fiddled with his keys.

"C'mon, Miranda, you know all of these practices with Jet have been takin' up your time."

"So?"

"So you've got a guy waitin' on you and wondering when we're finally gonna . . ." Kevin's voice faded, the car filling with the echo of his loud tone.

I focused out the window while Kevin shook his head. After an awkward, tense pause, he finally turned back to me.

"Forget it for now, okay?" He watched me running my thumb along the door handle, eager to leave, and hesitantly reached for my hand again, but I pulled away. Sighing heavily, he grasped the steering wheel. "Have a good class."

As Kevin drove off, leaving me standing on the sidewalk outside of the studio, I tucked a stray braid behind my ear, watching him go.

I never liked arguing with him, but ever since the accident it seemed as though we had grown apart. It wasn't that we didn't care about each other, but lately, I guess you could say Kevin's caring about me was beginning to annoy me.

"No cane today?"

I turned and looked to see Jet striding up the sidewalk, his sports bag slung over one shoulder.

"No," I replied shortly, though not wanting to answer his forward question at all. While allowing him to hold the door for me, though, I couldn't help but recall (and perhaps appreciate) the considerate tone in his inquiry, the hint of concern in his serious, dark eyes.

For the next two hours, I watched Jet and Bri move about the floor effortlessly, their dancing synchronized, purposeful, and simply beautiful. Jet seemed to be trying a little harder than usual these days, and his work was paying off. Come the last run through of the dance that afternoon, Jet had taken every critique I had given him, executing each move with precision and skill. Watching him dance out the soulful quality of the song, holding Bri in the final pose, I realized then and there that Jet was a natural at dancing. He had a gift.

Jet broke the pose a few seconds after the music faded, a little out of breath, his hands on his hips and eyes hopefully awaiting my approval.

Standing before Bri and Jet, Bri already being one of my favorite students and Jet now easing onto the list, I almost felt honored, and had to look away for a moment.

"There's no more work to do. You can go now," I stated quietly, pretending to be interested in the white stripe running down the leg of my workout pants.

Jet and Bri shared a glance, almost afraid to speak.

"I-it's only 6:00 . . ." Jet frowned. "No three-hour practice today?"

I smiled a little at the tone of disbelief in his voice, then nodded.

"No three-hour practice. Keep practicing, though—the recital's only a week away." I walked over to the tape deck, occupying myself with flipping through my CDs, trying to look as though I was preparing for the next class.

Jet silently watched me for a moment as Bri gathered her things, then he finally did the same, leaving the room.

Two long hours later, when all of the students and teachers had gone, and I was left only with Mr. Nelson in his office and Cicely filing papers in the lobby, I sat quietly behind my desk in the classroom, holding my head in my hands. I had dismissed my final class for the day only fifteen minutes earlier, and I wanted a moment to rest.

"Miranda."

I looked up abruptly.

"Are you alright?" asked Mr. Nelson from the doorway, himself looking a little drained from the long day (the whole studio staff gave their all before a big recital).

I smiled lightly.

"Yeah, I'm fine, Mr. Nelson. Just a little tired."

Mr. Nelson nodded understandingly.

"Alright. I'm leaving now and Cicely's done, too—the janitor will probably stop by in a few minutes. Are you okay with locking up?"

"Sure thing."

Mr. Nelson smiled and left, and a few minutes later the building was completely silent.

In the quiet of my classroom, I returned my head to my hands, wanting to allow my mind to settle down in peace. My parents had long-since learned not to wait up on me (believe it or not) and I had already called Kevin and told him I would be catching the bus home that night. I had to argue with him a little first, but eventually he relented, saying he would call me at eight to make sure I got in okay.

I was faced once again with the major changes my physical condition had escorted into my life. Many times, I felt as though I wasn't my own person, as though other people were running my life for me. Sure, it had pretty much always been that way, but adding what had happened to me certainly made it worse. I knew that I was blessed to have people who loved me so much, but still I desired to be free . . . maybe, especially, free to dance.

Images of Jet and Bri's final dance moved through my mind, and I sighed. It was truly remarkable; I couldn't even tell Jet how far he had come. But why couldn't I tell him? It scared me; I was afraid of what my teaching had done for Jet . . . jealous, maybe? No, that wasn't it. The thought of Jet realizing his potential actually made me glad, and honored to know that I had helped him to do so. But why was I so terrified all of the sudden of what he could become?

Just as the soothing sounds of the silence began to fade around me, and my mind escaped to a bittersweet state of relaxation, I jumped at the sound of my name.

"Miranda."

Jet, of all people, stood in the doorway, dressed in his brown leather jacket, a black sweater and slacks. Apparently, he actually had something to do on the Friday night, and it wasn't as though this came as a surprise. He certainly wasn't unattractive, especially since he wasn't as conceited as he once was.

Jet walked over slowly, stuffing his hands into his pockets. Blinking out of my thought process, I quickly decided to appear busy, and pretended to be occupied with writing gibberish onto a piece of paper on the desktop.

"You're here late."

I shrugged, wondering what he could possibly want, and why he was there when he didn't have to be.

"So are you."

Jet nodded thoughtfully, scratching his chin and seemingly unable to decide what to do with his hands.

"Yeah . . ." He glanced around the room as I waited for his explanation. "So, uh . . . can you, uh . . . can you teach me how to dance?"

I stared, then laughed shortly.

"Um, isn't that what I've been doing for the past month—"

"No—I mean . . ." Jet sighed in frustration, then corrected himself. "There's this . . . um . . . this . . . banquet . . . thing we do at the end of every football season. And, uh, y'know, there's dancin' and crap." He took a deep breath, rushing through the next sentence. "I, um, I wanted to show the guys that I learned something..." He paused. "They, uh, they might not come to the recital."

I nervously swallowed, my eyes focusing down on the desktop, and Jet continued.

"So . . . I was wonderin' if you could possibly teach me the, uh, the box step . . . maybe."

"Um," I began quietly, unsure of what to say, not realizing that this was the first time I had heard Jet stuttering or appearing shy. "Bri's, uh, she's-she's not here to . . . show you . . ." I pointed out, the stuttering obviously contagious.

Jet's whole face seemed to drop, and he nodded quickly, rubbing his arm as his eyes moved from me to the floor.

"Oh, uh . . . right. Yeah . . . cool."

I frowned a little, noting his apparent disappointment.

"Well, I mean, I could *tell* you how . . ."

"Really? Uh, okay." Jet moved a few feet away, watching his reflection in the mirror.

"Start by stepping forward with the left, and now step to the side with the right," I began to instruct him, and Jet did the first two steps. Before I could speak again, though, he had his arms up, as though holding an imaginary partner. Wincing and then chuckling a little, I noticed that his arms were reversed.

Jet waited for my next instructions, and I couldn't help but walk over to at least correct his arms.

"Here, the woman holds hands with the right—you use the left," I informed as I placed his arms into the proper position, and Jet laughed as well.

"Oh, my bad," he blushed a little.

I stepped back to examine his form, then sighed, noting that his shoulders were drooping.

"Keep your shoulders up—you're the frame, so your stance has to be strong," I explained.

Jet bit his lip as he raised his shoulders much too high, still a little confused.

"So, my arms go . . . where, again?"

Unable to keep from laughing out loud, I moved in once more, this time pushing his shoulders down a little and raising my hand up to his, placing his right hand on my back.

"There," I chuckled.

But then I looked up.

Jet had a look of surprise and almost amusement on his face, as well as a shyness I had never seen before. Gradually, my smile faded, and I was altogether locked into what must have been a silly gaze into his deep, dark eyes—eyes that I was just now realizing were intent yet soft, focusing directly into mine without faltering. Jet had no smile on his lips, but now a mature seriousness.

Before I knew it, I felt as I did when my dad first taught me how to swim, easing me father and farther away from the edge of the pool, until I was out in the deep end by myself. The next thing I knew, Jet stepped forward, and, without thinking, I stepped back. He stepped to the side, and I followed. In no time, we were dancing, starting out in a small, safe circle, until our strides were longer, braver—and soon, we were waltzing around the room. At first, neither of us knew just quite where to look, though eventually, into each other's eyes seemed most natural, and after a while, it didn't even feel all that awkward.

I'm not completely sure how long we danced, since there wasn't any music playing anyway, but I'll never forget the way I felt when we did it. My heart seemed to leap as though on a roller coaster, a joy rising inside of me, as well as an excitement for the future. I don't know if you've ever felt it, but sometimes, maybe while at work or studying, you'll pause suddenly and remember something in your future that makes you happy. The next thing you know, you're flying through the task, inspired by the fact that you have that one thing to look forward to. Maybe it's an event or a promotion; probably for some only the realization of being alive and breathing. But for me, I didn't know what it was that I was looking forward to. All I knew was that I hadn't felt that way in a very long time.

Waltzing with Jet that night was the first time I had truly danced since before my accident, and, suddenly, I no longer despised the once cynical fact that I was walking better that day—without a cane.

I didn't know how much time had passed, but the feeling of being both weightless and timeless came to a halt much too soon, and I held onto Jet's shoulders suddenly, feeling as though I was about to fall off of a cliff. Looking down, I closed my eyes, trying to help the room to slow down and stop spinning.

"Miranda, are you okay?" I heard Jet ask, and I frowned, not seeing the level of concern on his face.

"Um . . . yeah," I replied, taking a deep breath, then slowly moved away from him, limping suddenly to my desk. "I'm . . . sorry," I apologized quietly, holding my head with one hand as I grasped the edge of the desk with the other.

Jet quickly shook his head.

"Oh, uh—no. It's fine." He rubbed the back of his neck. "Did I... did I do okay?"

I swallowed, closing my eyes again, my back to him.

Who are you *to say anymore, Miranda? You can't even waltz with him . . .*

"Perfect . . . Jet—you did . . . perfect."

Thirteen

Jet

"Five minutes, Mr. Carmichael, five minutes."

I rubbed my hands together with a heavy sigh as the final call came from the hallway to my left. Just outside the dressing room was the rest of the backstage area, the curtain controls, producers, dancers, choreographers, and finally, the audience.

My true audience included Nana Jo, Coach Nagin, maybe Jonathan (a *big* maybe) and perhaps most importantly, Miranda. She had promised Bri and me in practice the day before that she would be there to help us backstage before we went on, but I still had yet to see her. I guess it was okay, though, since Bri was checking on me every now and then, answering any questions I had about the routine.

Standing up from my chair in front of one of the mirrors, I

examined my reflection. My costume was pretty simple (thank God) but nice nonetheless. A red, button-down shirt and black slacks seemed to fit Miranda's idea of "a young man struggling to find love." Oh, and I would be dancing barefoot . . . At least the assured embarrassment of ballet slippers was out of the way (and boy was it interesting getting all of that tape on the balls of my feet).

Rolling my sleeves up a little below my elbows, I began to dance out the routine in my head, approaching the event as if it were a football game. Every stride, every catch, had to be mapped out in my mind—for practice, I suppose—but mostly, for the sake of my nerves. My mind simply can't rest before a game, and apparently, not before a dance recital, either.

The recital, by the way, was hosted by the studio, and wasn't supposed to be anything too elaborate—well, not to my aesthetically untrained mind. Several solos would be featured, including hip-hop and jazz, all centered around various themes, such as family, relationships, and love. Entitled "Coalesce," the production was mainly about how all of these factors tie into everyday life. It was a good idea, and I was actually pretty proud of my role in it.

While smoothing my shirt, mentally rehearsing a leap I had been worrying about, I realized that my nerves weren't only due to the recital, but also Miranda's absence. I wanted her to be there for moral support as well as to see the performance, but I also hoped that she was alright. No one had been able to get in touch with her.

"Ready?"

I turned and nervously mirrored Bri's supportive smile.

"I guess I have to be."

Bri adjusted her ponytail. Miranda had chosen a nice costume for Bri, which was made up of a black tank top and a purple skirt. It was simple, yet complimentary to my costume.

"You're gonna do fine." She shook her head as another producer arrived to summon us.

As we followed the producer out of the crowded dressing room area, the music of the previous act began to fade, and the applause of a packed house exploded from the theater. With the producer waiting to give us the signal, and Bri preparing to leave my side to walk to the opposite end of the stage for her entry, my stomach seemed to split in half at the thought of Miranda's absence.

"Any word from Miranda?" I snuck a quick whisper over to Bri before she left.

But she shook her head.

"Cat says she must be running late—I gotta go."

With a reassuring squeeze of my arm, Bri hurried behind the back curtain of the stage to her station, and the producer to my right held up a hand signal meaning "fifteen seconds." Swallowing, I nodded, trying to compose myself.

Nana Jo will see it, Jet, and Coach too—maybe even Jonathan. It's worth it . . . yeah, it's worth it . . . Miranda will be here, don't worry.

As the time drew nearer, I questioned whether or not I could turn back. The audience, the press, Miranda, the pressure, *me*—it was all too much. I felt like I was being pushed to the limit. Jet himself was an obstacle now, and suddenly, it dawned on me that this was up to *me*.

I can't do it . . .

"Break a leg."

Jumping, I turned at the touch on my arm—the familiar whisper. I probably knew who it was before she even finished the sentence.

I didn't speak, a little too surprised, glad and still too nervous to even think anyway. Miranda merely smiled her classic half-smile. It was one of those moments where seeing a certain face you've mistaken in the crowd, someone you're expecting to see, causes your heart to jump, and suddenly, you feel embarrassed, childish and excited all at once. (Not to mention the fact that I was relieved that she was alright.)

As Miranda walked off and the music started, somewhere amidst the madness of anxiety in my mind, I wondered if I had misread her smile in the past—if maybe, just *maybe*, there was encouragement and affirmation there more often than I thought.

With more confidence than I held before, I took the first step forward onto the stage.

Fourteen

Miranda

An icy wind swept by the side of the theater building as I carefully started down the stone front steps. Car trouble had caused me to arrive at the theater late. Kevin had ended up driving me, insisting that he wanted to see what all the hype over Jet was about.

"You *never* wait, do you?"

Sighing, I paused on the second step and turned to see Kevin, carrying an armful of bouquets and teddy bears. He was hurrying out the heavy wooden doors of the old theater, a frown of disapproval on his face.

Reluctantly, I allowed myself to be helped down the steps, then shook my head.

"I've got it, Kev'—"

"Okay, okay." He shifted the flowers into one arm, placing the other around my shoulders as we stood on the sidewalk. "It wasn't too bad," he said with a light shrug.

I couldn't have been prouder of both Jet and Bri. Jet had blown the whole audience away. If I thought he had nailed the technique in the classroom only days back, I certainly wasn't expecting him to grasp the emotion of the piece. It felt good to know that my idea had been captured and expressed, but it felt even better to know that I had taught him.

I just couldn't help but feel a tinge of the familiar sadness. Watching Jet dance with such purpose that night had caused me to truly realize not only his potential, but the uncanny feeling that somehow, this was what he was *supposed* to be doing: dancing.

"You, of all people, thought it wasn't 'too bad,' Kev'? I'm shocked," I joked with a light smile as I slid my hands into my jacket pockets, searching for warmth from the nippy, autumn air.

Kevin chuckled.

"Why don't I pull the car up?"

"Kevin—"

"You look tired—it's cold anyway. Be right back."

As Kevin jogged off, I sighed as I lingered around the sidewalk outside of the theater, where mostly everyone had already left. After a few people exited the building, nodding to me as they passed, the door suddenly opened again, and I turned to see an elderly woman bending in the doorway, retrieving several bouquets of flowers from the ground.

Grasping my cane, I hurried up the steps and began to help her.

"Oh, thank you—but you don't have to," she spoke graciously as I gave her a hand.

"Not a problem at all." I straightened with a smile, handing her the flowers.

She smiled, a cheerful smile with a youthfulness in her eyes. Her well-kept, short snow-white hair blew gently in the breeze, and she wore a brown suede coat and scarf.

"You know what? I'm glad I'm out here droppin' things—I got to meet you," she beamed warmly, reaching out to squeeze my hand as though I was family. "You did an absolutely beautiful job with my boy, Ms. Phillips—it brought me to tears."

I stood surprised, then smiled.

"Thank you. So you're Jet's grandmother—it's nice to meet you. Please call me Miranda, Mrs . . . ?"

She chuckled.

" 'Nana Jo' is fine—it works for Jet."

I nodded and Nana Jo shook her head, crossing her arms as she cradled the flowers.

"Jet couldn't have gotten a better teacher—the most wonderful dancer we know."

I shook my head modestly with a shrug, though smiling inside. She had said "*dancer*," not "former dancer" or even "choreographer," but "dancer"—in the present tense. Usually the thought of still being a dancer pricked at my heart in a cruel, bitter kind of way, but this time, it felt good to hear.

Nana Jo seemed to hesitate for a moment.

"You know, Jet really . . . really needed this . . ." She paused, furrowing her brow in seriousness. "We all know he was headed down the wrong path, but," she sighed, then shrugged with a sad smile, "I guess it was just hardest to have to actually *watch* him first-hand. He doesn't have an easy life, like these newspapers and TV shows say . . ." Her voice faded for a moment. "He'll get me for saying this, but he's my baby boy still, and I want the best for him. He's been let down a lot—he needed someone to teach him and not give up on him." She beamed at me. "If you only knew how many times he's come to me talkin' about how Miranda taught him this or how Miranda said that—I can't remember the last time he was so. . . so genuinely *fascinated*."

I looked away, unsure of what to say.

Nana Jo quickly smiled disarmingly, relieving the atmosphere.

"Anyway, I'm sure this'll help with football, too."

We both chuckled lightly, and Nana Jo paused before leaving, touching my arm.

"Miranda, why don't you come over for dinner sometime—is tomorrow night okay?"

I cleared my throat, taken a bit off guard with her abrupt invite. "Oh, um . . . I . . ."

"We'd love to have you, and if tomorrow won't work then we'll set up another day."

Seeing that there was no painless way to turn her down, I finally shrugged, knowing that I would like to get more acquainted with the kind grandmother. Besides, this would give me a chance to say goodbye to Jet, as well as give him his parting gift. The recital did, after all, mark the end of his disciplinary course.

"Tomorrow night is fine."

Fifteen

Jet

Life was good after the recital. No guilt trips, no worries about practicing, and no having to stress over what the press would think of me—they *loved* the dancing and couldn't get enough of it. Yet with all of the rave reviews, why was I feeling down? I honestly couldn't understand what was wrong with me. Coach was proud of me—Nana Jo practically overflowing with pride—and even my boys on the team had more respect for me. So what was the problem?

I parked my car that Sunday night in a daze, having driven from the nearest neighborhood park, where I had taken a long walk.

Since I started college, I had found refuge in the park, whether in jogging or just sitting watching the kids playing or teens tossing Frisbees. It was therapeutic, and oftentimes I prayed—because I could actually remember to when I was there.

See, for me, it was easiest to think about God when I didn't have football practice, classes or even friends around me. Sitting by myself in the park, I was invited to acknowledge His presence, and that's usually when I did most of my praying—the hardcore prayers; that is, those that didn't fit into the category of "911" or "directory assistance." And, believe it or not, my prayers weren't the kinds you hear on TV from the especially notorious sinners—you know, that prayer that begins with something like "God, I know you haven't heard from me in a while, *but*" and ends with "so if you just do this *one thing*, I *promise* I'll never do x, y, and z again." Yeah, I was actually pretty experienced in prayer. I was taught that God was like your dad, so I talked to Him normally and freely. Being real with Him wasn't too much of a problem for me.

If I could record my prayers and play them back to you, you'd be pretty surprised that *I*, the infamous Jet Carmichael, was the one doing the praying. I was always asking that God would change my ways. I had been to the youth group sessions, seminars, and I heard the sermons, yet still, I struggled with applying obedience in my life. As much as I prayed to be a better person, I guess I just never really understood how much of it was on *my* part.

So God and I had a pretty good talk that day, and, for the most part, I was feeling refreshed. Not quite happy, but mellow and thoughtful. It's was one of those moods where you feel this tug playing with your feelings and confidence, though you just can't seem to trace its origin. In turn, you end up going through the day feeling incomplete and off balance, like you forgot something important that you were going to say. Anyway, I *hated* that feeling, and could only hope Nana Jo had fixed up a storm in the kitchen while I was gone.

"Nana Jo, I'm back," I called wearily from the back door, carelessly tossing my coat onto the hook in the vestibule, grateful for the toasty warmth of the house. My appetite quickly whetted at the aromatic blast of "comfort food no. 5" in the air. Hearing light voices coming from the dining room, I assumed it was the TV and moved to the stove, then lifted the lid off of the largest pot. "Nana Jo, you're a lifesaver for real—how'd you know I was wantin' gumb … o…"

I paused in mid-sentence, looking up to see Nana Jo appearing in the kitchen doorway, dressed up in a cashmere sweater and her reading glasses nowhere in sight—which could mean only one thing. Glancing around, I noticed the suede-and-wool coat in the vestibule—the cane leaning against the wall.

I swallowed. Nana Jo grinned.

"You took long enough! We're starving."

"Wait, Nana Jo—what . . . what . . . why?" I stammered and gulped, rubbing my head.

"Well, don't just stand there—we have company!"

My jaw dropped and I glanced down at my clothes, touching my old university t-shirt and jeans.

"I can't go in there like this!" I spat in a whisper, beginning to panic.

But Nana Jo shook her head with a sigh.

"Then go upstairs and change, child! But be quick, we've already waited a half hour."

Taking no time in asking more questions, I rushed up the steps to my old room, where Nana Jo kept a suitable change of clothes in the case that I should ever spend the night. After tossing on some slacks and a black sweater, I quickly checked the mirror, wishing there was enough time to at least shower again. But there wasn't, so I rubbed on some lotion and headed back downstairs.

Adjusting my watch in the hallway leading to the dining room, wondering why I hadn't been notified ahead of time about our dinner guest, I finally took a deep breath and made my entry.

The casual murmuring briefly ceased as I stood in the doorway, until Nana Jo spoke up, "Well c'mon in."

A very different-looking Miranda was watching my awkwardness with what must have been an amused smile—or was it a smirk? Her braids were down and her spirits high (I guess Nana Jo could loosen up anyone). Wearing a brown blouse, which accentuated her eyes, and black, pinstripe slacks, she was a slightly more elegant version of the casual Miranda from practice at the studio.

An uncomfortable (for me, at least) silence lingered after Nana Jo left the room to check on dessert, and I shifted in my seat, trying not to glance up from my plate across the table, where Miranda was quietly eating.

Think of something to say, Jet, it doesn't look right to just sit and say nothing. The weather? No, that's dumb. The recital? Yeah, that's it! Thank her for the lessons and stuff.

I cleared my throat, setting my fork down to reach for my glass of ginger ale. I took a quick sip before speaking.

"So, uh . . . thanks for the—"

The worst possible thing that could happen, happened. It was downright stupid of me to decide to take a drink before attempting conversation, because I was choking on the ginger ale in mid-sentence.

When I finished coughing, my eyes watering slightly, I looked to Miranda and saw the mixture of confusion, surprise and concern on her face. I felt like an idiot.

"Are you okay?" she asked slowly, and after I nodded, she chuckled a little—much to my embarrassment.

Thankfully, Nana Jo returned at that moment, smiling as though the evening was going swimmingly.

"How is everything?"

"Delicious," Miranda complimented.

"Great," I quickly added, scooting my chair a little closer to the table, only to jump up suddenly to pull Nana Jo's chair out for her. My mind couldn't have been in more of a whirl.

Once we were all seated again, Nana Jo engaged in light conversation with Miranda—asking her about the studio, her students, as well as school and her family.

For the most part, I listened in silence, noting how well my grandmother and Miranda hit it off, but also how . . . *normal* Miranda seemed at the dinner table. Hearing about her classes at school, her sister's jobs and how her parents were doing, I realized then that I really knew absolutely nothing about her. It was almost strange to sit across from someone whom I was so used to seeing as a teacher—someone to listen to and try to impress—and suddenly seeing that she was just a normal person.

Sometime around when dessert was served, it dawned on me that Miranda smiled more and laughed more—genuinely—that night than I had ever seen in class. It wasn't all *that* monumental, I guessed, since there was a big difference between a dance lesson and dinner over a home-cooked meal. All in all, by the time we had finished dessert, I felt very awkward and a little confused—unsure of how to sit, where to look, or what to say. How *are* you supposed to act when your teacher's at your dinner table, chatting with your family?

"Jet, why don't you show Miranda the flowers on the porch? I need to go put this food away and wash these dishes."

Blinking, I looked up. I had missed a good bit of the conversation, being too busy marveling at the situation at hand.

"Um . . . huh?"

Nana Jo looked impatient, and Miranda smiled, most likely amused.

"The pansies and chrysanthemums—on the front porch."

I felt unsure as to what to do.

"I can do the dishes if you want me to . . ."

93

The statement was very "foot-in-mouth"-ish, and Nana Jo wasn't pleased.

"I think I've got it," she replied reassuringly with a tone in her voice that I couldn't quite read.

After bringing Miranda her coat and cane, sliding my jacket on as well, we walked out the front door onto the porch. Nana Jo had always taken pride in having such a large porch and walkway, and spent a lot of time on her favorite swing and around her hanging pots of plants and flowers. By now, the temperature had dropped even more, since the sun had set, and I flicked on the dim porch light before closing the front door.

"So . . . you like flowers, too?" I asked after a moment, and Miranda turned and nodded from where she stood near the railing, studying some of the flowers.

"You have a really sweet grandmother," Miranda said with a small smile as she slowly sat down on the swing, her gloved hands resting atop her cane.

"Oh . . . thanks," I replied, leaning with my back against one of the wooden pillars of the railing.

There came a pause, and the noisy silence in the air seemed to vibrate at the mere nudge of our breathing.

"So you're going back to practice tomorrow?"

I stuffed my hands into my pockets.

"Yeah."

Miranda nodded, fingering the handle of her cane.

"You did a really good job, Jet," she said slowly. "I know it . . . wasn't always easy." She chuckled a little, but her smile quickly faded. "But you rose up to it and above it."

I looked down at the ground, surprised at what I was hearing.

There it was, the final (and perhaps most important) affirmation of my efforts. Receiving that kind of praise from Miranda was like winning the Nobel Prize, yet still, the persistent imbalance I had felt earlier returned stronger than ever. What was missing?

"Um, thanks," I said quietly, feeling freezing cold despite the warmth of my jacket.

Miranda was quiet for a long moment, twirling her cane in one hand. Was it just me, or was I not the only one feeling down?

"I need to get something out of my car. I'll be right ba—"

"Oh no, I can grab it for you."

Miranda shook her head at my quick interruption, waving a hand as she readied her keys.

"It's fine, Jet, you don't have to—"

"But I want to." I offered a smile. "What does it look like?"

Miranda finally handed me her keys as she sat back down.

"It's a flat box. A white . . . gift box."

I headed for Miranda's car, opened it and found the box with ease on the front passenger seat. Coming back to the porch, I noticed the broad smile on her face. "What?" I asked with a laugh.

She gestured to the box.

"Open it."

Puzzled, I slowly opened the box. Inside was a black t-shirt with over a dozen signatures and notes written on it in white ink. But what caught my eye the most was the front of the shirt, which held a picture of Bri and I from practice, executing one of the more challenging lifts from the dance.

I grinned, recalling the day when the photographer came in to take the shot.

"Wow, thanks."

Miranda smiled lightly.

"I got everyone to sign it last week—Mr. Nelson probably took up the most space."

We both laughed.

"It's your best lift, you know—the day you got it down," Miranda added, and I nodded.

95

Another silence followed as I continued to study the shirt, briefly reading a few of the notes.

"So what's next for you?" Miranda asked just as my eyes found the note she had written, and I shifted with a sigh.

"Football." I shrugged. "School . . . Maybe I can pick up the pieces."

Miranda nodded thoughtfully.

"Anything else?"

I blinked.

"Well . . ."

Miranda seemed to struggle with something in her mind, on her heart, and hesitated a little before speaking up.

"You know, Jet, I . . . I wasn't just saying that you rose above the challenge because I had to or whatever," she said hesitantly, brushing a braid out of her eyes. "I mean, you've really got a knack for dance—and I know dancers when I see them. So, um . . . if you want to take it further, then I think you've got a good shot."

I wondered just what had gotten into Miranda tonight. Now, complimenting me was one thing, but honestly telling me to pursue dance? For some reason, I didn't take her words as encouragement.

I cleared my throat.

"So . . . you think I could really be a dancer?"

Miranda shrugged.

"Yeah."

I smirked, shaking my head as I looked out across the street.

"You sound like everyone else now. They say to find something to do with myself—with my life—since I'm so reckless and naive. You didn't have to come all the way out here just to take pity on me—"

"Jet, you're not understanding." Miranda sighed. "Listen, I'm not prodding into your personal life or whatever . . . I'm just telling you the truth. You don't have to be so defensive."

I crossed my arms over my chest, knowing that *she* just didn't understand either.

"I just . . ." I shook my head. "I don't like trying new things, okay? I'd rather just stick with football, y'know? I know the ropes in it and everything's cool." I scratched the top of my head, unsure of whether or not to say what else was on my mind. "It takes too much trust to start somethin' new, and I'm . . ." I paused, sighing as I decided to let it out, "I'm not good at trusting people."

Miranda didn't reply immediately, and only nodded again, slowly and, perhaps, understandingly. She leaned forward, resting her elbows in her lap as I stood quietly wishing I hadn't said anything at all.

"I was probably twelve—maybe thirteen," she began softly, "and I had just started really liking dance. I didn't always like it, believe it or not, and when I was a little kid I almost quit a few times." She picked at the wood on the swing, and sighed. "But I came to love it over time—it's like it grabbed me and wouldn't let go. All it took was one mistake, though, and I would beat myself up. That's why I tried to run away from it—feeling like I wasn't good enough."

I was taken aback at her words.

"*You* didn't feel . . . good enough?" I questioned, dumbfounded.

Miranda nodded.

"But one day a good friend of mine told me not to ever let dance become hate and not love—a thorn and not a rose." She paused thoughtfully. "I haven't forgotten it since, but . . . I still can't always avoid dance's prick," she swallowed, "Especially now."

I looked down at my hands as the snow fell outside of the porch, and Miranda twirled her cane.

Sixteen
Miranda

"Watch your step!"

I looked up with a frown as I tried to carefully make my way down the icy front porch steps, the growl of my sister's sports car muffling her voice.

"What?" I called, and Nina braked while backing out of the driveway.

"Be careful!"

Gingerly, I arrived safely at the bottom of the steps.

"Later, Mira." Nina waved as she drove off.

I distantly nodded as I made my way to my own car, being careful not to let my cane slip on the ice. After unlocking the door and sliding into the driver's seat, I pushed my keys into the ignition. A pitiful cranking noise escaped the engine, and I frowned in concentration before giving another attempt. But the car only grumbled for a few seconds before the engine refused to start at all.

I sat quietly for a full minute, wondering what to do. Nina had just driven off for a job interview, my parents had already left as well, and Kevin was out of town again.

With a heavy sigh, I finally grabbed my cell out of my purse and was about to dial Cat's number, when I remembered that she, too, was out of town. Closing my eyes, I combed my fingers through my hair, pulling a few braids out of my face. There was nothing left to do but catch a bus, but my right leg was already feeling achy and vulnerable—I didn't think I could make the three-block walk to the nearest stop. Maybe on one of my better days, but not that day.

Watching the minutes tick by on the clock, I realized I had no other choice but to walk, and finally alighted the defeated car, hauling my backpack over my shoulder and holding my coat tighter around me. I noticed how empty the street was with a hint of dismay, almost hoping a neighbor would offer me a ride, but still knowing I wouldn't accept it anyway. I was much too headstrong for that, as my dad always said.

By the time I covered a block, now entering the commercial part of town, my leg began to state its disapproval, and I was limping quite a bit. Finally, I paused for a rest at a corner, leaning against the pedestrian traffic post, wondering if I could make the walk after all.

"Miranda!"

Frowning, I turned my face to the left, where the whizzing, morning commuters had just halted at the red light of the intersection. The car nearest the sidewalk was black—a Firebird like my own—only much more "tricked out" with purple and black chrome wheels. I was surprised to see its driver, though.

"Hey," I greeted, and Jet leaned over to open the passenger door.

"Need a lift?" he asked casually, glancing at the traffic light.

I blinked.

Of course *you're not gonna take any pity offers, Miranda*—especially *not from Jet Carmichael.*

"Um . . ." I hesitated. The morning sun was hidden behind the cloudy sky, and already I was beginning to shiver from the chilly air.

It is getting pretty cold . . .

"Hop in," said Jet, and I finally did so, deciding it would be insane to go any farther by foot when I was cold *and* crippled.

For a moment, all I was aware of was the comforting heat encountering my numbing face and hands from the dashboard, and huddled closer into my coat to try to get warm. Kirk Franklin, my favorite Gospel artist, was playing on the stereo, and I felt a little more at ease than minutes back on the sidewalk.

"So much for summer." Jet sighed, and I looked over at him, almost having forgotten he was there. Dressed in warmups and a black, puffy coat, he looked as though he was on his way to football practice, and I worried whether I should have taken his offer after all.

"Yeah," I agreed, deciding it was too late to do anything but ride along.

A few blocks later, I realized that I hadn't told Jet where to go, and sat up more, peering out the windows. We were passing Lenny's Pizza, Capstone Productions (my parents' talent agency), and a small Greek sub shop. I realized we were headed to the studio—he already knew where to go.

Duh, Miranda.

As Jet pulled the car over to the sidewalk outside of the main studio entrance, I rubbed the top of my cane.

"Hey, um . . . thanks—you didn't have to . . ." I hesitated, but Jet nodded understandingly.

"No problem." He waved his hand, reaching for a mug of coffee on the console as I opened the door.

I had just gotten out of the car when Jet spoke up again.

"Hey, when does your last class get out?"

I shrugged and closed the door.

"About five."

Jet nodded, putting the car into drive.

"Later."

As I walked into the lobby and greeted Cicely, I wondered why he had asked.

"Good class today, Miranda!"

I looked up from where I was browsing through a dance apparel magazine near my desk, and smiled as Chris, one of my jazz students, waved as he left the room.

"It *was* pretty good," Bri echoed from where she sat tying her sneakers by the mirror, being the last person to remain from my final class of the day.

I browsed through the catalog, highlighting a pair of workout pants.

"Usually you guys don't like suicides . . ."

Bri shrugged with a playful grin, her dark eyes scrunching.

"Only if it's hot outside."

I laughed as I grabbed my backpack and walked across the room to shut off the lights—Bri following with her bags.

"How'd it go last night?" she asked lightly.

I paused while closing and locking the classroom door.

"So who leaked it?"

Bri chuckled as she leaned against the wall, freeing her hair from its ponytail.

"Cat, Nina—everyone."

Exasperated, I asked, "And what was Nina doing here?"

Bri shrugged.

"Said something about checking on you—"

"I didn't see her come in today."

"It was during a water break—she only came to the lobby."

I nodded with a wry smile.

"Okay . . ."

"She said she went home around two to see your car still in the driveway, so she—"

"Worried," I finished for her, sighing as I shook my head. "So why'd she leave? Or is she parked outside, ready to drive me home?"

Bri yawned as we walked through the dimly-lit lobby to the front door.

"I told her I'd give you a lift—"

"Bri, c'mon." I ran my fingers through my hair as we stepped out into the frigid, evening air. "I'll catch the bus, okay?"

Bri sighed as well, zipping her coat and flipping her cell open.

"I promised, Mira—c'mon."

"Well, I give you permission to break it, okay? You've gotta pick up your brothers tonight anyway." I shrugged. "Gas costs too much for you to be haulin' me around."

"Are you sure?" Bri persisted, a hint of worry on her face.

"Yes, now . . ." My voice trailed as I focused on a particular car approaching on our side of the street, and frowned.

Bri looked over as well, and soon the black car arrived, pulling up to the sidewalk.

"Hey, Bri," Jet greeted with a smile, and Bri waved, almost as confused as I was.

"I guess I'll . . . see you later, Mira," Bri spoke quietly as we both watched in wonder as Jet exited, jogged around to the passenger side, and opened the door.

"Um . . . yeah." I tugged at one of my braids, taking a deep breath.

Bri cast me an interesting smile as she walked off for her own car, and I glanced around nervously, hoping the blush on my cheeks wasn't obvious.

"Um, Jet, it's cool—really." I tried to decline, but Jet only shrugged after glancing up at the hazy sky which threatened snow.

"It sure is," he finally stated with a grin, and I was unable to keep from smiling as I reluctantly slid in.

When we arrived at my house, having taken a detour to Popeye's after Jet announced that he was hungry and asked if I was too (I had argued that he shouldn't pay for me, but, of course, to no avail). Jet parked against the curb, and to my surprise, walked me to the front door.

After we said goodbye and Jet started down the steps, I paused with my key in the lock, then turned.

"Jet."

He turned as well, standing on the walkway with his hands in his coat pockets and black beanie adorned, shivering slightly with fresh snowflakes falling on his eyelashes. I couldn't control the smile twitching at my lip.

Not only was Jet charming and attractive, but there was something about the way he watched you when you spoke— something . . . *captivating*.

I glanced down at the icy front steps.

"Thanks, y'know . . . you didn't have to give me another lift..."

Jet nodded and smiled, then jogged off.

I entered my house slowly and thoughtfully, softly closing the door behind me before I dumped my backpack near the steps, distantly hanging my coat on the rack. As soon as I walked into the warm kitchen, all three pairs of eyes looked up at me, but I didn't notice. I must have looked quite distracted as I walked to the cabinet for a glass, since a curious sort of hush fell over the room.

Momma, who was hovering near a pot on the stove, glanced at me a few times, as did Dad and Nina from the dinner table.

After grabbing a glass and filling it with water, I finally sighed and set it down on the counter, just now noting the silent questions in the atmosphere.

Mom spoke before I could, though.

"I thought Kevin was out of town . . ." she mused aloud in a tone that was too casual.

I picked up my glass and took a sip.

"He is," I replied shortly, not feeling like playing games.

Mom was quiet for a moment, and I thought everything had passed over. Checking my cell, I began to sift through my calendar.

"Who brought you home then, Mira?"

Her tone was too innocent. This was bad.

"Jet, Mom," I had to reply, but wished I somehow couldn't.

Mom shared a look with Dad, who was taking slow sips of his coffee, a look of disapproval on his face. When *Dad* was quiet and serious, it was especially significant.

Mom cleared her throat as she rinsed her hands at the sink.

"Was there a lot of traffic? It certainly took you a while to get back—your last class got out at five and it's already 6:15."

I really hate that she has my schedule memorized . . .

"Mom," I began, a little more defensively this time, "we just grabbed some dinner, okay?"

This only fueled the fire, and Mom nodded slowly—*very* slowly.

"Well, wasn't that nice of him, Charles?" she asked Dad, and I rolled my eyes.

Here we go.

"Yeah," Dad agreed, raising an eyebrow, "maybe a little *too* nice."

Nina, who had been silent the whole time, finally spoke up.

"Hey Mira, did you hear about the pilot?"

I shook my head, trying to focus on my schedule.

"Well," she continued, "Kev's gonna get that cameo he wanted after all—I worked things out with the director and he's cool with it."

I nodded distantly. Nina frowned.

"Don't be so excited about it, Miranda—what's with you?"

I felt slightly annoyed.

"I already knew he'd get it, Nina."

She shrugged, gathering her loosened hair and pulling it back into a ponytail.

"But you didn't *hear* about it from him—Kev said he's been trying to reach you all day, and that your phone was off."

Glaring at her I said, "I was busy, okay?"

Growing tired of defending myself, I finally shook my head and left for my room.

Seventeen

Jet

I felt pretty good while walking up the iron flight of steps to my apartment that night, though I probably wasn't willing to admit to myself the reason why. Life was great nonetheless, though, and this was enough for me as I stepped inside of my bachelor pad.

It wasn't too shabby of a place, with its black leather seating and coffee brown walls—I guess that's the advantage of once flirting with a cute design major from school. Mainly, the hookups were thanks to my roommate, Luke, who had affluent, selfless and nurturing parents (a pretty nice mix, if you asked me).

I stretched my arms after tossing my coat in the closet, then tackled the warm, rich sofa before closing my eyes.

"Enjoy yourself?"

I opened one eye, then smiled lazily at Luke, who stood in the doorway cradling his black cat, Betty, and looking as though he needed sleep.

"I'll take that as a 'yes,' " he smirked, then let Betty down while scratching his blond, curly-afro head, making his way into the kitchen.

Luke's dad was black and his mom white, so he had springy curls which he wore in a signature 'fro. I guess finding girls through him wasn't hard, considering how they always talked about his tanned skin and gray eyes. He was a good friend to me, probably the closest one I had, and I couldn't have asked for a better roommate.

"Man I'm stupid hungry—you wanna grab somethin'?" Luke called from the kitchen over the rummaging through boxes and bags.

"No, I'm good—I ate already," I replied through a yawn, and a fleeting memory of Miranda's attempted argument to pay for her meal dashed through my thoughts.

I closed my eyes again, wrapping my arms around one of the cashmere pillows.

"What're *you* smilin' about?"

I frowned, opening my eyes once again.

"Who said I was smilin'?"

Luke grinned, then nodded very slowly while grabbing his keys and jacket near the door, apparently intending on going out despite the plaid pajamas he wore.

"C'mon, Jet, I know that 'look.' " He laughed. "Who is she?"

I rolled over, turning to lie on my back while lacing my hands behind my head.

"I don't know what you're talkin' about, man."

Luke pressed on.

"Let's see, it can't be Kayla, 'cause you just dumped her a month ago." He counted off on his fingers. "And it's not Meredith, 'cause she kicked *you* to the curb after she *found out* about Kayla."

"Hey," I complained, "leave it alone, okay?"

Luke chuckled.

"Whatever—so who is it? Gina, maybe—that girl whose number you got at Starbucks?"

"Luke, man, shut up," I grumbled with a sigh. "*You* were the one who got her number anyway, remember?"

"Okay, okay." He backed off, placing his hand on the doorknob. "I'm gonna go get some grub." He paused suddenly. "Wait a minute, you aren't still hangin' with that Miranda chick, are you?"

When I didn't answer, Luke became agitated.

"Jet, man, are you *crazy*?! I know she's fine and all, but she's already hooked up with that dancer dude—what's his name again?"

I shrugged and shook my head, wanting to change subject. Luke sighed heavily.

"Well, you be careful—she's got a big ol' net of protection around her. Everybody knows not to mess with her or that dude she's goin' out with," he snickered. "You may be Jet Carmichael the football player, but her boyfriend's got those ATL connections. Be smart about it, okay?"

"Luke, will you just go on? When did I say I was messin' around with her? All I did was give her a lift to work, okay?"

"Why?" Luke pressed.

I thought for a moment and then sighed.

"Her car was broken down or somethin,' I dunno,'" I fumbled.

"Hmm, well, just be careful. I'll be back in a little bit." Luke opened the door. "You need me to stay out for a little while or ... ?"

I shook my head, though I couldn't help but chuckle.

"And where are you gonna hang around at 7:00 in your pj's?"

Luke shrugged, letting out a yawn.

"Gina *did* ask about you today, so, uh, y'know . . . I can be gone tonight if you want . . ."

I sighed.

"Luke, man, I'm not expectin' anybody, okay?"

Luke shrugged again and finally left.

I rubbed my eyes for a moment, trying to forget Luke's words and our conversation. But when it all began to ring in my ears, deadening the calming effect of that day's memories with Miranda, I finally sat up. I didn't move for a long moment, trying to think about football practice or the English paper I had due in a few days, but soon, my thoughts were interrupted by the doorbell.

Frowning, I slowly got up to answer it. Standing before me was none other than Gina, smiling sweetly, still dressed in her green Starbucks apron.

"Oh . . . hey," I greeted a little nervously, suddenly wondering why in the world I had accepted her number from Luke in the first place. I barely remembered her anyway, since Luke was always flirting with someone new, and I technically hadn't even met her.

"Hey, Jet," she replied smoothly, her voice hanging onto each syllable.

As pretty as Gina was, with her long, dark curly hair and cocoa eyes, I still felt a little . . . annoyed, almost. Or maybe it was more like a sick kind of nervousness—questioning the timing of it all. A couple of months ago, I wouldn't have minded the situation at all, but now, it somehow felt . . . awkward.

"I called your little friend, Luke—is it?"

I nodded, and she slowly grinned, revealing perfectly straight, white teeth.

"Right. He said I might find you here."

I laughed lightly, then cleared my throat, tugging at the collar of my shirt.

"Uh, yeah . . . here I am."

Gina nodded, then glanced around me to the inside of the apartment.

"Can I come in?"

I blinked.

"Um . . . sure." The words came out automatically, and I could have kicked myself.

As I stepped aside, Gina moved fluidly into the den, and over to the couch I had collapsed on minutes earlier.

"So," she crossed her legs with another smile up at me, "I hear your recital went well."

I nodded silently, sliding my hands into my pockets as I stood a few feet away from the couch, already trying to figure out a way to get rid of her.

"Establish any . . . connections?" she questioned curiously, as my sense of awkwardness grew.

"Um . . . yeah, I made some friends."

Again, Gina nodded, twirling a strand of hair on her finger.

"That Phillips girl was your teacher, right?"

"Yeah . . ."

"You know," Gina leaned forward slightly, "I used to dance a little myself—"

"Hey, Gina, would you like somethin' to drink, maybe?" I asked nervously, flustered.

Gina shrugged and nodded, a bit surprised at my interruption yet amused just the same.

"Sure—water's fine."

I hurried into the kitchen, trying to figure out what to do. To a degree, I had always been nervous (though I learned to conceal it) around women, but this was ridiculous.

What's gotten into you, Jet?! She's gorgeous!

Taking a deep breath, I grabbed a glass and filled it with water, noting how much my hand was quaking. I couldn't afford to get into any more trouble with the team, but then I wasn't good at saying no to this kind of thing anyway . . . was I?

Holding the glass in my hand, battling the war going on inside

110

my mind, I suddenly tripped on a laundry hamper on the floor. Grumbling, I set the glass down and picked the hamper up.

While moving it toward the laundry closet off of the kitchen, though, my eyes landed on one of the shirts at the top of the pile. It was black, and filled with white writing. As crumpled and wrinkled as it was, only one note was in plain sight:

Jet,

You made it! I know you probably think I'm the worst teacher ever, and you'll most likely tell your grandkids about how horrible it was to learn how to dance from me, but know that I am proud of you. Everyone else is as well, and I know you'll be okay in the future. You displayed true responsibility and maturity in the classes, and I'm glad I got to teach you.

Let me know if you need anything.

~ Miranda

Now, I had read this note many a time since Miranda gave the shirt to me, but somehow, this particular time was . . . *different*— alive; almost as though I could hear Miranda speaking the words. I nervously set the hamper down, recalling all that had happened that day, the night before, the dinner and our talk on the porch . . .

I left the glass of water as I exited the kitchen, walked into the den and told Gina I was busy—that she couldn't stay. She was confused at first, then asked if there was a better time, but I shook my head, and she finally left.

When I went to bed that night, the joy from being with Miranda that day returned–guilt-free.

Eighteen
Miranda

"Looks like it might snow again."

"Yeah," I replied distantly as Mom and I walked down the front steps to her car the following morning.

With my own car in the shop, I was now completely dependent on family and friends when it came to getting around, and my mom insisted that she drive me to class that morning.

"Your hair looks cute, Mom," I complimented as I held my cane up while taking a few steps, "testing" my legs as I did at the start of each day.

Mom smiled, holding her long, brown coat closer around her, with her hair straightened and down, blowing gently in the early winter breeze.

"Thanks—your daddy likes it better curly, though," she sighed when we reached her car.

I smiled a little as we slid into the frigid Explorer.

"That's okay—as long as you're feelin' it."

Mom warmed the engine up as I yawned and munched on a cereal bar, going over that week's calculus notes, still trying to wake up.

In the passenger-side-view mirror, my reflection looked tired and cold. That day I had decided to wear my braids in a ponytail, and threw on a brown headband at the last minute. My hazel eyes were a little washed out and puffy, thus I kept my shades handy in my purse.

"The defroster's not gonna cut it," Mom sighed from my left. "Let me go scrape really quick—"

"I'll do it," I quipped as I opened the door, grateful for the chance to move, as I was feeling restless for some reason.

"Miranda," Mom protested with a sigh.

"Be right back." I ignored her as I exited the car with the scraper tool.

About a minute into my task, I noticed the rumble of an engine at the end of the driveway, in the street, and I finally looked over.

Jet . . . again?

Mom let her window down, frowning slightly.

"Mira, who is that?"

I blinked.

"Um, it's, uh . . ." I hesitated. "Hold on."

Walking over to where Jet had just gotten out of his car to open the passenger door, I scratched my head and sighed.

"I didn't know you'd come today . . ."

"Did I come at a bad time?" he asked slowly, a little concerned.

I looked down at the scraper in my hands, then glanced over my shoulder.

"Um," I hesitated.

He went out of his way to pick me up . . .

I finally shook my head.

"It's fine—can you hang on just a sec?"

Jet nodded, and I turned to go back to Mom, who was now alighting her car. I met her halfway between the Explorer and Jet, placing my hands on her shoulders.

"Is that Jet Carmichael?" she asked, still frowning a little as Jet nervously stood aloof, his hands in his pockets as he glanced from the ground to us. The two of them hadn't met yet, even though my whole family had come to the recital.

I nodded.

"Yeah, Mom, it's him."

"Oh . . . well . . . what does he want?" she asked slowly, keeping her voice down.

I sighed.

"He was gonna drive me to class today . . ." I attempted, but Mom looked concerned as she glanced past me at Jet.

"Was he, now?" She shook her head. "Miranda, I don't know what he thinks he's—"

"Mom, please, I just . . . I can't turn him away now—he drove all the way out here, out of his way, to get me."

"Did you ask him to?"

"No."

"Well, then—"

"Mom, c'mon. You know what I mean."

Mom sighed heavily, shaking her head.

"Listen," I tried again, "you haven't even met him yet."

"Mira."

"C'mon." I grabbed her hand and led her over to where Jet was studying his shoes. "Mom, this is Jet and Jet, this is my mom, Evangeline."

Jet extended his hand with a polite smile, and Mom gradually

114

accepted it.

"It's nice to finally meet you, Mrs. Phillips."

Mom smiled briefly, appropriately.

"Yes, you, too."

I cleared my throat.

"Well, I'll see you later, then."

Mom nodded at me, then Jet, and left for her car after I handed her the scraper.

After grabbing my things, I hopped into Jet's car and we drove off.

Jet arrived, faithfully, at the school after my class, and proceeded to drive me to the studio. When my final dance class got out, he was waiting on the sidewalk in his car.

While gathering my things from the back seat when we sat outside of my house, my backpack contents spilled out, and I sighed while retrieving everything. Jet gave me a hand, and I thanked him. Before he left, I explained that my car was supposed to be ready the next day and he wouldn't have to pick me up anymore.

Once upstairs in my room, I began to unload my homework, flipping on the radio as I did so. Tossing my cane on the floor, I fell onto my bed with my physics book in hand. While turning to the chapter I had bookmarked, a paper slid out. Frowning, I picked it up and set it aside, guessing it was a random sheet of notes or something. But my eyes quickly returned to it, and I looked to see that it was an essay, with the name Josiah Carmichael on the front.

It must have gotten mixed in when my stuff fell out. I'll have to get it back to him somehow . . .

I was about to return to my studying when I read the title: "The Second Wind Effect." Curious, I noticed the grade of "A +" on the cover, as well as the note of approval the teacher had scribbled. Sliding forward comfortably onto my stomach, I couldn't help but begin to read.

Josiah Carmichael
Professor Bailey
Creative Writing 1020
10/22/06

The Second Wind Effect

As a football player, I've had to condition myself for the game. I've built muscle, adapted to a healthy diet, and gotten into the habit of working out. In a world where just about everybody is striving for physical success, I guess you could say I've risen to the challenge.

However, there's one aspect—one obstacle—in football as well as in everyday life that I find especially difficult to overcome. This is the "breaking point," that so-called "limit" we approach when the goal is barely within our reach.

In football, this limit pertains to a myriad of things. For defensive players, football is about doing their best in protecting the quarterback or running backs—constantly keeping their eyes open for that interception that could decide the outcome of the game. It's not easy, though, having to keep so alert and ready to tackle, and this can cause you to want to give up—if you reach that "breaking point." And for running backs, we have to be able to not only catch the ball, but carry it safely to the first down; the end zone, if possible. Many a time, my legs have grown weary during these actions, but this happens especially when the end zone is in clear view and, at the very moment, the challenging question echoes through my mind of "can you reach it?"

It's when the goal is so close, so palpable, that the verisimilitude begins to almost mock, or perhaps encourage, our zeal for success, that we feel an agonizing mixture of potential and discouragement; confidence and doubt. The question of "can we really make it?" begins to sound louder, and this, as my coach always says, is when the pain arrives.

A weightlifter knows this pain well, and has to grow accustomed to the burning at his or her "breaking point." He has to train his mind, as well as his muscles, into believing that the breaking point truly can make or break him; it's either a "breaking point" or a *"making* point." It can encourage, or it can discourage—depending on how it's utilized.

This breaking point exists in everyone, no matter what the field or person. I often like to tell myself, "when I think I've reached the limit, simply raise it higher," and this is a method of thinking that I have used in many a football game or practice.

Not only does this breaking point exist in the physical realm, but the emotional and spiritual as well. One example of an emotional/spiritual breaking point is when one is challenged to gain more confidence or to, perhaps, give their total effort on a test. This breaking point can appear within relationships and forgiveness, as well, because it takes more courage and perseverance to forgive than it does to hate.

As challenging and intimidating as the breaking point is, there is always one thing that is essential to overcoming it; one aspect of comfort. This is the effect of the "second wind."

My coach has spoken to the team many a time about the second wind, and I'm sure everyone learns about it in the physical education of their childhood.

The second wind is best summarized with running a race. After the muscles have grown weary during the first half, or so, of a race, they reach this distinctly significant point (the breaking point) where they suddenly fill with energy, spurring the runner on toward the goal. Some may dispute that this energy has little or nothing to do with the emotional struggle inside of the runner and only pertains to the physical realm, but I choose to disagree with that logic. Without the initial *decision*, which can be engendered only in the heart and mind of a person, not their muscles, they can't possibly overcome the breaking point. It takes every part of us, our hearts, our minds and our bodies, to succeed the breaking point.

Where there is potential, there is always fear, because with the question of "Can I make it?" there's often the fear of what's on the other side—what it means to reach the goal. For some reason, true success and fulfillment of purpose has always frightened and even daunted humans. Perhaps it's due to the classic "fear of the unknown," or abandonment of one's comfort zone.

Whatever the obstacle, though, with the second wind guiding us and in our hands, the decision of whether or not to reach our goal—to raise the limit—is always up to us.

I set the paper down slowly; thoughtfully. It wasn't hard to see why the essay had gotten an "A +," and I found myself considering the depth of it as I returned to my Physics book.

The next morning, I stood up from where I sat on the front steps of my house with a sigh of relief, gratefully watching my car pull into the driveway. Dad parked the car and got out, then walked over to hand me the keys.

"Here she is."

I smiled as I accepted the keys and dropped them into my purse.

"Thanks Dad—you don't know how much I missed it."

Dad paused, adjusting his baseball cap and shivering slightly in the falling snow.

"You're welcome—at least you didn't ever have to walk."

Because I only had one class to teach that day at one o'clock, I had decided to grab lunch with Cat, and went on to drive to a local pizza buffet to meet her.

"So tell me about it. Bri tells me you've had free chauffeur service for two whole days—*and* a free meal."

I glanced up from my plate of salad and bread sticks, and sighed at Cat's amused smile.

"Well, that's it. What else am I supposed to say?"

Cat shrugged, wincing slightly at a sore muscle in her shoulder.

"I dunno,' you tell me."

I detected the curious tone in her voice and refused to justify her statement with a blush.

Cat smiled apologetically, though, and laughed lightly.

"Alright, Mira, okay. It's just . . . this kind of stuff doesn't happen every day."

"What kind of stuff, Cat?" I pressed quickly, suspiciously, and she paused in thought before dipping a breadstick into a dish of marinara.

"You know, Mira . . . It's not every day a guy . . . well, does that kind of stuff for any old girl."

"Here we go again with 'that kind of stuff'—and what do you mean by 'any old girl?' " I said while mindlessly shaking some parmesan cheese atop my salad.

"You know what I mean—as in guys have to be . . ."

I blinked, beginning to shake a little harder, taking my anxiety out on the salad.

"What? They have to be what?"

Cat sighed as she tapped the top of her straw.

"Well . . . either crazy or serious to treat a girl that way."

I shook my head as I glanced around the semi-crowded buffet. Why was everyone acting as though Jet's kind acts were so . . . serious? They weren't . . . were they?

"Everyone's talking about how different he is these days—they say it's not just in public, either," Cat continued, then smiled a little, "and it's not like he's bad-looking—"

"Cat, can we please just change the subject?" I pleaded as I coughed, having nearly choked on an olive during her ramble.

She sighed, and was quiet for a few seconds.

"So when does Kevin get back?"

I frowned at the inquiry.

"Um . . . tonight," I replied quietly, feeling my appetite escaping.

Cat nodded, closely studying her food, her blue-green eyes showing what I was certain to be a glint of sympathy.

"Do you think you two will do anything?"

I only shrugged, picking around at my salad while glancing sideways at my dance bag on the floor, which was slightly open. The tip of Jet's essay was barely visible.

After my two-hour-long class, I left the studio and hopped into my car, headed for La Salle University. It was about five o'clock when I arrived at the large football field, parking my car in the lot. The sun was considering setting as I walked into McCarthy Stadium, one hand hiding in the warmth of my leather jacket pocket, the other holding my cane and a folder.

A group of twelve to fifteen high schoolers stood at the fifty-yard line with a handful of older guys, and a man whom I recognized to be the La Salle coach hovering nearby. As I stood aloof near the base of the stands on the sidelines, I was able to recognize the guy in the middle of the huddle. Interested, I watched as Jet, dressed in a sports jacket, his black beanie and warmups, demonstrated a play to the boys. They watched him closely, laughing when he made a joke and painstakingly imitating his movements. I stood watching for a few minutes, until the coach dismissed the practice and the group dispersed.

I was finally discovered when one of the older guys, most likely a fellow teammate of Jet's, looked over at me. He went on to tap Jet on the shoulder, nodding in my direction. Surprised, Jet cut off his conversation with another player and jogged over.

"Hey, what're you doin' here?" he asked with a light smile, still a bit winded from practice.

"Well, I brought you someth—"

"Yo Jet, man! Come here!"

Jet quickly glanced over his shoulder as I was interrupted by a voice in the field.

"I'm sorry," he sighed. "Can you hold on for just a second?"

I nodded.

"Sure."

Jet started to jog off, then turned, moving backwards.

Don't go *anywhere*!" he called.

I smiled.

When Jet returned, ten minutes later, I had moved up to the front row of the stands to have a seat. Instead of taking the long route through the gate and up the steps, he ran to the wall and hoisted himself up.

"That's one way to do it," I chuckled after he had climbed up and sat down beside me.

Jet paused, very winded and, maybe, blushing slightly.

He had hurried all the way back.

"Oh . . ." He smiled, rubbing his hands together to stay warm. "Sorry it took so long—the guys are crazy."

I shrugged, curling a braid behind my ear.

"No problem." I paused, playing with a bangle on my wrist. "So... do you like teaching?"

Jet nodded with an immediate smile.

"Yeah," he replied, his tone becoming serious. "It, uh, it helps me take my mind off of myself."

I nodded as well, running my fingers along the smooth, grooved handle of my cane.

"That's why I like teaching, too," I voiced softly.

Jet looked at me.

"Really?"

I smiled lightly with a shrug.

"I've gotta have *some* kind of distraction—even though my distraction's a reminder." I laughed a little, and Jet nodded with an understanding smile. He was probably wondering if, given the irony of my words, smiling was even appropriate.

He glanced at the folder in my lap.

"What's that?"

"For you—it got mixed in with my stuff last night," I replied, handing it to him.

Puzzled, Jet opened it. It wasn't long before his expression snitched that he felt he had made a mistake.

"Aw man," he said quietly, placing his head in his hands, and I laughed.

"You don't have to be so upset—it's . . . amazing. I mean . . . really. It's good, Jet—and there's the A plus to prove it."

Jet finally grinned, distantly fingering the page with a shrug.

"But who woulda' thought *Miranda Phillips* would be readin' it?" he chuckled. "I need to be more careful next time."

I shook my head with a smile and studied his side profile as he looked out at the football field. For a moment, I stared at him, his seemingly perfectly-shaped, slightly-wide nose and barely-slanted eyes—his serious, angular jaw.

Was it just me, or did he mean something by saying "next time?"

I cleared my throat, sweeping the thought under the rug in the back of my mind.

"No worries—I gave it my stamp of approval."

Jet sighed, returning the smile.

"Thanks."

A few seconds passed as we both sat quietly wondering when the other one was going to say something and whether or not we should speak—desperately searching for a decent topic to break the ice.

"So, uh, I guess you won't be gettin' any more surprise football disturbances."

Drawing circles on my knee, I couldn't help but smile at his words.

"You weren't a disturbance, Jet," I replied quietly, but he laughed.

"C'mon, don't lie."

I looked at him, chuckling.

"Not always. . ."

"Just 99.9% of the time, right?"

I sighed, then noticed Jet's joking smile, and finally laughed.

"For real, though," Jet began quietly, "sorry about the way I blew up that night."

"What night?" I frowned.

Jet shrugged.

"When you came to Nana Jo's for dinner—I got all defensive at what you said, remember?"

I shook my head and smiled lightly.

"It's fine—I'm surprised you even remembered that."

Jet merely shrugged again, and sat studying his hands for a moment, his mind obviously weighed down by something.

"So what're you lookin' forward to these days—more recitals, maybe?" he finally asked casually, changing the subject.

I didn't reply immediately, my thoughts traveling to the Mayo letters, the doctors awaiting my decision . . . Kevin.

"I'm not really sure," I admitted softly, looking down at my hands, noting the lack of care I had given my nails in the past few weeks.

"Ah, I don't know," I lied.

"There must be somethin'—your classes look real advanced. It ain't like they've got a bad teacher." Jet smiled.

I grinned a little, but it quickly disappeared.

"I might not . . . be there to teach them soon."

Jet blinked, then frowned at my abrupt statement.

"Oh . . . um, really?"

I nodded.

"I've got some . . . decisions to make." I paused, resting my cane against the seat as I slid my hands into my pockets and leaned forward slightly. "I don't really know where it'll all take me."

Jet was silent for a long time, and I didn't expect him to pursue the subject any further.

"You're a lot braver than most people."

I looked up, searchingly, unsure of how I should thank him or what to say.

We sat in a more comfortable silence, although it was cold, at that, and almost sad.

"Tell me more," I hesitated, "about the second wind."

Maybe it was too straightforward of a question, but Jet didn't seem to think so, and he was silent for a moment before he began, leaning forward and resting his elbows on his knees.

"The second wind, to me, is like that God-given push you get— right when you're startin' to fall and always when you're nearin' the finish line," he said thoughtfully. "It's like . . . when you're learnin' how to ride a bike for the first time, and your dad lets go of you— it's when it's all up to you . . . when the power to move is put in your hands."

I looked down at my cane, feeling almost inspired, yet sad. Similar to how I felt when Jet led me around the classroom in the waltz; I felt a sense of excitement, as well as fear and reservation. As the wind stroked at our cheeks and the sun approached the horizon, I wondered if my second wind might be a little closer than I thought. . .

"It's gettin' pretty cold—I'll walk you to your car," Jet offered as he hugged himself, and we left the stands for the parking lot.

Nineteen

Jet

I yawned while moving down the hall, a towel slung over one slightly sore shoulder. The team had practiced hard that day, preparing for the division championship we once thought we'd never win.

I turned a corner, receiving a pat on the back from a fellow teammate, and stood before Coach Nagin in his humid, cramped office.

"Good practice, Carmichael," Coach Nagin grumbled with his eyes glued on a sheet of paper, his desk phone balanced on one stocky shoulder.

Eddie Nagin wasn't the type to dwell too much on any subject without multi-tasking, and I had learned, along with the rest of the team, to go with his flow. He was a tough coach, having graduated from the University of Tennessee years back with football victories under his belt. He wasn't the type of man to waste time or energy, and he made sure to extend this philosophy to the game of football.

I took a seat with a nod and mumbled a "thanks" that Coach probably didn't hear, and waited for him to end his call. As Coach half-argued, half-joked with whom I had guessed to be the university president, I allowed my mind to leave the moment slightly, my gaze fixed out the window behind Coach, my posture slouched in the metal chair before his desk.

Before I knew it, Coach's call ended, and my name was called.

"Daydreaming, Carmichael?"

I sat up a little straighter.

"Uh, no . . . sir," I lied.

Coach shrugged, shuffling some papers on his desk, scratching at the remnants of hair on his scalp.

"Don't lie, Carmichael—no harm in a daydream, as long as you don't do it on the field." He cleared his throat and coughed into one balled-up, thick fist, his breath carrying the sweet odor of a cigar. "You've changed more than I thought you would." I grimaced, shifting in the uncomfortable chair, ignoring the steady twitch in my shoulder, the twitch which suddenly seemed to activate in synchronization with my nerves.

"Oh, uh . . ." my voice trailed.

"Don't thank me." Coach waved his hand, narrowing his dark eyes, framed by bushy, gray brows. "Thank those ballet slippers— that Phillips girl."

I rolled my tongue along the inside of my cheeks, now focusing on the dirty, tile floor and attempting to will my frantic heartbeat to settle.

"But that's not all I wanted to talk to you about," he digressed, reaching for a gnawed pencil at the edge of the desk (he was attempting to quit smoking). "The Bledsoe team needs work. Those

127

boys are as hard-headed as our freshman line-up at the beginning of the season . . ." He paused, fingering the pencil. "The kids need discipline and more training. You've done a good job with them, but they can't seem to figure out how to carry what they learn onto the field. When Coach Shelton asked me what he thinks he should do, I told him I had just the plan." Coach leaned back in his tattered, leather chair, lacing his fingers behind his head as his black eyes squinted out at me. "Jet, I want those boys to learn the basics of ballet."

"Sir?" I found myself asking before I could think, and Coach looked determined.

"Of course," he waved a hand in my direction, "Look what it did for you. I wasn't just talkin' about your attitude change, but the way you play the game." Coach smiled his usual smirk. "There's almost as much muscle and balance training in ballet as there is in football." The smile disappeared as he leaned forward again, sifting through his papers once more. "I want you to get in touch with the Phillips girl and ask her to teach them—matter of fact." He paused, stalling an unprecedented five seconds before speaking. "I'll just go over there myself and ask her."

Twenty

Miranda

"Now, this won't hurt one bit, Miranda. You'll fall asleep, and when you wake up, you'll be a dancer again . . ."

I blinked once or twice, the glaring white light slowly fading into darkness above me. I couldn't wait to open my eyes again. I would be dancing when I did so—that's what the doctor had said. He had done research into my case—they knew exactly how to fix me. And then there was my full scholarship to Juilliard—the Alvin Ailey dance troupe, even, if I wanted . . . They were waiting for me—the nation, the world . . . me. I was waiting to be a dancer again.

My eyelids lifted. An audience sat before me in a large, vacant theater. My mom, Dad, Nina, Bri, Cat . . . They were waiting for me to dance. But I wasn't used to it anymore—I couldn't remember how to do it, could I?

I extended one leg, but suddenly fell forward. To my right, a hand was reaching out. I looked up into a pair of gentle yet serious dark eyes.

"Not that routine, Miranda. The other one—the one you taught me. It's easier. We'll take it slow . . . one step at a time . . . one step at a time . . ."

"Good morning Philly, I'm your traffic and weather man, Taylor King, with today's forecast. Right now it's 6:30 with a nippy 35 degrees outside and a fifty percent chance of snow. You may wanna grab those snowshoes before heading out, just in case—"

The thud of my hand atop the clock put an abrupt stop to the jarring radio alarm. I chided myself for setting it a half an hour earlier in order to get a head start on the day.

Rolling onto my back, I yawned and rubbed my eyes, allowing bits and pieces of my dreams to float back to me. Before I could recall the end of the last one, though, I sighed and climbed out of bed. When I reached my bureau, while fumbling through my clothes for something to wear, my sleepy eyes found the pile of letters from the Mayo Clinic, and I paused.

I breathed a deep sigh and grasped the surgeon's information card amidst the pile.

I concluded my last class on a weary note. I had been distant during school and while teaching that day, and this was mostly thanks to the long conversation with my doctor the day before and the near argument with Kevin over the phone when I got home.

Surgery grazed the horizon; that is, if I decided to go through with it. Kevin wasn't exactly excited about it, and voiced his concerns when we last spoke. As much as I respected his opinion and knew that he simply wanted what was best for me, I still couldn't help but feel slightly annoyed. It was my life and my decision (though it rarely felt like it). If I had the chance to dance again set before me, shouldn't I take it?

I hauled the final ballet bar to the mirror with a grunt, ignoring my flopping shoelace. Before limping back to my desk to finish cleaning up, I bent to tie my shoe, wincing only a little at the slight aching in my legs.

Barely had my thoughts dragged to Kevin and the possible surgery before voices floated from the empty hall outside of my door.

I frowned as I straightened—the studio would close in fifteen minutes.

At the preceding knock on the door, I sighed, not feeling like walking over to open it.

"Come in," I vaguely called while heading toward my desk, inwardly scolding myself for abandoning my cane to move the bars.

"Miranda Phillips."

I turned at the gruff voice, and there stood who I barely recognized to be the La Salle Explorers coach, with a husky boy of fifteen or so at his side.

I blinked in slight confusion. The coach extended a large hand while walking over.

"Eddie Nagin," he greeted in a business-like way, and I nodded with a shake of his hand.

I searched for a reply.

"What can I do for you . . . Coach?"

Coach Nagin crossed his arms over his chest, the sleeves of his blue-and-white jacket rolled up slightly.

"Well, I went to Carmichael's recital a few weeks ago, and I have to say that I never knew he could move like that."

I offered a light smile, leaning against the desk.

"He's a natural—you might have a dancer on your hands."

Coach Nagin seemed to consider my statement, nodding while twisting his rugged jaw in thought.

"Maybe so, maybe so. But what I know for sure is that if Carmichael can benefit from a few dance classes, then so can any other guy—take Gerald here, for example, from the Bledsoe High

131

team we mentor. He's been playin' football for ten years and still needs to work on his basic footwork." Coach gestured to the shifty-eyed, mop-haired boy, who looked as though he couldn't have felt any more embarrassed at being inside (let alone within a five-mile radius) of a dance room. "But that's nothin' a few twists and turns couldn't fix, eh?"

I shrugged with a smile and laugh, identifying his hidden request.

"I really don't think you're asking the right person, sir." I grasped for an excuse. "I mean, I only teach dancers, and the whole thing with Jet coming was really out of my element—"

"But it sure did work," interrupted the coach as he slid his hands into his pockets. "Jet's been putting the other boys to shame in practice."

I couldn't smother a smile, recalling the coach's public statement from the get-go that Jet's dancing was strictly for punishment.

"Listen, Coach Nagin, I'd be glad to teach Gerald, but I just don't know about guaranteeing that it'll help with footba—"

"Just Gerald?" Coach's heavy eyebrows raised two inches. "Well of course not just Gerald—*all* the Bledsoe boys need work! Gerald here's just the captain."

I blinked in disbelief.

The whole *football team?! That would be like an all-out attack on dance! None of the boys would listen and we wouldn't get through a single practice without dance being laughed at . . . No way.*

I swallowed, shaking my head with an apologetic shrug.

"Oh no—see, I can't really . . . I mean, there's so many to teach and so much they'd need to learn and—"

"So many reasons why you should accept—hey Coach, sorry I'm late."

Perturbed, I turned to the doorway.

"Jet?"

Jet cast me a blithe smile as he jogged inside, then turned to

Coach Nagin.

"No luck yet, Coach?"

Coach Nagin breathed a heavy sigh, holding up his hands.

"I used to think *you* were stubborn, but now. . ."

I smirked but Jet grinned all the more.

"Miranda's just . . . careful," he chuckled. "I'll take it from here."

I sighed, and Jet turned to face me.

"Miranda, I know you've had your share of crazy football player attitude with me alone, but would you please teach the Bledsoe guys—they really need your help."

I shifted my jaw, only hoping he wouldn't attempt the puppy-dog eyes maneuver, which would surely do me in.

"Jet, I can't—"

"Miranda, just this once," he practically begged, his eyes darting in thought before he snapped his fingers. "I promise if there's even *one* laugh out of any of the guys over a move or dance, then I'll . . . I'll. . ."

"Show them that video Bri secretly shot of you doing a jazz walk in slippers for the first time?" I quietly ventured, and Jet's hopeful expression transformed into an embarrassed grin.

He cleared his throat as Coach Nagin looked amused, and even the silent Gerald couldn't stifle a snicker or two.

Crossing his arms over his chest with a sigh, Jet finally shrugged.

"If that's what it takes . . ."

Impressed by his persistence, I finally laughed.

"You've got yourself a deal."

Twenty-One
Jet

Things were almost back to the way they were before the recital, when aches and pains turned into flexibility, hearing the "5, 6, 7, 8" count-off was daily jargon, and, well, seeing Miranda every other Sunday was normal...yet a privilege.

I attended the classes for the Bledsoe team at Coach's suggestion (orders) and only planned on sitting on the sidelines at first—offering a bit of help wherever needed. But boy did that change. All I know is Miranda snickered to me after class that she "knew that watching from afar wasn't gonna last long."

I'll admit I enjoyed helping teach the boys, and they even seemed to have a little fun with it.

The only person who *didn't* seem to be very pleased with Miranda teaching the boys was Kevin, who arrived to pick her up once or twice with a less than friendly demeanor.

Now, I don't mean to jump to conclusions, but I can't help but say that I noticed something...off...about him. I mean, I didn't exactly know the guy, but each rare time I happened to see him with Miranda, I always noted how different she was. I guess you could say she was practically the polar opposite of the Miranda I had eaten dinner with at Nana Jo's that one night. Maybe I was reading into things too much, but Miranda was quieter and a little more distant whenever Kevin arrived at the studio. I often wondered if they ever even laughed together, since Kevin seemed to be such a serious guy.

I jogged a little faster than usual the following Friday. The park was welcoming as ever as the day neared the late afternoon hours, and I didn't mind the occasional gust of wind—it kept me cool.

I hadn't seen Miranda since the last Sunday we taught the Bledsoe boys, since both of our schedules kept us busy. Many times, I had seriously considered calling her, but always decided against it. I guess I was a little more timid than I was willing to admit.

With each puff, my breath suspended in the air before me. Winter was almost here and Thanksgiving was only a few weeks away. While watching a couple some yards ahead, slowly walking the path hand-in-hand, I found myself wondering what Miranda would be doing for the holiday . . .

"Jet!"

Startled, my thoughts jarred and I looked to my right. A heavily-bundled, waving Bri stood on the adjacent path, smiling as she walked over.

"Hey," I greeted, stretching my legs slightly. "Just chillin'?"

Bri nodded, reaching up to adjust her white, knit beanie.

"Conditioning?" she returned.

I chuckled.

"You could say that—more like exercising my mind, though." I

135

paused to cough. "So what's new with you?"

"Nothing much. I've got a show to practice for—my boyfriend Jake's gonna be in it as well."

I nodded.

"He dances, too?"

Bri hesitated.

"Well . . . he *tries.* . . ."

I smiled.

"Got it—he's like me, a 'wannabe.' "

Bri laughed, shaking her head.

"I bet Miranda's still goin' crazy with the choreography and classes—teachin' left and right, huh?" I questioned, quickly rubbing my gloved hands together before zipping my coat a little higher.

Bri wasn't as quick to respond this time, though.

"Um, well . . ."

I frowned at her sudden change of expression.

"What is it?"

Bri sighed, kicking at a curled leaf on the cement path.

"She's about to have surgery."

My mouth hung open slightly, and I scratched my head.

"Oh . . ." I glanced around me, unsure of what to think. "Okay ... I didn't really . . . I mean—"

"No one did," Bri shrugged, speaking quietly. "I mean, we kinda' expected it, but then . . . it's still a lot to swallow, y'know?"

I nodded slowly, understanding the risks involved. Not only were there physical dangers, but there was always Miranda's own feelings, her durability and hopes, to consider. What if . . . what if it didn't work? What would that do to her? Would the disappointment be too much to handle?

"So," I picked at the corner of my lip, stuffing one hand into my pocket, "when does she leave?"

"Sunday night they head to Rochester. You know, the studio's holding a sort of 'best wishes' party tomorrow night."

"Really?"

"Yeah, you can come, if you want." Bri paused, smiling a little. "Miranda would love to see you before she leaves..."

"Oh." I cleared my throat. "Yeah, I'll, uh, I'll-I'll be there . . . then," I somehow managed to say, even though my thoughts were dwelling on Bri's last sentence.

After we discussed school and local events for a few minutes more, she continued with her stroll and I returned to my jogging, this time my thoughts revolving around the news I had just received.

"So after Iverson took the ball to the hoop, the ref wanted to call a charging foul, but Kobe's feet were movin'! Can you believe that?"

I nodded distantly from where I lay on the living room floor of the apartment, pretending to be listening to Luke's account of the 76ers game I had missed.

Obviously, Luke wasn't pleased, and eyed me from where he was sprawled on the couch, tossing a basketball.

"Dude, you haven't listened to a word I've said, have you?"

I frowned, lacing my fingers under my head as I stared up at the ceiling.

"Hey, do you think it's bad to have gotten a gift from someone who you owe and you haven't gotten anything for them?" I shot my own question.

Luke sighed with a shrug.

"I dunno' . . . yeah. I mean, if you owe 'em, you owe 'em."

"Hmm." I closed my eyes, recalling the signed t-shirt from Miranda, which now hung on the wall in my room. "What do you think I should get her?"

Luke smirked, leaning back as he noted my failure to uphold my ambiguity.

"Somethin' nice—somethin' girls like . . ." he shrugged again, ruffling his brownish-blond coils, "perfume, a teddy-bear or somethin.'"

I frowned. "Nah, man, that's too simple."

Luke grew impatient. "Well, what're you thinking then? A diamond?"

I breathed a sigh. "Whatever. I'll think of something."

"Hey, Jet, good to see you."

I smiled as I walked through the front door of the studio, grateful to escape the falling snow outside.

Bri grinned as she accepted the plate of homemade cookies Nana Jo had sent me off with, and lead me to the food table to set them out for the guests.

The lobby was packed, with everyone from students and teachers whom I knew, to others whom I had never seen before. A large banner swung overhead, with bold lettering reading, "Warmest Wishes, Miranda!"

"It looks great," I commented while looking around, and Bri chuckled as she unwrapped the plate of cookies.

"That's all Cat and Nina's doing." She looked up, noting the carefully sealed, purple envelope in my right hand. "Oh, I'll take that for you," she said.

I drew back nervously.

"Oh, uh—I . . . um . . ."

Bri blinked in confusion, then nodded slowly, understanding showing on her face.

I looked down at the floor.

"I've gotta go—I'll be right back." Bri moved away as she was summoned from across the room.

I nodded as Bri hurried off, realizing that I had no idea what to do next. The crowd was much too thick to be able to spot Miranda easily.

"Oh, excuse me."

I looked to my right after being nudged, and quickly spoke up, "No problem."

The man smiled, then paused. "Jet Carmichael, right?"

I nodded.

"Well, it's great to finally meet you." He grinned a confident grin, extending a hand and firmly shaking mine. "Harvey Willis—I work for Juilliard; I'm an intern right now."

"Oh, nice to meet you."

Harvey ruffled his hair slightly. "You know, it's crazy how many people Miranda knows."

I nodded, stuffing my hands into the pockets of my black slacks. "She's pretty famous."

"Tell me about it," Harvey agreed, helping himself to some chips and cookies. "Debbie Allen at one o'clock," he added, cocking his head across the room, and I quickly turned to look.

Sure enough, Debbie Allen, the famous dancer, was barely visible in the crowd, linking arms with Miranda's mom.

"Oh . . . wow." I blinked, feeling more and more like a nobody.

I turned back to Harvey.

"So . . . you know Miranda from . . . ?"

"High school," Harvey spoke up, then tilted his head. "I was her sort of stand-in partner when Kevin wasn't available—which was rare," Harvey added a slightly wry laugh, but I only nodded.

"Now I see her—standing by the front desk with Nina and Kevin."

I followed Harvey's gesture, and spotted Miranda, who was nodding while listening closely to something Kevin was whispering in her ear. Her braids were loose, and she wore a flattering green dress. Nina was nearby, listening as well, with one arm around Miranda's shoulders.

Just seeing how close-knit a group they were caused my spirits to drop, and I breathed a sigh. Here I was, inside of a room full of people who knew everything about the dance world—Miranda's world. Standing next to a dancer friend of Miranda's and watching Miranda associate with a famous sister and boyfriend whom she was practically engaged to.

I jumped slightly at the tap on my shoe, and recalled the envelope I was holding, which had fallen from my limp hand onto the floor. After I bent to pick it up, Harvey was gone, most likely having found someone else to talk to. Perhaps someone a little more up on things concerning dance and Miranda.

I blended into the walls for most of the evening, watching as Mr. Nelson thanked everyone for coming, extending an invitation for anyone to give Miranda some words of encouragement or gratitude. I hung back even more during that portion of the party, ignoring the nagging to go up and say something, hoping my palm wasn't sweating through the envelope to the card that was supposed to do all of the talking for me.

After words were spoken and some tears were cried, the party gradually came to an end, but Miranda was too busy with her guests for me to reach her.

I left the building with a heavy sigh, realizing how stupid it probably was of me to come in the first place. I wasn't really anybody at all—just Jet Carmichael, the guy Miranda had to put up with for a month or so. The people at the party were the ones who truly knew her—people she trusted and actually liked to be around.

I zipped my heavy coat with a sigh, my fingers quickly growing numb in the cold. The note was stashed away in my pocket, and was probably destined to be shredded as soon as I got home.

I didn't leave immediately, though, and, for some reason, I lingered near the door, mostly out of sight. After Miranda's family walked to their car, I guessed that only Miranda was left.

Kicking at an empty can on the sidewalk, I realized that it was pointless to think that I would be able to get the note to Miranda now. I couldn't just walk up to her when she came out, hand her the note and say my peace—not in front of Kevin, the obviously very-watchful boyfriend.

With one final sigh, I started to move, but paused when I heard voices hovering from the vestibule, slightly muffled through the glass door.

"Miranda, don't you think that's what I want?" Kevin was asking, his tone lined with a mixture of desperation and anger. "Don't you think I want things to be flexible in Atlanta?"

"No, Kevin, I don't!" Miranda returned, her voice filled with a pain and exasperation I had never heard from her before. "I don't feel like you listen to me anymore—not when you go off and make plans without talking to me first!"

"Miranda, would you just listen to *me* for once? You always wanna go off talkin' about how I'm not thinkin' about you, but wouldn't it take a guy who thinks about you to go all the way to ATL to make sure you get what you want?!"

"This was never about what I want, Kevin! It's about what *you* want, and you know it! How many times do I have to tell you that?!"

"Well, I'm just now hearing it!"

A tense silence followed Kevin's heated response, and I hesitated, feeling as though I should leave, but unable to walk away from the words I was hearing. All I could think of was how much Kevin had his foot in his mouth—*both* feet.

"Kevin, listen," Miranda was speaking softly now, and I stepped a little closer to hear, "I just . . . I-I wanna feel comfortable with all of this . . . but, I don't."

I nodded as though I was listening to a dialogue on a TV show, agreeing with Miranda's choice of words and noting her sincerity.

No guy in his right mind would debate her point, I thought with assurance. What I didn't realize, though, was that part of me was aching slightly, at the obvious hurt in Miranda's tone. There was a catch in her voice that could only foreshadow tears.

But Kevin didn't take the wise route, and I was surprised at what I heard next.

"Well, you keep drillin' me on how this isn't enough for you and this isn't this or that for you—well guess what, Miranda?" his volume increased, "This isn't about you anyway, and I can't keep gettin' shot down while tryin' to please you! There's no one else *but* me, Miranda—no one else would have stayed by your side through all of this drama!" He sighed. "I'm out—lemme guess, you can drive yourself home?"

Before I could even react, the door suddenly burst open, and an angry Kevin stormed out of the studio, hastily zipping his jacket. He paused for a second, obviously surprised to see me standing there, and proceeded to glare at me before crossing the street for his car.

I watched him go, feeling very embarrassed suddenly, but I'm sure it couldn't match the shame and embarrassment on Miranda's face when I turned to see her standing outside of the door, the blatant tracks of tears on her face.

I don't think I could have felt any more stupid for having heard the whole argument, and for not leaving when I knew I should. If I were Miranda, I would have been mad at me. She only looked down at the ground with a sigh.

"Sorry," she spoke quietly, taking me a little off-guard by her apology.

"Uh, n-no, it's fine . . . ?" I felt unsure as to what I should say. It couldn't have been a more awkward situation.

Miranda pushed a braid out of her face, hastily wiping at the tears, dealing with her embarrassment in what I witnessed to be a very professional, "Miranda" way. I guess I should have known it would take more than an argument with her boyfriend for her to let anyone see her sweat. I couldn't help but admire her toughness, but felt sorry for the way she had learned to hide or quickly cover her emotions.

"Can I walk you to your car?" I offered. There would have been no point in leaving Miranda by herself—as Kevin so politely did.

As we moved through the still, cold air to Miranda's car, we said nothing. Miranda moved steadily with her cane, and I could tell that she was trying to conceal her limp, her head held high and eyes casually scanning the area.

When we reached the car, Miranda briefly thanked me as she readied her keys. She reminded me very much of the cool, reserved girl I had met in the classroom that day so many months back, and not the Miranda I had seen begin to open up to me.

"This is for you," I said in one shaky breath, my hand still fumbling inside of my pocket for the note which I had come close to destroying.

Miranda paused, staring blankly at the slightly bent, pathetic envelope in my outstretched hand, her keys already in the lock of her car. Her expression softened only slightly as she reached for the card.

"Thank you," was her business like reply, but she seemed to hesitate after a moment, and looked up at me, checking for any sign for her to stop as she began to open it.

I, with all of my careful planning, down to the card, envelope, sentence and word, had not thought of this happening. I held my breath, the wind seeming to whip a little harder at my cheeks.

As Miranda's eyes scanned my painstakingly neat handwriting, I fiddled with my hands, desperately trying to recall exactly what I wrote and where I wrote it. Which paragraph was it that said how great I thought she was? How I admired her lack of fear? That I would be praying for her, and how I would think of her as a dancer no matter what?

I don't think I realized that I had been holding my breath until I felt my stomach move again, when Miranda's whole countenance changed and the note trembled ever so slightly in her fingers.

Miranda reached up a hand to wipe one of the tears cascading from her eyes, looking away from me a little.

I barely knew what to think, and found myself blushing, wondering if my note had really been *that* impacting.

Before I knew it, though, Miranda reached out to hug me, and whispered the sincerest "thank you" I had ever received.

And then she left, driving off onto the main street. I stood alone in the parking lot, my car a few yards away. I was filled with a humility, sadness and joy that I had never felt before.

Something had changed—or maybe I should say had been begun—about the way I felt about Miranda that night, and I didn't resist admitting it.

Twenty-Two
Miranda

The view outside of the tenth-story window of the hotel was calm and serene, and the lavender-orange clouds looked as though they were created by the delicate strokes of a paintbrush. Despite the heavy feeling in my stomach, I smiled a little, sadly, as I touched the cool glass of the window, wishing for a brief second that I could somehow fly out of the window and into the sunset, wherever it led me to.

"Mira, you thirsty?"

I didn't turn at Nina's inquiry, and only shook my head, not wanting to leave my rare, peaceful moment.

Nina and Dad were trying to quickly finish their dinner of hot dogs and French fries, taking care to stay away from me, since I could only drink clear liquids before the surgery the next morning. They had insisted that they eat out, but with some arguing, I told them it was fine with me—since I wasn't hungry anyway.

The door to our suite opened, and I saw my mom's reflection in the glass.

"How'd it go?" Dad asked from where he sat on the couch, his food spread out on the coffee table.

"Well enough," Mom replied with a sigh, removing her hat and scarf. "There's still the local press to take care of."

"You should have let me go with you—"

"Charles," Mom interrupted, then paused in her steps to the bathroom, frowning at the coffee table. "What's all this doing here? I thought we were gonna eat out?"

"We tried to tell her, Mom." Nina shrugged, tucking her legs underneath her from where she sat on the floor, already dressed in her pajamas.

"Charles—"

"Mom, it's fine," I cut in, not feeling like dealing with any commotion over petty issues.

Mom looked over at me, where I now stood leaning against the frigid window, not caring that my hand was going numb.

"Well, alright . . ." she said slowly, obviously unconvinced.

Eight hours later, when the sun was on its way to the horizon once again, I sat on the couch in the front room, wide awake and very much afraid. I hadn't gotten any sleep, and after four hours of praying, thinking, and a little bit of tearing up, I finally got out of bed to sit for a while—to do something with my restless mind. Thousands of questions and scenarios floated through my thoughts. What would it be like? Would it be very painful? Would I make it? Could the doctors do it? Would I be okay tomorrow?

"Miranda."

I looked up sharply from where I held my head in my hands, having forgotten where I was for a moment.

"You should be asleep," Mom spoke quietly, tying her robe around her.

I sighed while rubbing my burning eyes. I hadn't slept well for a good two or three days, and though I didn't feel my exhaustion enough to be sleepy, I certainly felt *tired*.

"I wish I was."

Mom nodded slowly, then walked over to sit beside me. The only light came from a nearby lamp I had flicked on to a dim setting.

"Momma, I feel like I'm all alone," I said softly, watching the curtains blowing lightly in the warmth of the vent beneath them.

Mom didn't reply immediately. "With all those people praying for you and thinking about you?"

I didn't say anything, and only hoped I wouldn't burst into tears. If I couldn't maintain my composure to some degree, I wouldn't be able to face the next day. I hated not being strong. In reality, I was terrified and very weak. Without a front, I would fall apart, and be unable to carry the load.

"I hear Kevin called while I was out . . ."

I shifted my jaw, trying with everything in me not to think about him—not to remember the last words he had said to me.

Mom continued.

"I doubt he's not thinking about you, Miranda." She hesitated. "You should have spoken to him—"

"Mom . . ." I closed my eyes. "Please," I whispered, shaking my head, knowing I was emotionally unable to handle discussing Kevin at the moment.

"I'm just trying to remind you, baby," Mom sighed after a few seconds of silence.

I swallowed, turning to face her.

"But I don't *need* you to remind me of that right now." I tried to

147

keep my lip from quivering. "I . . . I just need you—I need everyone . . . to let me face this not as 'Miranda the teacher' or 'Miranda the cripple,' but as *Miranda . . . me*."

I lost the battle against the tears that night, but at least I was wrong about one thing: I wasn't alone.

I started out the long preparation process for surgery a nervous wreck the next day. The drive to the hospital, though it was only down the street, was a hectic one. My family was trying to remain calm for my sake, but they altogether failed. Dad forgot to bring some important papers, and we had to turn around to go back to the hotel. My parents almost got into two arguments about which entrance to use and where to park, and Nina's uncharacteristic silence quickly picked at my nerves.

Everything changed, though, when I was finally on the moveable bed in the recovery room, having been briefed by the caring surgeon on what would happen for the umpteenth time, as "knock-out" medication flowed through my veins from the I.V. Both of my legs had been numbed from an uncomfortable "nerve block" procedure, but I didn't seem to mind anything as the medicine took effect and the ceiling lights seemed to dance.

Mom sat in a chair beside the bed, most likely in the exact opposite frame of mind, but hiding her emotions like a pro now that the moment had arrived.

"Miranda." She spoke softly, leaning in close, in case I couldn't hear her. "I told the doctor to fix you up well—that you're a dancer."

I smiled weakly, my eyelids drooping as her voice suddenly sounded as though it was miles away.

"Mom," I whispered as the steady "beep" of the heart monitor lulled me to sleep, "I'm sure he already knows."

Mom smiled sadly as I gave in to sleep, her hand gently

smoothing the braids from my forehead, breathing a silent prayer that all would work out.

The next twenty-four hours were a haze, and surprisingly, I didn't feel any pain. But the numbness in my legs was only temporary, and very gradually, an intense aching, not dissimilar to what I felt when I first had my accident, rose up in my legs to the point that I wished I could somehow detach myself from my lower body for relief. Narcotics were on hand, but they did little for the constant, altogether inescapable pain. By the second day, living from minute to minute became both a physical and mental struggle, since my very mind was beginning to grow exhausted from the pain.

Somehow, I managed to fall asleep after downing some pills, but was soon disrupted by a sudden jerk and, consequently, a sensation of sledgehammers pounding my legs as my muscles suffered from a new obstacle: spasms.

My cry must have summoned a nurse and awakened my dad. After explaining that it wasn't quite time for my next dose of medicine and asking if there was anything else she could do, the nurse left. I gripped the rail on the right side of the bed, beginning the torturous exercise of counting down the two hours left until I could take more pills.

My dad got up from the recliner he had been sleeping in and sat down in the chair near the bed, taking hold of my hand.

"You're hangin' in there, Tutu." He smiled gently down at me, trying to stay positive for my sake.

I nodded quickly while shifting a little, trying to ignore the pain. As I squeezed my eyes shut, my heavily-medicated and exhausted mind pictured a vivid memory involving a music box in a store window. I opened my eyes, a few tears escaping as I squeezed Dad's hand.

"Daddy, you-you remember that time you took Nina and me

shopping in the city?" I asked softly, swallowing back the lump in my throat. "A-and how I looked in a toy store window and saw that ballerina music box? I begged and begged for you to get it for me." I took a deep breath. "Well, I-I wish you never bought it for me.

"I mean, it didn't take me anywhere—all of the practices and lessons . . . all of the work and dreams I had." I paused as the tears clouded my vision, and Dad hung his head. "I-I don't see them as anything but curses now. Why did God do this to me? Why did He let me love to dance? I wish I never did. It's always hurt me—always hurt me . . ."

"Miranda, everyone is born with something." Dad held my hand tighter and touched my cheek, his own voice catching a little. "God gives us all something that we love to do on earth, and He takes that and uses it to give people joy and hope—all for His purpose." He swallowed. "He gave you dance, Miranda. No matter what you do or what people tell you, dance will always be one of the things He assigned to you, baby. You've been beating your fists at it all your life, trying to run from it sometimes. But when it's in you, Miranda, it can't leave. God's plan will work in you—it will."

I continued to sob as I held my dad's hand, the pain of dance's hold on me conquering the physical pain in my legs.

But Dad's words echoed throughout my thoughts and heart for the rest of the night.

I was mostly bedridden for two weeks, wheelchair bound by the third week, but after a month had passed, I was finally able to walk gingerly with the aid of crutches. The staff at the hospital applauded my efforts when I was finally able to stand on my own two feet, and I was glad to be making progress, as hard as it was. Upon first standing on my own, I nearly cried like a baby from the throbbing in my legs. This was to be expected, but I didn't know the pain would rival that of what I felt after my accident.

On the brighter side, I was constantly receiving words of encouragement from my friends and family back home, and it felt good to know that people were praying for me and thinking about me.

"You won't believe who I saw in the lobby!"

I looked up from where I sat reclining on the hotel bed, my legs propped slightly on pillows, a dance magazine in my hands.

"Who?"

Nina grinned as she removed her suede coat, tossing it onto a chair and sliding onto the adjacent bed. My dad had returned home to run the studio after my surgery, and Mom stayed behind with me. Nina was currently on one of her weekend visits.

"Just some people," she said as she loosened her dark hair from her winter hat, then grabbed the room service menu. "I think I'm feelin' sushi tonight . . ."

"Nina." I rolled my eyes, stretching my arms with a yawn before dusting some potato chip crumbs from my oversized t-shirt. "Who was it?"

"W-e-ell . . ."

There came a knock on the door.

I looked warily at Nina. Mom had just left a few minutes earlier, and she had a key; I hadn't ordered anything from room service, either . . .

"Nina?"

"I guess that's them." She smiled, ignoring my apprehension.

My jaw dropped as Nina got up and headed for the door, and I took no time in tying my braids into a ponytail, tossing the magazine aside and quickly checking my reflection in the window to my left.

"Mira!" came a squeal from the doorway.

Before I could process everything, Bri came running over and wrapped me in a hug.

I chuckled, and looked in the doorway to see a grinning Cat, and,

151

to my surprise, Jet—both of them carrying flowers, teddy bears, DVDs, and sacks of junk food.

"So, how was the flight?"

Jet looked up at me with his casually lazy smile, a half-eaten bowl of Pizza Rolls in one hand.

"Crazy, with those two," he chuckled, and I laughed.

Just in the other room, the chattering of Bri, Cat and Nina floated through the doorway as my sister showed them her latest promotional shots for a perfume ad. Cat and Bri had insisted upon seeing them, and Nina took no time in whipping them out.

Jet stretched his legs out before him as he leaned against the opposite bed on the floor. I was entertaining myself with staring out the window into the Rochester city lights. I couldn't help but be glad that my mom was out taking a much-needed shopping trip, as I was certain she might not be too pleased to see Jet at the hotel—not with the Kevin situation still on the horizon, that is.

"Was it really hard?"

I blinked, turning to Jet and alighting my train of thought.

"Oh . . . um." I twirled a braid, trying to think of an honest way to answer his question about my surgery, but eventually shrugged.

Jet nodded slowly, setting his bowl to the side.

"Sorry I didn't come sooner—I kept trying, but I had games and coach wanted me to practice."

"Don't worry about it—it's fine. Thanks for the card, by the way." I waved my hand, knowing I wouldn't have wanted Jet to see me in the shape I was in a month earlier.

"Speaking of cards," Jet spoke up, reaching into his pocket and fishing out a small, red envelope. "Nana Jo wanted me to give you this."

Opening it, I began to read the note inside. When I had finished, I smiled, noticing the gift card attached.

"She remembered I like Outback—it's a free dinner for two," I said quietly, and Jet nodded with a smile.

"She doesn't forget anything."

I chuckled.

"You'll have to give me her number before you leave—I've gotta call her and thank her."

Both of us were silent for a moment, and the others continued to chat in the other room.

"So how are the boys coming with their dancing?"

Jet smiled. "They're enjoying it. I'm still learning new stuff, too with Carl."

I grinned. "That's good to hear."

"So . . . what now—with your recovery?"

I picked at the Velcro strap of one of my leg immobilizers, recalling the days when I was able to walk and dance freely.

"Physical therapy," I replied softly, forsaking voicing my true fears. We all knew the therapy wouldn't be easy, but it was the ultimate deciding factor of whether or not I would dance again.

Jet rubbed his arm, then looked up with a comforting smile.

"I'll be praying for you."

I smiled a little as well, grateful for his concern and faithfulness.

"Thanks, Jet."

"All the way from Philly."

I looked up with a light smile, twirling a French fry in my hefty bowl of ketchup, and Nina chuckled.

"I can't believe they came," I replied, as the sound of Mom's breathing floated from the other room, where she was sleeping. "Especially Jet," I added, then reached for my cup of Sprite.

Nina was silent for a moment as she finished her bowl of trail mix, laying on her back on the floor below the couch I was reclining on, a hint of contemplation in her dark, almond-shaped eyes.

"I can," she responded after what must have been a full two

minutes, surprising me a little.

Before opening my mouth to speak, I paused, suddenly realizing what she meant. I set my bowl down on the end table, feeling an excited fear rising inside of my chest.

Nina rolled onto her stomach, propping herself up on her elbows, looking up at me.

I looked away from her expectant stare.

"He's just . . . being nice, Nina."

"Miranda." She shook her head with a sigh, speaking quietly. "There is a red flag of seriousness in the air, and it's right on your doorstep—"

"He hasn't really done anything, though."

Nina shrugged at my hasty interruption, then contemplated.

"That doesn't mean it isn't on his mind."

I scratched my head, sinking a little lower into the warm fuzziness of the couch, trying to ignore both the ache in my right leg and the truth in my sister's words.

"I don't know," I said quietly with pretend disregard, slowly pulling a cashmere throw over myself, suddenly wishing I was a child and void of young-adult drama.

"Miranda, what's keeping you from admitting that I'm right?"

"I'm scared, okay?" I quickly replied, listening to my voice raise a little, then sighing as I snuggled into the pillows.

"I know, Mira," Nina said softly, pulling her own pillow beneath her chin. "But we're not talkin' about a jerk, here . . . not anymore, at least." She smiled lightly. "I mean, he's sweet, caring, attractive, strong . . ."

I closed my eyes and picturing Jet's warm smile in my mind, remembering the many times I had recently found myself trying desperately to keep my heart from fluttering at his smile, or the way he watched me very closely when we spoke, never taking his eyes off me . . .

"That's why I'm afraid."

"Hey Mira, they're here!" Nina's voice called from the front room.

I sighed as I studied my reflection in the mirror, parting my braids on the side, then grabbed my crutches and hobbled out of the bathroom.

Outside, Bri, Cat and Jet stood chatting with Nina, and after talking a little longer, we finally hugged and said goodbye. Jet lingered to talk with me in private as Nina explained that she was going to call mom and see how things were going with the press.

"So," Jet began slowly as we both sat on the couch, me with my legs propped on the coffee table, Jet sitting casually at my side as we waded through a long goodbye. "When do you start therapy?"

"This Monday . . . the day after tomorrow," I replied, and Jet nodded.

He stared down at his hands for a moment, then looked up at me, smiling broadly with a boyish twinkle in his dark eyes.

"I bet they'll be pretty psyched out having Miranda Phillips as their patient—you might be signin' autographs."

I chuckled, shaking my head as I looked down.

"You know somethin,' Jet?"

He looked at me, and I swallowed, trying carefully to formulate my words.

"You, uh . . ." I picked at a loose thread on the edge of the couch, having to look away from him. It was getting harder and harder to look him in the eyes without my lips twitching into a smile, feeling my cheeks growing warm, or forgetting what I was going to say. Before I could finish my sentence, though, my right leg twitched, shooting a signal of pain to my brain. Involuntarily, I grabbed the arm of the couch with one hand, and Jet's wrist with the other.

"Are you okay?" he asked, frowning in concern, immediately taking hold of my hand, noting the obvious pained expression on my face.

Holding my forehead, I took a deep breath.

"Yeah—I'm-I'm fine . . ." I let the breath out, and we both slowly, hesitantly, released the other's hand. I smiled apologetically. "Sorry."

Jet shook his head.

"No, no," he quickly replied, then hesitated. "*I* am . . . that you've gotta go through this to get to your goal."

Once again, I broke the gaze between us, almost wanting to wish that his blatant sincerity was feigned, in order that I could be relieved of the hovering "red flag" Nina had spoken of.

Twenty-Three
Jet

Cat and Bri's giggling echoed from my right, and I shook my head with a sigh as I laced my fingers behind my head.

The hum of the jet engine rumbled around us as we waited for the plane to land in Philadelphia.

"Tic Tac?"

I looked at Bri's extended palm, holding a packet of Tic Tacs, ready to dispense.

"Why, do I need one?"

She chuckled.

"Most definitely," she exaggerated, and Cat glanced over with a laugh.

"Very funny." I grinned, then yawned. "Cat, can I have a section?"

Cat blinked, then shared a mischievous grin with Bri.

"Do you prefer celebrity gossip, 'what guys are *really* thinking,' or makeup tips?" Bri giggled.

"The *newspaper*, Cat—not *Vogue*," I bristled.

Cat chuckled.

"Okay, okay." She handed me the newspaper, and I accepted it with a sarcastic thank you.

Settling into my seat, I sighed as my eyes scanned over the headlines. After failing to find an interesting story, I flipped over to the sports section to see how the Eagles were doing. I paused while doing so, as I was certain I had seen Miranda's picture somewhere. Leaning forward a little, I skipped back a few pages, searching for the photo. Sure enough, I found it, and carefully began reading the article:

The Dancer with a Second Chance
Allyson Hernandez

The hotel room is filled with warmth and laughter when I visit the Phillips family, but perhaps the glow is coming mostly from the young lady sitting across from me, her hazel eyes dazzling despite the bulky braces and bandages her legs were set in, her long braids swept into a ponytail with a few dangling over her eyes and shoulder.

Miranda Phillips, 21, is your average college-aged girl at first glance, but you wouldn't know what she's been through until you sit down to hear her story. Born and raised in the urban, North Philly setting, Miranda and her sister, Nina, followed in the footsteps of their mother, Evangeline Sylvester Phillips, former Broadway actress, by dancing and acting at a young age. Coached by their father, Charles Phillips, co-owner of Capstone Productions, and guided by their mother, the girls both found a love for artistic expression. Nina has narrowed her love down to acting and modeling, Miranda to theater and, now, dance.

With a beyond-auspicious beginning and a future as bright as her sister's famous smile, Miranda's path was paved for her. Evangeline tells me, with a mug of hot cocoa in one hand and the other wrapped warmly over her daughter's arm, that "Miranda could have gotten into any prestigious dance school or troupe without a problem." She was that talented, to the point that numerous troupes, schools and, once, even R&B superstar Beyoncé, were constantly inviting her to join their host of professional dancers. It was as though every CEO who made money off of the dance industry was simply waiting for this gifted young woman to grow up.

The mood changes slightly in the hotel room when we approach the subject that seems to have been lingering in the air, manifested in the braces around Miranda's legs. When I ask Miranda to tell of the night of her accident, she begins slowly, but is unable to finish as her eyes moisten. Evangeline, always the loving mother, explains that Miranda's been unable to recount the accident since she remembered what happened. Due to the shock, Miranda couldn't recall exactly what happened, but when she did, it came in the form of a nightmare that chills her to this day. As Evangeline smoothes her daughter's hair, Charles speaks up. "It was the night of June 15th . . . she had just gotten out of a class at the Capstone studio on 79th street," he begins, sitting next to Nina on the couch, as she places her arms around his shoulders, "she had just graduated a week earlier, and was packing her things into her trunk, when a car came speeding through the empty parking lot." Charles finishes that Miranda looked over with a scream, and, being unable to move quickly out of the way, she was crushed by the speeding car, sandwiched between the two vehicles, her legs receiving the worst injuries—altogether leaving her crippled. "He drove off," Nina speaks up quietly as her father pauses to wipe at his eyes. "He just . . . left her," she swallows, trying to control the tremor in her voice. "He'll be brought to justice, though . . . he will . . ."

"Jet? Are you okay?" Bri's voice came crashing through my

thoughts as I was unable to finish the article, and I dropped the newspaper, the sound of a scream and screeching tires piercing my brain.

" . . . *June 15th, the Capstone studio on 79th street . . . she had just graduated a week earlier . . .*"

"*He'll be brought to justice . . .*"

"I, I . . ."

Before Bri could ask anymore, and as she and Cat watched in concern, I jumped to my feet and hurried to the bathroom.

Twenty-Four
Miranda

Everything was perfect about the physical therapy department of the hospital. The therapists were friendly and humorous, the machines and gadgets looked fun, and the place even smelled good—like warm vanilla extract. It was almost like a gym mixed with a toy store.

My sessions would be private, but while moving gingerly on my crutches to the room I would be using, I watched the handful of patients at work. A few were teens, most of them with knee-related injuries, and the others were elderly, some sitting at tables with blocks and other tools for helping range of motion, others sitting on neon exercise balls with their arms extended. Two of the therapists were stationed at a table with an adolescent girl lying on her back, her knee slowly, painfully, bending from a straightened position with their help. When one of the therapists whipped out a measuring tool and enthusiastically called out, "87 degrees already!" the girl's entire expression transformed into a smile, filled with pride and achievement.

"Miranda, I'm Mandy, it's nice to meet you."

I smiled as I reached out to shake Mandy's hand as my mom and I entered the small room. Mandy looked to be only a few years older than I, with a sparkling diamond on her left ring finger, short blond hair, and a youthfully round face.

The room looked a lot different than the open area outside, and was nearly bare, with the exception of a simple chair against the wall, a box of tissues, the black-cushioned examining table I would lie on, and an inspirational photograph in plain sight on the wall. While removing my jacket and handing my crutches off to my mom, I found myself staring at the photo, which was comprised of a silhouette of a runner on a track against a large sunset, and the graceful script of a poem reading:

> *When you see the finish line*
> *You may feel you're out of time*
> *But don't forget what's at the end*
> *It's then you get your second wind*

I was a little surprised at the coincidence of the poem, and immediately thought of Jet and his essay. Little did I know, though, just how applicable it would be in the minutes to come.

"Shall we begin?"

"So how'd it go, Tutu?"

I sighed shakily, closing my eyes at the sound of Dad's caring, concerned voice from the other line. I could barely remember ever feeling so disappointed in all of my life, and I could have cried my one millionth tear of the day at that moment.

Mom rose from where she was sitting across from me on the opposite bed, and I rubbed my eyes, trying hard not to cry. She had spoken with him already, most likely, and what he really wanted to know was how I was taking things.

"I couldn't do it, Dad," I answered quietly, a tear slipping down my cheek, and I felt a mixture of anger, pain, and sadness.

Dad seemed to be giving me a moment to add something else, and didn't speak immediately.

"It takes time, Miranda," he said gently, sighing a little.

The therapy session started out in the expected way, with questions and discussion about what would happen, and then the exercises began. When I was asked to merely flex my upper-leg muscles, I did so, however, painfully. But as soon as I tried to lift my legs off of the mat, my weakened, sore muscles twitched and filled with pain. Two more hopeless attempts left me in agony and tears, and I soon went back to the hotel, feeling as though a massive door had been shut in my face—the door leading to my healing . . . to dancing again.

"But Dad . . ." My voice faded, and I became aware of my mother's silence from the other room, then recalled just how much of this she was carrying herself. "I don't know," I finished darkly, not allowing myself to vent, as I did not want to hurt my parents further.

"Don't you give up yet, Miranda," he encouraged, then seemed to smile sadly. "I'll be flying over there at the end of the week, and I'm sure you'll impress me."

Twenty-Five
Jet

"Did your practice go well today?"

"Mm-hmm."

"School?"

"Yeah."

"Any word from Miranda?"

I didn't reply this time, and Nana Jo shook her head with a heavy sigh, scooting out of her chair at the table and coming over to take my half-eaten plate.

"Lord, I don't know what's gotten into you, child." She placed a hand on her hip. "Ever since you got back from Rochester, you've been quiet as a mouse—and eatin' like one, too."

I wearily rubbed my forehead, ignoring her concerned stare.

"Nana—"

"Is there somethin' you need to talk about, Jet?"

I merely shook my head, getting up and heading to the front porch for solitude.

"Miranda phoned me to thank me for the gift card before you got back," Nana Jo called from the dinner table, and I paused as I stood with one hand on the doorknob, closing my eyes as I felt gripped with emotional pain. "I pray every day that everything's alright with her . . ." Nana Jo added softly, "and you."

I closed the door gently behind me, but still, it somehow sounded like a slam in my suddenly-sensitive ears. I lowered myself down to the swing with a sigh, the swing which Miranda had sat on months earlier, fingering her cane and openly trusting me with her own fears and insecurities concerning dance. Holding my head in my hands, I felt as though I could . . . cry.

It was the first time I could ever remember feeling that way for a girl—for once not even thinking about what she thought of me or if there was a chance we could be together, but merely *caring* about *her*. It had never truly hurt me before to think of another girl going through something painful, at least not to the degree I was feeling at the moment, and suddenly, all I could think about was the fact that I had actually hurt Miranda—caused something to happen in her life that cut a very deep wound in her heart. It was unbearable to even think about, and the feelings of chemistry I had grown for Miranda in the past few weeks, as silly and trivial as they now seemed, only made the matter worse.

What do I do now? How can I face this?

The sound of car engines soon interrupted my thoughts, and I looked up.

Bri's white Neon sat against the curb, and surprisingly, Luke's yellow SUV was parked behind it.

Both of them, whom I was sure had never met, moved slowly up the walkway, Bri with her arms hugging herself and Luke with his

165

hands stuffed awkwardly into his jacket pockets.

I listened to them introduce themselves to each other as they approached, and waited for what they had to say.

Luke went first, at Bri's gesture, his green eyes finding me every so often.

"Uh, so . . . y'know, I've been worried about ya,' man."

I looked down at the ground, leaning forward onto my elbows.

"You haven't been around much—not talkin' too much since you got back," Luke continued, trying to be gentle.

"It's fine," I lied after a heavy silence, my breath suspending before me in the frigid air. "Everything's . . . fine."

Luke glanced over at Bri, and she nodded, clearing her throat.

"Jet, uh . . . I came because I need to tell you something." She squeezed her fingers to warm up, and I realized how strange it was to see Bri so serious and nervous.

Immediately, I sat up more, my thoughts rolling over all kinds of scenarios. Was Miranda okay? Was there a complication with the surgery that was just now surfacing? What had happened?!

"What?" I asked hastily, feeling my pulse quicken and heart nearly bound out of my chest.

Bri sighed, tucking a strand of hair behind her ear. "Well, Miranda started her therapy the other day, and, um . . . it's not looking good."

I swallowed heavily, feeling as though the world had turned upside down, once again.

"W-what . . ." I stammered for words. "I . . . what happened?"

"She can't do the exercises." Bri paused, leaning against the icy, iron porch railing. "They're just too hard for her—too painful. And, um . . . if she can't do them now, then her knees will be locked in a straight position, and . . ." she sighed again, shakily, obviously herself a little upset—and rightfully so, as she had always looked up to Miranda, "she won't be able to walk again."

Luke stood quietly, his face down and hands in his pockets, and Bri turned away a little, wiping at her eyes.

Without warning, I shot up, jogging to my car and speeding off, with Bri's final sentence ringing in my ears.

The apartment was pitch black when I entered, and I left it that way, choosing to sit in the darkness. I hugged my knees to my chest like a five-year-old in the silence of the living room, feeling reminiscent of the days when I would huddle in my room when my father was sick—after my parents' pivotal argument . . . the morning when my mom was gone.

I didn't know if I would cry, at first, but the tears came before I realized it, and soon it was altogether normal.

Before, I couldn't understand why I cared so much, but I think I did then. It wasn't so cryptic that I was numb or confused, but in a painfully cruel sort of way, I felt as though I understood everything, though nothing at all made sense. Why Miranda? Why me? Why was I the cause of all of this? What had possessed me that night when I should have disobeyed my adolescent whims and stayed at home with Jonathan and Nana Jo—the only people involved with me who were still around . . . still loving me.

My actions were more than ridiculous, and it was hard not to curse myself for them. Yet, I was afraid—no, *terrified*. And I don't think I really knew if it was of my future in jail if I were to turn myself in, or the way it would hurt Miranda to find out.

So I organized. I would have laughed at myself if it weren't for the gravity of the circumstances. I don't know why, but I took it upon myself to organize my bedroom the next morning after waking up in a daze on the living room floor, the previous night's revelation fresh in my mind. Luke peeked in once or twice, most likely concerned, but quiet and respectful nonetheless.

My mind was blank the whole time, my cell phone off and home phone ignored. Nana Jo called several times, and I worried she would drive over. But I didn't do anything about it, and only continued with my organizing, feeling what my mother must have felt on the many nights she could be heard shuffling through papers and vacuuming in her room, going off on one of her therapeutic, "cleaning" binges. She dealt with the burden of expensive doctor's bills in her own way, a way that I had seemed to inherit. I sighed heavily, feeling as though I could pass out. I had been organizing for hours on end, maybe four or five—I had lost count at three. I didn't eat breakfast, and I could only thank God that it was a Friday—the day when I didn't have any classes or football practice.

I rose to my feet, pulling off the shirt I had been wearing since the night before, and shuffled through the fresh load of laundry I had forsaken to fold. While rummaging through the pile on my bed, I looked up randomly, and my eyes fell on the black shirt—the note I had memorized. Closing my eyes, I hung my head for a moment, then finally grabbed a La Salle football t-shirt from my laundry and put it on. Deciding to at least get some water to drink, I hopped off of the bed and headed for the door, but stopped at the sound of a crinkle under my foot.

I bent over; I was met with my essay, the one Miranda had read, and I quickly determined to shred it to pieces. For some reason, though, I paused, recalling the day we sat in the stands, discussing the second wind effect, and I was struck with an idea.

After glancing at the calendar, I grabbed my jacket, hastily folded the essay, stuffed it into an envelope and jogged out the door.

After parking my car, I got out and walked up the driveway, trying to control my breathing.

"Mr. Phillips, sir?"

Miranda's father looked up from where he was about to lift a suitcase into his green truck, a hint of confusion on his face.

"What can I do for you, Jet?" he asked, reaching up to adjust his winter cap as a stinging breeze whipped through the air, bringing a few snowflakes with it.

I felt nervous, suddenly beginning to wonder if this was such a good idea after all.

"Um, could you . . . could you give this to Miranda?"

Mr. Phillips looked at the envelope in my outstretched hand, frowning a little. He looked pretty weary and burdened, and I realized that I wasn't the only person struggling with the latest news.

"Of course . . . I'll do that." Mr. Phillips nodded with a light smile, and I thanked him and left.

Twenty-Six
Miranda

I awakened with a slight start and looked around in confusion from the medication. Out of habit, my hands touched my legs, and I breathed a sigh of relief that there wasn't pain. After weeks of waking up to agonizing muscle spasms, I had become terrified of falling asleep. I was taking muscle-relaxer pills that left me drowsy and listless.

The hotel room was silent, and, still feeling the effects of the drug I had taken some seven hours earlier, I had to calm myself before I could panic. I hadn't had a distinct nightmare, but for the past few days, I hadn't liked waking up alone.

Exhausted, I pressed my back into the large, comfy chair I was sitting in, my legs propped before me on an ottoman. After a moment, I found myself gazing out the window directly to my left, at the mid-afternoon, gray winter sky. This was not my first stay in the city, at the Mayo Clinic. When we were seven or eight, Kevin's mom had to have an emergency brain procedure done. My family and I flew over to be with her. To this day, Mrs. Cannon has been just fine, and hasn't had to make any more trips to the acclaimed facility. Thinking back, I couldn't help but wish I had as good fortune as she did.

Two suitcases sat half-packed against one of the beds— reluctantly packed. My mom had been quieter that day than I had ever witnessed in all my life, and though she never implied it, I felt as though I had shattered not only my own dreams, but hers. Though my mother had always been the primary, driving force behind my dancing, she had never pressured me concerning my injury, and I had always appreciated that. But I knew that it secretly hurt her, as well. Unfortunately, I just didn't really know if it was because I was crippled, or because her dreams couldn't be lived out through me.

I closed my eyes, and bitter memories of my two attempts to lift and bend my legs darted through my mind—the way the therapists urged me on, my mom holding my hand. It felt like I was in some sort of nightmare, and I wanted desperately to wake up. The shock of my failure had worn off the night before, when I cried myself into a troubled sleep. Sitting in the dim, silent room, lit only by the clouded sunlight outside, I didn't quite know how I felt. I was tired of feeling, tired of pain, in more ways than one.

I heard the front door opening after a couple of minutes, and quiet whispering in the other room. Expectantly, I looked at the bedroom doorway. Seconds later, my dad appeared, and the next thing I knew, he had rushed over and I was sobbing into his collar. Dad held me back some after a minute, and I brushed the tears from my face with a heavy sigh. I soon noticed that he was quietly looking down at the floor, from where he knelt on one knee against the chair. I couldn't have felt worse, for all of the lessons and money spent, and now the progress which had led to a dead end. Reaching out to touch his face, I fought back the tears as I spoke,

"I've disappointed you, I've let e-everyone down—"

"Miranda," Dad interrupted firmly, taking my hand in his, looking me in the eye, "you've *never* let me down—none of us." He sighed, speaking softly. "You've overcome more than any of us deal with in a lifetime."

I swallowed and looked down, feeling as though I had failed the world.

But Dad smiled sadly, wiping a few tears from my cheeks.

"You hold your chin up, Miranda—everything happens for a reason. You've done your best, and that's all we've ever asked of you."

After one last hug, Dad reached into his jacket, bringing out an envelope.

"Who's it from?" I asked, frowning a little.

He merely smiled.

"I'm gonna go talk to your mother, okay?"

After kissing my forehead, Dad left, and I stared down at the envelope in my hands. It was blank, and I tried to guess who it was from as I opened it.

The only thing inside was two sheets of paper, hastily folded and stapled together. Once I saw the first page, I recognized it in an instant. After reading it through twice, I finally let the paper drop in my lap, and covered my eyes as my shoulders trembled and tears fell. If ever I had been faced with a second wind, it was then. There were two things I could do, and one was clearly harder.

Slowly, I lifted my head up, and took a deep breath.

"Mom, Dad, we've gotta unpack!"

The tiny room was gripped with silence the next day, and all eyes were focused on the table where I lay. All of them, the therapists, my mom, Dad, and Nina were watching, and waiting. I was scared, terrified of whether or not I could do it—whether my legs would lift or not—but also of the pain. Finally, gripping my mom's hand on one side and my dad's on the other, I tried to think of the task as though I was doing it before the surgery—as though it was simple.

My vision quickly blurred with tears, and in the earsplitting stillness, I saw the picture across the room, the poem and the coincidentally-fitting words. Praying that I would either succeed or be able to live with not being able to dance again, I willed my legs to lift. The pain came like one long, drawn-out, mental replay of what I could barely recall of the accident. It wouldn't leave, and it was my only opponent.

And then, I had to stop. The pain intensified and my muscles weakened. I doubted myself for a moment, but quickly determined to try again. Although it hadn't worked the first time, I had to keep trying.

Now, counting off all of the people who had impacted my life—my family, Bri, Cat, Kevin and Nana Jo—I arrived at Jet and saw his faithful smile; I felt us waltzing in the classroom, reading the note he gave me after my sending-off party, discussing his essay . . .

I don't know if I really heard Mandy say "You did it!" but the cheering, applause and bear-hug from Mom, Dad and Nina confirmed it all.

Touchdown.

Twenty-Seven
Jet

I was a nervous wreck for the next couple of days, having given the essay to Miranda's dad the day before. I hadn't heard anything from Rochester, and Bri was without updates.

With Luke having left to have dinner with his parents, I took it upon myself to fix a meal. As I sprinkled some salt into the boiling, bubbling pot of water and spaghetti, I realized just how busy I was actually making sure that I was. I cooked for myself fairly often, but never anything quite as intricate as real spaghetti that wasn't frozen, and even Luke, as light as he was trying to be on me lately, had joked that I was becoming quite the chef.

Yawning, I flipped off the football game I was watching on the TV in the corner, and listened to the soothing gurgle of the boiling noodles.

With the regular football season over, life was fairly quiet.

Somehow, I still had my eyes on the future—football and, most likely, the NFL.

Now becoming hypnotized by the boiling noodles, my thoughts circled around Miranda, but the doorbell quickly interrupted me.

I sighed and headed to answer it.

"Josiah."

I blinked at the caller, a little surprised that he was there.

"Jon . . ." I replied slowly, still blocking the doorway.

My brother was older than me, and when we were younger, he never ceased to remind me of this. He was my parents' eyes and ears (and belt) when they were too busy to tend to me, and had practically raised me. Jonathan was a very serious, mature guy, with little tolerance for frivolity. Though he played sports for fun in high school, and was actually good, he never got as involved as I did. Instead, Jonathan devoted his interest to politics and social matters; everyone thought he would become a lawyer or politician.

"Sorry I couldn't make the recital," Jon said slowly as he stepped inside, forsaking removing his coat but walking over to the couch to take a seat.

I shrugged, knowing it wouldn't have been like him to be interested in my dancing anyway.

"Don't worry about it." I leaned against a wall opposite the couch, and Jon looked at me while resting his elbows on his knees, his eyes narrowing curiously—eyes that were shaped in the same serious way as our mother's.

"You didn't quit, did you?" he asked carefully, rubbing his hands together in a professional, doctor-like way.

Confused, I asked, "Um . . . quit what?"

"Dance."

I laughed shortly.

"Of course. Why wouldn't I? All I had to do was follow Coach's orders . . ." My voice faded after my attempt to sound cool, my heart secretly slapping me for acting as though the past months meant nothing to me. I stared at the floor.

"Well, I thought you liked it—that's what Nana Jo said." Jon spoke in a very laid-back way, as he always did, and leaned into the sofa, casually placing a hand behind his head. "I hear you got a famous teacher."

I nodded, feeling as though I was standing before my mom during a confession of forsaking to do my chores. I sat down in a comfy chair, trying to match Jonathan's composed nature.

"Yeah, Miranda Phillips." I said her name matter-of-factly, and to Jonathan she was just another dancer—from a whole other world.

Jon nodded slowly, rubbing his hand over his closely shaven head.

"I've heard about her, y'know—the surgery."
Jon brushed a remnant of melting snow from his knee.

"Are you two close?"

I didn't reply immediately, the events of the past week flipping through my mind. The mere thought of Jonathan learning about my crime made my skin crawl, and I suddenly felt very small.

"Yeah," I replied quietly, feeling the familiar fear of wondering what was going to happen next.

Jonathan must have nodded again, and spoke up after a few seconds.

"You know, Mom called me the other day."

My eyes darted up, and I quickly frowned.

"She, uh, she's living in L.A. now," Jon continued steadily. "She's got a boyfriend out there—takin' care of her and what not."

I didn't reply and only sighed while shaking my head. I always dreaded hearing updates on my mom. It only made me mad, and I never liked being angry with her.

"Did Nana Jo tell you?" asked Jon.

I shook my head.

"I haven't really been over there much this week." I paused, hesitating a little and rubbing the back of my hand. "I, uh, I guess I wouldn't know all of this since I don't get these calls."

Irritated, Jonathan rubbed at the thin hairline on his angular jaw. "C'mon, Jet—"

"I don't care," I interrupted, getting up to finish preparing my spaghetti as Jonathan's cell rang.

"Bri, it's been a week, nearly, and you *still* don't have any updates? Every time I try to call Miranda's cell she doesn't pick up!"

Bri's sigh was casual over the phone.

"Jet, I'm sorry, I just . . ." I waited patiently for her to finish. "Listen, I've gotta go—I'll talk to you tomorrow."

I was unable to get a word in edgewise, and set my cell down with a heavy sigh.

"Hey, Jet! Come teach us that new play!"

I turned, watching my high school boys eagerly waiting on me to return from the water break I had taken as an excuse to call Bri. A football-loving yet not-quite-savvy Luke was giving me a hand that afternoon, since Coach was unable to make it.

Taking one last drink from my paper Gatorade cup, I tossed it in the trash and jogged back over to the group in the middle of the field.

"Hear anything new?" Luke snuck the question over to me before I began to instruct, and I only shook my head with another sigh.

I spoke for a few minutes, my throat a little raw from the cold and my mouth running automatically—since my thoughts were miles away, in Rochester. The boys were aware of Miranda's situation as well, and had gotten together to send her a card a few weeks back.

Apparently, I must have said something wrong, as each boy's jaw dropped and eyes widened while I was in midsentence. My voice trailed and I frowned. But then Luke tapped my shoulder, instructing me to turn around.

Twenty-Eight
Miranda

Jet stood staring open mouthed, a football dangling lifelessly from one hand. Despite the cold, as well as the pain in my palms from having crutched from Dad's car to the field, I smiled.

Turning to my dad, who stood quietly nearby, I thanked him and handed my crutches off to him, saying I could go the rest of the way on my own. Dad looked concerned, but soon relented with a supportive smile. He handed me my cane, then turned and went to wait in the car.

For a moment Jet was paralyzed with shock, until I started over—moving slowly and carefully with the aid of my cane. When he saw me approaching, he seemed to snap back to reality and started toward me. I quickly held up my hand, wanting to walk the ten or so yards to him by myself.

When I arrived, a couple of feet in front of him, we were both silent, and the high schoolers and Luke looked on. A bird sang overhead, a few snowflakes finally began to fall. I chuckled a little at the obviously awkward silence, and Jet managed a nervous smile.

Finally, I shrugged, almost shyly, running the thumb of one hand along my cane handle and pushing a stray braid from my face with the other.

"Um . . . it's like I keep ending up with this, huh?"

I withdrew the folded essay from my pocket, looking up at Jet with a meaningful smile. A broad grin slowly spread across his face, and he reached out to wrap me in a warm hug.

I moved slowly while making my way down the hallway into the kitchen, following the warm, rich aroma of Mom's famous caramel cake. She didn't hear the knock of my cane on the oak floors, and I paused in the doorway, watching her fumble with the noisy oven racks.

I didn't say anything, but watched in silence, my thoughtful mind, fresh from a nap, running very slowly and consciously. I thought of how glad I was that my mom liked to cook, especially holiday desserts, as I had always associated food with warmth and family. With her medium-length, hazel-dyed hair pulled up hastily into a ponytail, and a fluffy bathrobe adorned, along with a little bit of flour on her forearms, she was beautiful. Momma never really liked to dwell on such "trivial" things as her own beauty, but it was true that she was able to hold her own and radiate loveliness no matter where she was. Whenever I thought about myself years into the future, I always knew that, whatever I was doing in life, I wanted to possess that quality.

"Miranda," Mom spoke through a sigh, barely turning to spot me, exercising her sixth sense of knowing where I was at all times.

"Awake already?"

I smiled lightly, slowly moving to the kitchen table and taking a seat.

"I wasn't all that tired."

Mom paused as she brought her pot of freshly-cooked caramel frosting from the stove.

"Don't lie."

I chuckled, already tasting the melt-in-your-mouth caramel on my tongue, and Mom shook her head.

"Well, as for me," she began slowly, voicing her opinion, "it's like as soon as I walked through these doors I could have collapsed."

I grinned, deciding to finish her sentence for her—the part she was thinking but wouldn't say.

"But Daddy *had* to have his caramel cake for energy to put up the Christmas lights."

Mom laughed with a nod, carefully pouring some of the icing over a layer of cake.

Even from the kitchen and over the light, jazzy Christmas CD Mom had playing in the den, I could hear the voices of working men from the front yard, surprising since I thought Dad was by himself.

"Let me know when it's ready," I said before leaving, heading for the front door to peek out the window. I was taken aback when I saw the other person helping my dad, standing at the base of a ladder with a spool of lights in one hand.

"What in the world . . . ?"

I turned to look over my shoulder at the kitchen doorway, where I could hear Mom singing along with the CD and rummaging through a drawer. Satisfied, I made my way up the steps to my room. After changing out of my comfortable pajamas and throwing on some jeans, a sweater and my puffiest, warmest coat, I went back downstairs and quietly let myself out through the front door.

". . . go ahead and grab those other lights for me, please, Jet—Tutu, what're you doin' out here in this cold?"

I shrugged from where I stood on the front porch, watching my Dad hang the last of the spool of lights over the bay window. Jet, who was sifting through a box of lights and decorations, looked up suddenly, and smiled at me.

I grinned back, wondering how he had ended up helping my dad hang our overdue lights.

"Jet here, was driving back from football practice when he saw me working and decided to help," Dad commented what sounded matter-of-factly, but I thought I caught a hint in his tone.

Nodding slowly, I smiled. "Oh, okay."

Jet awkwardly continued to search through the box.

"We're out of icicle lights, Mr. P.," Jet said after a moment.

"I'll get them," I offered.

I turned to open the door and retrieve the box, secretly being amused with Jet's "Mr. P."—noting that students at the studio and on the job called him that. Being able to call my dad "Mr. P." meant that he was cool with you, and you were cool with him.

After spotting the box and grabbing it, I returned to the porch and started down the steps to where Jet was approaching to take it from me. Because I had rested my cane against the door, I was moving on my own, with my balance still re-training itself and a box in both hands. Before I knew it, though, I had missed the next step and felt myself falling forward.

The box went flying, and in a split second, I was bracing myself for the impact with the ground. That never came, though, as I fell against Jet, my arms wrapped fearfully around his neck, his securely around my waist. Somewhere along the way, our lips landed together. I'm not sure how long we were like that. Our first response was not to break away, as we were both in shock. After the initial moment of extreme awkwardness had passed, our eyes wide

182

open in terror, we must have closed them and relaxed a little, forgetting ourselves and surroundings. We drew away slowly, but soon I quickly looked to my left, realizing that my dad must have seen the whole thing. Somehow, though, the whole thing was unnoticed. Dad was busy adjusting the lights while on the ladder, singing obliviously to himself.

When I turned back to Jet, both of us still holding each other, I could barely look at him due to my embarrassment, but, thank goodness, he smiled and laughed after a moment. I grinned, then joined in, we both felt a mixture of relief and self-consciousness.

Of course, there was also that classic "fuzziness."

Twenty-Nine
Jet

Fine, I'll admit it: I *did* have a bit of a bounce in my step later that evening as I jogged up the iron steps to my apartment. Okay, maybe it was more like a leap.

Luke must have noticed it too, and he was, for once, without words as he stood in the kitchen, waiting to spread a slice of bread. He watched as I entered the apartment, bellowing "I'm singin' in the snow" at the top of my lungs.

I subconsciously passed him, not minding the fact that he was unquestionably onto me. I headed to the 'fridge for some soda, then left for my room.

The light-heartedness and singing did stop, however. While lying in bed that night, I stared up at the ceiling and realized something.

Jet, you hurt this girl, remember?! What are you doing?!

Frowning, I turned onto my side, trying to ignore the voice. But it was right—I *had* hurt Miranda, and if she ever found out . . .

Who *was* I to want to be with her? No one. I might as well have been worse than the inconsiderate Kevin at that point.

Who says she likes you anyway . . . right?

There was a . . . strangely nonchalant, open kind of vibe I had received from Miranda lately—ever since she got back from Rochester only the day before, but maybe even since I came to visit her. Maybe my male, egotistical side was imagining it, but why did it seem as though Miranda was acting very . . . "here I am, it's your call now-ish?" I realized that Miranda was showing signs of liking me. But then again, I kept telling myself that I was wrong . . . I had never felt like I would be enough for Miranda, and even the way I perceived her behavior didn't change that—heck, even if Miranda was in love with me, it wouldn't change that.

But yet, still, I couldn't let go of the crazy notion to pursue what might be there . . .

Somewhere between wakefulness and sleep, I pictured a blush on Miranda's cheeks after we kissed, and didn't know if it was wishful reconstruction of the event, or a factual memory.

Thirty

Miranda

"The temperature's still dropping."

I looked up from where I sat at Cat's desk in her classroom, watching her twirl a coffee stirrer in a Styrofoam cup.

"It's coming down fast out there, too," I added, looking out the window to my right, the city street lined with traffic and covered with snow.

Cat sighed, wiping the back of her neck with a towel, having just dismissed her hip-hop class.

It was Tuesday, a couple of weeks before Christmas, and my Dad had driven me to the studio to meet with my students and the other teachers. I had received a warm welcome on my first day at the studio since my surgery, and was grateful for all of the love I had received. But now, with a blizzard rushing in and traffic already backing up at 4:00, the studio was closing for the day. Mr. Nelson had already left and was sending everyone else home.

"Your Dad's coming to get you?" Cat asked, taking a seat on the floor a few feet away.

I nodded, playing with Cat's favorite stress-reliever ball on the desk.

"Yeah, but you don't have to stay with me—"

"Miranda." Cat rolled her eyes and smiled a little, tucking a strand of hair back into her ponytail. "You sure you don't want me to get you some hot cocoa?"

I nodded again, then yawned as I rested my elbows on the desk.

"I think I'll call him and see where he is," I spoke up after a moment, realizing how afraid I was of silence—having sensed, as best friends do, the question in Cat's mind which she was likely to vocalize if given enough time.

After only being able to reach Dad's voicemail, I closed my phone and spun it on the wooden desktop.

Cat continued to contemplate, now watching me.

"So how's Jet—what's he up to these days?"

Oh well, I tried.

I cleared my throat, pretending to be casual as I continued to poke at my phone, avoiding Cat's stare. "Oh, the usual, I guess. Football . . ."

Cat nodded slowly, leaning back on her palms, an amused smile curling at the corner of her mouth.

"I see," she replied calmly, and I was about to breathe a sigh of relief, when Cat suddenly laughed. "Mir*anda*!"

"What?!" I nearly jumped, feeling terrified yet being unable to hide my own smile and blush.

"You *have* to tell me what happened."

"Who says something happened?"

"Nobody—it's obvious, girl!"

187

"What's obvious?!"

"I don't know, you tell me!"

We paused in our friendly argument, and both of us began to laugh.

"Ugh, Cat, c'mon . . ." I groaned into the desk as I lowered my forehead, wanting desperately to change topic, though *not* wanting to just the same. I was cornered, and I never liked being cornered.

Cat beamed, her suspicions obviously confirmed based on my current behavior.

"Miranda, you like him . . . don't you?"

I slowly looked up and back out the window, still smiling a little.

I was nervous and afraid, and yet, everything was so . . . peaceful—so fresh and new. I guess I couldn't help but be excited.

The sound of footsteps floated from the hallway, and soon the door opened.

"Jet, we were just talking about you." Cat grinned.

I sat up straight in my seat, feeling very embarrassed.

Jet smiled slowly, a little unsure, as he walked in, shivering slightly despite the heaviness of his warm, black coat. His handsome face was a little red from the cold, but sudden bashfulness couldn't be ruled out either.

"I'll go on then, Mira—see you tomorrow." Cat rose, gathering her bags and pulling on her coat. "Later, Jet."

Once alone, both of us were awkwardly silent for a few seconds too many, until Jet cleared his throat, one hand stuffed into his jeans pocket and the other scratching his chin.

"So, um, you ready?"

Flustered, I slowly stood up and grabbed my cane.

Jet must have noticed my confusion, and smiled a little.

"Oh—your dad asked me if I could come get you. We were finishing up with the lights and he had his hands full."

I was flabbergasted. Dad *sent Jet? Wow.*

"Oh, okay. Sure . . ." I acquiesced. "Thanks, Jet."

Due to the weather and traffic, it took us a whole hour to get to my house, but the delay allowed plenty of time for us to talk. And talk we did, mainly about local news and the like at first, but when a long pause arrived, I began to feel the unspoken yet obvious topic begging for me to speak up—the topic that was on both of our minds.

I swallowed, I ran my finger along the black door handle of Jet's car, looking out at the blankets of snow covering Philly, watching the cars inch along around us.

Go on, bring it up.

"Um," I cleared my throat, "Jet . . . I, uh . . . you know . . . yesterday . . ." My voice faded when I realized that I didn't know what to say, and my stuttering wasn't exactly making me look any better.

But Jet quickly came to the rescue.

"Oh . . . yeah . . . um . . ." He stumbled into silence, not fairing any better than I had after all.

Both of us nodded slowly, avoiding looking at each other and instead focusing out the windows as the traffic remained at a standstill.

"Miranda," Jet finally said, turning to me.

"Yes?" I quickly replied, facing him as well, hoping he was about to say something that would bring some sort of ease to the awkwardness.

Jet seemed to falter a little, glancing from the console back to me, twice, until he eventually smiled.

"This is pretty ridiculous." He chuckled, and I laughed, grateful for the ease in the atmosphere.

"Yeah, you're right . . ." I replied, twirling my cane against the warm, leather seat. "Ridiculous," I added slowly, looking back up at him, "but . . . nice," I offered with an almost hopeful shrug, a hint

189

of a question in my voice.

Jet nodded slowly, his eyes holding what I thought was some sort of sadness, although I didn't understand it.

"Yeah . . . nice."

When we arrived at my house, the blizzard was hammering down in full swing; the streets were covered in thick snow. Not wanting Jet to travel home in the dangerous weather by himself, I invited him inside, and after a little bit of arguing, he finally relented.

I guess cold weather really does bring people together—even the most . . . stubborn of people. The minute Jet and I walked through the door, Mom was rushing to the kitchen to prepare us some hot cocoa. Dad threw a couple of logs in the den fireplace, and Nina, who had just gotten in for her holiday vacation, didn't hesitate to crank up Mom's Nat King Cole Christmas album.

After Nina stretched out on the leather sofa opposite the fire, I decided to sit on the warm, carpeted floor, near the Christmas tree.

"Miranda, you wanna sit on the cold *floor*?" Mom questioned, aghast, when she returned with the mugs of cocoa and coffee, and I sighed.

"It's not cold, Mom." I shook my head, unable to keep from smiling a little just the same.

Dad winked at me as he sat down in his and Mom's favorite overstuffed chair.

"Nina, scoot over so Jet can sit," Dad suggested, and Nina seemed to jump out of an entranced stare at the fireplace.

"Hmm? Oh, okay," she mumbled, dealing with her jet lag from flying in from California.

Jet shrugged from where he stood slightly aloof near the doorway, rubbing his shoulder and acting very shy.

"Oh, uh . . . it's fine. I can sit somewhere . . . else."

Nina hadn't moved, and was already dozing off.

I chuckled, and Jet, who was acting as though my parents were ready to pounce on him at any minute, hesitantly, walked over to sit beside me.

Mom, who had gone back with the tray of mugs, having forgotten spoons, reappeared, dispersing them throughout the room.

Once everyone had been served, and she had taken her own mug, she sat down next to dad.

To my right, Jet was quietly adding his marshmallows to his mug a little bit at a time, and I couldn't help but laugh to myself, noting that I had always done the same.

I watched the steam dance above my mug, the "hiss" of the dissolving marshmallows like music in the silence. Soon Dad spoke up, filling in the quiet with one of his favorite stories.

"It was snowing like crazy outside, just like now," Dad said quietly, setting his mug down as we listened. "I had decided to make a stop at the church I had just started going to before I went back to the dorm. A Christmas play rehearsal was goin' on, so I just sat in a back pew to watch for a bit. And that's when I saw this young lady. She was standin' there, showing the kids what to do. They listened to her very closely, and she spoke kindly to them.

"And I remember thinkin' to myself, 'Why in the world is a gorgeous girl like this spendin' her Saturday night directing a Christmas play?" Dad chuckled warmly. "But then again, I admired her for that, and as I watched, her knack for what she was doing and her love for the kids was obvious. When they finished, I walked up to her and asked her what her name was. She said, 'I'm Evangeline.'" Dad paused, smiling at Mom as she blushed. "That's when I knew for sure that she was the one.

"I was on the brink of starting a career in producing and she was close to getting a big Hollywood break, so even though we went out for a while, we didn't know where things would go. But one day, Eva and I had an argument. I wish I could tell you what it was

191

about, but both of us have forgotten. So we decided to 'split up,' and went our separate ways. A few friends of mine had gotten everything set up for me to start my production business, but any time I thought about life without her, it hurt me.

"Eva was doin' her own thing in Hollywood—having visited there and met with some agents who wanted to give her some roles that could pave her way to stardom. So one day, she was about to pick up her phone and call them to accept." Dad smiled distantly. "But 'Vangeline decided that her heart was in Philly . . . that she was gonna get married to a crazy, oftentimes hard-headed business major with a wild dream to see a successful, Christian production agency." Dad laughed richly, then continued. "She told me that I needed her in order to do it—that I would mess it up by myself." With a sigh and a smile, Dad turned to look Mom in the eyes. "And she was right—I haven't stopped thanking her for that yet."

The room was silent again after a moment. The only sounds came from the fire, the falling snow, and the deafening, unanswered question in the air.

Thirty-One
Jet

"Where are you off to in such a hurry?"

Sighing, I turned from where I stood in the vestibule, ready with my coat in one hand.

"Football practice—"

"Jet," Nana Jo chuckled as she took a seat at the kitchen table, "Don't lie. Now sit down and talk with me, child."

Slowly, I did as I was told, returning my coat to its hook, plucking at the collar of my polo shirt as I sat across from my grandmother at the table.

"Jet," she began slowly, smiling a little, "I'm not gonna ask what's gotten into you because I already know."

"Nana—"

"No, you don't need to worry," she breathed an airy laugh, beginning to snap green beans from a metal bowl. "Young people always think they've been cornered or did something wrong when it's this obvious."

I slouched slightly in my chair, knowing that, to me, her words could hold a double meaning. As good as I had felt in the past few days with Miranda's return, the guilt was only pricking me harder and harder. Lately, I had kept choosing to ignore it . . . but it wasn't easy.

I sighed again, setting my elbows on the table and rubbing my forehead. "Nana Jo, what in the world am I supposed to do?"

Nana Jo smiled wisely, focusing on the vegetables between her trained fingers.

"Help me snap these," she replied, and I reached to grab a handful from the bowl. Nana Jo caught my hand, though, and in one swift movement, I was suddenly holding two plastic cards. Grinning, she stood up and went to tend to a pot on the stove, leaving me staring in confusion at my hand.

They were two tickets to the last showing of *The Nutcracker Suite*—the big-city production which Miranda had wanted to see this year but didn't think she would be able to due to her surgery and therapy.

Smiling, I shot up and rushed out the door, but quickly returned from the freezing outdoors, having forgotten my coat and something else. After placing a kiss on Nana Jo's cheek, I finally hurried off, leaving her beaming after me.

I watched Mr. P. move from the driver's seat of his car to the back, all while on his cell phone. I swallowed heavily, taking a final deep breath before leaving my parked car by the sidewalk to help and, hopefully, strike up the conversation I needed in order to get my question answered.

194

"Here, lemme help," I quickly offered as I arrived at his side, lifting one of the boxes of Capstone Studio promotional equipment from the car.

Mr. P. paused when he noted my presence, and smiled slightly in gratitude.

"Thanks, Jet," he said between sentences on his phone, balancing it on one shoulder, with a box in his arms. "Follow me inside."

As I followed his lead into the garage, up the steps into the kitchen, I couldn't help but be glad that he was busy taking a call. That way, he couldn't ask or worry about what had brought me to his home on the busy Thursday afternoon. I had intentionally chosen this day and hour to meet with him, because I knew Miranda would be watching one of Cat's classes at the studio, Nina would be at work, and Mrs. Phillips would be teaching a drama class.

After being silently instructed to set the box down near the kitchen table, I stood watching Mr. P. begin to wrap up his conversation while opening the 'fridge. The moment had almost arrived. I rehearsed my lines for the umpteenth time, just to be sure.

"You thirsty, Jet?" asked Mr. P. once he set the phone to the side.

I cleared my throat with a nod, feeling a slight boost of confidence at his easygoing nature.

"Sure."

Mr. P. grinned, lifting a pitcher of sweet iced tea from the 'fridge.

"Mrs. Phillips makes the best tea in town, and I hear you're from Memphis, so maybe you could give her an expert critique?"

I shrugged.

"Tea sounds great."

Mr. P. poured two glasses of tea, then handed me one while motioning for me to take a seat.

"I take it you didn't just come to help me with those boxes—you need to talk about somethin'?"

Here we go. Don't screw it up!

I breathed a nervous sigh.

"Yes, sir," I somehow managed to say without stuttering, and cleared my throat again as I recalled my opening line. "Mr. P., I was wondering if I might possibly—"

"Jet—so sorry to interrupt you—but don't you think this tea could use just a little more sugar?" asked Mr. P. with complete coolness, sliding across from me at the table while frowning into his glass.

Bewildered, I continued, "Oh, um. . . well, mine's great. . . actually."

Mr. P. shifted his jaw with his brow still furrowed, not once taking his eyes off of the glass to look at me.

"You know what? I think I'm gonna sweeten mine more."

I nodded silently as he rose and headed for the sugar canister, frantically trying to figure out how to get back onto the original subject.

But Mr. P. was too quick for me.

"What do you think about spaghetti? I think I'll make things a little easier for 'Vangeline and throw some noodles on. Which do you like more, Jet, basil-and-onion or mushroom-and-veggie sauce?"

I was taken off guard by the question.

"Well . . . basil and onion sounds good . . ." I mumbled stupidly.

Mr. P. studied the two jars in his hands, then finally nodded with a gracious smile in my direction.

"Yeah, that'll work just fine," he sighed, opening the jar and pouring the sauce into a pan. "You know what, Jet? Today has been a long day, and a long year, too," he paused as I listened in polite silence, "or a long *few* years, I should say. But it still feels like just yesterday I had two little girls runnin' around this house."

I smiled a little, taking a drink of my tea (which I actually thought to be perfectly sweetened).

"Yes, sir," Mr. P. sighed, leaning a palm atop the counter, "it was only yesterday Nina was playing with her Barbies and Miranda askin' me to help tie her ballet slippers." He smiled wistfully. "But when they got to that age where they liked boys—" he remembered with a chuckle. "I thought I was gonna have to put extra locks on the doors..." I laughed softly as Mr. P.'s voice faded, nervously deciding my conversation could wait, given the topic at hand.

"And then they grew up some more, and got serious about their standards . . . You know, I still remember the day Miranda came runnin' down the steps, maybe a few months shy of 16, wavin' a piece of paper and wanting me to look over it." Mr. P. smiled while filling a pot with water. "It was her list of standards—and preferences—for her future boyfriend and husband, and she wanted her dad to give her an 'okay' on it.

"So we sat down at the kitchen table—Miranda sittin' right where you are and me beside her—and I read each one aloud. At the top was 'on fire for Jesus,' and there were also qualities like strength and dignity." Mr. P. shook his head with a small laugh. "And then of course, right under the character qualities, was dance—he *had* to be a dancer. And when I asked her if it would be okay if he wasn't—tryin' to remind her that we don't always get all of the preferences we want in life—Miranda, with her headstrong self, shook her head and said, 'Daddy, if he doesn't dance then I'll just be an old maid!' "

Mr. P. let out a laugh which I nervously joined in, easily picturing the scene in my mind.

"She was bent on having her way or the highway," he added quietly with a bit of a grin while wiping at a spill on the countertop. "But she did tell me that day that she wanted me to be the one who made sure the boy lined up with her list—said that I would do better than she would at that." He sighed. "So I've held to my side of the agreement ever since—Miranda hooks 'em, I screen 'em, and if I don't like him, we all move on."

197

Though Mr. P. was still smiling when he spoke the last sentence, I noted the seriousness in his tone, and shifted ever so slightly in my seat, feeling my palms begin to sweat.

"Look at me," chuckled Mr. P., "Sittin' here runnin' my mouth like the old dad that I am when you came over here to ask me something. Sorry about that, Jet—what were you gonna say?"

The floor turned upside down, the ceiling was below me. My stomach churned and my heartbeat galloped. My mouth went dry.

I did my best to clear my throat, wondering what in the world to do next. Could I really...? Did I have the nerve to...? Even after all that he said about the standards and...?

Just say it!

"Mr. P., I . . . would like to . . . I mean, I was thinking maybe I could . . . if-if it's *okay* with you, I would like to . . ." I swallowed, the glass trembling in my numb hands. "I want to take Miranda out . . . and maybe . . . start to . . . see . . . her . . ."

The silence that followed was deafening.

Shoot me now.

Mr. P. moved from the counter to the stove behind him to stir the sauce, what little I caught of his expression seeming to be perfectly expression*less*. It was all over. I just wasn't the guy who lined up with the list . . .

Before the pain of this realization could hit and overtake the numbness, Mr. P. spoke up.

"Jet, what you said took a lot of bravery, and I appreciate that."

His back was to me as he spoke. Appreciation didn't automatically mean agreement, and bravery was pointless right about now.

I hung my head with a slow nod.

"Yes, sir."

"But you know what?" Mr. P. turned, scratching his cheek. "I never told you what the very first thing Miranda had under a

198

relationship with Christ was on her list, did I?"

I shrugged with a small, forced smile, for the sake of courtesy. "No sir."

Mr. P. leaned with his palms atop the counter once more, looked me in the eye with a meaningful smile and said, "Bravery."

I shivered a little outside of the house, admiring the decorations I had helped hang, unable to keep from smiling. Next to Nana Jo, Mr. P. had to have been the only person I knew who was able to make you feel at ease within a few seconds of meeting them. When I dropped by only a few days back to help decorate, he quickly removed any awkwardness I originally felt. Though I still had enough sense to be smart and respectful around Miranda's father, I still felt comfortable around him, and knew that I would be cool with him no matter whose father he was or wasn't. This was especially true after the deep conversation we had only a day earlier, following my stammered question to begin to see his daughter.

A few seconds after I had knocked, the door opened, and Nina appeared with a portfolio and cell phone in one hand, obviously busy.

But a smile slowly spread onto her face when she saw me, and I found myself kicking at the steps, nervously glancing around.

"Jet," she spoke slowly.

"Hey, Nina," I greeted, fidgeting with the tickets in my pocket and hoping I wouldn't accidentally fold them due to my sudden case of nerves.

What if Miranda's not home, or says no?

I cleared my throat, noting that Nina was too busy being amused with my presence to ask what I wanted.

"Is Mi—"

"She sure is, c'mon in."

"Uh, thanks."

The house was slightly dim inside due to the cloudy day. I paused upon stepping aside for Nina to close the door, expecting her to say something like "I'll go get her," or "wait here."

"She's in the den—probably still napping—"

"Oh." I frowned suddenly, feeling as though I had caused the world's end. "Well, I'll just come back later. I don't wanna distur—"

"Jet," Nina interrupted, chuckling a little. "Miranda, with her creative self, *rarely* sleeps like normal people do. She just . . ." she paused with a laugh, "rests with her eyes closed. Go ahead in— she'll be glad to see you. I've gotta go make a call."

With Nina gone, I stood in the foyer feeling very confused and unsure. Eventually, though, I walked toward the doorway up ahead, and took a deep breath.

Thirty-Two
Miranda

I woke up from my slightly unconscious state, the only state of rest I was truly accustomed to in the late afternoon hours, and after a moment of gathering my thoughts, I suddenly feared that I was late for my 4:30 class. I jumped a little, but stopped myself before I could get up, recalling that it was December, and I had surgery and therefore wasn't teaching anymore.

Sighing, I pulled my warm, knit throw closer around myself, grateful for the dimness of the room and the twinkle of the Christmas tree. I had plopped onto the couch barely a half hour earlier, having just gotten back from a long, tiresome physical therapy session. I had told Nina I was going to nap, but I knew I would probably just "rest," as I usually did.

I started, certain I had awakened at the sound of something—voices in the foyer, maybe? I turned to my left, and the last person I was expecting to see (but was happy to see, nonetheless) stared back at me from the doorway.

"Jet!"

My eyes widened in horror at the thought of how hideous I must have looked, and I quickly fumbled for the hair tie I had thrown onto the floor, hastily tying my braids out of my face into a ponytail. I would deal with Nina later.

Jet smiled lightly, shyly, looking as though he himself might turn around and run out the door. He hesitated a little, then stepped forward from where he was seemingly half-hiding behind the door frame and coat rack.

When I started to sit up and make room for him on couch, Jet quickly held up his hand, shaking his head. I reluctantly leaned my upper body against the armrest, feeling impolite but remaining where I was just the same.

Jet walked over and sat down cross legged on the floor in front of me, fiddling around with his hands as I waited for him to speak.

"Um . . ." He sighed after a moment, then finally looked up at me with a hopeful smile, displaying two tickets in one hand. "Still got a place for ol' Drosselmeyer in your heart?"

Slowly, a smile spread across my face, and I quickly nodded, reaching out to hug him.

With a lot of persuasion from Nina, Cat and Bri, I wore a floor-length, spaghetti-strap, satin, pearly gown, my braids pulled up into a classy bun with a braid or two framing my face. My legs were, thankfully, concealed by the dress, thus I was able to wear the braces I was still required to use.

I felt extremely self-conscious, this being the first time I had gotten dressed up since before my surgery. But once I had arrived downstairs, waiting for Jet, Mom said I looked "gorgeous," Dad, "wonderful," Nina, "fantastic," and Jet, when he came to escort me out, "beautiful."

I have to admit that I felt very classy walking into the Kimmel Center Theater, with my handsome escort on my arm, in his sharp, black suit over a black-satin shirt with a pearly-white tie. Being that I knew so many people associated with dance, and Jet knowing so many people as a star college athlete, we were waving and fraternizing our way through the lobby. Both of us were feeling very happy with the atmosphere, but mainly with each other's company.

It was a . . . silent declaration, I suppose, looking back on it now, though I'm not even sure if it crossed either of our minds. Though we were on our first date and publicly displaying ourselves as a couple to the public eye, I think Jet and I were a lot more comfortable than we thought. We were simply enjoying ourselves.

The play was as charming as it was every other one of the hundred times I had seen it, and I was glad to see that Jet enjoyed it as well. While exiting the theater into the packed lobby, he leaned over to me once and told me that he had come to see me in the community theater's production of *The Nutcracker Suite* one Christmas with Nana Jo. Chuckling in amusement, I asked him if he liked it. Jet shrugged at first, then grinned and said that he loved it—especially the Sugarplum Fairy.

As we strolled along to his car, Jet patiently matching my speed as I moved with my cane while holding his arm, a light snow fell, and Jet let out a thoughtful sigh.

"What?" I asked, turning to him.

Jet shrugged, and didn't reply immediately. "How much . . ." he hesitated, "how much training do those guys have to have?"

I tilted my head in consideration. "Hmm, I guess it depends . . . Some theaters require two years and others ten," I smiled comfortingly at Jet's surprised expression. "But they go by fast . . ." my voice trailed a little, and I looked up at the tall, Philadelphia skyscrapers and the lively Christmas lights of the city. It was still a little hard to watch my favorite ballet, even with the progress I was making with my legs.

"Good advice, comin' from the best dancer ever."

I turned, not having noticed Jet's eyes on me.

Blushing, I shook my head and looked away, smiling just the same.

Thirty-Three
Jet

"How does dinner sound?"

I sensed Miranda's smile from the other line.

"Sounds great—where at?"

"The best place in town—Nana Jo's."

Miranda chuckled.

"I'm game."

"Alright, I'll be there at six."

"Okay."

"And wear your hair down—I like it that way." I paused, realizing my foot might have been in my mouth. "Well, you could rock it any way, but that's my favorite," I quickly added.

Miranda laughed, and we finally hung up.

Tossing my cell aside, I fell back onto the couch, breathing a content sigh while propping my feet up on the armrest.

"Someone's havin' a good day."

I looked up, noting Jonathan, standing in the kitchen doorway in jeans and a t-shirt. He was staying with Luke and me until New Year's, when he would have to leave for a job interview.

"More like a good week," I replied, opening my cell once again and smiling at the wallpaper, which was a picture of Miranda and I from when we saw *The Nutcracker Suite* only a couple of nights ago. I couldn't remember ever feeling so lightweight and heavy all at once. I kept promising myself that the guilt would eventually fade away, though. In the meantime, I was going to continue as I was, to keep on seeing Miranda.

"Hey, you got any plans for tonight?" I sat up a little, realizing that Miranda hadn't met Jonathan yet.

Jon shrugged casually, leaning in the doorway and stuffing one hand in his pocket. "Nope." He paused, then smiled. "I've been missin' Nana Jo's cookin' lately anyway," he added, revealing that he had overheard my phone call.

"Jet, man, my car is dead," Jon sighed.

I frowned as I jogged down the steps to the apartment complex parking lot, watching Jonathan close the hood of his green Taurus.

"You wanna ride with me, then?" I offered, zipping my jacket closed and glancing at my watch.

Jonathan quickly shook his head.

"No, of course not—I'm not gonna intrude."

I encouraged him, "Jon, c'mon. Miranda's cool, she wouldn't mind."

"Nice decorations," Jonathan commented when we arrived at Miranda's house, and I chuckled.

"Guess who helped," I said with a sideways glance as we got out of the car, stomping through the layers of snow.

Jon noted my grin.

"You're warmin' up fast, aren't you, little bro'?" he chuckled.

Jonathan stood slightly aloof as I rang the doorbell, surveying his surroundings, staying true to his observant, careful nature.

"Lookin' sharp, Mr. Carmichael," Miranda commented when she opened the door, and I laughed. I ended up in a brown, button-down shirt and slacks, and since I had been growing my hair out a little, I decided at the last minute to add a little bit of gel to define the curls.

Miranda, on the other hand, looked stunning in her brown leather boots, denim skirt and white sweater with a belt tied around the waist. "You look beautiful." I smiled, speaking in all honesty, and Miranda grinned as I assisted her with her jacket.

It was when I heard a thud from my right that I recalled Jonathan, and quickly turned. Both Miranda and I looked to see Nina, who had just driven up, standing near her car, looking down at a pile of folders and papers she had dropped.

I started over to help, but Jonathan was two steps ahead of me.

When Miranda and I arrived at the scene, Jonathan had just found out who Nina was.

"Nina . . . Nina Phillips?" he asked slowly, his jaw dropping—which it rarely did.

Nina smiled politely, appearing self-conscious. I had never witnessed her meeting anyone new, and I suddenly realized that it must not be easy being so famous. But what I couldn't understand was how Jonathan Carmichael, my laid-back, business-minded brother who had yet to find out what women's perfume was, knew about Nina Phillips.

"Yes," Nina nodded. "And you are . . . ?"

It could have come across as an annoyed question, but Jonathan didn't take it that way.

"Um . . ." Jonathan's pause was too long. "Jonathan—Jonathan

Carmichael." He continued to smile in an obviously smitten way. "Wow, it's really great meeting you—I see you on *No Way* all the time."

I turned to Miranda, trying to keep from laughing out loud, and whispered, "All the time?"

Nina smiled, looking as though she was beginning to enjoy the celebrity moment. "Really? Well, I'm glad you watch it."

Before Nina could say any more, Miranda cleared her throat, and I realized that there were still introductions to be made.

"Jon, this is Miranda, Miranda this is Jon, my brother."

Miranda smiled as she shook Jonathan's hand.

"I didn't know Jet had a brother," she chuckled.

Jonathan laughed, glancing at Nina.

"I didn't know you had a *sister.*"

After all the introductions were out of the way, Jon and I walked to the car—Miranda hanging back a little to chat with Nina. I looked over at Jonathan, who was still grinning childishly to himself.

"Since when did you watch *No Way?*" I snuck over to him, readying my keys.

Jonathan grinned slowly, then paused as he turned to look over his shoulder, his tone serious when he spoke.

"Since Nina Phillips joined the cast."

"Jet would never tell you, Miranda, but this dancing thing is really nothing new to him."

Nana Jo chuckled, Miranda looked amused, and I placed my forehead in my hands, knowing where Jonathan was going.

"Is that right?" Miranda asked, then shook her head at me with a laugh. "You don't tell me anything, Jet."

"I'm not tellin' you *this*, that's for sure," I promised, sighing and smiling a little, realizing that Jonathan wasn't to be stopped.

"The truth is," Jon continued, "Jet used to do the Hammertime dance better than anyone else, and every Christmas, when all of our family was visiting, we would have to get him to do the dance. But Jet would never do it, until Dad finally told him one year that he would get Jet a new bike if he did Hammertime." Jonathan grinned. "So, sure enough, this was all it took, and Jet did the dance that Christmas—I bet Nana Jo's got the tape somewhere."

"Not if I burned it!" I laughed, and Jonathan snickered.

"Didn't I tell you that you had it in you?" Miranda said between peals of laughter, and I became flushed, ready to hide under the table.

Nana Jo shook her head, chuckling as she began to cut the dessert of sweet potato pie with whipped cream.

"That child was an unofficial dancer, alright." She smiled, handing Miranda a plate of pie.

"That's for sure," Jon quipped.

"Just don't tell the newspapers," I sighed.

"It sounds like I should've given you and Bri a Hammertime piece instead," laughed Miranda.

Jonathan nodded, amused as he reached out to slap hands with her.

I picked at my slice of pie, aggravated but grinning just the same. I was glad that Miranda and Jon were hitting it off, as I had worried that they wouldn't get along since they were practically polar opposites.

We all laughed a little more, until the doorbell rang. Nana Jo started to get up and answer it. "I wonder who that could be . . ."

Jonathan wiped his mouth with his napkin, looking up as he swallowed his food.

"I'll get it, Nana—"

"No, it's fine," I spoke up, rising from my seat and heading for the door.

I opened it quickly and was thoroughly shocked to see who the caller was.

"Josiah?" she spoke softly, calling me the only name she really knew me as.

She was shorter than me now, and it was strange to look down on her. Her face, which I had always thought was warm and beautiful, was now drawn, wrinkled and scrunched, holding only a few hints of the person I used to know. Dark circles hung under her deep, brown eyes, and her hair, which was once long and braided—not dissimilar to Miranda's—was cut to about an inch long, with a few speckles of gray at the temples. She was still petite, though, especially in her heavy, fur coat, and my eyes quickly noticed the expensive gold jewelry around her neck, wrists, and fingers.

For a moment, I thought for sure I was going to cry, more so at the realization of how different she was from how I remembered her than at seeing her again, but I didn't. Instead I just stood—staring blankly, feeling empty.

"Josiah," she said again, finally reaching out to hug me, and I caught the nicotine on her breath and in her clothes.

From the dining room, one could see the front door, and suddenly recalling our audience, I felt ashamed . . . especially in front of Miranda. Without a second thought, I grabbed my coat from the rack and quickly stepped out onto the porch, swiftly closing the door behind me.

It was silent outside, with the exception of a passing car and chattering on a neighbor's porch.

She looked at me with confusion, but there was a hint of gladness on her face. I walked over to the railing, leaning my back against it and crossing my arms over my chest as I stared coldly at the ground.

"Josiah—"

"Mom, why?"

Mom blinked at my interruption. "I just . . ." She didn't finish her sentence—I'm not sure that I expected her to.

"What are you doin' here?" I asked quietly, still looking down at my shoes, at our footprints in the snow.

"I came to see you . . . and your brother."

"That wasn't on your mind when you left, though."

Mom sighed heavily. Her cell phone rang as if on cue, and I rolled my eyes as I looked out at the street.

"R.J., I'll call you back . . . no . . . no . . . I'm at Joelle's right now... yes, I'm talking to him. . ."

I shifted uncomfortably, suddenly wishing she would just leave in the taxi waiting for her in front of the house.

"Okay . . ." she sighed again in frustration. "R.J., just leave it alone—I'll call you later."

When she hung up, the silence returned. Mom glanced nervously at the cab in the street, trembling slightly.

"Josiah, I have to go. I'll be back tomorrow."

"What makes you think I'll believe you?" I quickly shot, finally managing to look at her.

Mom nodded slowly, awkwardly glancing around, perhaps a hint of hurt in her eyes.

Before I knew it, I suddenly wanted to beg her forgiveness, though I don't know what for. I just wanted her to stay—to not leave like she did before. I wanted things to be normal again, to put the past behind me.

"I'll-I'll be back," she repeated quietly, then started to go, but not before placing a kiss on my cheek, a kiss that felt more like a stab in the back.

As she hurried to the cab, retrieving her cell phone from her purse and dialing what must have been R.J.'s number, I felt the tears on my face and rushed into the house.

Thirty-Four
Miranda

Jet came back in as suddenly as he had left, interrupting what little, awkward conversation there was after an uncomfortable, vague briefing from Nana Jo on who the caller was. She said that she had a feeling their mother would come back in town—seeing Jet for the first time in eleven years, and Jonathan three, since he had gone to find her once before.

Jonathan got up to go to the door, but Jet stopped him with a rough voice, saying, "She's already gone."

Seeing that Jet was clearly upset, I stood up, intending on going after him into the kitchen where he disappeared, but Nana Jo quickly rose instead, touching my arm and heading for the other room.

About an hour after church got out, I slid into my car and drove to Nana Jo's house, my right leg finally well enough to drive. A note was tucked away in my jacket pocket, a note which I had written the night before after a very silent Jet drove me home. I had worried about him, and not wanting to prod too much, I decided to express my concern through a note. That way, he could talk about it when he felt ready, I supposed.

But as I shut off the ignition, noting Jet's car in the driveway, I couldn't help but feel slightly . . . hurt by the whole thing. I mean, it didn't feel good to know that Jet was having trouble with his mom, but there was an obvious distance between us, as a result of it. I wanted to be in on everything and solve all of Jet's problems, and yet, I didn't want to be in on anything at all. I didn't really want to know about the dark aspects of either of our lives that could possibly separate us. I wanted to ignore them.

I didn't knock immediately when I stood on the porch, and instead looked down at the welcome mat, my hair blowing gently in my face from the breeze.

The most unexpected thought crossed my mind, and it was of how much I found myself comparing things now with back when I was with Kevin. I remembered when I first started liking Kevin, and though the feelings I had were now hidden by the pain, I could recall them as though they were alive and new. I remembered how there were, virtually, no problems with the ambiguous relationship we had—no long-lost relatives popping up out of nowhere and bringing division. No drama at all, really. No, there was only the drama *I* created. My life had been relationship drama free.

But now with Jet in the picture, a key part of the picture, I saw just how sharp of a turn things had taken in my once-planned life. I knew that I wanted things to be "perfect" for Jet and I, and how afraid I was of the difference between my past relationship with

Kevin and my current one with Jet. With Kevin, and even life before surgery—before the possibility to dance again was tangible—everything was meticulously planned and carefully directed. But with Jet, I honestly had no clue as to what would happen next.

Brushing my braids out of my face, I sighed. I once told you that I needed direction in my life, and at that point, I saw that I still did.

I knocked, realizing I had been standing and thinking for over two or three minutes, my gloved hand, surprisingly, shaking a little.

A few seconds passed, and I waited patiently to greet either Jet or Nana Jo, tilting my cane from hand to hand.

The door opened, and I looked up, but not into a face I was familiar with. I opened my mouth to speak, but knowing I didn't really know what to say.

She spoke for me. "Miranda Phillips."

I swallowed, feeling very small all of a sudden under the obviously disapproving stare of Jet's mother.

"Yes . . . yes ma'am." I spoke quietly, wishing I could pretend to ignore the sarcasm in her tone.

Jet's mom nodded slowly, raising a cigarette to her lips and skillfully lighting it—never taking her eyes off of me once.

"So you're the girl who changed my boy . . . got him off of the football field and onto a dance floor—a stage." She paused, her dark eyes narrowing at me ever so slightly, scanning me as though I was an enemy. "I guess you never had to worry about payin' for college—havin' to take on football like Jet did," she smirked. "I suppose havin' rich parents, expensive dance lessons and your own studio has paved the way easy for you, huh?"

I bristled, staring down at the ground and feeling my cheeks grow warm in the chilly weather. Coming all the way from L.A., being so removed from Jet's life, she couldn't have known about my physical situation—but even if she did, I wouldn't have been quick to doubt that she would change her tune.

214

I could have gotten angry, and I could have blown up in her face and set the record straight—told her about all the hours of painful therapy, the agonizing surgery, the initial accident, or the way my family had nearly gone broke several times while trying to pay for my medical bills. I *could* have . . . but I didn't. To be honest, I wasn't angry. I was just hurt. The verbal beating I was taking was confirming my fears that I was insufficient for Jet.

"No, ma'am," was all I said, meekly disagreeing with her fallacious rant.

Jet's mom slowly lifted the cigarette again, and then exhaled a breath of smoke.

"I hear he's taken to you," she began quietly, evenly, then smirked again. "I remember when you two were little, and Joelle, Jet and I would go to the park down the street—we'd pass you and your mother on the path, and Jo would always say that you two would 'cross paths' again." She shifted her jaw, watching me hang my head in silence. "I never was one to believe in superstition."

"It wasn't superstition, Evelyn."

I turned at the voice from behind. Jet's mom narrowed her eyes.

Nana Jo, in her long winter coat, with her scarf blowing in the wind and a paper sack of groceries cradled in one arm, was moving up the porch. With all of the sounds of neighbors arriving home from church around us, we hadn't heard her pull up.

"I always told you that," Nana Jo added when she reached the top step, casting me a casual, warm smile at the same time. "No, it was providence—hungry, Miranda? C'mon in."

Confused and still trying to process everything, I blankly followed Nana Jo into the house as she took hold of my hand. Leaving Jet's mom glaring in the doorway, we left for the kitchen, where Nana Jo set the bag down on the table and removed her coat and scarf.

Inside the enclosed kitchen, with the smell of Sunday dinner wrapped around me, it was like waking up on the right side of the bed; it was like starting a new day altogether. The prick of the previous "conversation" was just as sharp, though, with the contrast, and I held my forehead, fearing I was going to break down and cry.

I slowly sat down at the table. Nana Jo moved efficiently and casually through the kitchen, her business with the many pots on the stove providing noise, and my only reason not to sob. My mind hung on Evelyn's harsh words. Was she right? Was I really just too... "perfect" for Jet? I sighed to myself, realizing I certainly didn't feel this "perfection" people were so quick to point out from afar.

Before I knew it, though, the soothing sounds of cooking ceased, and a neatly-plated ham-and-cheese sandwich was slid before me.

"Thank you," I said quietly, accordingly.

Nana Jo sighed.

"I'm sorry you had to put up with that. I wouldn't take it personally, though." She hesitated. "Evelyn's wary of...people."

I nodded without speaking, poking at the sandwich, knowing I should eat it to be polite, but my stomach was as torn up as I was feeling.

Nana Jo was silent for a moment, then she sat down across from me, placing her hands over mine.

"She's got her own growing to do—don't let her words sink in, Miranda," she said softly, and I only nodded once more, knowing her advice wouldn't be easy to follow.

Nana Jo sighed again.

"An old teacher once told me, 'when there's resistance, you're doing somethin' right.' " She smiled warmly, consolingly. "You don't have to change who you are or be ashamed of who you are, Miranda. Everyone else may be lookin' at you as the girl with the accident or the popular dancer. Or in Evelyn's case, the girl who's stealing her son." She paused, speaking softly. "And they can come up with a thousand different definitions for you, Miranda, but it's *you,* not any classification or title, who your family, friends, me . . ." she smiled with a light chuckle, ". . . and Jet, love."

I could only smile gratefully, feeling my voice catching in my throat as I reached up to wipe at my eyes.

"Amen," came a sound of agreement from the bottom of the staircase behind me. Turning, I saw Jet, standing with solemnity in his eyes and a smile on his face.

"More water, Mira?"

"Oh, uh, no . . . I'm fine. Thanks, though."

"Jet?"

"Uh, no, no, Nina. I'm fine . . . thanks."

Once Nina had left, Jet and I looked at each other and laughed, covering our mouths to keep her from hearing us.

Jet had received a call from Nina, telling him to dress up, buy a bouquet of roses, and bring them to our house. As for me, I was told to dress up and wait in the dining room. Nina had also taken it upon herself to advise me on what I would wear, and eventually we agreed on a flowing, brick-red skirt, brown-satin kimono blouse (borrowed from Nina) my favorite ruby chandelier earrings, golden-maroon eyeshadow, and half of my braids swept up into a ponytail, the others hanging down my back.

When I came down the stairs, holding my cane in one hand and the banister in the other, a tasty blast of the gourmet meal Nina was preparing met my nose. I smiled. Upon reaching the dining room, though, my jaw dropped a little. The table was spread in a classy white tablecloth, elegant glasses and the best china, as well as an empty vase, which, I was told, Jet would bring the finishing touch to.

Jet arrived on time, sporting a white button-down shirt, a red tie and black slacks with the roses in hand.

We were sitting, laughing and talking lightly, halfway through the main course and carelessly poking at the sirloin strips that my sister had burned. Nina had appeared for the fifth time that evening, asking if either of us wanted any more water (our glasses were full)—most likely to release her guilt from burning the steak. The cell phone in her hand couldn't rule out up-to-date news flashes to Bri and Cat, either.

When the steaks were taken away, Nina ushered out two cups of delicious crème brulée, even going through the trouble of toasting the top before us with a pastry torch (I love my sister).

Jet chuckled once he finished his dessert, and I laughed.

"What?"

He shook his head, wiping his mouth with his napkin. "Your sister is too much. She didn't have to do all this."

I smiled, setting my spoon down and taking a sip of my water. "Yeah, she didn't."

"We should thank her somehow."

I nodded, watching the floating candles in the bowl near the vase. "Don't let her act fool you too much, though," I warned quietly, a smile inching across my face.

Jet, quizzically, "Why?"

I grinned, cocking my head toward the door leading to the kitchen. "If she's not sitting by the door eavesdropping, she's not Nina Phillips."

Jet smiled with a chuckle, the candlelight dancing in his deep, brown eyes.

Neither of us spoke for a moment, and eventually, Jet glanced around the room, out at the den. After spotting something, he looked back at me with a silent request to be excused. I smiled.

I watched Jet walk up to Mom's record player and begin to sift through her stack of records.

"Let's see, Diana Ross . . . Aretha, Dionne Warwick . . . ?" He held a few records up for observation, and I merely shrugged.

Chuckling, Jet carefully placed one of the records on the turntable, then twisted the volume knob up just enough. When he returned, his hand was extended, a hopeful smile on his face.

"Nothing too fancy," he promised.

I slowly smiled as I gave him my hand.

Taking a few steps away from the dinner table, Jet and I began to dance slowly to "The Look of Love" by Dionne Warwick, a song that I had always liked. I placed one of my hands on his shoulder; his was around my waist as our fingers intertwined.

For fun, we sang along with the record, until both of us hit a shamefully-sour note. We both laughed.

"You know," Jet spoke up, a smile playing at his lips, "it's pretty weird to be standing here right now when only a couple weeks ago I was askin' your dad if I could start to see you—well, more like stuttering if I could see you."

I laughed a little at the thought and Jet chuckled.

"Yeah, I was . . . pretty nervous. But it was worth it," he admitted seriously, glancing from me to the floor, "especially gettin' to hear your list of standards."

I smiled slowly, recalling my list. "I figured Dad would have run that by you—we made a pact a while ago that he would take care of all of that."

Jet grinned. "And as your dad said, you'd 'snag them' while he 'screened them'—and boy was I screened . . . but definitely snagged."

I blushed and looked away, noting the seriousness in his trailing voice.

We didn't speak again for a moment or two, until Jet chuckled suddenly.

"What?" I questioned slowly.

Jet shrugged.

"It's nothin'—I was just remembering something . . ."

I shrugged as well with a laugh.

"Care to share?"

"Well," he sighed, apparently a little hesitant. "You remember when I came into your classroom that one night and asked you to teach me how to waltz?"

I demurred, then smiled. "Definitely . . ." I paused, frowning somewhat. "But you never told me how that banquet went—did you actually dance with anyone, or . . . ?"

Jet cleared his throat a little nervously, a hint of laughter darting through his eyes. "Well, see . . . I didn't dance with anyone because . . . because the banquet didn't exist . . ."

Puzzled, I shook my head. "I don't understand."

Jet chuckled at my confusion, meeting my gaze.

"I only made that up." He hesitated again, his eyes shifting around. "All I really wanted was to . . . watch you dance—to dance *with* you."

I couldn't help but falter slightly at the sincerity in Jet's words, in his eyes.

My surprised silence must have caused Jet to worry, and he quickly spoke up with a frown, "I mean, I wasn't meaning to be cruel about it or whatever—I hope you don't think I lied because of that . . ."

A smile gradually lit my face.

"Jet, just . . . shut up," I chuckled. "I didn't know what to say because that was probably the nicest thing anyone's ever done for me after my accident . . ."

Jet's concerned expression eased into a smile, and I sensed him beginning to relax.

As we danced in silence, avoiding each other's eyes, I found myself mentally walking through the past months, and just how much had changed for me . . . good changes. It didn't take me very long to realize that a lot of those changes were thanks, mostly, to

220

Jet.

"Jet, I want to, um . . . thank you," I began slowly, wishing I could find the perfect thing to say. "I mean . . . things are so much... different now, and I want you to know how grateful I am for your friendship . . . for you. You've taught me so much . . ."

Jet didn't smile modestly or say anything, but only looked down at the floor, sternness evident on his face.

"You're the one who taught *me*, Miranda," he spoke quietly, breathing a small laugh before becoming serious. "Miranda, I . . ." Jet's voice altogether faded as he finally looked me in the eyes, and we soon stopped swaying to the music.

Swallowing, I looked away, having the strangest and scariest feeling of knowing what he was about to say. "Jet—"

"No," he quickly interrupted, taking a deep breath as he placed his other hand over mine on his shoulder. "You don't have to say anything . . . just me." He sighed. "See, I . . ." He swallowed as well, seeming as though he was trying to find the words again, but finally shook his head.

"Would you . . . would you be mad at me if I didn't finish that sentence," he hesitated, "right now?" His eyes filled with what I saw to be a genuine fear.

Trying to keep from smiling suddenly, I cleared my throat, and with a straight face, I asked, "Would *you* be mad at *me* if I didn't respond to the end of your sentence," I looked up at him, "*right now?*" I added meaningfully with a light smile.

Searching my eyes, Jet soon grinned with a nod.

Both of us continued dancing to the soft music, neither of us speaking for a long time.

Thirty-Five
Jet

"Sir, could I interest you in one of our latest arrivals?"

I blinked, realizing just how long I had been standing and staring.

I had decided to spend my Thursday Christmas shopping in the mall, since the holiday was only four days away. I was standing in front of the counter at Kay's: a place, months back, I wouldn't have given a second glance.

I felt overwhelmed as I gazed at the silver-banded diamond a second longer. "No, no . . . I-I was just looking."

The salesman, in his suit and tie, looking as though he was no older than me and sporting his own wedding band, smiled amiably. "Sure? You were looking pretty serious, there. She's worth it, isn't she?"

Smiling again, I nodded. "Oh yeah, she's worth it alright." I raised my eyebrows, easily recognizing the understatement in my words.

The salesman shrugged, grinning broadly through perfect teeth. "Well, don't let her slip away."

As I walked off, his words hung in my mind, and I sighed once again, sliding my hands into the pockets of my hoodie.

More like "don't scare her away . . ."

I spotted an artist's kiosk to my right and walked over to look at it. Quietly, I watched the artist glance up from her work only once, deeply focused on her painting. The pieces were made of watercolor and held anything from an ocean scene to, surprisingly, a football field. I studied them closer.

"Jet Carmichael, that one was inspired by you."

Blinking, I turned at the sound of my name. The artist, whom the kiosk revealed to be "Julia McPherson," was looking up again, over her thick, red glasses through clear, blue eyes, looking herself like a painting on her stool beside the kiosk. Her hair, long and white as snow, was pulled back into a ponytail, and her face was slightly aged, yet pretty.

Julia smiled. "My husband's a diehard college football fan," she explained, and I chuckled.

"Wow," was all I could say, and took another look at the wide range of paintings. "These are real great."

Julia beamed, dipping her brush into a splotch of pinkish orange on her palette. "Thank you," she graciously replied, then sighed. "I just wish I could say the same about this one."

I frowned, turning to look at the painting. Julia gestured for me to come closer so that I could see. The painting, to me, was just as good as the others, and, interestingly enough, it was of a dance classroom. A mirror sat on one side of the scene, with a ballet bar in front of it, and orange-ish-tan light flooded in through a window on another wall. But where I expected there to be dancers on the wooden floor, there was no one.

Julia looked up at me as I studied the painting.

"See, I don't have an idea for the actual *dancer*—no pose or inspiration at all." She laughed. "It's about to become an abstract painting."

I shrugged with a light smile. "It's beautiful anyway. . ."

"But something's missing," Julia finished for me, pondering for a moment as we both looked at the unfinished piece.

An idea had flashed through my mind the moment I saw the painting. Unlike Julia, I had pictured the dancer she was looking for, vivid and clear in my mind. I didn't speak up, though, since I didn't feel that it was in my place to do so.

"Any suggestions? I'm open to anything at this point."

"Well. . ." I hesitated. "I have a dancer in mind."

I felt perfect during the next week. I hadn't been so happy in a long time, and it was as though everything was simply too good to be true. The air at the park was lighter than usual. My thoughts were cleared and I didn't have one care—that is, nothing but the guilt I had been shouldering for the past month or so. I breathed in the fresh, cool winter air deeply as I jogged along, planning the day and the week to come. With Christmas only two days back and New Year's Eve four days away, I was excited. I hadn't given Miranda her present yet. It wasn't finished. But I had been promised that it would be done by New Year's Eve, when I was going to present it to Miranda at midnight. In her classic, low-maintenance style, she hadn't once asked me why I hadn't given her a Christmas present, but I knew she was wondering just the same.

I was interrupted by a voice from behind on the path.

"Jet, wait up!"

Gradually I came to a stop, turning to see Luke quickly

approaching, winded and hastily bundled in a jacket and cap.

I laughed, wondering what had brought *him*, with his non-athletic self, all the way to the park.

"Luke, man, what're you doin' here?"

Luke bent when he reached me, placing his hands on his knees and continuing to pant. When he looked up, he wasn't smiling his usual grin.

"I had to hurry over." He paused, holding his chest, looking as though he had run all the way from the parking lot.

I shrugged, beginning to stretch my legs.

"Well, what for?" I laughed again. "Oh, you must've heard about the Chiefs' loss—sorry, man, but the Eagles took your team to school—"

"Jet!" Luke interrupted, suddenly grabbing my shoulders. "The press is onto you! The-the police—there's a warrant out for your arrest!"

I frowned, shoving his hands away.

"Hey, what're you talkin' about?!" I shot, feeling my old paranoia kicking in.

Luke sighed, "Jet, they're sayin' *you're* the one who hit Miranda in that accident and crippled her! Some dude came forward with a security tape." He shrugged with another frustrated sigh. "Somethin' with your old license number—claims he's the store owner of the shop at the scene of her accident." Luke withdrew his cell phone, his fingers rapidly dialing a number. "But don't worry about it, man, my dad and his firm will quickly get this taken care of…"

Luke's voice seemed to fade into silence although his lips continued to move. He explained how he would call his father, have the store owner thrown in jail for trying to frame me, and ultimately get me off the hook. I just wish he knew that there wasn't anything to defend. I was the one in the car—the store owner was right. He was bringing me to justice. I hadn't turned myself in, but someone else was now.

Before I could feel the grip of fear and panic, another thought came to mind: the other person involved. The firm pavement swam beneath me.

The press knew my secret; it would only be a matter of minutes before Miranda found out, that is, if she hadn't already . . .

The screech of tires, the scream of pain—everything came crashing back to my memory, but this time, I had a face for the faceless girl I hit, memories, a name, a friendship and . . . a love.

I left Luke chattering into his cell phone about clearing my name, rushing to my car with one thought in mind: to reach her house, to get to her in time . . .

As I blankly sped down the street, I don't think I knew just what I was going to do when I got there; I didn't know what I was going to say. Was there anything *to* say at all? What could possibly fix this? Would it matter if I somehow got there before the press reached her?

I had to talk to her—I had to at least let her know that I was sorry . . . that the past months meant something to me, that *she* meant something to me. Even if she hated me for the rest of her life, she would know where I stood.

The drive to her house was instant yet never ending, and I arrived without recalling any of the trip. But as I approached the house, less than a block away, I could have ripped the steering wheel right out of the car from frustration.

The press had beaten me there.

I don't know what possessed me to get out of the car, but I did, right into the sea of cameras. I was overwhelmed by the crowd at one shout of "Jet Carmichael's here!" From there, the questioning around me came like a roar from a packed football stadium. But this time, they weren't on my side.

"Were you drunk that night?"

"Is it true that you're her boyfriend?"

"Did you ever plan on coming forward?"

"Is it true that you withheld the information just to gain your own limelight with the Phillips family?"

"Was it an act of malice?"

Despite the chaos, I continued to try to press toward the house, still hoping I could get to Miranda. I must have only reached the area where the driveway met the front walk when all eyes abruptly shifted from me to the door.

Standing with her parents on either side of her, along with whom I guessed to be a lawyer, was Miranda. Her head was down toward the ground; one hand was raised up to her face for privacy.

Of course, she already knew what was happening, but I moved nonetheless, perhaps foolishly. I pressed through to the vehicle the family was about to leave in. Standing at the car, I tried to think of what to say or do. But when Miranda arrived, I froze.

All at once, she saw me, standing less than two feet away, her mouth open. Now that her face was visible, I noted that her eyes and cheeks were wet with tears. I can't tell you how it made me feel to see the pain in her eyes—the distrust, betrayal, and disbelief. I felt as though she was looking at someone she didn't know, and it made me ache beyond words.

And yet, all I could do was swallow, trying to say something—to say the very thing I had been subconsciously rehearsing the entire drive over. But it didn't come out. I was unable to speak, unable to move. I wanted to take Miranda in my arms and apologize until my voice really did leave me.

In the moments that Miranda and I stared at each other, paralyzed, I had failed to hear the sirens or see the police pushing through the crowd.

I was grabbed from behind, and roughly moved to the police car.

They pressed me onto its side. As my rights were recited to me by one of the officers, I was instructed to place my hands on the car. While my pockets were searched, I watched as Miranda was driven off.

My past had finally caught up with me.

Thirty-Six
Miranda

I didn't go to the studio for two months. I didn't really leave my house much. I even went to my grandparents' place in Florida for a few months to escape the press. My family sheltered me the same way that they had after my accident. Dad handled the legal matters and the press, with the ultimate decisions up to me. And Mom, well, she was just "Mom." She was there for me emotionally, knowing when I needed to rest, talk, or have a shoulder to cry on. Still, it was bittersweet in that we were finally on the same page concerning Jet.

I didn't press charges. For Jet, this really only meant that he wouldn't have to spend six months in jail. He would, however, have his license suspended. He would also have to pay for my medical bills.

I wish I could say that this made me feel better, but it didn't. Suddenly, Jet was a villain in the eyes of my loved ones, and they wanted justice to be served. They wanted me to get every ounce of payback that I could. I tried with everything in me to be as angry with Jet as they wanted me to be, but I never did get there. Yes, I was mad at him for the accident, for not telling me from the start. . . but more than anything, I was heartbroken. Maybe it was because any and all traces of a future I could have had with him had evaporated. I don't know. I just know that I was angry and hurt, but more so with my inability to detest Jet than with Jet himself. I had no release.

One day, a mere two or three months after the revelation surfaced, I found myself climbing the ladder to the attic in my house—the room I once practiced in when I was younger. I hadn't been up there in a good year or so, and there wasn't as much dust as I thought there would be, thanks to my mom.

The wood floor was obstructed only slightly by boxes and chairs, and I didn't have much rearranging to do. After pulling back the curtains in front of the small window, I squinted at the light which delicately bathed the room. A foggy reflection stared back at me from the dusty mirrors, and I withdrew a cloth from my pocket to wipe them clean. On one wall, in plain view, yet ignored by my cautious eyes, were trophies, plaques and framed photos—all of them mine, from my glory days. And beneath them, leaning against a shelf, was my first cane—the one I was presented with by the physical therapist who helped me walk again after the accident. I pretended not to see it as I stood before the mirror, forcing myself to face my reflection.

It was hard to see me in dance surroundings those days. It only reminded me of my inability to dance, but this time, it scared me more than ever before. This time, I had gone through the surgery which had corrected my legs and was in the middle stages of my rehabilitation process. This time, there was potential in the person standing before me in the mirror.

I closed my eyes for a long time, standing still in the silence of the room, and every possible move seemed to race through my mind at once. I danced in my head, as I had done many a time during my crippled phase, and wondered if my body could follow.

Soon enough, though, I took a step, feeling embarrassed despite the fact that I was alone. I felt like I was on a stage in a packed theater. It was real to me, and my heart began to pound faster and faster. I started out carefully, but then dared to add some emotion to my movements. For what felt like a long time, I forgot the imaginary audience, and suddenly, I was alone again. My movements came bolder and freer; I was the Miranda I used to be—the Miranda everyone was proud of and satisfied with—the Miranda with a future.

All it took was an ambitious *assemblé*, a leap requiring strength and balance, and I was on the floor. I was crippled again, the girl who had hidden behind her inabilities for two years.

I panted heavily, my head throbbing as I lay on my back, my fists pressed against my closed eyes. My legs were mocking me, the silence of the room—my cane, the mirror. Who was I to think I could dance like that again? I had been robbed and forced to face my predicament; I didn't have a right to try to dance again.

A burning tear squeezed out of one eye, and I began to feel every bit of the anger I couldn't discover before. Not just with Jet, but with everything. Anything that played a role in my injury and heartbreak: walking to my car the night of the accident, parking so far away from the building . . . meeting Jet and falling for him. If only those things didn't happen . . .

I opened my eyes and rolled my head to the side, staring wearily at the dusty cane on the wall. With one swift move, I had grabbed it and shattered the mirror.

"So I saw *No Way* last night."

Nina grinned before plunging a chip into the bowl of ranch dip she, Bri, Cat and I were stationed around. We were gathered together in my room for a girl's night in.

"And what'd you think?" came Nina's customary response.

I rolled my eyes at Bri, and she chuckled.

"Well," Cat began slowly, stroking her chin. "It was good. *But*, I definitely think you should end up with that Marco guy instead of Ben."

Nina chuckled. "If only I could get Allen to see that." She shared a glance with me, speaking of the show's director.

"That's what they all say," I commented with a light laugh, and Nina nodded with a shrug.

The four of us sat quietly munching on our snacks, sitting or lying on the plush carpet, a dozen DVDs scattered around us and abandoned Mad Gab cards nearby. I poked mostly, though, at my plate of Chex Mix, enjoying feeling comfortable around my best friends.

It didn't take me long to note the periodic glances between Nina, Bri and Cat, and I picked up my cup of water for a drink, knowing I would need it.

"Mira," Nina spoke first, "we think you should get away."

I shifted to a cross-legged position, confused with her statement. "What do you mean?"

"Away from your parents," Cat cut in, flicking at one of the Mad Gab cards with one freshly-painted, maroon fingernail.

I frowned, subconsciously running my fingers along the scar on my left knee.

"Where would I go?"

"Just, somewhere . . ." Bri took up for Cat slowly, her voice fading as she chewed her lip.

"Where no one knows who you are as much," Nina finished for her, watching me closely, her clear, brown eyes knowing me well and filled with seriousness. "Or at least where you can get a fresh start."

Perturbed, I looked away from the concerned stares of my girls, feeling the fear of the future I had left unacknowledged since the revelation.

Bri tucked a strand of her black hair behind her ear, squinting as she looked at me.

"You didn't come this far for nothing, Miranda."

Getting away for me meant moving out of my parents' house into a New York City apartment which Nina had helped me find. It wasn't far from her own place near her show's studio.

I was at my parents' house on West Oak Lane once a month or so, thus life wasn't entirely different. But I was definitely on my own, for a change, working under one of the costume designers and makeup artists for *No Way*, and I was secretly considering taking dance lessons again. I was around the stage on the job, so it wasn't as though I was working too far out of my passion. But I knew I wanted more. I just didn't know how to tell anyone—that is, anyone but the only person who might actually take me seriously.

"What do you think, Mira—red or brown?"

I tilted my head from where I stood in the kitchen doorway, holding a newspaper.

"Um . . ." I sighed passively before yawning. "I dunno'…"

Exasperated, Nina stepped down from the stool with the two swatches in her hands.

"Mir*anda*." She shook her head, then stroked her chin in consideration. "Okay, we'll go with red."

I paused from where I was making my way to the makeshift couch of crates in my new living room, and shrieked, "*Red* walls?!"

Nina turned around with a lopsided grin, her almond eyes laughing.

"You never liked bright wall colors." She chuckled, stuffing the patches into her purse before grabbing her hoodie and pulling it on.

With a light smile, I carefully laid across the crates, holding the newspaper as I looked out the floor-to-ceiling window. I stretched and bent my knees once or twice. They hadn't given me any pain for almost four weeks now, and the therapists were impressed with my progress.

"We need to find you some good artwork," Nina mumbled to herself more than anyone else, flipping through an interior-design magazine as she took a seat on a pillow on the bare floor.

I closed my eyes, envisioning the Alvin Ailey Dancers performance ad inside of the newspaper, picturing the choreographers and dancers.

I had stumbled across the ad for the prestigious troupe earlier that day, and couldn't help but read it over once or twice. For some reason, I had been feeling a boost of confidence lately. I had a lot of time to think about my life and what I would do next, and as much as I tried to ignore it, my ambitions kept returning to dance.

"Nina."

"Mmm?"

I took a deep breath, calmly placing one hand on my forehead.

"I wanna dance again."

Nina looked up briefly from the magazine, her expression still that of concentration on the task of finding the right design for my bare living room.

"Hmm? Oh, yeah, I know . . ." she paused, then seemed to recall that we were dealing with a delicate subject, "and you will, Mira." She added optimistically, returning to her sifting.

I smiled a little to myself.

"No, Nina, as in I want to *dance* . . . like I was planning to before

234

anything happened to me."

Nina paused in her browsing and set the magazine down.

I opened my eyes, turning to meet her bewildered stare. I had trekked into uncharted territory this time; not even the doctors were brave enough to hope that I could professionally dance again. They just told me I could have fun with dancing to some degree. To be honest, I wasn't even brave enough to hope for it myself . . . until now.

Nina's mouth was open, and I wondered if she would speak.

"Mir-Miranda . . ." she stammered. "Wow. . . wait . . ." A smile slowly formed on her face. "Really?" She breathed, and I nodded, smiling as well.

"Really." I sat up, propping myself on my elbow as I opened the newspaper to the ad and Nina came over to see for herself. "Alvin Ailey's been on my mind for a while..."

The bookstore café was lively and mellow. A few groups of people sat around my corner booth—reading, sipping, blogging and socializing to the grinding hum of the coffee machines behind the counter. I didn't drink much of my caramel apple cider, since my stomach was already a bit jumpy. My eyes searched the sidewalk beyond the window. "See u in 5" was the last text I had gotten on my phone, but I had received it a good fifteen minutes back.

"Where is she?" I murmured, continuing to watch the sidewalk before smoothing my braids.

The soothing, earthy aroma of coffee and spice swam through the air, and I tried to relax into the lush leather of the booth, silently chiding myself for being so jumpy.

I sighed again, but finally caught a familiar face in the crowd. Smiling, I watched her skillfully maneuver through the bodies, even in her high heels, carefully reaching up to pat at her hair.

Within seconds, I was standing up with my arms outstretched.

"Miranda, baby, it's so good to see you!" Mom declared warmly after we hugged, holding me back to look at me. She shook her head. "Look what New York's doing to my baby—"

"Mom." I glared.

"You look beautiful," she finished, ignoring my suspicion, "and older than you were when I last saw you on New Year's."

I shrugged as we slid across from each other in the booth. "I should—I'm twenty-two."

Mom nodded, grabbing a menu from a holder as she swept a bang out of her eyes.

"Alright, alright." She paused. "That makes it a little over a year now—I can't believe it," she added, her tone serious and voice lowered.

I slowly sipped my cider, studying the lettering on the side of the cup.

"Yeah," I replied quietly, evenly, myself a little surprised that it had been a whole year since the revelation.

"Well, here it is—New York," Mom digressed, her eyes scanning the menu, looking as though she was trying to make herself appear busy. "What do you think?"

I shifted my jaw. "Hmm, I don't know. It's okay . . ." I glanced out the window at the crowded streets and tall buildings. "Not what I thought it would be, though."

Mom looked up, a hint of concern on her face. "What do you mean?"

I wanted to say that New York would have been amazing if only I was actually *dancing* and not working as a random costume designer's apprentice. But I didn't, and only sighed.

"It's colder here . . ." I lied about my answer, "than it is in Philly." I finished quietly, staring at the disappearing cider and remaining whipped cream in my cup.

Mom frowned in confusion, her lively, brown eyes questioning.

"I thought you loved the cold." She chuckled. "That's why you never liked visiting your grandparents in Florida."

I smiled distantly as Mom sifted through her purse for her wallet. I noticed that she had been glancing out the window periodically.

"How is everyone?" I questioned softly.

"Pretty good. Your Daddy's looking at that new building again—did Nina tell you?"

I nodded, and she continued, though casting more seemingly hopeful glances out the window.

"And the studio's still doing fine—they ask about you a lot, you know." She sighed as she withdrew her wallet. "Cat's got a lot of auditions coming up, but you probably already know that—I'd better go order—"

"What do you want? I'm about to go get some water."

Mom shook her head. "No, Miranda, it's fine—"

"Mom, c'mon."

She sighed, but finally pressed a five-dollar bill into my hand with a pat.

"Alright—a mocha-caramel latté, and no whipped cream . . ." her eyes shifted, and she lowered her voice, ". . . my diet."

I chuckled and got up, moving slowly since my knees were still trying to remember how to bend under my weight.

"You do *not* need to be on a diet, Mom."

Mom cast me a look that said otherwise, and we both laughed as I moved off for the front counter.

"May I help you?" asked the teenage girl after abandoning one of the coffee machines to tend to the register.

"Um, yeah, I'd like a—"

"Caramel apple cider," came a voice from behind, and I quickly turned, immediately recognizing it.

Kevin smiled, stuffing his hands in his jeans pockets, his serious eyes locked into mine.

"You never did like coffee."

My mouth hung open until I recalled the girl taking my order.

"Uh, just water and a mocha-caramel latté, please." I chewed my lip as she nodded and typed the order into the cash register.

"Will that be all?" she asked in a somewhat annoyed tone, and I zoned out as I felt Kevin's eyes on me.

"Um . . ." I swallowed, wanting to run away all of the sudden. "You know what? Just make that a mocha-caramel latté—here's the money, it's for the lady in the corner."

I was out of the café in no time, not pausing to look at Kevin as I left.

Barely had I walked a few yards, hurrying to summon a taxi, before I heard my name from behind.

"Miranda, wait!"

I crossed my arms over my chest, wishing a taxi would stop.

"Miranda," Mom said when she reached my side, frowning in confusion and, perhaps, disapproval. "Where are you going?"

"Why did you invite him?!" I returned heatedly, ignoring her question.

Mom sighed, shaking her head. "Because he's been trying to reach you forever, Miranda!"

"So?!" I shot, unable to believe that she thought I wanted to see Kevin again. "He has nothing to do with me anymore!"

"He's your *best friend*, Miranda—"

"No!" I clenched my jaw. "He's not." I held my forehead, trying to control my temper, realizing I was allowing the situation to get to me too much. "Mom . . ." I sighed. "I-I just don't need to talk to him right now—"

"Miranda—"

"*Mom.*" I held up my hand. "I'm on my own now—I-I've got a job and my own place." I paused, feeling as though I could cry suddenly. "My legs are getting better, and my life is trying to

238

reassemble, okay?"

Mom's expression softened at my pleading tone, and she nodded slowly.

"I know, Miranda . . ." she said quietly as the sounds of the busy city echoed around us, and I almost felt myself relax, hoping the argument was over and that she had understood.

"Thanks," I whispered.

But Mom sighed. "But he's not Jet—he's Kevin."

I frowned again, closing my eyes, knowing I shouldn't have gotten my hopes up.

"When will you stop comparing them?" I asked slowly, trying to keep my volume down.

"When *you* stop, Miranda," Mom quickly returned, her voice level and serious.

I swallowed in surprise at her cloaked accusation, and was about to open my mouth to speak again when I caught site of Kevin. He stood at the door to the bookshop, concern on his familiar face. "I-I'm sorry," I managed to voice as my eyes filled with tears, then hurried off into the heavy New York City crowd.

If I thought Kevin would get tired of trying to see me, I was wrong. Every day after my argument with my mom, he came to the set while I was working, but I refused to see him.

One whole month of this had gone by. I could only hope in the fact that Kevin didn't know my address. But one day, my hope would be proven false.

Ding-dong.

"Ugh," I grumbled as I reluctantly shut off the TV on which I was watching that night's episode of *No Way*. It was a tricky episode to shoot, and makeup-wise, it was a nightmare. We had to make several cast members look forty years older, and I had been given my first task of actually putting a whole face on by myself. I took longer than I was supposed to, but it came out pretty well.

Weary from a long day at the studio, I dragged myself up, my bare feet brushing the lush brown carpet. My apartment had long since been finished, and Nina had ended up giving it a modern feel, with brown-and-gold walls, dark carpeting and suede furniture. I'll admit I liked the outcome, and it was nice having a beautifully-decorated space of my own.

Before checking the peephole, I brushed a few of the crumbs of my panini sandwich from my gauchos, and pulled my braids back into a ponytail, guessing it was only Nina anyway. But when I looked through the peephole, I was surprised to see Kevin.

He had finally gotten my address.

I exhaled a heavy sigh.

Maybe if I just go on and talk to him, he'll leave me alone . . .

I came only seconds away from touching the doorknob, but instead I walked away, letting him think I either wasn't home, or, better yet, that I didn't want to see him.

"Miranda, we've got twenty minutes left before they shoot the prison-cell scene and I still don't have Marty's costume."

I sighed, trying not to prick myself as I quickly sewed the ID tag to the orange jumpsuit—by hand, since the only machine available had given out.

"Miranda!"

"On my way, Ms. Davenport—ouch!"

I dropped the needle upon impact with my skin, and bit my tongue.

Miranda, it's just a needle—get a grip!

You could say I was a little jumpy—okay, maybe *a lot*. With Kevin constantly seeking me out, I was close to calling the police.

"Fifteen minutes, Miranda!" The executive costume designer passed the door to the workroom for what seemed like the one hundredth time.

"Yes, Ms. Davenport!"

"And make sure there are no mistakes this time!"

"Okay, Ms. Davenport!" I mumbled under my breath as I pushed the needle through the fabric. "Whatever you say Ms. Davenport, I'm you're *slave* Ms. Davenport, *as you wish*, Ms. Daven—"

"Mira!"

"Ms. Davenport!" I whipped around, my heart pounding. However, I didn't face my boss, but Nina. She was grinning from ear to ear, dressed in her usual courtroom attire of a stylish suit and heels.

"You don't know how glad I am to see you." I held my chest with a laugh, and Nina chuckled.

"Right back at ya'—today has been crazy!" She stepped over the many articles of clothing strewn about the floor and gave me a hug.

"Tell me about it." I smirked, briefly setting the prison outfit down in order to touch Nina's bangs, which were recently cut for the show. "When was this damage done?" I inquired, disapprovingly.

Nina knew I never liked the idea of her hair being cut.

"Miranda." She sighed, being familiar with my ways. "C'mon, I think it's cute."

I shrugged. "Yeah, it's cute." I held up one hand before she could squeal with victory. "But *next time*, you need to demand braids, girl, like *moi*—natural, *and* cute."

Nina shook her head.

"Yeah, whatever, sis.'"

We both laughed, and Nina picked up the unfinished jumpsuit after scanning the worktable.

"Uh-oh," she said, noting the active needle and thread. "I'd better go before your tail gets whupped."

I smirked. "Yeah, no lie." I accepted the outfit, carefully taking

241

the needle. "Nina, we work on the same set, live on the same block, and hardly ever see each other." I chuckled lightly at our predicament.

Nina shrugged. "I know, but once the sweeps are over," she grabbed a cracker from what was left of my lunch on the table, popping it into her mouth as she walked backwards for the door, "You won't be able to get rid of me—oh!"

All of a sudden, one of Nina's stilettos got caught in a scarf on the floor, and she started to fall backwards.

Before I could react, another person appeared in the doorway, and in one swift motion, rushed forward to catch Nina from her fall.

My mouth went dry, and Nina looked up in surprise at her rescuer.

"Kevin?"

Ms. Davenport appeared, her chunky arms crossed over her chest as she placed one hand on Kevin's shoulder. "He's been trying to see you for a whole month now, Miranda. Don't make me get the security guards."

Kevin helped Nina back to her feet, and she straightened her suit, stepping away from him a little, looking very confused.

"No, it's okay. I'll show him out," I voiced reluctantly.

"Just make sure you get that suit done," pressed Ms. Davenport before leaving.

Oops.

Looking down, I quickly bent to retrieve the fallen outfit.

"Miranda, do you want me to stay?" Nina asked slowly, her voice fading in her discomfort.

I quickly shook my head. "I'll see you later, okay?"

"Okay," Nina replied hesitantly, and walked off.

I didn't look at Kevin, but continued with my sewing.

"Look, I know you're busy…" he began, watching me closely.

"Could you just hear me out?"

I did a slow burn, wishing he would go away, but remembering I would be getting off in only a few minutes. All I had to do was ignore him as the minutes ticked by, and I was free.

Kevin sighed, pulling at one of his short dreads. "Miranda, please—"

"Please *what?*" I returned hotly without a glance up at him, unable to keep silent any longer.

"We really need to talk."

I hesitated, but considered the situation. If I kept putting it off, he would only return to the studio again.

"Okay, here we are—what do you wanna talk about?" I asked quickly as we left the set for the employee parking lot, finally allowing Kevin to walk me to my car. (Although he was struggling to keep up with my intentionally-fast pace.)

"Well," he began slowly, glancing sideways at me, "I . . . want you to come with me to Atlanta."

I halted in my steps, finally turning to look at him. "What?" I shot in disbelief, shocked that Kevin was still singing the same tune.

Kevin took a deep breath and nodded, his coal-black, intent eyes watching me closely. "Yeah, I mean . . ." He chuckled. "I told you I'd wait a thousand years for you—maybe more."

I shook my head, looking away from his lopsided grin. "Kevin..." I sighed, not knowing what to say.

Don't let him get to you, Miranda!

"Miranda, listen," Kevin began seriously, running a hand along his dreads. "It wasn't right of me to leave you like I did, when I did. And I'm sorry." He sighed, kicking at the dirty concrete. "But . . . I can't get over you—I've known you since I was a kid, for as long as I can remember." He looked up hopefully at me. "I love you, and

I...wish we could be together, for the rest of our lives . . . like we planned." He laughed at a sudden thought. "Remember back when we played Romeo and Juliet, and how I asked you to marry me during one of the rehearsals? You thought I was crazy . . . but you *did* say you'd think about it." Kevin became serious again. "I can't see myself with anyone else, Miranda. . . please. . .?

While Kevin spoke, I had been thinking about our last argument—the things he had said. Hearing the Kevin I used to know and love once again, it seemed as though it was another person I had spoken with that night.

What was I supposed to do? What now? I did have to admit Kevin was right—we used to be so close. I had grown up automatically picturing myself with only one person whom I'd spend the rest of my life with . . . until recently.

Yet . . .

"You hurt me, Kevin," I finally spoke, my voice quiet.

Kevin lowered his head. "I'm so sorry," he murmured.

Frowning, I realized that I felt as though something was missing, as though I had forgotten something. My hand was fidgeting at my side, unable to find something to do. It didn't take me long to figure out what I was picturing in my grasp: my cane. I felt as though I needed my cane, as though I was crippled again. It was a scary feeling, but I tried to ignore it, not realizing just how much Kevin reminded me of my injury.

"I . . . I need time . . . to think, please." I pushed a few braids out of my face as the wind whipped around the tall surrounding buildings.

Kevin quickly nodded. "Of course, Miranda."

I did a lot of thinking for the next week. It didn't take me long to come to the conclusion that Kevin was perfect for me, and he pretty much always had been. There was just this one thing that kept causing me to reconsider my decision . . .

It was a rainy Sunday night that I sat on the edge of my bed, staring at the red clock display which read "7:30," my phone in one hand, feeling very much as my mom must have felt when she turned down Hollywood.

With one final sigh, I dialed his number.

"Hey, you called," Kevin's voice answered in a slightly rushed, eager tone after it had barely rung once.

I closed my eyes, resting my elbows on my knees and leaning forward. "Yeah, I called," I repeated quietly, the tap of the rain sounding like voices on my window.

Kevin remained silent after that, and I knew it was all on me now.

I kept my eyes closed, feeling the familiar sensation that an audience was watching me. "You used to say that I would do administration at your company . . ." I swallowed heavily, suddenly feeling afraid to voice the rest of what was on my heart. Kevin didn't pressure me to go on, though, and didn't say a word as I gathered the boldness to continue.

"I can't . . . I-I *won't* . . . marry you, unless I'm not behind a desk but on a dance floor . . . in a classroom . . . at least," I managed to finish, my voice hanging in the air.

I thought I caught Kevin chuckling. "Miranda," he began slowly, collectedly, "the arrangements have already been made for you to teach."

My jaw dropped slightly, and I pulled my legs underneath me. "Really?" I asked, breathless and dumbfounded.

Kevin smiled from the other line.

"I *promise.*"

Thirty-Seven

Jet

"Jet, man, you ready?"

I looked up from the newspaper in my hands, still mumbling the criteria for the last job advertisement I had read.

Jonathan opened the passenger door of his car and beckoned me inside.

Folding the paper, I got up and walked across the sidewalk to the car, sliding in with a dull sigh.

"Thanks," I said quietly after a moment as we rode along, and Jonathan shrugged.

"Don't worry about it."

I had been relying on public transportation, family or friends (the few I had left) to drive me around, since my license would be suspended until March of next year, two years after standing before the judge. I didn't exactly have anywhere to go, except for the unemployment agency or the park. It was strange that the park in which I used to freely jog, I now cleaned as volunteer service. Other than that, I went to church with Nana Jo.

I was flat-out broke. My name had been dragged in the dirt, and my departure from the football team was immediate. I was also kicked out of the university.

I wearily rubbed my chin as I stared out the window at the passing shops and markets, feeling the brush of stubble on my palm. Every day I thought of Miranda, and every day I remembered the last time I had seen her in person. If I thought the guilt of hitting an unknown person was bad, the knowledge of just *who* that person turned out to be was almost unbearable. More than anything, it was the drama my actions created that hurt the most. I would probably never see Miranda again. Any and all chances of a future with her were destroyed.

"Nana says she's makin' dinner tonight and wants you to come," Jonathan said quietly from the driver's seat, keeping his solemn eyes on the road.

I didn't reply and only sighed again, tapping at the empty wallet in my pocket.

Nana Jo didn't judge me. She didn't want me to distance myself, and proposed that I stay with her until things blew over. But I didn't want to burden her, and instead decided it would be better if I room with Luke and pay him back as soon as I was able.

Jonathan pulled the car up to Nana Jo's house, and I alighted into the crisp, springtime air.

When Jon and I stepped into the kitchen, we were met with the familiar smell of a home-cooked meal, and Nana Jo's warm hug.

After we had finished dessert, the three of us sat in the den with mugs of coffee, and rain began to pour onto the house. Jonathan sat on the sofa across from me, I took a seat on a cushy foot stool, and Nana Jo eased into Pap's old recliner.

247

"How did the job searching go, Jet?" Nana Jo spoke first, her voice quiet as she leaned forward slightly.

I stared down at the swirling coffee in my mug. "Not so good. . . as usual."

Jonathan cleared his throat. "Why don't you let me set you up with some friends of mine —"

"Law friends?" I quickly interrupted, frowning severely.

Jonathan sighed defensively. "Well, you've always been picky, Jet." He shrugged. "If it's not football then it's not a possibility—"

"That's not true," I shot, my voice rising slightly as I gripped the mug tighter, my eyes lifting to meet my brother's condescending stare.

Nana Jo sighed.

I shook my head, not feeling like arguing with my brother that night.

Clearing her throat, Nana Jo turned to Jonathan, who was distantly fiddling with one of the tassels on the sofa. "Jon, did you talk to her again?"

Jon hesitated, and I looked up slowly, furrowing my brow as I watched them.

"Um, yeah . . . she did call me back," Jonathan replied softly, avoiding my questioning eyes.

Jonathan, unlike me, didn't go out with just any girl at any time. It was a big thing when a girl was announced concerning Jon. And yet, for some reason, this girl was obviously supposed to be a secret.

"You're seein' somebody?" I ventured, wondering why I wasn't in on everything.

Jonathan glanced up at me, then nodded silently.

I turned to Nana Jo for an answer. "Well, why's everybody so secretive about it?" I laughed shortly. "Shouldn't this be a good thing?"

"It is, Jet," Nana Jo spoke abruptly as she set her mug down on the coffee table.

I smiled wryly in disbelief at everyone's peculiar actions. "So who is she?"

Jonathan seemed to take a deep breath, and I shifted my gaze to him. I wondered what could possibly be so wrong about the girl Jonathan, the perfect guy, chose.

"I'm . . ." Jon shifted his jaw as he stared down at the floor, "I'm thinking about seeing Nina Phillips."

Thirty-Eight
Miranda

I brushed the drops of perspiration from my forehead as my chest burned slightly, though I was unable to suppress a bit of a smile. It had been a long time since I had been so winded, and though I was slowly getting used to it, I liked it. The feeling of my muscles energizing, the air exploding throughout my lungs, the sweat cooling on my skin; it was everything I had been afraid to dream of since my accident.

I was back, and loving it.

After reaching down to pull my workout slacks up to my knees, and brushing some dirt from the tape wrapped around the balls of my feet, I pressed the earphones into my ears and tapped "play" on my iPod. As an energetic CeCe Winans song played, I prepared to execute a series of leaps across the floor. I tried to do them as powerfully as I used to.

The East Studio branch hadn't been used for a long time, and I had found it once while completing an errand Ms. Davenport sent me on. My apartment wasn't exactly the best place to practice, thus I began my training as soon as possible in the abandoned studio. I would shed my work clothes and change into jazz slacks.

Once I had reached the far wall, I paused, then turned to leap back again, but halted at the sight of a figure in one of the dimly-lit doorways.

"Not bad!"

The person walked forward and I grinned sheepishly, pulling the earphones out as I slowly walked over.

"Thanks, Nina," I panted.

Nina smiled, stepping toward the middle of the floor to stand against one of the many industrial pillars. "You weren't joking, were you?"

I carefully lowered myself to sit on the floor, leaning back on my palms as I looked up at her. "What do you mean?"

Nina shrugged, sliding down as well, crossing her stiletto-bound feet at the ankles. "About dance—those leaps were lookin' good."

I laughed shortly, stretching my legs before me and leaning forward a little to rub my knees. "I've still got a long way to go."

Nina retorted, "You're just as hard on yourself as you were before."

I shrugged, starting to bend one knee. "I have to be." I drew my breath in sharply, feeling the aching in my joint. "Wow, my body's about to kill me for this . . ."

Concerned, Nina warned, "Be careful, Mira—no need to take this too far and hurt yourself."

"Nina—"

"Hey, I'm just sayin.'" She held up her hands, and I sighed.

"I know, and I'm okay . . ." I traced my finger along one of my

251

scars, a smile forming on my lips as I looked down. "You know, . . .
I really like it—dancing again . . . I mean, it feels so good—like . . ."
I chuckled, "I dunno,' like eating somethin' you haven't had in a
long time, somethin' you loved . . ." My voice faded, and I sensed
Nina smiling as she watched me.

"Not to mention the kick-butt scars you have to prove just how
much you went through to get here," she noted, and we shared a
laugh.

A silence filled the air, and I yawned as I tucked my iPod away
into my purse, Nina stretching her neck from a long day of work.

"I'm glad you're happy, Miranda."

I looked up at her with a light smile. "Thanks, Nina—me, too."
Rubbing the back of my neck, I knew there was something I needed
to tell her. "I, um . . . I talked to Kevin again last night . . ."

Nina paused, her copper, makeup-lined eyes watching me closely.
"What'd he want?"

I nervously swallowed, realizing I hadn't ever actually thought
about how Nina felt about Kevin. We didn't talk about him often.

I tried to brush my anxiety off.

"Well," I began slowly, trying to choose the right words, "he . . .
uh, he apologized... And we talked. He told me his offer was still
open . . ." I looked up at Nina, who was remaining dangerously
quiet, staring down at her hands. I inhaled a deep breath before
continuing, "So I told him that I wouldn't go with him to ATL . . .
unless I would be dancing—teaching."

"And he said 'of course I'll let you dance,' and now you're going
to Atlanta—just like that?"

I shifted my jaw, feeling apprehensive at how precise Nina was
with her replies. "Um . . . yeah," I managed to say as calmly as
possible, although growing all the more nervous.

Nina nodded slowly, then shrugged with a sigh. "Miranda, Kevin
never . . ." Her voice trailed, and she shook her head as she finally

looked up at me. "He never wanted you to teach—"

"That was then, Nina, it's different no—"

Concerned, Nina interrupted, "Miranda, Kevin has his own agenda, and he'll do anything and promise anything to make sure that agenda's carried out."

My face became flushed as I looked away. "What are you tryin' to say, Nina?" I asked, struggling to keep my tone down.

My sister seemed to take a deep breath, and when she spoke, her voice was firm and sincere, "I know how Kevin is, okay? There are some things about him that you don't know—things he won't tell you . . ." She sighed again, wearily. "When we worked together last year, right after your surgery, he asked me if I wanted to go to lunch with him and some friends. Obviously, he and I weren't exactly on good terms because of how he walked away from you, but I went anyway, since a few other friends of mine were going, too.

"I left with my friends, then I realized I had forgotten something, so I went back. When I was within earshot of his table, I could hear them talking. They brought up the ATL agency he's been trying to start." Nina's tone darkened after a pause. "Someone had asked him how the funding was going, and Kevin said that he would . . . 'pull some strings, do some swindling,' as he put it." Nina sighed. "I thought he was joking at first, but then I realized they weren't.

"After that, my worst fears were confirmed . . . because he started bragging about how the man who owned his sponsor company is skilled in making 'fast cash,' along with a lot of other things that I don't even wanna repeat... " Nina shook her head, looking me in the eye. "Kevin's about to run a corrupt business, Miranda, one that you don't need to be a part of."

As she spoke, I stared down at my hands, at my legs and the scars. I didn't want to believe her, though I knew she would never lie over something like this. But still, it hurt . . . it hurt me to think that I had gotten the wool pulled over my eyes once again. I felt so...stupid. I mean, how many more times would I have to be the one getting fooled?

I was tired, and this was the last straw. It was time for *me* to be on top of things, for a change. "Why didn't you tell me all of this if he's so 'corrupt?' " I asked quietly, though my voice trembled slightly with anger.

Nina sighed again, twisting one of the buttons of her pinstripe jacket.

"It wasn't exactly the best time, Miranda—you were about to have physical therapy. . ." She shrugged. "Besides, I thought you wouldn't want to have anything to do with Kevin anyway. . ."

"Who says?" I quickly shot, feeling an infuriated lump forming in my throat. "You act like you know everything I want, Nina!"

Nina's jaw dropped in disbelief. "Miranda, c'mon—"

"No!" I stood up, angrily stomping the floor as pain shot through my legs for moving so hastily. "I'm tired of all of this! Of my stupid injury, of—of being ruthlessly lied to, of having to learn how to dance all over again!" I swallowed, clenching my jaw as I glared at her. "And of people who think they can run my life." I shook my head in frustration. "I'm tired of this, and I don't have to deal with it!

"Why is it okay for everyone else to live their lives in peace and freedom, while I have to go from beat-down to beat-down?! I can't live this way, Nina!"

"Nobody said you had to, Miranda!" Nina rose as well, placing her hands on her hips as she matched my tone. "And I can't help the fact that you've had your letdowns, and I've never acted like I enjoy that, but you need to start distinguishing between the real people in your life and the fake ones!"

I smiled bitterly as I crossed my arms over my chest.

"Okay—alright. Fine." I threw up my hands. "You couldn't help but squeeze that last command in, could you?" I narrowed my eyes.

"Well, I'll be sure to follow it—don't you worry." I bent, snatching up my things. "'Cause this time, I'm making my *own* decision."

"Almost there." Kevin pressed a Styrofoam cup of cheap coffee in the cup holder between us as he slid back into the car. With a sigh, he twisted the keys in the ignition.

I blinked a couple of times as the motor roared to life, my squinting eyes gradually adjusting to the loud, eerie fluorescent glow of the gas station lights overhead.

"Tired?" He glanced over at me as he maneuvered back onto the main highway.

I yawned as I sat up a little more, my cell phone falling out of my lap to the floor as I did so. "Yeah," I chuckled as I retrieved it. "I fell asleep on a text convo with Bri."

Kevin laughed, reaching for his coffee to take a sip.

We were driving to Atlanta. Kevin fueled up his car and came for me at about three p.m. on Friday, when I got off of work. Kevin insisted we make it to the dinner he had planned for us with all of the executives I had yet to meet in a few hours.

"Bri getting boring these days?"

Kevin chuckled at his own joke, and we continued on through southeastern Tennessee as the clock neared six and the sun flirted with the mountainous horizon.

I re-braided some of my hair as we rode in silence, worrying that there would be barely time for a shower and makeup as it was.

I felt him glance over at me every now and then.

"You should wear it down," he commented after a moment, and I nodded as I moved on to another braid, watching the scenery.

"Yeah, I will."

Kevin set his cup back in the holder and shook his head, reaching up to smooth his own recently-shaved scalp. "No, I mean loose—no braids. You should try it sometime."

I looked at him somewhat indignantly. "What, you no like my braids anymore?" I asked jokingly, and Kevin shrugged, smiling only a little.

My own smiled faded. I guess I wanted him to say, "Of course not, Miranda, I just want you to try something new." But he didn't. I shifted my jaw slightly, turning back to the window. *You've known this guy since you were a toddler, Miranda. This isn't the first time we've disagreed. Now get it together—stop being so sensitive.*

I jumped at the sudden rumble on my lap, and I quickly picked up my phone.

Thinkin about u sis

I turned off my phone after reading the text, not wanting to think about Nina or our argument. I was off to Atlanta with everyone's blessing but hers, and as much as I tried to ignore it, it did bother me. Maybe it was the fact that I knew she wouldn't lie to me, or that our relationship had practically been severed . . .

Kevin fumbled with the radio, and I swallowed as I persuaded myself to turn the phone on again.

My thumb trembled a little as it hovered over the screen, ready to type a reply to the text message.

One question had been lingering in my thoughts, keeping me up at night, since the argument with Nina. I was afraid to ask it, but it was driving me crazy not knowing the answer. As to why I thought Nina would know it, I'm not sure. Maybe it was because she suddenly "knew" Kevin better than I did . . .

Whatever it was, I knew I had noticed something that I had been too afraid to address for a while now—especially during the hours spent with Kevin on the road.

Do u think Kev is jealous of me? If so, y?

I typed so quickly that Kevin glanced over at me. I was afraid, not only of what Nina's answer might be, but of the question itself. Why did I really have to ask? Was it just because I was tired of the burden it put on me?

BUZZ.

I jumped. According to the clock on the console, only two minutes had passed since I sent my message off.

I looked at my phone, and the glowing "1 New Message" icon seemed to be jumping off of the screen. My finger touched the area of the screen that would open the text, yet the moment I did so, Kevin reached over to take hold of my left hand. He smiled at me as he brought it up to his lips.

I smiled back at him uneasily.

I swiftly locked the cell again, unable to read Nina's reply.

"You almost ready?"

"Yeah, it's open!"

Kevin walked inside of my hotel room upon my invitation, and I came out of the back room to meet him, twisting one of the chandelier earrings on.

"Look at you, Mr. Clean," I joked as I reached up to rub his unusually-bare scalp, still not used to the absence of his mini-dreads.

"Hey," Kevin pretended to complain before we closed in for a quick kiss. He chuckled when we drew away, and I adjusted his black tie, though he had tied it almost perfectly. "Makin' fun of me already—how come you can look good but I can't?"

I laughed at his joke, but as the phone suddenly rang, I couldn't help but read into his statement.

"Hello?" I asked as I sat down to answer it on the couch, reaching down to adjust the buckle on my t-strap heels.

Kevin helped himself to the candy dish as he watched me take

257

the call, stuffing one hand in the pocket of his pinstripe suit.

"Ms. Phillips? This is Denny with Guest Services."

I rubbed the satin of my classic black evening gown, crossing my legs and clearing my throat as I replied, "Yes, what can I do for you?"

Denny spoke slowly, carefully.

"Well, there's a woman here at the desk who says she has something to give you—an artist by the name of . . ." the clerk seemed to hold the phone away for a second, "An artist by the name of Julia McPherson. She's from Philadelphia and says it's very important that she sees you. Obviously we respect your privacy and want to check with you first before we send anyone."

After some contemplation, I said, "Sure. You can send her up."

Kevin, who had been watching me closely, inquisitively, stepped forward to join me on the couch as I hung up the phone.

"Who's comin' up here?" he asked, touching my hand.

But I rose as soon as he sat, thoughtfully picking at my lip despite the gloss I had just applied.

"Julia McPherson . . ." I replied distantly, wondering what she wanted.

Kevin shrugged, his piercing eyes leaving me for a change to rest on his watch. "Well, who's that?"

"An artist," I answered shortly as I stood before a mirror on the wall, parting my braids on the side and sweeping a few over one eye. With all of Kevin's persistent interrogating, I was liking my braids more and more.

"Loose" indeed. It's a good thing you're attractive and *a dancer, or else we wouldn't have been an item to start with!*

"Oh . . ." Kevin, shifted his determined jaw, tossing a peppermint from hand to hand. "What does she want with you?"

I sighed heavily, beginning to grow annoyed with his questioning, and I turned to face him as my voice rose. "Kevin, do you *have* to be

258

so—"

"Wait!" Kevin held up his hand as he stood to his feet, the other reaching to his inside jacket pocket. "Now before you bite my head off," he withdrew a tiny black-velvet box with a golden clasp, and extended it to me, "let me at least allow the record to show that I managed to give you the ring *before* you pushed me out the window to my death."

Kevin chuckled, watching my expression change from exasperation to bewilderment as I opened the case to reveal a large, stunning diamond surrounded by a host of sapphires atop a solid-glass band.

After the initial shock from the extravagant rock in my hands wore off, I swallowed and opened my mouth slightly, not knowing what to say.

In that moment, any and all reservation and annoyance faded, and I threw my arms around his neck in jubilation.

The doorbell quickly interrupted, though, and I sighed as we drew away. I had started off to answer the door, when Kevin swiftly grabbed my hand and slid the ring onto my finger. "Can't forget that, now can we?" he asked with a lopsided grin.

I was still smiling as I opened the door to a bellhop and a middle-aged, white-haired woman standing slightly behind him, a hefty, draped canvas at her side.

"Ms. Phillips, Mrs. Julia McPherson," the young bellhop introduced us, and I held out my hand to Julia.

"It's very nice to finally meet you, Ms. Phillips," Julia spoke warmly, her bright smile accentuating her youthful face. "I live in Philadelphia, just like you."

I couldn't help but grin in return at her amiable nature, and held the door for her to come inside as Kevin reached into his wallet to tip the bellhop.

"Likewise, Mrs. McPher—"

"Oh no, dear," Julia protested, holding up her hand as she toted the canvas in with her, "just call me 'Julia'—it keeps me young." She laughed, her clear eyes shining, and I smiled.

Kevin cleared his throat, having become idle after doing his duty to the bellhop.

"Oh, Julia, this is Kevin Cannon—my fiancé. Kevin, this is Julia McPherson," I introduced them, and Kevin nodded with a polite smile as he shook Julia's hand.

"Please sit down," I offered, but Julia shook her head.

"Oh no, thank you, but I can't stay long." She glanced at the unexplained canvas at her side. "I'm sure you're wondering what I'm doing here," she began, but was interrupted by Kevin.

He cleared his throat. "Well, by the way, Mrs. McPherson, I'm Miranda's manager and I'm sure we could discuss this at a later date—we were just about to leave for an important dinner—"

"*But it can wait*, Kevin," I quickly cut in before he could say another word, smiling at Julia apologetically. "Please continue," I said to her as she observed us nervously, sensing the tension in the air.

"Yes, of course. I will be brief." Julia kept her friendly smile as she unveiled the painting, and my eyes widened as I stared at it. "You see, this work is one of my self-proclaimed 'masterpieces,' and I take great pride in it. It started out as a painting that was soon to be thrown away, unfinished, until I was given some inspiration by a very . . ." she hesitated, "caring and creative person. They wanted to get it to you year before last as a Christmas gift, but were . . . unable to. When I finished it, I promised them I would make sure you received it." Julia paused, looking on fondly at her piece. "This is, like I said, one of my personal favorites, but it belongs to you now—it always has, I think," she finished with a smile, her tone almost motherly.

"Looks kinda' like you, Miranda," Kevin noted, tilting his head as he studied the painting. He popped a peppermint into his mouth.

With all of its careful lines and lovingly-selected colors, Julia was right in deeming her work a masterpiece. But I was altogether speechless, *honored*, to see that I was the subject of such a painting.

A dancer, seated on the floor of a sunset-kissed dance room, had her head lifted and eyelids closed, her face bathed in the glow of the peach-orange light, her braids dangling down her back. There was just enough of a smile hinting at her lips to cause you to look again—almost like the *Mona Lisa*. She was seated, with one knee bent upwards and the other tucked beneath her, but her arms poised in such a way that it was suggested that she was in the process of standing up.

"Wow . . ." was all I could whisper, but that was before my eyes rested on what was probably the most poignant element of the scene: a cane, abandoned only inches away from the dancer's palm, as though she had left it behind.

"It's called *Her Second Wind*," Julia answered my silent question, looking on with a wistful smile.

I swallowed, feeling the lump in my throat.

Her Second Wind . . . My *Second Wind . . . I know exactly who this is from.*

"I . . . um . . ." When I couldn't find the words of thanks, I hugged Julia instead.

"So why did you come all the way from Philadelphia just to give her that?" Kevin interjected, taking the painting from Julia and eyeballing it.

"Well, I've been trying to track this lady down for a while now, but I also have family in town," Julia answered graciously.

Kevin handed the painting back to me, then reached for the doorknob.

"Oh. Okay. Well, it was nice meeting you."

Once Julia had gone, I slowly lowered myself down to the sofa, holding the painting—the portrait—on my lap. I gazed down at it, trying to keep from crying.

Jet had asked her to make it for me—finish it for me. It was because of him that it was now *my* painting, as Julia had so proudly called it. The picture touched me a great deal. It was the most beautiful thing I had ever owned; I didn't quite know what to do or say. Holding something in my hands that was made with such care, and given to me by someone I cared about so much, made me feel strangely alone in the Atlanta hotel, even though my soon-to-be husband stood only a few feet away.

"You ready, Miranda?" Kevin probed, and I snapped out of my reverie as I silently rose and followed him out the door.

Thirty-Nine
Miranda

"Now remember, Mr. Singleton's *the* man—the one you wanna talk to the most and socialize with, as well as his wife and son, Tye. Kelly's his girlfriend, but don't talk to her too much about our engagement—she's sensitive about that since Tye hasn't popped the question yet. And whatever you do, don't let Mitchell bring up his old high school football stories—he's Tye's uncle and will bore you to death."

My head swam with names and personalities as we stepped into the marble-floored, gold-buttoned elevator that would lift us up to the Singleton penthouse.

"Okay, so I want to talk to Mr. Singleton, and . . . Mitchell is . . . who, again?"

Kevin sighed as he pressed the "54" button in the empty elevator. "Mitchell is Tye's uncle—Mrs. Singleton's younger brother. But he's just like a brother to Tye."

Visibly overwhelmed, I was unable to keep up with so much information about people whom I hadn't even met. "Alright, alright. So whose girlfriend is Kelly?"

"*Tye's*, Miranda, *Tye's*."

"Oka-ay." I sighed heavily, turning to check my reflection in the mirrored walls, making sure my navy-blue eyeshadow hadn't managed to melt off under the hot lamps above. My stomach was dreading meeting people who knew so much about me through Kevin, and the warm, lengthy elevator ride wasn't exactly helping.

When the door finally opened, Kevin took my hand and we walked into the silent, empty hallway—it too, lined with marble, gold, and plenty of mirrors. At least it was cool, though, unlike the elevator. We arrived at extravagantly-decorated, oak-framed double doors at the end of the hallway. I could only imagine what the *interior* must look like . . .

"Alright, here we go," Kevin stated quietly as he reached up to ring the doorbell. "Just be the Miranda everyone loves, and it'll all go smoothly."

I couldn't help but glance sideways at Kevin, watching a queer sort of smile light his face as he patted my hand, looking straight ahead while adjusting his flawless, black tie.

And just who is she? How about the Miranda I really *am?*

The door opened, and I held my breath.

"Good evening, Mr. Cannon," the young maid greeted. "Miss Phillips," she added, her tone changing in a way that I couldn't understand, and she almost seemed to falter. "Please come in."

She was only a few years younger than Kevin and I, with micro-braids similar to my own, a small frame and a benign smile. There was something graceful about her, though . . . something artistic.

264

Kevin merely nodded politely, and I murmured a last-minute "good evening" in response to her greeting, thinking it rude that he hadn't done so himself.

We stood in a mid-sized, candlelit entryway as the maid closed the door behind us. The walls were painted in a burnt orange. A sculpture of a dancer sat on a black, wooden table to the left, and rustic-gold chargers rested on the wall on either side of a large, oval mirror.

Light laughter and soft music floated in from beyond the hallway up ahead, and I felt my stomach tense as Kevin checked his reflection one more time.

"May I take your jacket, Miss?"

I removed my light jacket from my shoulders myself. I didn't really like being waited on hand and foot. "Oh, thank you." I smiled graciously, and the maid murmured a quiet "you're welcome" as she accepted the jacket and placed it over one arm.

"Please follow me—*hors d'oeuvres* are just being served."

Kevin smiled reassuringly as he placed my hand on his arm, and we followed the maid through the dim, sconce-lit hallway toward the light coming from a bend up ahead. While looking forward, I noticed the maid, walking with a limp.

"Polio," Kevin whispered in my ear.

I frowned, and he added, "Danielle was a dancer once—probably why she was trippin' so much back there to meet you. You've got yourself quite a fan base among the disabled community, Miranda." He seemed to be stifling a chuckle. "If she gives you any trouble, just let Singleton know—"

"Of course not!" I responded firmly, looking at him in annoyance and disbelief, wondering why he would say such a thing.

"There they are! C'mon in, you two."

The hearty welcome came as soon as Kevin and I turned the corner behind Danielle, as she skillfully disappeared with the jacket.

265

"Miranda Phillips, we thought we'd never meet you," said the voice again, and I saw that it belonged to a tall, husky, light-skinned African American man, with a round nose, bright eyes and a booming voice.

The living room was just as beautiful as the taste of the grandeur I had seen on the way up, and I felt strangely self-conscious as conversation ceased and all eyes shifted to Kevin and me. There were more people there than he had told me to expect.

The man who had greeted us walked over, bringing an elegant lady at his side.

"Well, Kevin, I have to say she's even more beautiful than she looks in pictures and interviews." He grinned broadly, speaking to Kevin but looking at me, extending his hand. "Marshall Singleton. It's nice to finally meet you, Miranda."

I nodded, smiling appropriately as we shook hands.

"Likewise, Mr. Singleton," I replied as Kevin looked on with a proud sort of smile, his arms crossed in front of him.

"And my wife, Aisha," Mr. Singleton added, gesturing toward his wife.

"Hello, Miranda—it's so nice to meet you."

I turned to Mrs. Singleton, shaking her delicately-extended hand.

"Nice to meet you, Mrs. Singleton," I returned, noting how much she reminded me of my old dance teacher from high school.

She was tall, like her husband, with smooth hair cut stylishly close to her scalp. Her complexion was a medium brown, and her dark eyes small and defined. I knew she was a dancer just by looking at her, with her long, graceful limbs and straight posture—posture which only years of serious ballet training could teach.

Both husband and wife were in their late thirties, and held a business-like yet artistic quality about them. I was reminded of my parents in those traits, but that was as far as the familiarity reached.

We gathered closer to the rest of the group, where I met Tye, the

266

Singleton's son who was about my age, taking mostly after his father in looks. There was also his girlfriend, Kelly, a nice yet quiet girl, and finally Jeff and three or four more friends of the Singletons. I knew Jeff already from high school, and he was a close friend of Kevin's. He was a dancer as well with bronzed-olive skin and a handsome face.

I tried to stick close to Kevin as we circulated throughout the group of guests. When he was off discussing sports with some of the men, I stayed back, hovering around the tall fireplace, watching Mrs. Singleton chat with her other guests. Jeff walked over to me after noting my aloofness.

"Well, Miranda, here you are." Jeff smiled, holding a drink in one hand and smoothing his cornrowed hair with the other.

I nodded with a light smile. Jeff was always an easy person to get along with, and he was good at including everyone and making friends. I often told him that he needed to pass that trait on to his best friend sometime.

"Yeah, crazy, huh?"

"So how do you like it—ATL?" he continued.

"Oh, uh . . . yeah, it's . . ."

"Not Philly?" he guessed, and I hung my head, not realizing how much I was allowing my true opinion to shine through. Jeff chuckled comfortingly, noting my sudden change in expression.

"It's okay—I had to adjust to it, too." He shrugged, kicking lightly at the floor. "I hear you're in New York now. *No Way's* doin' pretty well, huh? My little sis' is a big fan."

We both laughed and grew silent with a pause in our conversation, a question weighing on my mind.

"Um, Jeff . . . how's this whole studio idea of Kev's sounding to you?" I tried to sound casual, and watched Jeff closely.

"I think it's pretty cool," he replied slowly, lost in thought, then smiled apologetically. "Sorry, I'm actually just now getting back from a long tour I did with my troupe in Europe, so I'm not too up on things here."

I nodded with an understanding smile as I twisted the engagement ring on my finger, feeling a little reassured.

You wouldn't be in on any 'corruption' anyway—you were always an innocent person.

An eruption of laughter sounded suddenly from the group of men on the other side of the room, and a call soon followed, "Jeff, come here!"

Before leaving, he congratulated me on my engagement to Kevin.

I watched the guests socializing for about five minutes more. I felt ridiculous standing by myself, but I was too terrified to move or speak. Mrs. Singleton glanced at me several times, and when she looked as though she was about to walk over, I quickly headed down the hallway Danielle had brought Kevin and I through. I thought I remembered seeing a bathroom.

Once the door had closed on the laughter and chatting, I felt only a little more at ease. I didn't move for a lengthy moment in the small, marble powder room, my ears tuning in to the smooth jazz music playing in a speaker overhead.

I turned to the gold-leaf, framed mirror, carefully watching my reflection. I didn't toy with my hair or check my makeup, but just stood there, and asked myself, *"Do you really know what you're doing?"*

When I failed to answer my own question, I swallowed, slowly looking down as I rested my palms on the sink.

"Kevin's about to run a corrupt business, Miranda, one that you don't even need to be a part of anyway."

I closed my eyes, trying not to remember the honesty in Nina's tone when she and I last spoke. But her voice rang in my ears, and I sighed.

" . . . You need to start distinguishing between the real people in your life and the fake ones . . ."

268

" 'This time, I'm making my own decision.' "

My final words echoed through my mind, and I held my head before finally slamming my fist down on the sink top.

"Lord," I whispered slowly, my voice trembling as the sounds of laughter slithered under the door. "I don't want to pray this . . . not at all." I swallowed again, feeling scared and confused. "But I need to know," taking a deep breath, I quietly continued, "if Kevin really isn't right for me . . . if-if Nina was right . . ." I breathed a shaky sigh, trying to restrain the eager tears as I looked down at my ring, "then I want You to show me—I want You to show me exactly why I shouldn't be with him. I want You to expose him for what he might really be, no holding back . . ." I blinked the tear out, "even if it crushes me. And if You do," I lifted my head, staring at my reflection once again, "then I'll leave here and go back home."

I stood in the hallway after leaving the bathroom, still trembling a little. If I thought I was terrified before, now I was absolutely dreading going back in to the party. But I didn't regret my prayer.

"Miranda, there you are—they're about to give a toast," Mrs. Singleton said as I re-entered the living room, and quickly led me into the dining room where everyone was starting to seat themselves.

Kevin took my hand as soon as he saw me, and he frowned in concern.

"Where were you? I thought you'd left for a second there."

I didn't answer him.

Mr. Singleton cleared his throat as he held up a glass at the head of the table.

"Friends and loved ones, I would like to give a toast," he grinned his abnormally-wide smile, his eyes roaming over the faces before him, "to Kevin and Miranda, our newest faces in the business, as they start their life together. And tonight, we welcome Miss Miranda Phillips, Administrative Chairwoman of the Golden Productions empire . . ."

I don't think I even heard the rest of Mr. Singleton's toast, but altogether, glasses clinked and light applause sounded. Kevin wrapped his arms around me with a kiss on my cheek as I tried to keep from choking on the drink I robotically raised to my lips.

Administrative Chairwoman? Had I heard him correctly?

Everyone sat down to dinner, which was served by Danielle and another maid. The food was delicious and the atmosphere light and joyous, yet I was unable to enjoy any of it. It wasn't the place to talk to Kevin, to ask him what Mr. Singleton meant by "Administrative Chairwoman."

When Kevin began explaining to one of the guests how we met as toddlers, I swallowed and excused myself, unable to bear sitting at the table with such troubling news on my mind.

Kevin must have decided to catch up with me this time, since I heard him excusing himself behind me.

"Miranda!" he called in a low voice when I was halfway down the entryway hall. "Where are you going?!"

I halted when he grabbed my arm, and faced him.

"What happened to dancing—teaching?" I came straight to the point, my voice clear, firm and demanding.

Kevin threw up his hands.

"What are you talking about?"

"You forgot already?" I shook my head with a sigh, placing my hands on my hips. "You promised me I would be teaching dance—not an 'administrative chairwoman' or whatever he called it in there!"

"Okay, okay, okay," Kevin quickly replied, trying to calm me down with a nervous glance behind him. "Listen. Apparently, Singleton got it wrong. There must have been a problem with our communication—a-a simple misunderstanding—"

"Kevin," I lifted a hand, briefly closing my eyes. "I want you to be

270

honest with me," I pleaded softly, and he sighed.

"When have I not been, Miranda?"

"C'mon, Kevin . . ." I sighed heavily. "There have been times, and you and I both know—"

"Wait a minute, Miranda," Kevin quickly cut in, shaking his head with a frown. "If you're trying to pin somethin' on me from the past, then that's not even fair." He shrugged in frustration. "It's like ever since the whole Jet thing, you've been comparing me to him or something. Well, I'm not him, Miranda—I never hurt you the way *he* did, I never would have—"

"What does he have to do with this, Kevin?!" I shot in disbelief. "You're the one who brought him into this, not me!"

"Well then why is it that every time I turn around, you're annoyed with me. Even *before* homeboy turned on you, you were actin' like this!"

Unable to respond, I turned away from him, feeling hurt by the argument, though I knew it would come someday. Everything had been building up to it for a while now.

"Miranda," Kevin sighed, speaking softer this time, "I'm sorry. I just . . . I want you to trust me. I don't know how we're gonna make this work if you don't." He rubbed his forehead. "And I hate to bring Jet into this, but it's true—I didn't hurt you like he did, Miranda. He kept the truth from you and acted as though he was gonna be there for you all the while. He put himself over you—his own feelings over yours. You deserved the truth, but he gave you a lie. You weren't free with him, but you are with me." Kevin watched me before hanging his head. "And I'll clear everything up with Singleton, because I love you, and I want your dreams to be reached."

I swallowed.

Kevin was right. He was actually the first person who had pointed out exactly how Jet had treated me—the only person brave

271

enough to say it in my presence. And somehow, it felt reassuring to know that he had realized what Jet had done. It showed how much he really did care for me . . . right?

Slowly, I turned back around, and he waited silently, hopefully, for me to speak.

"I love you too, Kevin." My voice was weary, yet sincere, and Kevin smiled as he took my hands in his, raising them up to his lips.

"How 'bout we go back to this dinner?"

I finally smiled, suddenly feeling a lot better—reassured and at peace with everything.

"Okay."

Taking my hand in his, Kevin and I walked back to the party and guests, and the dinner progressed on a lighter note.

After all of the other guests left, Kevin and I conversed with the Singletons in the den. They were interesting people, and I admit that I enjoyed speaking with them. But as midnight approached, Kevin announced that we should leave, and we rose while saying our thanks for the evening.

"Miranda, let me show you those photos from the Alvin Ailey show before you leave," Mrs. Singleton offered, and I accepted as she led me to a nicely-decorated, well-equipped studio off the living room.

"Wow, this is nice," I commented as I stepped inside. Mrs. Singleton smiled, opening a closet and withdrawing a box.

"Why, thank you. Marshall insisted we add one—for the clients, you know. Here you go." She handed me a small stack of photos from the box. "The first ones are from the New York show, and the others were taken during a rehearsal—I actually have to take a call really quickly, but I'll be back before you leave."

I thanked her, and stood alone in the studio after she left, sifting through the photos, secretly dreaming of what it must be like to tour with such a renowned dance troupe.

The sound of footsteps came from the hall outside of the studio, but I didn't look up, guessing them to belong to some maids. I heard familiar laughter and voices after a moment, and assumed Mr. Singleton was speaking with Kevin in private—perhaps Kevin was clearing up the confusion from dinner.

Smiling lightly, I set the photos down on a desk and caught sight of a clock. It was half-past twelve, and I was beginning to get a little tired. Sighing, I left the studio to return to the living room and ask Kevin if he was ready to go.

When I was within a few feet of the opening that would lead me to the living room, I paused, hearing Kevin and Mr. Singleton speaking to each other in low voices.

"It was a dinner to remember, alright." Mr. Singleton was chuckling, then became serious. "You did straighten her out, didn't you—work some Cannon charm?"

I felt my heart stop, and froze.

"Yeah," Kevin sighed wearily. "It took some doing, but I've got her thinkin' she'll be teaching again—told her there was a mistake. All we need to do is get her to sign the contract, now."

Mr. Singleton sighed blissfully.

"Yes, this certainly will make our job easier promotion-wise."

Kevin let out a complacent chuckle.

"No lie," he agreed. "You don't know how long I had to chase after her to get her back. It was absolutely ridiculous."

Mr. Singleton laughed.

"Well, we needed her celebrity—surgery or not." He paused, his tone icy. "It's a shame she had it, you know. This new freedom's got her acting like she runs the world." He laughed acrimoniously. "And we can't have that at Golden Productions, soon to be the most powerful Christian production company in the country."

Kevin snickered, and I had to hold the wall as the hallway seemed to shift.

"No, we can't," he chimed. "We need a crippled Miranda to pull this off—the sob story's much more gripping," he spoke sarcastically, the words sliding off of his tongue like oil, and they both laughed.

"Hey, maybe you're onto something there, Cannon," Mr. Singleton joked.

Their voices faded as they moved off to another room.

I held my head, feeling sick to my stomach yet glad that they had walked off, since I couldn't bear to hear another word. No tears escaped my eyes—I was too shocked to cry.

I finally moved, hurrying for the front door. The trip down the elevator and luxurious halls was a blur. When I made it outside of the building, I summoned a cab and rode back to the hotel. I didn't pause to gather my thoughts until I stood against the door to my room, holding my forehead as my thoughts collided.

I couldn't believe it; it was simply too much to take in. And to think I had actually trusted Kevin.

I started forward for the bedroom, eager to pack and be on my way to the airport, but paused suddenly at a beeping noise coming from the coffee table on my right.

Startled, I went over to see what it was.

Hidden behind the candy dish sat my cell phone, which I had forgotten when Kevin and I left. I sighed, about to toss it and worry about charging the battery later, but paused, my heart leaping at a thought.

Slowly, picked up the phone with trembling fingers, and was met with the same "1 New Message" icon which had been begging me to read it for so long.

Running my fingers through my hair, I looked at the painting I had left on the couch.

I held my breath, and finally opened Nina's text.

I think Kev is jealous of u b/c u were the 1 who got all of the publicity by only being crippled. In fact, he's afraid of u since ur not crippled anymore. Please don't go thru w/ this Mira

Forty
Jet

I opened my eyes with a start, blinking in confusion. The dingy, yellowing ceiling of my apartment gradually came into focus, and I sighed as I rolled out of bed, sending a cascade of papers and books onto the floor as I did so.

After stumbling into the narrow bathroom, I flicked on the light and was about to splash some water onto my face, when I caught my reflection in the mirror. My barely-slanted eyes were weary, and I no longer wore my hair closely shaved to my scalp, but in a two inch, curly "afro."

After I finished getting ready, I remembered that I had to turn in my philosophy paper at 8.

The clock beside my bed read 8:24.

"Jet, my favorite student."

I panted slightly from my jog to the door of Professor Jennings' office, and sighed.

"I'm so sorry I'm late, Professor—"

"No, no, it's fine," the older man excused, taking the paper from me, his squinty eyes slowly scanning it, and he chuckled dryly. "It's early anyway—it wasn't due 'til Friday, remember?"

I looked down.

"Oh . . . right."

"How's that dancing coming?" Professor Jennings inquired, stroking his short, white beard.

I shrugged, fiddling with the zipper on my windbreaker.

"Okay, I guess."

About a year and a half had passed since the incident with Miranda, and I was gradually getting my life back on track, taking classes at a local community college and getting involved as a leader with the youth ministry of a church I had joined. Originally, it would have still been another six months before I got the chance to get another driver's license, but I had been let off the hook about a month earlier for good behavior. It felt good to know that I was winning back some sort of trust, but it still wasn't from the one person whom I had actually hurt.

I was taking dance lessons, as Miranda once suggested I do on that night at Nana Jo's. Monday, Wednesday and Thursday, I took jazz and hip-hop classes at a community studio, and had been doing so for almost a year now. Not only that, but I had long since moved from Philly to Brooklyn, and was in the process of finding a job with the acclaimed Alvin Ailey dance school. I thought of football often, and how much I missed the sport. It wasn't easy being kicked off the team, but over time, I began to realize that my heart hadn't been in it as much as I thought it was. All of the fame I had generated for myself through it had tricked me into thinking that it was what I wanted to do for the rest of my life. Though I loved football, it had become a hobby since I found dancing.

It might surprise you that I had become so closely associated with dance, but it almost seemed to draw me, and it helped release some of my anguish. Many times, I wished Miranda could see me doing what she loved so much, and now, what *I* was beginning to love as well.

"Mr. Carmichael, Mr. Billings is ready to see you now."

My eyes darted from the sports magazine in my hand with a start. The elderly secretary was standing with a few papers in her hands, her glasses resting at the tip of her nose.

I rose from my chair in the waiting room, smoothing my black suit and tie as I did so, wanting to make a good first impression.

I had received the call I was waiting for a couple of days back, finally hearing word from the Alvin Ailey School. I was asked to come to the office, where I would be interviewed by their chief employer, Bradley Billings.

I was nervous as I followed the secretary through a door and down a long hallway, passing various offices behind closed doors. Each job interview was more and more serious these days, due to my criminal record.

The secretary went ahead of me, opening the door with an announcement.

"Mr. Billings, Mr. Carmichael is here."

"Send him in."

When the secretary summoned me to enter, I stepped inside the mid-sized office, and she left, closing the door behind her.

The walls held paintings and photos of dancers, all in grayscale, and a few sculptures and awards sat on the surrounding shelves.

"Mr. Carmichael, nice to meet you. Have a seat." Mr. Billings motioned toward the small, leather chair before his desk.

"Yes sir, thank you."

After we shook hands, I sat down across from the desk, noting the intricately-carved wood.

Mr. Billings removed his black-framed glasses and rubbed his eyes. He was a casual man in his early forties, with pictures of his family on his desk.

"So you'd like to work for our school."

I sat a little closer to the edge of my chair.

"Yes, sir."

"Well," Mr. Billings began. "You seem to be a very smart young man." He reached for a paper to his left, and I recognized it to be my résumé. "This superb essay states that plainly." He paused, tapping the paper on the table, then chuckled. "I mean, have you ever considered writing?"

I shook my head.

"Um . . . no, not really, sir. I wrote it in college."

Mr. Billings nodded slowly.

"Well, how about we hire you as one of our stage directors, and then we'll see if we can squeeze some writing in there somewhere—perhaps in the newsletter or pamphlets."

I opened my mouth slightly, realizing what had just happened.

"I'm . . . I'm hired?"

Mr. Billings nodded, smiling as he extended his hand.

"Welcome to the Alvin Ailey School, Mr. Carmichael."

As usual, I entered my modest apartment to silence that night, weary from a hard day's work. My hip-hop class had learned a difficult dance that day, and I was starting to feel the physical effects.

I wasn't exactly in a bad mood, though, with my recent promotion fresh on my mind. All my thoughts were dedicated to my new job as I prepared a hot dog for myself.

My cell phone rumbled from the adjacent coffee table, and I continued to eat as I looked at it. I had lost a lot of contact with a lot of old friends since the arrest, and really only stayed in touch with Nana Jo and Luke—sometimes Jon.

Jon and I hadn't talked much since he disclosed his relationship with Nina. I mean, it isn't exactly comforting to hear that your brother's about to start going out with the sister of your ex-girlfriend whose life you just happened to ruin. To be honest, I was jealous of the fact that Jonathan was the unblemished big shot who had the freedom to do as he pleased, and that I was the one with a criminal record now—the girl I was in love with hating me.

I was angry with him, true. Because, of all the girls out there, Jon had chosen the one most closely associated with the one I had fallen in love with.

I allowed the phone to ring three more times, wondering when the caller would give up, sighing at my lack of regard for my social life. As it kept ringing, I finally tossed my napkin and arose, reaching down to pick up the cell.

A familiar number caused me to I hesitate before answering.

"Hello?" was my uncertain greeting.

"Jet . . . um, hey."

I stepped toward the couch.

"Um, hey . . . Bri," I chuckled awkwardly. "I wasn't expecting to hear from you . . ."

Bri didn't answer immediately.

"Um . . . yeah. I'm . . . sorry about that, Jet." She sighed, and I couldn't help but laugh again.

"You don't have to apologize. I only meant that I didn't expect you to call because of how things are." I shrugged, lowering myself down to the couch as my side ached a little from the dance lesson.

Bri hesitated, and there came another break in the conversation.

I felt uncomfortable as an argument erupted from the apartment next door.

"So what have you been up to lately?" Bri asked, trying to sound casual.

"Well," I began slowly, carefully choosing my words, "job searching, for one . . . I got a new job recently . . . one I've had my eye on for a minute now."

Bri seemed to nod in interest.

"Oh, really?"

"Yeah," I sighed, glancing through the open doorway of my box-like bedroom, my eyes automatically finding the signed shirt on the wall. I guess I wasn't able to get rid of it. There was a question on my mind, but I didn't know how to ask it, or if I should ask it at all.

I pulled at the collar of my polo shirt.

"So . . . uh, how is . . . how is she?"

It came out a little faster than I planned, and I felt my palms become sweaty as I waited for Bri's response.

"Oh . . ." she hesitated. "She's . . . okay," she cleared her throat, obviously meaning to say more. "But she's had some trouble. She went back to ATL with Kevin and stuff, but it . . . didn't really work out."

I nodded slowly, frowning.

"Really?"

Bri sighed softly.

"Yeah."

I shifted my jaw while trying to figure out how Kevin could have possibly let Miranda go. I would have given anything to have had his opportunity. But then, I guess I already did at one time, and didn't do the greatest job either . . .

"I'd probably better go now—"

"Oh, wait," I quickly interrupted, a realization coming to me. "Did um, did Miranda ever get a painting?"

"Well, yeah, actually," Bri spoke slowly, a hint of curiosity in her

281

voice. Apparently, Miranda hadn't told her much about the painting.

"Okay . . . good." I smiled a little, glad that the painting had reached her.

Before Bri could ask any questions, I told her I would talk to her later. Our conversation ended.

Forty-One
Miranda

"Hold still—you're *never* this nervous."

"That's because this time, I actually *have* something to be nervous about!"

Cat's delicate, strawberry-brown eyebrows nervously twitched as I attempted to apply a layer of dark-green shadow to compliment her eyes, and I sighed, though I was unable to suppress a smile.

"The show of her life," as Cat called it, and perhaps rightfully so. "Choreographer's Carnival," was its actual name, and it would be the performance that could decide her immediate future concerning dance. All the top choreographers, talent scouts, and producers in the area were dotting the seats behind the curtain, and my talented friend was nervous.

"You don't have anything to be nervous about." I dabbed one last time with the brush, then assessed my finished product. With a final nod of approval, I noted the uncharacteristically diffident look on Cat's face, and shook my head, placing my hands on her shoulders.

"Cat, you have nothing to worry about—"

"But Miranda—"

"One minute!" came the stage director's warning.

Both of us glanced over at the busy backstage hallway adjacent the makeshift dressing room. Cat shook her head as if to jiggle the nerves off, and anxiously straightened her flawless, jazzy black leotard and skirt.

"Um . . ." she sighed, nodding slowly, mentally reassuring herself. "Okay . . . yeah, you're right. I can do this. I *can* . . ."

I smiled again, sympathizing with her nervousness.

"Yes, you can! Remember what we always used to say—that corny saying back before those crazy shows Ms. Peterson had the whole troupe do?"

Cat beamed lightly.

"I was *born* ready," she murmured, reaching out to squeeze my hand. "Thanks, Mira."

Cat and I shared a hug, until the stage director summoned the dancers once more in a shrill voice.

We both laughed, and Cat finally turned to jog off for her entrance, but paused, turning back to me and saying, "This is for you, Mira."

I watched her go with a light smile, then turned and left the backstage area.

I had only been in New York for a week, and my eventful return to the city from Atlanta was still fresh on my mind. I had been welcomed back from my flight by a mob of press at the airport. Apparently, the news of my departure from Golden Productions had leaked.

I was trying to piece things together again. I had been on so many rollercoasters that I found my plans constantly shifting. Though I wanted to take a much-needed break, I was restless, and immediately took on as many guest teaching sessions with dance workshops as I could, maxing out my schedule.

It continued to surprise me that studios and companies were still jumping at the chance to have me as a guest choreographer, but I guess it actually boosted my résumé that my story was becoming so drama filled and unpredictable.

As I moved down the back hallways of the theater to the seats, I remembered the way my mom was silently disappointed when I explained to her that Kevin wasn't right for me. As hard as it was, I didn't tell my parents about Kevin's corruptness—especially my mom. He was still her best friend's son. My dad took the news quietly, but eventually reached out to hug me, and told me that things would get better.

Of all people, Jet was on my mind more than ever these days. Just when I thought I had forgotten about him, I realized that I found myself comparing everything to him. Even when I was around Kevin again, I knew that I was secretly thinking about Jet. Not once did I stop and consider what this might mean.

I sighed, recalling my mom's constant reminders that I compared everything to Jet. With my eyes distantly focused on the floor, I continued down the hall, past the mingling guests and ushers.

"Hey, Mira."

"Yeah?"

"Um . . . is it okay if I start to see Jonathan Carmichael?"

The question came as a bit of a slap, I'll admit. Though I knew Nina had been getting to know Jonathan in the past few months, I had always thought of them as friends. Nina was picky when it came to guys, and had turned many down whom I thought to be perfect for her. It did hurt at times when I saw how well things were working for them. Though I hadn't been around Jonathan much, and as different as the brothers were, he was enough like Jet to remind me of him.

I tried to appear blasé, shrugging. Nina had dropped by my apartment an hour back with a bag of popcorn to watch a movie, but I never thought our get-together would include such a question.

"Um . . ." I twirled the remote on the floor as I stretched out on my stomach, and Nina watched me from where she sat cross-legged against the sofa.

I shrugged again.

"Why wouldn't it be?"

Nina raised her shoulders as well.

"I mean . . . is it okay with _you_, Mira?"

I managed a weak smile, ignoring my half-eaten bowl of popcorn.

"Jon's a great guy . . ." I was unable to continue, my voice fading, as thoughts of Jet flickered in my mind. "And, uh . . ." swallowing first, "you shouldn't have to be held back from him just because of my situation."

Nina's head hung a little. She didn't reply.

I cleared my throat.

"Why . . . did you ask me, anyway?" I questioned slowly, distantly tugging one of my braids.

Nina picked at her thumbnail, rolling her almond-shaped eyes.

"Miranda," she began softly, smiling a little, "you don't actually think I would have gone out with him if you weren't okay with it, do you? I mean, I care about your opinion, and about you. In this case," she shrugged, "I couldn't just go out with him without asking you first . . . he's not just any guy."

I considered her words after she finished speaking, drawing circles in the carpet with my finger. Our whole conversation was very . . . _unfamiliar_, to me, I realized. I was used to having to conform my opinion to someone else's; I wasn't used to having someone ask me what my opinion was. As much as it would be painful for me to accept the relationship, I knew that I wanted my sister to be happy, and I also knew that Jonathan was right for her.

What else was I supposed to say?

"I hope it all works out," I voiced quietly, sincerely, and Nina smiled. "You know? This has gotta be the weirdest conversation I've ever had."

Nina tilted her head at my statement.

"Why?"

"Well, because . . ." I shook my head, feeling ridiculous suddenly. "I mean, nobody's seemed to care about my opinion or feelings lately . . ." my tone dropped, ". . . ever."

"Besides Jet . . . " I sadly thought to myself.

Nina sighed, leaning forward on her elbows and looking me in the eyes.

"Well, *I* do," she stated firmly. "And long after there's Jonathan or modeling or TV shows," she chuckled, "there's still gonna be you, and I'll still be there," Nina finished sincerely.

I grinned slowly, gratefully, as an understanding was made. I laughed after a moment, though.

"Unless, of course, you finally get that call from Ralph Lauren or Tyra . . ."

Nina chuckled, waving her hand with pretend complacency.

"Girl, you know they've already got me on speed dial."

Forty-Two
Jet

I thought about Miranda more than ever those days. With constant reminders of Jonathan and Nina's relationship, and despite the new friends I was slowly making, I felt more and more alone. Many times, after getting back from work or a draining dance class, I would wonder how different things would be if I had simply turned myself in the moment I knew that I was the one who had caused Miranda's accident.

Sometimes, I came to the conclusion that I probably wouldn't have even met Miranda if the accident hadn't happened, as she would have probably gone on to be famous at Juilliard or somewhere other than the Philly studio where I ended up taking classes. Though I knew that I wouldn't have traded knowing Miranda for anything, the fact that it was something painful that brought us together was constantly tormenting me.

Nana Jo called me every now and then, and I visited her on holidays and breaks. Mom had recently left her boyfriend and worked as a telephone operator now, making a modest living for herself in California. I hadn't seen her since she decided to show up in Philly years back at Nana Jo's. Sometimes I considered calling her, but I never actually went through with it.

Since Miranda had broken up with Kevin, I wondered if she had accomplished her dreams with dancing, if she had given it another try. There were days when I also wondered if she ever thought of me.

I didn't get my hopes up.

It was the end of a long week, when a hasty pounding on my apartment door awakened me from an unusually sound nap on the couch. Grumbling and looking around in confusion, I lifted the open textbook off my stomach, placing it on the floor before rising to answer the door. I could not imagine who could be so impatient.

"Jon?" I blinked in surprise when I swung the door open. Jonathan was actually trembling, a look of fear in his eyes that I had never seen before. His t-shirt was rain-soaked and he hadn't bothered to wear a jacket.

"Pack your bags—we've gotta go to Memphis immediately!"

My heart paused in paralysis before I opened my mouth, afraid to ask anything at all.

"What's happened?"

"Dad's sick—very sick."

Forty-Three
Miranda

"Miranda . . ." Mom stared at me in surprise.

"Can I come in?" I asked after a moment of standing on the doorstep in the muggy rain.

I'm not sure of exactly what made me go back to West Oak Lane. Though it was only for a spring break visit, I knew it wouldn't be an easy trip. My mom and I hadn't been on the best of terms since the breakup with Kevin.

I guess there were some things we needed to talk about—some things I needed to make clear.

"Of course, come in before you get soaked."

I stepped into the house, the warmth and familiarity immediately setting me at ease. It had been a long time since I had been home, and I couldn't help but feel glad to be back.

With a smile, Mom gave me a hug.

"It's so good to have you back."

I closed my eyes as I caught the smell of caramel and cinnamon in her hair, and smiled sadly, realizing just how much I had missed her.

"It's good to be back," I said quietly sincerely.

A timer interrupted from the kitchen, and Mom sighed.

"Oh—that's my pie. Let me get that really quick and I'll be right back. Have a seat; you must be tired from the drive."

As she hurried off, I smiled at her faithful concern. Exhaling with a sigh, I strolled into the den after abandoning my drenched raincoat on the coat rack.

The house hadn't changed much; I noticed a few new paintings and a vase of fresh roses on the coffee table. It was bittersweet to see how much it was the same, and I lowered myself to the sofa with another sigh, perhaps a sad one.

My thoughts were relatively empty as I sat, surrounded by the silence of the house—silent, with the exception of the radio playing softly in the corner, set as always to Mom's favorite easy listening station.

I stared at an old picture of me on the coffee table, taken a good ten or so years back, looking up only when I heard a footstep across the room.

"Tutu?"

Dad grinned broadly as he placed his hands on his hips, wagging his head from where he stood in the kitchen doorway. He wore his Capstone Productions baseball cap and a company sweatshirt. He had grown a bit of a mustache, but other than that, he was still the same, tall, husky guy with the easygoing smile.

I stood up beaming, and Dad set his briefcase down, walking forward with his arms outstretched. He paused when I jogged over and wrapped my arms around his neck.

"And to think there was a time when you couldn't do that!" Dad exclaimed after a moment, holding me away some, chuckling warmly. "Look how far you've come, Miranda. I hear you're doin' a lot of teaching in the Big Apple."

I laughed, shaking my head with a shrug.

"You know I wouldn't have it any other way."

Dad smiled.

"C'mon, let's sit down—you've gotta catch your ol' dad up."

After we sat on the comfy couch, Dad removed his hat and leaned back into the sofa with a sigh.

"So, how is everything?" he asked, lacing his hands behind his head. "I hear *No Way's* gettin' good ratings."

I nodded, rubbing my knee.

"Yeah, Nina's really excited about that . . ."

Dad smiled lightly.

"She told us about Jonathan Carmichael," he spoke quietly, watching me stare at my hands. "You okay with it?"

I quickly nodded again, managing a light, reassuring smile.

"Yeah, Dad. She asked me already—"

"But seriously, Miranda . . ." Dad pressed softly.

I swallowed shakily, then sighed.

"I . . . I want her to be happy," I replied slowly, saying the same thing I had told Nina.

Dad nodded understandingly, reaching out to pat my hand.

"Okay," he stated simply, as though I had made perfect sense, and I smiled gratefully. He had always been the only person who really knew when I was lying or telling the truth. And this time, he knew that I was making a good, though difficult, decision.

"Charles, you're back early."

Both of us looked over to the doorway, where Mom was standing with the phone in her hand.

"Nelson called for you," Mom quietly explained, and Dad quickly nodded, then turned to me.

"Sorry baby—we'll talk soon, okay?"

"Okay Dad," I replied with a nod, and Dad smiled lightly, touching my cheek before rising and taking the phone from Mom—greeting her with a quick kiss.

"Sorry it took me so long," Mom apologized as Dad left.

I shrugged, and she sat down in a chair across from the couch. "It's okay."

Mom sighed, brushing a stray brown curl out of her face.

"It feels like a lifetime has passed," she spoke softly, and I nodded quietly, looking down at my hands.

Mom cleared her throat, leaning back and crossing one leg over the other.

"So how's Nina doing?"

"She's doing okay," I replied vaguely, choosing to omit the fact that Nina's relationship with Jonathan was going well, since Mom wasn't exactly happy about the two of them being together.

Mom nodded, running her long, graceful fingers along the wide arms of the chair.

"I hear the show's going into its fourth season."

"Yeah," I confirmed, glancing casually about the room.

We continued like this for a few minutes more, Mom throwing me a conversational question and me replying appropriately. But both of us were secretly wanting the other to say what was really on their mind. Mom sighed again during a break in our awkward talk, then she leaned forward onto the edge of her seat.

"So how are things looking job-wise?"

"Um, it's looking good . . ." My uneasiness was evident since I felt as though I could scream if I had to answer one more question. "Mom?" I quickly stated before she could make another inquiry.

Mom nodded, looking slightly expectant.

I shifted in my seat, not knowing where to begin now that I had changed course.

"I, um . . . I want to audition—I-I'm *going* . . . to audition." I swallowed after speaking in one stammering breath, feeling the atmosphere seem to jolt.

At first, her face was expressionless. But after a moment, when my words had registered, she appeared stunned.

"Dancing?"

I cleared my throat at her level question.

"Yes."

"For whom?"

"Alvin Ailey."

"When?"

"Soon . . . as soon as I feel I'm ready."

A heavy silence followed the abrupt line of questioning. I swallowed shakily as Mom looked away, nodding very slowly.

I had been dreading telling her this for a long time, and you're about to find out why.

"Miranda," she began carefully, seeming to try to keep her voice calm. "I just . . . I don't," she sighed, "Miranda, you can't—"

"I can, Mom, and I will . . ." I spoke quickly, my words sounding unfamiliar in my ears.

She sighed again.

"Miranda, ever since you left Kevin you've been distancing yourself more and more from the things you used to love—"

"What things?" I frowned, shaking my head. "Things that held me back? Things that I *settled* for when I was crippled?" I laughed wryly. "Mom, I'm better now—things don't have to be the same anymore—"

"But you're biting off more than you can chew, now, Miranda." Her voice was firm. "Isn't what you have now enough for you? Can't you be glad that you're walking and teaching?"

"Yes, I'm glad, Mom, but it's not what I was trying to do all along."

"Miranda, you're telling me you left safety and a good life with Kevin over an old dream?"

I sighed in frustration at her insistence that Kevin was still the best choice for me.

"I didn't leave safety, Mom, I left bondage! Being with Kevin would have been the worst thing I could do to myself—"

"But *why*, Miranda?"

"Because I was gonna be treated like a piece of land to be bought or some kind of prize!" I finally explained, disclosing for the first time the details of our breakup.

"Miranda—"

"No, you don't understand—you never did understand! Kevin wasn't the perfect guy you believed him to be—"

"But at least he didn't cause your injury in the first place and then hide that from you, Miranda!"

The sound of our rising voices bounced off of the walls, and I shook my head and looked away. Things would never be straight between us as long as she was blind to the truth.

I held my head in my hands, staring down at the white carpet, my eyes moistening.

It didn't make any sense to me. Why would she insist that Kevin was right for me, even after I told her the truth about him?

"You knew, didn't you?" I asked quietly, not wanting to know the answer, though. "You knew that Kevin was really just gonna make me a business manager and not a dancer…"

Mom didn't reply, and this only confirmed my suspicion.

Swallowing, I blinked a tear out of my eye, allowing it to slide freely down my cheek.

"Miranda . . . you were . . ." Mom appeared flustered as she tried to find the words, "so bent on dancing. But you just don't know for sure if it would have worked. You could have hurt yourself again . . . or—or now with this auditioning business . . ." She sighed. "Who knows what might go wrong? I just . . . I don't want you to get hurt—it's a harsh world out there…"

"And yet you encouraged me to have the surgery so that I could dance again…" I spoke dryly, a defeated sarcasm in my voice.

"Yes, Miranda, I did." Mom's voice rose in defense. "I did it because I *did* want you to dance again, and I still do." She looked away, wringing her hands slightly. "But I…I just didn't think you would try to audition again…"

I shook my head, bitterly shifting my jaw as I listened to her in disbelief.

"Because you never wanted me to try . . ." I finished for her, speaking quietly, my tone dark, as my heart ached. "You never even believed I could do it . . . you never believed in me . . ."

I couldn't see it, but Mom was fighting back her own tears, and sighed heavily.

"Miranda, that's not true—"

"Mom," I interrupted, holding up my hand. "Please . . . just . . . let me say what I need to say—"

"What you *came* to say," she cut in quietly, correcting me as she looked down at the floor.

I felt my heart begin to sink lower and lower, and I hung my head as well, feeling my tear ducts moistening all the more.

It was a long time before I spoke again, and we both sat silently attempting to bear our injured relationship, perhaps both feeling hurt by the other in some way.

"I'm going to audition, and I know you don't like that." I took a deep breath, talking softly but honestly. "But . . . I need to do this. I didn't come this far for nothing . . . a-and even though everyone has their thoughts on me." I exhaled the breath I had been holding. "I *am* a dancer, and I will *always* be a dancer—no matter what I'm doing or where I end up." I hesitated. "And I had to go through a lot to realize that.

So as soon as I'm ready, I'm gonna go to the closest Alvin Ailey School audition . . . and I'm gonna dance my heart out . . ." I paused, feeling my voice beginning to catch as the quiver in my throat gained more strength, "no matter who's behind me or against me . . . no matter whether those people are family or not . . . I'll do this whether I fail or succeed. But in the end, no matter what . . . I'll still be a dancer."

Forty-Four

Jet

Every second of the walk down the hallway of the hospital's intensive-care unit was agony. Jon moved with a jerky sort of step at my side but slightly ahead of me, reaching up to rub his head every few seconds, sighing shakily every now and then. I tried to keep my display of nerves to a minimum due to Nana Jo, whom I walked with both arms around. I could feel her trembling, but she was clearly the strongest out of the three of us. Her eyes were serious and focused as we neared the cubicle Dad was in, but her grip on my hand was firm—perhaps for my sake more than her own.

Pneumonia—it had come over him out of nowhere. The doctor we had spoken with minutes back said that they would do their best to care for him, but I refused to trust any of their words.

When the curtain-drawn cubicle was only a few yards away, I realized that I had been wondering where my mom was for a while now—during the whole flight and drive. I tried to push her out of my thoughts, though, and took a deep breath as a nurse came to meet us outside of the cubicle.

Jon and Nana Jo spoke with her quietly after she explained more of the details of the illness, but I hung back some, sliding my hands into my jeans pockets and anxiously glancing around the busy, dreary area. A man was staring at us from the inside of his cubicle nearby, his glazed eyes filled with fear. Heavy breathing sounded from another cubicle, and somewhere a woman was groaning and crying.

My hands shook as I reached up to wipe my eyes.

"Jet."

I looked up, feeling Nana Jo's hand on my shoulder.

She nodded with a very slight, comforting smile, and I took hold of her hand as we followed Jon into the cubicle.

Dad was asleep, but when he heard our tender footsteps, his eyelids lifted as though they weighed tons, but he smiled weakly nonetheless. He looked older than he did when I last saw him a good two years back, with hints of gray speckles in his dark hair. A short, slightly-graying beard sat on his jaw, and despite the illness, his large, brown eyes were as lighthearted and keen as ever—eyes like his mother's.

Nana Jo went to her son, hugging him and whispering something in his ear. Standing slightly aloof near the curtain, I thought I heard her say something like "look at these grown men I brought with me."

Jon took his cue, moving slowly as he held Dad's feeble hand in his own, smiling sadly.

Dad grinned broadly up at Jonathan, speaking quietly to him, and after a moment, his eyes shifted to me.

"Josiah," he whispered, slowly beckoning me over.

Jon stepped aside, and I somehow moved forward, my legs feeling like lead. I was nervous and afraid, and suddenly wanted to run off in the opposite direction.

"Hey, Pop," I managed to say, trying to be as calm as my brother as I took Dad's hand.

Dad, apparently, saw right through my act, and nodded with a knowing smile.

He pulled me into a hug, and after a moment I began to cry as he held my head to his collar.

"Don't be afraid . . ." Dad whispered, over and over.

It was a long night sitting outside of the cubicle. Jon and I were silent as we sat in the cold, metal chairs a nurse provided, and Nana Jo remained where she had been the whole time—at Dad's bedside. I was feeling only a little better, and Jonathan, as solemn and composed as he usually was, would ask me every half hour or so, "Are you okay?"

A bottle of water quivered in one hand as I leaned forward on my elbows, staring down at the multi-colored, scratched, linoleum floor. If it hadn't been for my fear, I would have been angry. Dad had come so far with his recovery, but now with this sickness, I didn't know what to think or feel.

An older man in a long, white coat approached after a moment, and introduced himself as Dr. Olsen, one of the doctors working with Dad. Jon told him that our grandmother was in the cubicle, and Dr. Olsen nodded, saying he needed to speak with her.

The doctor's somber tone caused my initial fear to return afresh, and I sighed heavily as I hung my head, wishing it was all just a bad dream.

I felt a nudge from Jon after a few minutes, and I blinked in confusion as I looked at him. His eyes were focused to my left, at the hallway leading to the ICU area.

I followed his gaze, and watched as he rose and walked over to a woman in a heavy coat, a hood adorned due to the rain. As he embraced her in a hug, her hood brushed off, and I immediately recognized her to be our mother.

My first instinct, what with all of the turmoil going on, was to run over and join in the hug, but I quickly refrained.

I don't know whether I was glad to see her or angry; I suppose it was a strange mixture of the two. On one hand, it made me feel good to know that she had come, but then again, why should she care anyway? She had left us altogether once; she had left Dad.

I looked away from their reunion, irately shifting my jaw. It shouldn't take a serious illness to bring her back.

Mom and Jon parted, and she nodded as Jon spoke quietly to her, her eyes focused on me. Out of the corner of my eye, I watched her slowly walk over, her hands in her jacket pockets and head slightly down.

I didn't really want to, but I must have been planning on ignoring her altogether, and that's just what I did.

"Josiah," she whispered, reaching out to touch my shoulder, but I immediately stood up, stalking a few feet away.

Mom must have gone into the cubicle after watching me for a moment, and I sighed heavily, angrily, as I folded my arms over my chest.

Jonathan must have been watching as well, and he laid his hand on my shoulder after a while.

"C'mon, Jet," he assuaged quietly. "Not right now . . . not with all this goin' on."

I clenched my jaw, spinning swiftly to face him.

"*Yes*, with all this goin' on!" I exclaimed heatedly, struggling to keep my voice down. "There's no better time—she walks up in here

301

when Dad's sick as I don't know what and you want me to be forgiving?!"

"Okay, Jet. Alright," Jon replied diplomatically, trying to calm me as he held up his hands. "I know you've got some stuff to straighten out—"

"Why *me*?" I demanded. "What about you, Jon? Don't make me look like a bad guy—she walked out on you too, you know—"

"But I know when to move on and let things go!"

I shook my head, feeling as though I could explode. "Don't start that with me." I narrowed my eyes. "Don't you act like you're the only grown-up in this situation—" I halted my rant in mid-sentence, suddenly hearing what sounded like a sob from the cubicle.

I quickly rubbed the back of my neck, turning and closing my eyes.

I stood with my back to Jon for a long time, both of us fearing the worst, until we heard a voice from the cubicle, "Excuse me."

I turned, slowly, reluctantly, to face Dr. Olsen, who had exited with Nana Jo and Mom.

To my dismay, Nana Jo's eyes were red, and a few tears were rolling down Mom's cheeks. Her arm was around the older woman's shoulders, and her face was down.

"Doctor?" Jonathan spoke expectantly, his voice trembling uncharacteristically.

I wanted to leave—the room was spinning, I was certain of it.

"Mr. Carmichael," Dr. Olsen began slowly, placing one thick hand on Jon's shoulder, his gray eyes sympathetic, "he might not pull through the night."

Jonathan's head slowly hung, and he sighed heavily, a few tears escaping his eyes.

I'm not sure how soon after the doctor's words I found myself tearing off down the hallway, blindly fighting to get away.

Jonathan grabbed my arm but failed to stop me, and I was twisting and turning down various hallways, not knowing where I was headed. It was a Baptist hospital, and I must have caught the word "chapel" on one of the signs overhead. The next thing I knew, I was sitting inside of the small room, dimly lit and adorned with crucifixes and stained glass. I rested my forehead on the pew in front of me, and cried into my elbow.

Nothing was making sense. Why did it have to be Dad? He had gone through so much in the past decade, and now this . . . I felt like I could have visited him more often—called him more. And just as I did with Miranda, I felt guilty. I wasn't able to do anything right.

I don't think I heard the sound of the chapel door closing softly, but I did note another's presence at my side on the pew.

I was crying too hard to hear, and I didn't care who it might be anyway. I just kept on praying and crying aloud as I had before they entered, wishing I could change everything that had happened to my family and friends.

"Amen," said a shaky voice after I finished my rambling, desperate prayer, and I didn't have to turn to recognize her.

I didn't even try to be angry that my mom had dared to come after me—I was too exhausted. Nothing added up anymore—not my feelings, grudges, or how I thought things should be. It was all out of my hands . . . it always had been.

Mom didn't attempt to console me at first, but let me continue to cry silently for a few more minutes. But after a while, I leaned over to cry into her shoulder, forgetting the past for once.

"He's still asleep?"

"Shh."

"Oops—sorry."

A door closed, and I stirred.

Discomfited, I tried to remember where I was. There were no cushioned, wooden benches in my apartment, so I wasn't at home...

I opened my eyes a hair, feeling as though my head weighed a thousand pounds. My eyes barely adjusted to what looked like an altar, and bits and pieces of the night before floated back to my memory.

"Momma?"

I was leaning on someone's shoulder still, and they chuckled.

"No."

I recognized Nana Jo's voice, and suddenly the situation came back to mind.

"Nana..?" I sat up, my heart pounding in my chest as I waited for her to tell me Dad's condition.

But Nana Jo only smiled, reaching out to touch my cheek.

"Didn't I tell you prayer works?"

After her words registered, Nana Jo and I hugged, until the door to the chapel opened.

"Here's the juice—oh, sorry."

Jonathan stood at the entrance, holding a can of orange juice in one hand and a doughnut in the other. His eyes were lively, although he looked as though he needed to sleep.

At the sight of my brother, and with such good news in our midst, I jumped up and wrapped him in a hug—not caring that we were both acting highly out of character.

Jonathan chuckled, but when we parted, there was a question on my mind.

"Where's Mom?"

Nana Jo stood up slowly, yawning and stretching her arms as Jonathan took a seat in one of the pews, looking as though he was about to nap.

"With your father," she replied with a light smile, and I chewed my lip.

"I'll . . . be right back."

It felt as though a whole day had passed as I walked to the ICU, but when I came to a window-filled hallway, I saw that the sun was barely lighting the horizon.

On my way to Dad's cubicle, I ran into Dr. Olsen, who smiled when he saw me.

"He's gonna be just fine."

I grinned, extending my hand.

"Thank you."

Dr. Olsen nodded as we shook, then walked off to tend to his other patients.

I sighed as I neared the cubicle, noting that the curtains were slightly parted.

I didn't go in, but stood silently watching my mom sitting beside the bed, holding Dad's hand as they spoke quietly.

I knew that they couldn't have talked much to each other over the years—most likely only through business-like phone calls and letters dealing with the separation ordeal. Stuffing my hands into my pockets, I realized that they had yet to actually divorce.

But Dad was going to get better, I reminded myself, not wanting to dwell on the negative side of things. That fact was enough for me to forget about anything else, even if only temporarily.

It was nice to see my parents together again—strange, but nice. I didn't know what they were talking about, as I couldn't really hear, but it gave me a good feeling to know that they were at least talking (and even smiling) at each other.

Dad was still on his medications, and looked pretty drowsy, but after a moment, Mom glanced over and must have noticed me.

I quickly lowered my eyes to the ground and began to move away, starting to realize that I wasn't sure why I had come.

"Jet," came a call from behind when I had reached the end of the hallway leading out of the ICU, and I turned.

Mom was walking over briskly, and I waited.

"Can we talk . . . outside?"

I nodded, and we walked along to the cafeteria area, where there was a common area with benches outside.

For the first time since she had appeared, I noticed that Mom looked different than she had when I last saw her. She wore her hair in long braids, and though the weariness in her eyes was the same, she still looked . . . younger, perhaps—more like the way I remembered her to look, and not like the unfamiliar woman who came to Nana Jo's two years back.

The only reminder of the previous night's downpour was in the crisp, sugary scent in the air, and a few birds sang overhead as we sat down on one of the benches in the garden.

Neither of us said anything for a very long time, but instead we watched the sun rising in the distance.

It was awkward at first, sitting beside someone whom I had so much trouble with, someone who I barely knew anymore. Yet, it was serene.

"I had a lot of things wrong when we last spoke," Mom began quietly, rubbing her hands together.

I listened in silence, looking down at the moist ground.

"And I know about what you went through—your grandmother told me," she continued. "Josiah—*Jet*," she corrected herself, "I . . . I wasn't right to judge Miranda like I did, and I'm sorry for it." She hesitated, reaching up to rub her forehead. "And I know it's strange for me to say that under the circumstances . . . but I'm being honest, and it's true."

I cleared my throat after a moment, and nodded slowly.

"It's okay," was my soft reply, and I swallowed.

Mom's hands fidgeted, and she chewed her lip with a sigh.

"That's not all, though, and not all you need to hear." She seemed to swallow as well. "See, I . . . I hurt you years ago, a-and you obviously know that. But you deserve to know why."

I felt my muscles tensing, and I braced myself for what she would say next. I would have never guessed what I would hear, though.

"Jet . . . I got myself involved with illegal gambling when your father got sick—when the medical bills piled up." She sighed. "I was afraid . . . and I didn't know how I was going to support you, your father and your brother. So I reconnected with some old friends who contacted me and told me they could help me out. They had an illegal business, and I joined in. They were caught, though, and our gambling was discovered.

"I got very scared . . . for what it would mean for us if I was arrested, so I ran away to Toronto, first, and then Texas—where Jonathan found me. And finally, I landed in California. I met some people . . . and got caught up in selling drugs with them." She paused, shaking her head in shame. "I didn't get addicted, though. I never tried them—not the illegal ones, that is, but I did start smoking cigarettes.

"Believe it or not . . . I have been clean for about six months now, but I'm still dealing with some problems with the acquaintances I had." Mom sighed shakily, and cleared her throat. "I kept telling myself I would come back with money for you, but . . . I just . . ." Her voice faded, and she shrugged sadly. "I don't know. I was afraid. I got addicted to being away, even though it hurt me to be away. But now, I'm free from the ring, for the most part, and I served my time in jail after I was arrested a few years ago. I know I should have come back as soon as I could, but . . . again, I was too scared.

"But Jet, I want you to know that none of all of this had to do with you, your brother or your father. It started out as me wanting to help out . . . but soon I realized it was my own personal issues surfacing . . . to the point that I couldn't trust anyone anymore." She smirked. "You don't know this, but I almost stood your father up at our wedding—I was scared of family and marriage. Maybe because I didn't really know what I was trying to imitate anyway—I don't even know who my own parents are." Mom paused, hanging her head as her voice softened. "But I'm slowly getting things back together for myself." She turned to me. "I'm sorry I wasn't there before . . . but I will be from now on."

I didn't say anything for a while, and held my head as I looked away. Everything I had heard was a lot to swallow, yet it was freeing to hear. I had always thought that my mother simply didn't care, but now, hearing that her initial decision to leave, though it was a foolish one, was out of a desire to help us, actually brought a closure to my own insecurities; a peace, I suppose.

I wrapped her in a hug after a moment, and we sat silently crying as the sun rose on a new day, neither of us knowing what lay ahead, but finally being on the same page concerning what was behind.

Forty-Five
Miranda

Harpeth Studios had me impressed from the moment I saw the building. It reminded me of a larger version of my old studio back in North Philly, and I couldn't help but smile to myself as I opened the front door.

I stood in a sizeable lobby/reception area, where a young guy was leaning on the marble front desk, talking lightly with the receptionist, a thin, red-haired girl in her early twenties. The guy, I couldn't see, though, since his back was to me, and I stood still by the door for a minute or two, waiting to decide what to do and taking everything in at the same time.

The lobby gave away much about the free sort of youthful yet classy feel of the studio, with its warm, orange walls and modern black chairs. A large, grayscale, panoramic mural of a line of dancers hung over the front desk, and gentle mood lighting glowed from hanging café-style lamps.

I cleared my throat very lightly, and was certain that I couldn't be heard, but the girl finally noticed me at the door, and her jaw dropped slightly in what I guessed to be surprise.

I self-consciously chewed at my lip as she gestured for the guy to turn around, and I was a little surprised myself to see who he was.

"Miranda." He grinned, and I smiled.

Jeff's hair was no longer cornrowed, but instead he wore it cut close to his scalp. His hazel eyes scrunched into a smile when he saw me, and I finally walked over to greet him with a hug.

"You work here?" I asked after we parted, noting the black Harpeth Studios shirt he wore, and he nodded.

"Yeah," he replied, looking as though he wanted to add "Didn't Kev' tell you?" but didn't. "So what brings you here?"

I opened my mouth to reply, but a voice spoke from a doorway on the right.

"Can you copy these for me, Trace—"

A woman appeared, in her late twenties or so, with long, red-tinted dreads and deep-brown skin. Everything from the black golf-cap she wore to the Vans sneakers screamed "dancer," and she carried herself in a youthful sort of way.

It didn't take me long to recognize her, despite her new hairdo. Samantha Black, the dancer who had left the biggest impression on Philly, the impression I had once attempted to succeed. She had grown up in my neighborhood, but by the time I began to get truly serious about dance, she had graduated from Juilliard and gone on to bigger and better things. My parents often joked that she was my only competition, but after my accident, I had let all of that go. As close as most dancers from North Philly are, Samantha and I had never even met.

"Look who's here, Sam," Jeff turned to Samantha, grinning as he took my arm and led me over. Any and all confidence I had about coming to the studio was quickly fading, and I nervously cleared my throat as I extended my hand.

An amused, yet friendly, sort of smile slowly lit Samantha's face, and she shook my hand.

"Miranda," she spoke as though I was an acquaintance, "It's good to see you without the cane."

I didn't dance immediately upon joining the studio, and I don't think I even would have if I had been asked to. All of Samantha's dancers were superb, probably some of the best undiscovered talents in New York. There were classes available to the public at the studio, but mainly, it was a place for Samantha's elite troupe to refine their skills.

Jeff had joined easily, and Paul, who turned out to be one of the top dancers, was constantly trying to persuade me to join as well. I wanted to, but I would, of course, have to audition first, and I wasn't exactly looking forward to it. Adding to this, the troupe was a tight one, holding only 8 dancers at a time (4 guys, 4 girls), and the opportunity for me to join only existed because there was an open slot—one of the girls had gone off to travel with another troupe.

For the first week, I came and sat in on a few of the hip-hop classes, which were taught by Samantha and Jeff, but it was when I came to watch the acclaimed lyrical jazz class that I felt put to shame.

"That was amazing," I commented to Jeff as he walked over to where I was sitting against a wall before the mirror, tossing his water bottle from hand to hand.

Jeff grinned, wiping his brow as Samantha went over a move with her partner (and fiancé), Vince, a tall, friendly guy with short dreads that matched hers.

"Maybe it'd be better if you'd jump in sometime," he returned, taking a seat beside me on the wooden floor, kicking a random jacket and backpack out of the way.

"Hey!" shouted Lena, Paul's partner, the youngest girl in the troupe, pulling her dark curls into a ponytail as she paced the floor near the mirror. "Be careful—that's my stuff!"

"Don't put it on the floor next time!" Jeff shrugged as he adjusted his white headband, and Lena rolled her eyes.

I chuckled at their hint of rivalry, poking at the tongue of my Chuck Taylors while twirling one of my braids.

"So?" Jeff continued hopefully, and I sighed.

"I can't just jump in, Jeff. I'd have to—"

"Join first," he finished for me, nodding as he twisted the cap on his water bottle. "What do you think we're all waiting for?"

I shook my head, watching Vince lift Samantha in the air, Paul doing the same with Lena as they choreographed more to the song.

"You guys are so good," I smirked. "And I'm just some girl who used to dance but couldn't do it anymore and now . . ." My voice trailed, and I furrowed my brow as I looked down at my hands, picking at my fingernails.

"Now all you need to do is get a fresh start," Jeff suggested gently. "And there's no better place than here."

Though I didn't think it was worth it, I continued to train in the following weeks, maybe even harder than before. I didn't want to audition for the Harpeth troupe, but I wanted to see if I could make it just the same. It wasn't exactly like I hadn't ever tasted failure before, though, but I didn't want to deal with it again, either.

Not only was there me and my own lack of confidence to consider, but the other dancers. Samantha was one of the best dancers I knew—you could say I had tried to emulate her before the accident. She wasn't the most famous dancer (yet) but she had grown up on West Oak Lane, Philly (just as I had) and was passionate about jazz (as I was) and had a somewhat famous family (just like me). The only major difference was Samantha had actually *pursued* her training, road-block free, and had more experience than I did. How could I possibly live down blowing an audition in front of her and the rest of the troupe?

I found myself answering this question as I stood before the troupe one evening, a mirror before me and eyes waiting for me to dance, to prove myself to be more than just the "sob-story" dancer trying to make a comeback.

It was as though the audition was inevitable, and in the silence of the room, I was afraid they could hear my heart pounding.

"Just dance," were Samantha's last words from where she stood by the tape deck to my right, and I nodded, closing my eyes with my head lowered.

I don't remember the music starting, but somewhere in the middle of the song, I realized my movements. I was afraid for a good length of the dance, trying to remember the movements I had choreographed, as well as my technique—pretending nothing had ever happened to me, no accident. It seemed to go on forever, and I did my best to ignore the trained eyes which followed me. Yet before I even knew it, the song had finished, and I had stopped.

The room was silent once again as I stood, a little more winded than I would have expected myself to be, my eyes down, unable to face my audience for fear that I had blown the audition.

Samantha spoke first, and I couldn't have been more taken off guard by her words.

"I don't know about anybody else, or what they may say or think, but girl, this is what you were born to do."

"Hear, hear!" shouted Paul, and the others began to cheer.

"Amen to that!" Jeff chimed, and Samantha smiled as applause filled the air.

313

"Welcome to the troupe."

Forty-Six
Jet

The next few months were like a dream for me. Almost everything I prayed for and wished to come true, came true.

My dad continued to heal steadily from his sickness, even to the point of being nearly independent for the first time in years. Though I couldn't go see him often, we talked on the phone every week, and each time he had a report that he had improved. Within six months or so, he was back on his feet, and soon in search of a physical therapy job in Philly.

Mom was still getting her own life back on track, and she had moved in with Nana Jo a few weeks after we visited Dad in Memphis. She and I spoke every now and then, and I was slowly remembering what it was like to trust her again.

Life with Alvin Ailey was relaxing and fulfilling. I enjoyed helping dancers get into the school, and I even had a weekly column in the newsletter, as Mr. Billings had suggested long ago when I was hired. Bri had dropped by my office once, having been in town to visit Miranda, and it was when I showed her around the school that I learned she was seeing Luke. I was happy for them, and glad that Luke had chosen someone as sweet as Bri. After all, she could teach him how to dance, which he was suddenly (not surprisingly) taking an interest in.

I sighed contentedly as I watched my dad sitting on the edge of one of the therapy mats, patiently explaining an exercise to a pre-teen with a sprained ankle.

I couldn't have been more reminded of old times, when I used to watch Dad work with patients after school, and smiled a little to myself from where I stood near the reception desk, unnoticed. I was visiting North Philly for Thanksgiving, which was only a day away.

A little over a year had passed since Dad's illness, and he was back to doing what he loved—helping people strengthen themselves, as he had himself. Most of the doctors didn't think he would be able to return to normal life, but he was constantly proving them wrong.

Dad glanced over after a moment, and smiled with a quick wave. After he wrapped up with his patient, he walked over and we headed to the clinic's break room to chat.

"Your day going okay, Jet?"

I nodded lightly, taking a seat on one of the countertops, watching Dad gather his things into his bag, having finished with the day's work.

"Pretty much—what about you?"

Dad looked up with a small grin, adjusting his glasses on his nose.

"Same," he replied with a small shrug. "Your grandmother wants to invite the whole world to dinner tomorrow, but I told her it'll

316

have to be a small gathering this time."

I tilted my head, tossing my car keys in one hand.

"What for?"

Dad paused, a smile slowly lighting his face.

"You'll see," was his furtive response, and I chuckled with a shrug of defeat.

"I hear your brother's getting in from New York tomorrow morning instead of tonight," Dad mused, stroking his short beard as he studied his scheduler.

I was distracted, focusing out a window to the parking lot, watching a mother helping her daughter, who was on crutches, to their car.

Dad must have noted my silence, and cleared his throat.

"You okay?" he asked quietly, following my gaze out the window.

I quickly looked away, scratching my head with a sigh.

"Yeah, I'm fine."

Dad nodded slowly, tapping lightly on the table.

"Does your friend Bri have any updates these days?"

I shrugged with a weak smile, running my thumb along the slightly tattered pocket edge of my jeans.

"She just says Miranda's 'okay' or 'moving on'—the same thing she's been saying for the past year."

"But that's not enough," Dad added for me, and I sighed again in frustration with myself.

"No, I mean . . ." my voice faded. "I just . . . I don't know . . ."

"You want to know more," Dad attempted carefully, "because you care about her."

I didn't reply at first, knowing he was right.

"It hasn't been easy to just . . . not be around her, even though I know things couldn't work out between us."

Dad was thoughtfully silent for a moment, and he leaned on his palms, frowning a little.

317

"Your grandmother used to always tell me, 'Don't stop runnin' just because you can't see the finish line.' "

I blinked, then frowned as Dad hoisted his bag over one shoulder and started to leave.

"Why not?" I asked, and he paused, turning with a light smile.

"Just because you can't see it, doesn't mean it isn't there."

For a moment, I felt like I was back in Memphis as a little kid that Thanksgiving. The title of the holiday couldn't have been more personal for me, what with all of my family being around me at the dinner table.

The dinner was incredible, the dessert even better, and the fellowship timeless. Everyone was either laughing or smiling, and I noticed how joyful Mom was in particular. She had been stressed lately with the move to Philly and the process of getting her life back on track, but now, with her hair down and eyes shining, I knew that she was finally beginning to be at peace. Jonathan and I were getting along, having watched the afternoon football game with only the expected team rivalries, and Dad's easygoing presence and Nana Jo's warmth tied the whole evening together.

But I'm sure none of us (but one) knew what was coming that would change everything even more, for the better.

All of us were laughing and reminiscing about old times in the den over coffee, Jon sitting beside me on the floor near the fireplace, Nana Jo nestled comfortably in her overstuffed chair, and Dad with his arm around Mom on the couch. We had just finished a funny story about Jon's first day at elementary school, when Dad cleared his throat.

"Jet, will you bring me my jacket?"

I nodded, and got up to grab the jacket, wondering why he needed it.

When I returned, Dad accepted the coat with a nod of thanks, and I took a seat as we all began to quiet down. Mom sat twirling her spoon in her coffee, a light smile on her face, completely unaware of what Dad was about to do as he rummaged through his jacket pocket.

"Evelyn," he finally spoke up, a small box in one hand as he went down on one knee, and Mom's eyes widened as our jaws dropped, "We've both been through a lot together . . . as well as apart. But, to be honest, I've known all along that it's you that I want to be with. So," Dad opened the box, revealing a ring, "will you marry me . . . one more time?"

Forty-Seven
Miranda

"Perfect, Miranda, perfect."

I smiled as I continued with my advanced jazz solo, showcasing it for the first time to my new boss, Samantha.

Jeff glared, pretending to be impatient, crossing his arms over his chest from where he stood a few feet away, waiting for me to finish so that we could tackle our *pas de deux*, or "dance for two."

"When you quit showin' off we can start," he called.

I finished my final leap to a round of applause from Samantha, Vince and Paul, and walked over to Jeff to playfully shove him.

"It's called choreographing—you should try it sometime."

Vince chuckled at my comeback as he tied the laces to his sneakers, preparing for a hip-hop class he would be teaching.

"Yeah, you do kinda' leave ya' girl hangin' in that department, Jeff."

Paul snickered before going into a handstand with his feet against the mirror until Samantha noticed and quickly swatted him down (she was a neat freak when it came to the mirrors).

"Okay, okay, I'm down—and yeah, at least Miranda's not too busy doing interviews with magazines to actually put a dance together."

"C'mon." Jeff waved his hand in denial at Paul's indication, and Samantha shrugged with a laugh, ruffling her dreads as she stretched her legs.

"He's right, Jeff. You need to brush up on that—you two have to get your dance done by Wednesday. The Kelsey gig's Friday night and Carnival's only a month away," she reminded.

"It's okay." I defended my partner with a chuckle as I straightened a support brace on my right knee. "We'll have it done in time."

"Hey guys, popcorn's ready for whoever wants some."

All eyes turned as Tracey, another dancer as well as the secretary, stood in the doorway.

"I'm starved." Vince sighed as he stood up and headed out of the room, and Paul quickly followed behind.

Samantha started to go, but paused, turning back to Jeff and I.

"You can have some *after* you get at least an 8-count down," she joked with a laugh, and Jeff and I smiled.

"You have any song ideas?" Jeff asked after Sam had gone, and I shook my head, resting my palms on my lower back as I paced the middle of the floor.

"Not really. Anything lyrical is fine."

Jeff sifted through the CDs near the tape deck for a moment, until he found one and popped it into the player.

"How about this one? I was listening to it last night and thought it might work."

Jeff walked over as the song started, lost in thought as he choreographed in his head.

321

Before I could even worry about putting one move together, I recognized the song, and immediately felt my heart sink.

Jeff must have noticed my sudden change in expression, and frowned as he went to cut the song off.

"Sorry . . . is it a bad choice?"

I quickly shook my head, then sighed.

Only the song Jet and Bri danced to for the recital.

"No—no, it's . . . it's just that I . . . have some memories associated with that song . . ." I winced, "painful memories."

Jeff nodded understandingly, then paused, debating with himself as to whether or not to search for a different song or put off choreographing for the moment.

I placed a hand on my forehead as I walked over to the mirror, and Jeff tossed the CD case from hand to hand.

"Sorry, we can still use it if you want," I spoke up as I leaned against the mirror, lowering myself to the floor, and Jeff shook his head, his brown eyes sympathetic.

"No, Miranda, don't worry about it. We'll just use somethin' else—we've got tomorrow to work on this anyway." He paused, then smiled a little, walking over. "Why don't you show me your Alvin Ailey audition piece?"

I looked up at his extended hands, his eyebrows raised hopefully, and I eventually smiled.

"C'mon—"

"No, I'm serious. I know you've got somethin' cookin' up. So let me see it."

I sighed, tilting my head, and finally allowed him to help me up.

"Okay, but this is *only* because you requested it," I warned as I moved to the tape deck to put my song on.

Jeff laughed, leaning his back against the mirror and sliding his hands into his jeans pockets.

"You make it sound like it's bad or something."

I turned with a chuckle, pressed the "play" button, and finally moved to the middle of the floor to show my audition piece for the first time.

"Miranda, Nina's here."

I glanced over at Sam's reflection in the dressing room mirror, briefly pausing in my eyeliner application.

"Okay. Are we wearing the red-and-green sneaks or the blue ones, in the final number?"

Sam scratched her cheek, glancing down at her own red sneakers.

"Unless you two wanna look like a Christmas tree, blue," she replied with a laugh, and I smiled, shaking my head as she disappeared behind the black curtains of the dressing room.

My first performance at the acclaimed Choreographer's Carnival was only an hour away, and I was trying not to let my nerves show as I applied my makeup with the rest of the troupe backstage. Lena was constantly telling me not to be nervous, though, so I must not have been doing a good job of covering up my anxiety. I couldn't have been gladder to have such good friends with me in the troupe, especially Jeff, who had been very encouraging and positive through the most hectic times of our practices. It took us until the last minute to get the perfect piece together for our lyrical routine, but everyone was impressed and excited for us to perform it.

However, I'm sure no one was as nervous as I was, since this would be my first major show with a partner since before the accident.

"Hey, sis'!"

I jumped at the voice directly behind me, dropping my eyeshadow case, which immediately shattered into a fine, useless powder.

"Wow, you're really nervous, Mira," Nina's tone was serious and slightly concerned, but I only held my chest, laughing at myself for being so jumpy.

"Sorry . . . I know, it's crazy." I sighed, and Nina bent to pick the case back up.

"Were you done with this?" she asked, an apologetic smile on her face.

I nodded with a chuckle and wave of my hand.

"Yeah, it's just some eyeshadow—it's my fault."

Nina smiled, adjusting the collar of her suede, wool-lined trench coat.

"You look good—I love the outfit," she complimented, and I glanced down at my flowing, white skirt and leotard. Jeff would be wearing a white dress shirt and tie (which he would most likely need me to tie for him).

"Thanks—you, too. I'm gonna have to cop that jacket sometime." I cocked my head at her coat, turning back to the mirror to straighten my hair in its bun. I had begun to wear it wavy and free of its braids, as I used to.

Nina chuckled, and I caught a glimpse of Jeff pacing the hallway outside.

"C'mon." I grabbed her arm, leaving the dressing room for the hall.

"There you are—this tie is crazy," Jeff sighed when he spotted me, and Nina placed her hand over her mouth, stifling a laugh.

"All ties are crazy, Jeff," I noted with a smile as I worked with the tie, which Jeff had managed to unskillfully knot.

"I don't know what I'd do without you, Miranda." He shook his head, his tone almost serious (surprisingly, he was nervous as well—it was the whole troupe's first Carnival), and I merely smiled. "Hey, Nina," Jeff greeted with a quick wave.

"Hey, Jeff—you seem a little nervous," Nina replied, briefly stepping out of the way for a couple of dancers and stagehands to pass.

"Of course not," Jeff lied, and I couldn't suppress a laugh.

"Hey, guys."

I turned to see Jonathan walking over, pausing when he reached Nina's side.

"Hey, Jon," I greeted him with a hug, finishing Jeff's tie.

"Doesn't she look amazing, Jon?" Nina took hold of his arm, pretending that we couldn't hear her.

Jon smiled with a nod, stuffing one hand into the pocket of his leather jacket, the other arm around Nina's waist.

"You look beautiful Miranda," he paused, "better than your sister," he joked, and Nina glared, then grinned just the same.

"Now wait a minute . . ."

Jeff managed a chuckle despite his nerves, and I smiled.

"Thanks Jon, but Nina will always have me beat in that field," I replied as I finished Jeff's tie. "Okay partner, you're all through—why don't we go over the dance once or twice. I'd feel better if we did."

Jeff nodded, running a hand along his smoothed hair.

"Me, too. You two can watch."

After the four of us moved off to an open, empty back-lobby area, Nina and Jonathan stood off to the side as Jeff and I started in our opening pose. I felt my nerves beginning to leave me as we arrived at the halfway point of the dance, and smiled in return to Jeff's encouraging grin, both of us trusting each other with the lifts and holds. One particularly-challenging lift was toward the end of the dance, and each time we rehearsed the piece full out, we silently prayed that we would execute it without any trouble—injuries, mainly. We had yet to truly fail at the lift, and I was feeling confident as I ran into Jeff's arm and he proceeded to hoist me up over his head with one hand, my body parallel to the ground. I had never liked heights, and didn't enjoy the extremely high lifts I used to do with Kevin. He often joked that it was my only fear in dancing.

Nina and Jonathan cheered a little as Jeff spun around, and I held my breath as he let me down, and I slid safely and smoothly back to the ground. With all of the dangerous moves behind us, we shared another smile of relief and continued the dance in complete confidence.

As we parted to *chassé* into our own separate, yet synchronized, leaps, I found my mind traveling to the Alvin Ailey audition I would have in the future. I pictured my sister and Jonathan as judges, and took Jeff out of the picture. An audience of empty chairs substituted the industrial walls, and the dim lamp overhead became a bright, blaring stage light.

My heart skipped with an excitement mixed with fear, and I threw my head back as I stepped into the leap, everything suddenly moving in the slowest of motion.

With both legs extended and arms gracefully poised, I closed my eyes for a split second where I seemed to freeze in mid-air, feeling as close to the warmth I felt in my stomach when I once danced injury-free as I had ever felt. But I had to land, and my left foot touched the ground first. To my surprise, though, my knee seemed to twist abnormally outward, and the rest of me came down as well.

With a cry of pain, I crashed into the floor and lay holding my knee, my reverie shattering.

Forty-Eight

Jet

I never thought I would be attending a wedding that holiday season, and definitely not with the bride and groom being my parents. I sure wasn't complaining, though. Mom and Dad had the best wedding I had ever attended, of the few I had gone to. Jonathan and I were co-best men, and the ceremony was flawless. It wasn't too big of an event, with a medium-sized amount of family and friends, but the love we all received was immeasurable. My parents' love for each other was blatant and pure, and to this day, I think of their second wedding as one of the best days of my life—all of our lives; my parents, Jon, Nana Jo and I.

I moved out of Nana Jo's crowded house, where the reception was taking place, to the porch, smiling at the fellowship inside, as well as my memory of my mom, smiling beautifully as she walked down the aisle, and my dad, waiting with an emotional gleam in his eyes.

I let out a neutral sigh as I sat down on the bench, the sounds of laughter and chatter from inside muffling behind the closed door.

It was New Year's Eve, marking about three years since Miranda learned of my secret. I tugged at my black tie, pulling it loose as I leaned forward onto my elbows, staring down at the ground. I had stepped outside onto the porch at Nana's Jo's; inside, friends and family were celebrating the holiday. I wasn't all that much in the mood for festivities, since being back in Philly brought painful memories to mind.

I missed Miranda. It hurt to be away from her; I never even got to apologize.

As rough as it all was, I was beginning to realize what this was teaching me about love. Deep down, I had always thought that love was merely a temporary feeling. This was until Miranda came along...when everything changed.

To be three years out of a relationship that had barely even started and still having strong feelings, I knew without a doubt that I still loved Miranda—I loved her even more than before. This had taught me that *true* love is simply eternal, and independent of the circumstances.

But still, the heartache remained...

Lately, I had been praying that God would allow me to at least see Miranda again, and maybe I could even tell her that I was sorry...

"Jet?"

I nearly jumped, turning at the voice at my side. The front door was open, and Nina stood there with a concerned look on her face. Sometimes, she resembled Miranda a little too much.

"Oh, hey, Nina." I smiled lightly, standing up politely. "Wanna sit?"

Nina returned the smile and nodded as we sat.

I saw Nina every now and then, since she and Jonathan had

gotten serious. We had never really spoken about the whole ordeal in the past, though. But to my surprise, she had never shown anger toward me. "Well, it's about 11:50 . . . you bringin' in 2008 all alone?" Nina asked with a light chuckle, and I smiled.

"I just wanted to think for a second," I replied quietly, wondering why Nina had come out to check on me. I had yet to get over the guilt I always felt when around her.

Nina nodded quietly.

"Jet, um . . ." she sighed, running her fingers through her hair, "I know we haven't really talked . . . about the things we . . . well . . . you know."

My discomfort was evident as I felt the atmosphere change.

"But I want you to know," she continued, "that I . . . I don't have any bad feelings for you—not anymore." She shrugged. "I mean, it's not like I felt good about what happened to Miranda, but . . . I don't know, I just thought about it one day." She took a deep breath, twisting a bangle on her wrist. "And I pretty much came to the conclusion that things happen . . . and, well, even though my family wouldn't agree with me, and I've never told them this . . . I'm at peace with it."

"But also," Nina rubbed her hands together for warmth, choosing her words carefully, "I want you to know that I thought almost from the start that Miranda should be with you . . . and no one else."

I scratched my jaw.

"Even now?" was my soft inquiry, almost afraid to ask, and wondering why I had in the first place.

No answer came from Nina for a long time, and I could have kicked myself for being so ridiculous.

Of course *she doesn't think you should be with Miranda now!*

But to my surprise, Nina smiled at me.

I let out a heavy sigh.

"Wow . . . I . . ." I shook my head. "I don't know what to say . . . I don't even know why I'm acting like this—I mean, there's no possible way Miranda and I could . . ."

"You never know, Jet . . ." Nina offered quietly, hopefully.

I leaned my head back on the brick siding of the house, still surprised with the conversation we were having.

"Nina," I began slowly, pausing to sigh again, "I know this is all a crazy mess—all of it my fault. But . . . I do love Miranda, even though it didn't seem like it back then." I smiled sadly, listening to the cheers of "Happy New Year" sounding from inside of the house. "I *still* love her, and that'll be the case for a long time, no matter what happens."

Forty-Nine
Miranda

The ice pack was frigid on my knee at first, a sensation I had forced myself to forget after my legs began to heal. But I was having a rough day, my legs feeling uncertain. I was beginning to doubt my upcoming Alvin Ailey audition, despite all of my practice. I was worried; it had been so long since I had auditioned, and I wondered if I really was ready.

My argument with Mom replayed in my mind, and I swallowed. *Am I making the right decision?*

I rested my head back on the brick wall of the vacant New York studio, the place I had come to call my own. Distantly, I traced the sunset rays cascading through the windows and over my outstretched legs. When my knee began to grow numb, I closed my eyes. Everything went numb eventually—had I really forgotten?

"You look just like the painting hanging in your living room, you know."

I blinked my eyes open, turning to the doorway to my right.

Nina's silhouette approached.

I sighed wearily as she sat down beside me, and I poked at the melting ice on my knee. "I'm jealous of the dancer in that painting...I always have been."

Nina, annoyed by my pessimism, pondered before replying. "It is you, though," she insisted softly, but I shook my head, combing my fingers through my braids.

"Is it?" I laughed shortly. "I'm wondering today..." My voice faded, and I frowned out the window, watching a bird circle near the sun. "You know, I . . . I broke those old dance awards in the attic once, with my cane—I was so frustrated . . ." I shook my head. "I was mad . . . at nobody but myself. Maybe I need to throw in the towel—to stop chasing something I can't really have . . . Maybe Mom is right."

Nina was silent for a moment, and I touched one of the scars on my knee.

"Or maybe you need to stop listening to the distractions and do what *you* feel is right, Miranda," she responded. "Do you really think it's worth it to turn your back on your dream?"

I did a lot of thinking in the next few days. The Alvin Ailey audition was only a week away from my conversation with Nina. Somehow, despite my discouragement, I still wanted to audition— to at least try. Maybe it was just that I had been building up to this, working for it all my life. Through the surgery, training, and now . . . well, I wanted to finish what was started.

I woke up the day of the audition with butterflies battling in my stomach. After staring up at the ceiling for about fifteen minutes, praying and thinking, my eyes eventually found the painting on the living room wall, in plain sight through my open bedroom doorway. Without a second thought, I willed myself to get up.

I had an audition to catch.

"Name, please?"

"Miranda Phillips."

The woman seemed somewhat suspicious before she scanned my résumé once or twice, moving hastily.

"Miranda Phillips indeed . . ." I thought I caught her murmur in only slight amusement. "237. Here's your number. Head to the end of the line and your audition will be up shortly." She snapped back to attention, swiftly sliding my résumé under a pile of those belonging to other applicants.

I moved quickly, taking my number from a pile nearby and tacking it to the front of my black tank. I adjusted my dance bag on my shoulder and headed for the backstage area of the auditorium.

The line was long. I took note of the dancers around me, the way they carried themselves, what they wore and said to each other.

I was nervous at first, yet I knew the line wasn't going to move anytime soon, since we were only waiting for instructions as to what would happen next.

"Miranda?"

Someone nervously cleared their throat behind me, and I turned to see a guy who looked a bit younger than me.

"My-my name is B.J.," he stammered. "I think we're partners?"

I nodded with a polite smile; his awkwardness only added to my nerves. He seemed to be uneasily surveying his surroundings as he spoke, and rarely did he actually meet my gaze.

"Oh, okay, I'm Miranda," I replied appropriately, reaching out to shake his hand.

B.J. and I stood in silence for almost a half hour, until finally, someone came to address the dancers.

"You will be split up into four groups," the petite woman stated, "and each group will learn the partner dance. Each pair will learn the same dance to perform before the judges. After you perform your partner dance, we'll take a break. When you come back, we'll form the line for the solo auditions. I suggest that y'all take this time to stretch and warm up, if you haven't already. Thank you!"

When she finished, the loud chattering that had hastened most of the wait didn't resume. Everyone began to stretch and meditate as the reality of the audition began to take effect.

"Well, I hope we're last," B.J. squeaked, wringing his shaking hands.

I shrugged, reaching up to glide my fingers through my braids.

"But going sooner gets it over with faster," I tried to console, but B.J.'s face seemed to pale.

I stood on one foot for a moment, hoping my legs wouldn't grow too weary from standing up for so long.

"Oh no . . ." B.J. suddenly groaned from my left, holding his stomach and looking as though he was about to throw up.

I frowned. "You okay?"

B.J. quickly shook his head and tore off down the hall.

My jaw hung as I watched in disbelief. I didn't know what to do. I couldn't go after him, since he was most likely headed for the men's room.

What now?

I sighed heavily and walked toward a wall, deciding to take a seat on the floor to rest my legs.

My partner was sick and our audition was quickly approaching. What if he got sick again during our audition? What if he didn't come back?

I sat cross-legged and zoned out of the moment as I flipped on my iPod, wondering what would become of our audition.

As the chattering gathered volume around me, I tried to persuade myself to relax, and closed my eyes.

Fifty
Jet

"Hey, Jet, ready to walk it through?"

I nodded as I hoisted myself up onto the spacious, empty stage. "What about you?" I asked.

Marcia, one of the school's choreographers, sighed heavily as she cued the sound guy to play the CD.

"Sure, I'm ready." She tucked her short, dark hair behind her ear.

I rolled up the sleeves of my white, button-down shirt. "Let's walk it through."

As confident as I was trying to appear, I was pretty nervous. This was my first year choreographing the partner dance the school hopefuls would learn for their auditions. I hoped the dancers would catch on to the piece, since I had put a lot of time and effort into it and had enjoyed my first real shot at choreographing. It was a contemporary lyrical number, and Mr. Billings had already praised it.

We walked through the dance a few times, until we were comfortable with each step and lift—completely ready to teach it to the 250 dancers waiting backstage.

As Marcia stretched nearby, I grabbed my water bottle and sat down to rest up for the first group.

Amy, the head director, walked in from backstage. She looked up from her clipboard. "Are you two ready for the first group?"

"Yeah, we just finished walking it through," Marcia spoke through a yawn.

Amy nodded, reaching for the walkie-talkie on her belt. "It'll probably be another 15 minutes, so you guys can chill for a bit."

As Amy left, I rose to my feet. "I'm gonna grab a Snickers. You want anything?"

Marcia shook her head, checking her cell phone. "No thanks— but you can tell me what our groups are lookin' like when you come back," she laughed.

I nodded and headed backstage.

In the main backstage hallway, the line of dancers snaked from one end of the auditorium to the other. All of them were teens or young adults, no older than their twenties. Some were standing and fraternizing, others sitting and listening to music.

I had started for the back wall where the vending machines were, but my eyes found a particular face in the crowd.

My whole world froze.

Her eyes were closed, thus she couldn't see my stare. She sat against the wall, knees bent up and arms resting at her sides, looking very much like the painting I had commissioned for her. She was beautiful, just as I remembered her, and I had to look away, wondering if my frantic heart was going to escape from my chest.

"Jet, congratulations."

I turned swiftly, the voice sounding like a shout in my ear.

337

Mr. Billings was all smiles, dressed in a staff shirt with an ID lanyard around his neck.

I managed a weak attempt at a smile.

"For w-what?" I murmured, glancing back at her for a moment. "I-I mean...um..."

Mr. Billings smiled, not noticing my awkwardness. "Yes, you must be excited about getting your moves out there. Know any of these dancers?"

I nervously cleared my throat, my eyes trailing back to her.

"Um. . . yes . . . yes, sir. I do."

Fifty-One
Miranda

I opened my eyes with a slight start, having managed to fall asleep. I sighed as I stretched my arms and tucked my iPod away into my bag. Looking around, I saw that the first group must have left to learn the dance.

Seeing that B.J. still hadn't come back, I sat up a little straighter, tucking a braid behind my ear.

I winced as I unfolded my leg from beneath me, realizing that I had slept with it bent too far. Having my knees bent for a long time had always been painful, and it made them stiff.

I can't believe I let myself fall asleep like that.

"Group two, you're up!"

I felt my stomach tense.

That's me.

B.J. was nowhere to be found. Who was I going to dance with?

Sighing in frustration, I stood up to look around for my partner. After searching the line for a couple of minutes, I realized that B.J. must have left altogether while I was asleep. When I asked other dancers close to my spot in line, to my chagrin, I learned that he had, in fact, left. Worrying even more, I leaned against the wall. My knee had stated its disapproval when I stood to my feet, and I was reminded of all of my hard work with merely getting to the auditioning process.

Trying to control my fear, I moved robotically with my group around the corner up ahead, and finally onto the stage. It was packed with about twenty-five couples. I stood alone, wondering what to do. All of the stage directors were busy speaking into their walkie-talkies or working with other staff. I wondered if they would even notice that I was learning the piece by myself . . .

From where I ended up near the back curtain, it was hard to see the front of the stage, where the teachers were standing. But thankfully, they had microphone headsets, and a female voice said, "Can everyone see?"

A chorus of "noes" met her inquiry, and she chuckled.

"Okay, everyone spread out—make it easier for us."

I did my best to make do with my tiny bubble of space, continuing to crane my neck to see the teachers. I still wasn't sure how I was going to learn the dance alone.

"Check, check," came a familiar male voice over the PA, testing his microphone, and I frowned. "Am I on?"

He sounds so much like . . .

"Okay everybody, listen up," the girl continued. "I'm Marcia, and this is Jet . . ."

What?!

As Marcia continued to speak, my heart seemed to drop from my chest to my stomach.

Jet . . . Jet Carmichael?

I'm not sure if I wanted her to be right or wrong; I don't know if I wanted to see Jet in front of me or someone else. I couldn't have felt more torn, and my heightened nerves weren't helping.

"Today you'll be learning a jazz dance," the guy's voice picked up from where Marcia left off.

By then, I was certain it was him.

He went on to briefly explain the level of difficulty of the moves, how to dance with a partner. Finally, I was able to see him from where I stood.

Jet was facing us, at first looking quite a bit different from the Jet I remembered. He seemed more serious, more sure of himself. His face was more . . . mature, but not in an aged sort of way—maybe it was his eyes. Where he used to lack genuine confidence, he was cool and composed. But when someone asked him a question from the front row and he smiled his broad grin, he was the easygoing Jet I remembered. Confident, attractive and as carefree as ever, Jet was everything I had hated to miss for the past three years.

Somehow, despite the raging apprehension in my stomach, I learned the dance. Jet must not have seen me at all, but I was glad of this. Honestly, I had wanted to run away as soon as I spotted him, but at the same time, I wanted to stay . . . I had never felt such a mixture of reservation and longing.

While I watched Jet and Marcia's interaction as they danced the moves for us to learn, I couldn't help but ask myself the obvious question. As much as I was still hurt, I couldn't ignore the fact that I absolutely didn't like the idea of them being together.

After somehow learning the dance, I returned backstage, not knowing what to do about my lack of a partner. Without Jet on my mind, I still had my destined-to-fail partner audition to worry over. I couldn't be sure that the strict school would simply grant me another partner . . .

Wondering what to do next, I turned randomly to my right, meeting a gaze at the other end of the hall. I stood stunned, unable to move.

Jet seemed to falter, his lips moving without a sound coming out, and finally looked away and quickly moved off out of sight.

"Miranda Phillips and B.J. Morrison."

I took a deep breath as I stepped onto the stage and walked to the front, facing four judges seated in the front row before me.

One of them, a man in his early fifties, who reminded me a lot of Marshall Singleton, looked up at me over his glasses, condescendent at my silence. "Where's Mr. Morrison?"

I swallowed and cleared my throat. "He left."

The man, whose nametag introduced him as "John Solomon," smirked after a silence, and turned to his fellow judges to mutter, "Kids these days—ungrateful."

I didn't respond to his judgmental remark, but held my tongue as I tried to keep my chin up, bracing myself to face whatever my fate may be without a partner.

"Well, I'm sorry Ms. Phillips, but you won't be auditioning toda—"

Mr. Solomon was abruptly cut off by the same petite woman who had briefed the dancers on the audition process. She walked over to whisper something in his ear, glancing up at me every now and then.

Mr. Solomon nodded once or twice, and sighed impatiently a little too often. When she finished, he regarded her indignantly, and she nodded before hurrying off backstage.

He addressed me through the microphone on the table before him. "Ms. Phillips," Mr. Solomon began in a professional, dry tone, "since your partner is not here, and it is out of your hands, we will supply you with a substitute. This person cannot be another

342

applicant though, since that would interfere with our being objective." He waved one hand shortly, apparently summoning someone from the seats behind him (which were shrouded in shadows due to the glaring stage lights). "You will be dancing with today's instructor, Jet Carmichael. You will have no extra time to practice, since you both already know the dance, but you may take a minute or two to discuss it, if you wish."

I opened my mouth, though I'm not sure if I would have protested, declined, or murmured incoherently. Words had up and left me after I learned who my new partner would be, and I suddenly felt the stage begin to rock.

Jet soon appeared at the foot of the steps, moving at a medium pace with his eyes down, his face almost somber.

I reached up to rub my forehead, wondering what I was going to do. I could barely focus enough as it was, but now with *Jet* in the picture . . .

The butterflies in my stomach danced for me as Jet approached. What in the world were we going to do? Would he say anything to me? What would I reply? *Would* I reply?

This is too much—this is too uncomfortable . . .

"Sir," I heard my voice say, and Mr. Solomon looked up, as did the other three judges, with a look of impatience.

"Yes?"

My eyes slowly found their way to the black floor beneath me, and I let out a sigh, unable to find my voice.

"Ms. Phillips?" he prodded, and I must have been quiet for too long for his depleting patience.

"I'm . . . sorry." I let out a shaky breath, racking my brain for a substitute question to make my interruption worthwhile. "How long is the song?"

I suppose I was originally going to ask if I could leave—throw the audition completely. But as much as I wanted to run away, I

343

knew that I couldn't.

Mr. Solomon's face dropped in annoyance, and he sighed, tapping a pen on the tabletop.

"You have one minute. Whenever you're ready . . ."

I nodded quickly, knowing his suggestion was a command in disguise.

"Thank you, sir," I mumbled.

Jet was standing awkwardly to my right, a few feet away, and I finally turned to face him. I could only hope my body would go into auto-pilot, since my mind was begging for me to give up and go home.

Just dance with him. This has nothing to do with anything else—all you need to do is dance with him for one minute and you're done.

Jet's eyes lifted to meet mine, and he seemed to be patiently waiting for me to signal that I was ready.

Knowing I couldn't bet on Mr. Solomon's patience any longer, I stepped forward. Jet responded by doing the same as he held out his hand.

With a deep, terrified breath, I placed my trembling hand into his. Gently, he pulled me closer into the opening pose.

We were dancing before we knew it. My body did take over, and after a while, I began to realize that I was focusing on remembering the moves. I was actually grateful to be dancing with the one who choreographed the piece, as he could help me with any moves that I might forget. This was, after all, my first time actually dancing the piece with a partner.

About halfway through the dance, since I was so emotionally disoriented, I missed Jet's cue for me to come out of a basic lift. I remained in the air, with one arm around Jet's neck and his around my waist. I panicked, not knowing where we would pick up, but Jet quickly improvised, twirling and smoothly setting me back down. I still forgot the next move, though. Suddenly, we paused, our faces within inches of each other. Jet's eyes were sad as he took my hand in his, walking toward me as I stepped back into a spin away from him, trying desperately to remember the moves.

The dance was almost over, and we stood side by side, about to execute a double *pirouette*. As I came out of the complex turn, my knee suddenly stated its disapproval, and I couldn't help but wince a little as Jet guided me into the final turn into him and the dip. The music faded into silence as we held the end pose, Jet cradling me parallel to the floor, my arms gracefully extended back.

Out of nowhere, someone began to clap, and soon the whole auditorium was filled with applause and cheering. I held onto Jet's shoulders as he helped me to my feet, and I looked out at the audience, my jaw dropped in bewilderment. Apparently, our performance had generated an audience.

"Miranda."

Jet's voice brought me out of my shock, and I turned back to face him.

As the applause continued to sound, I looked up into Jet's eyes. He faltered only a little, looking more serious than I had ever seen him.

"Miranda," he repeated my name, his voice quivering, "I... love you."

The words struck me. I didn't move. I didn't speak. Jet's voice was sincere, fading into the slightest whisper.

I must have blinked eventually, feeling the room continuing to rotate, as though we were still dancing. My initial reaction was complete surprise, but later speechlessness.

And yet, I believed him.

Somehow, I managed to swallow back the tremendous lump in my throat, having to look away from his searing gaze in order to keep from falling into pieces on the spot.

"Thank you, Ms. Phillips—Jet." Mr. Solomon's voice escorted us back to reality, and I turned from Jet and left the stage as the next pair was announced.

My mind was complete madness as I stood before the mirror in the bathroom, staring at my reflection. Everything was happening all at once. My audition had been rescued. . . by Jet. Someone I never thought I'd see again or speak to again. And now here we were, *dancing* again.

Blinking out a tear, I quickly wiped it away, and exited the bathroom into the semi-crowded hallway. I knew I still had one more piece to audition: my solo.

As I paced the floor, I cringed, noticing a growing pain in my knee. I pressed a hand to the wall as I bent to rub my leg. It was feeling more unstable than before, and the stiffness seemed to gotten worse.

Sighing, I turned to lean back against the wall, wearily pulling my hands over my face.

"Jennifer Rudge."

The girl directly in front of me took a deep breath and stepped onto the stage, and I could only stare at the floor as I listened to her music playing.

In all the years I had been dancing and auditioning, I had never felt as nervous and as I did at that moment. I had the strangest feeling, somewhere in the pit of my stomach, that I wasn't going to be able to dance the way I wanted to—to the fullest. Every ounce of confidence I may have had when I arrived at the audition had left.

As I waited for my turn, I could hear the voices of those who had opposed my dancing in my ears. My heart ached as I pressed my hands on top of my head.

Are they right? Do I only belong in an office—away from a dance floor? Maybe I really am chasing the wind . . .

"Miranda Phillips."

My legs moved mechanically to the stage once more, and I halted at the center, waiting with a pounding heart for my music to begin. *This is it.*

The song began. I danced.

My whole body felt as though it was floating, and the music was showcasing my heart. Each step was *me*, a reflection of my being. I poured every drop of my yearning to dance into the moves. Every step, every leap, I executed it with passion.

I was free, finally. I would make it through the dance. I could do it, I was able. They were wrong. I had proved everyone wrong. I had gone from being crippled to enduring surgery, being used, and now...

My legs had the final say-so.

I fell to the ground as my knee suddenly jumped out of place. I landed gingerly, on my knees, before the judges and audience of dancers. My leg was gripped with pain, and I hid my face in my hands, the song continuing to play as my palms quickly moistened with my tears. I cried from both pain and defeat—but mostly the latter.

Finally, it was over. Everything was finished.

As the music drew to a halt and the theater was overcome by an astonished silence, I panted, telling myself I had failed. I told myself this before the judges could, as I was sure I was unable to stand up to another blow. This way, it wouldn't hurt as much. I would be okay if I finally admitted it to myself . . . admitted that I wasn't a dancer. This is what I had been running from all my life, but now it was time for me to face the truth.

The only sound in the auditorium was of footsteps, rushing onto the stage from the audience and pausing at my side. I didn't look up. They knelt down after a moment, and I saw a hand to my right.

Jet. Of all people to be at my side at such a time . . .

It no longer mattered that he was the one who hit me with the car—not even that he had hidden this from me. None of that mattered to me now, and I could only allow him to help me to my feet.

When my defeated knee began to give way, Jet quickly caught me, his arms around me as I held onto his shoulder for support, both of us facing the judges together.

"Ms. Phillips," Mr. Solomon finally began in his business-like tone, his eyes scanning a paper before him as he spoke, "as you most likely know, we at the Alvin Ailey School expect excellence from our dancers. We make it our priority to see to it that we find the dancers with the most potential, talent and dedication, and then," he shrugged, his eyes remaining down, "we simply train them to be professionals."

I swallowed, continuing to stare down at the floor, realizing just how much I was shaking. Somehow, I could sense Jet's own nervousness beside me.

"Therefore, since you are obviously dealing with an injury . . . we simply cannot accept you." He spoke matter-of-factly, then looked up at me. "However, I would like to note, based upon what we *did* see of your dancing, that your skills are superb."

Not surprisingly, I didn't accept his compliment, nor allow myself to believe it. All I had heard was that I was rejected.

Nodding very slowly, I struggled to find my voice. "Thank you, sir."

Barely had the words left my mouth before Mr. Solomon called for the next dancer to enter the stage, but he, too, was interrupted.

"Excuse me! I would like to say something, please."

I couldn't have been more shocked at the voice rising from the audience, and I lifted my head to see. Sure enough, my mom was hurrying from the back of the auditorium to the judges' table, her expression serious.

All eyes turned to watch her, including the judges.'

"And who might you be?" asked Mr. Solomon in an annoyed tone.

Mom cleared her throat.

"Evangeline Phillips—I'm that young lady's mother." She smoothed her hair. "I would like to say that I don't find your decision to be fair. Now . . . my daughter's story is known nationwide, and I don't say that for attention but to point out that she never once demanded any kind of recognition. She's worked harder than probably all of these dancers put together for this audition, and yet never used her fame to her advantage.

"Not only that, but Miranda's healing from something no one else had to go through, and yet what she was able to do in her solo was, in your own words, sir, 'superb.' " Mom paused, standing up a little taller. "This is Miranda's life-long dream—to dance with your school," she swallowed, "even though it's a dream that's been tested and opposed by many . . ." She took a deep breath. "But it's still alive, and stronger than ever. So no matter what happens," Mom looked up at me, her expression meaningful, "I *will* be behind her no matter what you, anyone else—or even Miranda . . . decides."

A silence lingered, until, slowly, someone started to clap. Soon, applause filled the entire auditorium.

As I felt the tears returning afresh, I lowered my head. I had been waiting to hear her speak those words for so long . . .

"That means me too," Jet whispered beside me, smiling only a little.

"Jet . . . I—"

"Well," Mr. Solomon spoke loudly over the clapping, adjusting his glasses on his nose, "Mrs. Phillips, your daughter has, as we've both pointed out, displayed just what we look for at our school," he admitted as the audience was silenced. "Therefore, if she chooses to accept, we'll offer her a guaranteed chance, no fees or lines, to audition again whenever she's ready."

As the cheering and clapping erupted once more, I was soon crying into Jet's shoulder.

"We'll take a break—I think we all need it," Mr. Solomon's weary voice said over the PA system as the applause began to die down.

Having gotten a hold of myself, before I could say anything to Jet, I felt a touch on my shoulder. I turned to face my mom, standing with a small smile on her face.

Jet politely moved away, and I was unsure of what to feel.

Mom sighed.

"Whether you believe it or not, I'm proud of you," she said, and I reached up to wipe at my eyes, a smile forming on my face.

"I believe it," I confessed quietly, reaching out to hug her.

"Look at us." She chuckled once we drew away, brushing at her tears.

I laughed, then glanced over my shoulder, hoping to see him standing nearby, but the stage was empty.

"We'd better get some ice on that knee—are you ready to go?" Mom's voice broke into my thoughts.

I turned with a small smile, a sad one.

"Yeah . . . sure."

A month later I stood quietly watching Cat instruct her students at the old North Philly studio, marveling at how much things had changed since I left for New York. A lot of the kids were older, taking more advanced classes. But Cat was still the same, a fresh face for the new students who arrived.

"Bye, Erica, good job today." Cat waved at her final student, grinning before turning to the other door and noting my presence. "Miranda!"

I smiled, welcoming her with a hug. "Your class is about to graduate from high school!" I joked with a laugh, and Cat smiled with a knowing nod.

"I know, I feel so old," she sighed lightly. "So what are you doing here? I thought you had a show tonight."

I tucked a loose braid into my ponytail. "I decided to cancel—knee pain. The doctor wants me to take it easy."

Cat nodded again, playing with the zipper on her pink hoodie.

"Well, you'd better listen to her—we can't have you getting hurt again in that big Alvin Ailey audition coming up."

I smiled, stepping a few feet toward the middle of the dance floor.

"True," I replied, recalling the days when I had my cane. "You know what, Cat?" I turned. "It's been six whole years since we used to dance on the school dance team. Isn't that crazy?"

Cat chuckled, gathering her CD case and bags. "I know—not to mention it seemed like yesterday you choreographed that dance for the recital—" She caught herself, realizing the touchy topic at hand. "Sorry, Mira, I—"

"No, it's fine." I breathed a sigh. "It doesn't really . . . hurt as bad as it used to . . . I guess . . ."

Cat frowned. "Have you spoken with him since . . . ?"

I silently stared at the scuffed wood floor. "No," was my quiet reply, but I quickly adorned a smile for my friend. "Not . . . everything we want is supposed to happen. Sometimes things just go a certain way and . . . you have to flow with it . . . y'know?"

With a slow nod, Cat returned the smile sympathetically. "True...but life's full of surprises."

I merely smiled as I headed for the door. "I think I'm gonna go check out my old classroom—see how different things are."

Cat grinned. "They haven't changed much at all—the two teachers we've had since you left were always afraid you'd come back and scold them."

I laughed. "Thanks, Cat—we'll do dinner tomorrow or

something."

"Sounds good."

With Cat having gone and the remaining staff concluding their final classes, I stood alone in my silent dance room. I remembered as many classes as I could while moving slowly about the room.

When I reached my desk, I placed my palm atop the smooth, wooden surface as a particular memory came to mind.

I had once laughed at the thought of teaching the football player arriving at the studio for disciplinary action, but now I couldn't help but smile somewhat sadly at the fun I had with him as my student... as my friend.

My smile slowly vanished. I missed the simplicity and spontaneity of life before Jet's revelation, but I also missed the audition only weeks back when I saw him again, when I danced with him . . .

He loved me, and I knew that I loved him. But there was absolutely nothing we could do about it . . . or, at least, nothing we *would* do about it. I was afraid, still terrified. I didn't know if it could work. There was so much taboo in the air, and yet, if it weren't for the taboo created by the people around us, I couldn't help but believe that I wouldn't be nearly as uncertain. Perhaps people had ruined things between Jet and I more so than the accident itself. After all, it *was* what brought us together.

But Jet was gone now. Most likely he was in a relationship with his co-teacher from the Alvin Ailey School, or at least someone else. He had forgotten the girl who had pushed him away.

I turned to gaze sadly into the mirror, painfully remembering the days when I could barely face my reflection. Slowly, I walked to the CD player, sifting through the stack of music. After selecting a song, I set the disk onto the tray and pressed "play".

I slid my feet out of my flip flops, standing barefooted on the cool wooden floor. My head hung, arms hovering at my sides as the music filled the room. I rolled my head to the side, and my arms followed as the violins cried. The voice began to sing, and I began to dance.

I twirled around, leaping, flying, spinning, dancing. Completely free, completely lost in the emotion. I rolled gracefully onto the floor, finishing seated, knees bent, elbows propped onto my legs, forehead in my hands and eyes closed. I didn't hear when the door had opened when I'd started the music, I didn't see who had been watching me as I moved.

I sighed softly.

A footstep sounded from the stillness. I blinked out of my lonesome reverie, having forgotten where I was. Frowning, I looked up, realizing I was being watched.

Every part of me froze, except for my heart, which hammered in surprise. I opened my mouth, but I didn't say a word.

Jet glanced awkwardly about him, then gathered a deep breath as he walked a few steps more.

Finally, he met my gaze and asked, "Would you teach me how to dance?"

I failed to move, and after a long moment, I had to look away to keep my tears at bay. It was hard to imagine that there was once a time when I had to answer "no" to this question . . . for more reasons than one. But this time, we had both come a long way. Jet was a dancer; I had been healed. Jet was in love with me, I was in love with him. I knew of Jet's feelings for me, and Jet knew of . . .

I . . . hadn't ever told him how I felt.

I swallowed heavily. "There's nothing left to teach," was my defeated reply, yet honest in every sense. The roles had changed. Nothing was the same nor ever could be the same anymore.

Jet wasn't finished, though. "But there's plenty left to learn."

I looked up to see his sincere expression and extended hand.

Silence met his words, but I made a quick decision.

Placing my hand in his, I allowed him to help me to my feet. We were dancing, waltzing like that evening years back when my legs were crippled. But it was sad this time, not free and careless as before. This time there was baggage and heartbreak, painful memories and tears.

I stopped, overcome with fear, and walked off to my desk as I had in the past.

"I'm sorry," Jet apologized from behind, looking down. "You're right. I . . . I shouldn't have come." He let out a deep sigh. "I just . . . I wanted to see you and apologize and maybe . . . ." His voice faded and I heard him swallow. "Never mind. Nana Jo was wrong . . . she was wrong about us."

I squeezed my eyes shut as Jet turned, each of his steps to the door urging my fear to multiply. But now, I was afraid of something else: losing him.

"Jet, I love you," I spoke in one breath as I turned around. A weak smile spread across my face. "And she was right."

Jet paused in his tracks, and slowly faced me. Smiling a bit hesitantly, he stepped forward, offering his hand once again.

"Then may we finish this dance?"

*

Jet

Five years have passed. Miranda and I are married, and we'll celebrate our fourth anniversary this weekend. I want to get her something perfect as a gift, but I couldn't think of what for a while. After giving it some thought, though, I came up with an idea.

After discussing it with Mr. Phillips, I decided to lease out the building next to Capstone Productions, where we'll open up the dance studio Miranda never got to co-own. *Relevé* will also be a therapy center for teens in need of rehab, where Miranda can either teach dance or train those in need of rehabilitation. She's glad to have gotten get her degree in physical therapy a couple of years ago.

I've finished my degree in journalism and I'm now working as senior editor of a local West Oak Lane, Philly newspaper. Miranda and I moved back home to Philly shortly after we married. We're expecting our second child, a girl who we'll name Relevé, after the ballet term meaning "raised."

Dominic, our three-year-old son, is already showing signs of liking football more than dancing, and Miranda's constantly joking that he represents the other me, the side that still has a love for football. Whatever he chooses, we'll support him and encourage him.

Jonathan and Nina got married exactly a year after Miranda and I, and Jon is quick to challenge me to see who can remember their anniversary the best. Nina's still acting, and was recently cast to be in a movie.

My relationship with Miranda's parents is still growing, and I'm glad to say that Mrs. P. and Nana Jo are the best of friends. Cat's still dancing and gaining more popularity, and Bri's fresh out of Juilliard.

As for me, I continued to study dance and train, and, according to Miranda, I've gotten much better at jazz and hip-hop. Miranda's trying to get me into ballroom. We'll see.

I would like to say that Miranda's dancing more than ever, but I can't. Five years ago, she auditioned for Alvin Ailey again and passed with flying colors. She went on to become one of their most famous dancers, becoming world renowned and living out her dream. Her legs, though, were a constant struggle for her, and she's had to step down from her spot on the acclaimed dance team. However, she isn't bitter about it. Miranda's grateful for what she achieved, and says that it wouldn't have mattered if her name was known or not—she's still a dancer.

Julia's painting hangs in our living room, as well as a copy in the Capstone lobby. Sometimes, while locking up, I'll watch Miranda pause in front of it, staring for a long time. I used to wonder what she thought as her eyes rested somewhat wistfully on her painting. But I do know now that it's no longer a stranger she sees on the floor of the dance room, the girl with eyes focused ahead and cane behind her.

No, Miranda finally sees herself.

44925809R00199

Made in the USA
Middletown, DE
12 May 2019